Fragments of Tom

The man who couldn't die

J. H. Wallder

*To Peter,
The best Art Director
I ever worked with!
Jeff Wallder*

Copyright © 2015 J. H. Wallder

All rights reserved, including the right to reproduce this book, or portions thereof in any form. No part of this text may be reproduced, transmitted, downloaded, decompiled, reverse engineered, or stored, in any form or introduced into any information storage and retrieval system, in any form or by any means, whether electronic or mechanical without the express written permission of the author.

This is a work of fiction. Names and characters are the product of the author's imagination and any resemblance to actual persons, living or dead, is entirely coincidental.

The views expressed in this work are solely those of the author and do not necessarily reflect the views of the publisher, and the publisher hereby disclaims any responsibility for them.

ISBN: 978-1-326-28929-4

PublishNation, London
www.publishnation.co.uk

Contents

1: Action Replay.	1
2: The day von Ribbentrop went paddling in Bognor.	15
3: Don't spend all your money on the dodgems.	45
4: The War Office regrets to inform you.	74
5: Is there anybody there?	104
6: The voodoo witch doctor's dance of death.	137
7: Flo attacks an SS Panzergrenadier with a broken brolly.	166
8: The faceless spectre in the shadows at Ray's wedding.	187
9: Tom meets the Goddess Aphrodite on a charabanc in Devon.	251
10: Just one more night.	330
11: Glossary.	360

1: Action Replay.

Saturday June 14th 1975
The Beach Hotel, Worthing, West Sussex.

The bride's mother ordered another bottle of Champagne, why not since her ex-husband was paying the bill? After all, she had organised the whole wedding and everything had gone swimmingly. Now she could relax, nothing could go wrong from here on and if it did nobody could blame her.

Anyway, what possible dramas could unfold now?

Then her gaze chanced to fall on Flo sitting alone. Clutching the Champagne bottle she crossed the room and took a seat next to her.

'Let me freshen your glass,' said Mez's mother and without waiting for an answer filled the crystal goblet to the brim with bubbly. 'We haven't been properly introduced but you're Flo, aren't you?' she continued.

'I am - and I'm most pleased to meet you,' gushed Flo. 'You really are to be congratulated on arranging such a wonderful wedding, it must have meant endless hard work.'

'It did mean burning the midnight oil and the usual last minute cock-ups to sort, if you'll pardon my French. But it's all been worthwhile in the end - only have the one daughter, you see.'

Then after a moment's reflection: 'You're Jeffrey's grandmother aren't you so you must be Vera's mother? I know I should know but there's simply been no time to take anything in.'

Flo laughed. 'No, not Vera's mother - Jeffrey didn't even know I existed until quite recently.'

Flo thought some explanation necessary but decided to keep the convoluted family connection as simple as possible. She also decided a little white lie was in order.

'What it is, I had a son called Tom who was killed in the War who was Vera's first husband. They met down in Selsey where he was stationed. They had twin boys: my grandson Ray who now lives in Australia and Jeffrey.'

Suddenly, time juddered to a halt for Mez's mother whose brain ceased registering anything beyond 'Tom'…'killed in the War'…'Vera'…and 'Selsey'. It was all such a long time ago but there are some of life's landmark moments that remain crystal clear even until the chiming of the hour. Everything began falling into place - but could it possibly all be coincidence?

Then came the second thunder bolt out of a clear blue sky. Her eyes were drawn to Flo's place name among the wedding table debris, carefully typed and encapsulated in a clear plastic holder. It had been pushed to one side but she had no difficulty reading it.

'Mrs. Florence Harman'.

'*Harman*'. That was the clincher, it was beyond the leeway of chance. Mez's mother's brain jumped back into real time.

'Did you say that your son was Tom Harman and that he was stationed in Selsey during the War?' she asked.

'Yes,' replied Flo with growing interest. 'Did you know him?'

In that instant Mez's mother determined that nobody should ever know. But she would have to live with the knowledge that every time she saw her new son-in-law Jeffrey it would remind her that his father was the only man she had ever really cared for.

What luckless fate to fall for a fellow on a one-night stand!

If only she could have had just one more night with him it might have been a different story. Just one more night and she might have rekindled his childhood infatuation for her. She might even have persuaded him to try for an officer's commission in which case he might never have died.

'No!' she lied to Flo, quickly recovering her wits. 'It's just that my parents took me on some lovely holidays to Selsey when I was a child.'

Just then a voice called from across the other side of the room.

'Kate! You're needed over here! We're going to cut the rest of the cake!'

Sunday October 4th. 1970.
Chichester Railway Station, West Sussex.

Flo was sad on that last taxi journey up to Chi from Selsey knowing she would never see Tom's old wartime stamping ground again and her extended family much less frequently now they were emigrating. But then she looked at her grandson Jeffrey, her new charge and live-in companion, and knew that looking after him would help to fill the void. Her weird energy would not be wasted from now on.

They arrived at Chichester Station with only minutes to spare before the arrival of the London train. Jeffrey dashed off to buy the tickets whilst Flo settled up with the minicab driver.

'That's ten shillings, luv,' the cabby told her. 'Seven bob plus a shilling for each passenger.'

'But there were only two of us,' replied Flo. 'Surely that makes it nine shillings?' The cab driver gave her a funny look.

'Excuse me, but there were two young men in the back. One was wearing blue jeans and the other was in army uniform. They both got out together,' insisted the puzzled driver.

Suddenly the answer dawned on Flo, she was in no doubt about who the third passenger could be. 'I'm so sorry, dear, of course there was. I don't know what I was thinking of,' she apologised giving him a pound note and without waiting for the change hurried into the station. Flo looked both ways up the platform and all around her but there was no sign of anybody in army uniform nor any other uniform come to that. Then she went back outside and had a good look round there and after that checked the waiting room but it was all in vain.

Then she heard Jeffrey calling her: 'Come on, Gran, we're going to miss the train!' Just then the engine thundered past the ticket barrier and shuddered to a stop and they both climbed aboard, though Flo continued to scan the platform from the open window of the carriage.

'What's up, Gran? Lost something?' asked Jeffrey perplexed by her strange behaviour.

'No Jeffrey, I thought I saw someone I knew,' she said as the platform guard blew his whistle and the 6.05 evening train to London started to inch forward. Flo sank back in her seat and began to think. 'Why couldn't I have seen him too?' she wondered. It would have meant so much just to gaze on him again, even if only for a few seconds. She would have given anything just to see his lovely face once more. But at least she knew he was always near, he was leaving Selsey for the last time with her and his youngest son. How lucky she was to have a son whose love was so great it even transcended the end of mortal life itself.

Saturday September 12th 1942
The Astoria Dance Salon, Charing Cross Road, London.

Round and round the Astoria's eight-sided dance floor they went, whirling and twirling, posing and posturing, more like ballet than ballroom dancers, until there were only six or seven couples left and all the others were watching.

Tom and Kate were among the survivors. Kate was surprised he was keeping up, never missing a step, no matter how far she pushed the envelope. For Tom, all those Saturday evenings spent at Wimbledon Palais, Streatham Locarno and Hammersmith Palais were paying off.

Finally the music came to an end and everybody applauded – Kate was in her element. As they left the dance floor she slapped his arm with the back of her hand and told him: 'Hey, you didn't tell me you could dance, feller!'

'One of us had to,' replied Tom. This time Kate whacked him harder.

'Just remember, Ginger Rogers did everything Fred Astaire did - only backwards and in high heels!' said Kate.

They found a small table and Tom ordered a bottle of sham Champagne. They each lit another cigarette and the smoke drifted up to join the thin haze that hung over the Orchestra and ballroom.

'That was quite something, my lady,' said Tom. 'You weren't joking when you said you could run a dancing school.'

They returned to the dance floor many times, got through at least two more bottles of sham Champagne and flirted outrageously. Their last number was 'Let's Dance at the Make-Believe Ballroom' – another big Joe Loss and Chick Henderson hit.

'Is this ballroom make-believe too?' Tom whispered in her ear as they slowly rotated round the wooden sprung dance floor. 'Are you really here with me?'

'In the flesh, my dear,' answered Kate. 'Are you enjoying it?'

'You've no idea...' he replied and kissed her firmly on the mouth. She responded in kind. Tom put his right hand behind her head to press her closer, just as she had done to him on that first kiss on the beach in Devon the year King Edward abdicated.

5

It was getting late and time to leave - after all who really wants to stay for the clichéd last dance of 'Goodnight Sweetheart'? It was simply too non-U.

They stepped out onto the pavement and both welcomed the rush of fresh air but saw nothing incongruous in immediately lighting up another Capstan Full Strength cigarette. There was no brand loyalty in wartime, you smoked whatever you could get.

No searchlights pierced the sky that night and no ack-ack banged away in the distance.

'Looks like the bastards will be late tonight,' said Tom noticing the unbroken cloud that heavy bombers hate.

'Or possibly won't come at all,' Kate hoped.

They continued walking arm-in-arm down Charing Cross Road towards the Station in silence. Tom gave Kate a sideward glance, she seemed deep in thought. Suddenly she stopped and turned on her heels to face him.

'Look Tom, would you think me an awful tart if I suggested we book into the Strand Palace Hotel for the night? People are doing it all the time, the desk clerks don't care. You see, it's this bloody war, I've had enough of it. You meet some nice boy and before you know it he's...he's shipped off to Egypt or something worse.

'Every morning that I catch that bloody train from Crystal Palace I ask myself, will it be the last time? Who knows when the next tip and run raider will strike? Did I tell you my older brother's hunting U-boats in the Atlantic and...and I've had enough of "Keep your chin up and carry on as normal..."' She began to sob.

Tom put his strong arms around her and guided her into the privacy of a nearby doorway.

'Hush now, sweet lady, you've nothing to fear,' he said as he cradled her to his chest. 'Nothing's going to happen, *nothing*

I tell you. You're far too good-looking to die.' And after a second's pause he added: 'And so am I.'

He leaned back to look at her and they both laughed at his pretended lack of modesty and Kate's shadows passed.

'Sorry Tom,' she said as they continued to walk arm in arm. 'It's nothing really but after a while it all begins to get a girl down.'

'Did you mean it about the Strand Palace Hotel?' he asked.

She turned to look at him again. 'I've never meant anything more in my life.' So saying she stroked his cheek with her fingers and looked to his eyes for their answer.

'You would make me the richest man in England because for one night I would possess its greatest treasure,' he whispered.

'That's the loveliest thing anybody has ever said to me, Tom,' Kate replied with conviction.

They walked on faster down the road towards the Strand.

'Do you have anything?' she asked him eventually.

'No, I hate those things,' replied Tom.

'So do I - and I don't give a damn what happens. I'll face that if it comes,' she added.

'I'll make sure it's alright. Just a matter of timing, just like in dancing,' he said.

'You look after your women then,' she answered with a smile.

The elderly desk clerk at the Strand Palace Hotel looked at the guest book and took a sharp intake of breath.

'I don't know, sir, we had a large party of American Officers book in for the night earlier. I've got a nice single room with its own bathroom at the back of the hotel, away from the noise of the traffic, but that's all.'

'We'll take it!' Kate interrupted almost snatching the key and heading towards the lift.

'Room 501. That'll be one pound five shillings in all, including the breakfast,' said the desk clerk. 'Seeing how it's only a single really.'

Tom gave him thirty shillings and told him to keep the change. As he finished filling in the guest book the old man looked at the entry.

'Thank you sir, I hope you and…er...Mrs. Harman have a comfortable night.'

The room wasn't bad for wartime Britain and the bath turned out to be the rare luxury of a shower. There was a stool and a little dressing table with a jug of water and two glasses standing on it.

Kate kicked off her shoes and flopped onto the bed as if exhausted. Tom loosened his tie and stood beside her before sliding a small silver hip flask from his jacket pocket.

'Fancy a brandy, sweet thing?' he asked. 'A small night cap maybe?'

She sat bolt upright on the bed. 'Brandy? You're a dark horse! You let me drink Champagne made from pears when you had this all along. I haven't had a brandy since before the War.'

The dark liquid, warmed to just the right temperature by the hip flask's closeness to Tom's body, set their taste buds glowing and slipped down their throats like nectar. They finished the brandy in two gulps as they stood facing each other in the small bedroom.

'That was good,' said Tom.

'Yes, but not half as good as this,' Kate replied slowly turning.

'Unzip me, but be careful. This dress is pure silk.'

Almost an hour later they lay together motionless on the narrow bed. Kate's head nestled against Tom's bare chest and his hand rested gently on her thigh. They basked in the lingering pleasure of the postprandial moment and for the first time since she could remember Kate knew perfect peace.

She broke the silence. 'Sorry for blubbing before, Tom. You know, when we were walking down the street. It's this war, just gets me down sometimes.'

'We're already three years in and no nearer the end than when it started.'

'Everyone has their dark moments, sweet lady,' Tom reassured her.

They both raised themselves up on one elbow until they were facing each other sideways.

'What adorable eyes you have, Tom,' she told him. 'Like doorways to your deepest thoughts drawing me in. A girl could lose herself in the labyrinth of those eyes.'

'Tell me, why did you get to know me all those years ago in Devon, show such interest in a much less worldly soul? You were way out of my league,' asked Tom.

Kate thought back to those carefree pre-War days. 'You were a sweet boy, Tom. You were like the little brother I never had. I wanted to play with you, protect you…even teach you how to kiss.'

Tom felt a flicker of resentment that at the time she saw him as her little brother and not the potential sweetheart he had wished for, even though the triumph of this evening made it all irrelevant.

'So you're saying you've just fucked your brother?' he asked her. Almost immediately he knew he had crossed a line. Kate's countenance changed and there was more than a hint of anger.

'Don't *ever* use that ugly word in my presence again!' she told him firmly.

'I apologise,' answered Tom.

She thought for a few seconds and eventually told him: 'I accept your apology.'

They both lay back on the single bed and embraced, each simply enjoying the closeness of the other. There was no time for lovers' tiffs in this war.

Sunday August 9th. 1936
Scout and Guide Camp Ramble, Holcombe, Devon.

About ten minutes along the path to Holcombe, just as Tom was wondering how far in front Kate must be, he heard behind him the voice of she who was fast morphing into a cross between movie maiden Dorothy Lamour and the Goddess Aphrodite.

'Tom!' she called. 'What's this I hear about you having a fight over something to do with me?'

News spread fast among the scouts and guides on the ramble who loved nothing more than passing on gossip of some outrage or scandal just like everybody else.

'It wasn't my fault, Kate,' Tom replied quickly. 'Mervyn Jones was saying rude things about you and I let him have it.'

'What did he say?' Kate demanded to know.

'He called you Lady Lah-Di-Dah and said you were going to have a baby.' Tom thought it better not to add that he was supposed to be the father.

'What a beastly boy!' Kate said with a passion, just as a crack of thunder sounded not too far away.

'I think we're going to have a shower,' she added and just then large spots of rain began to fall making a sudden pattering noise on the ground. They both ran for the shelter of a modest oak tree in full leaf and stood leaning against the trunk.

Just then Kate noticed the slight gash above Tom's eye. 'Tom, you're bleeding!' she said sympathetically. 'Come here.' So saying she pulled out a small folded handkerchief from the pocket of her shorts, licked it with her spit and began to unhygienically wipe away the excess blood.

Tom suddenly became aware of the closeness of her face to his which gave him a strange feeling.

Suddenly she paused and looked at him: 'Do you know, that's the first time any boy has been in a fight over me. I think you deserve a reward.'

Slowly she moved forwards until their lips engaged whilst holding him by the shoulders. He gently held her waist and became aware of her firm body beneath her blouse. Whilst this was going through his head, he began to feel the tip of her tongue probing into his mouth and in return he rubbed his tongue against her's. All too soon for Tom it was over.

Kate pulled back and said cheerfully: 'That was a French kiss, did you like it?'

Tongue-tied for the first time Tom could only smile his approval.

'Come on,' she said: 'It's stopping raining – we'd better catch up with the others before they scoff all the scones. "Stands the church clock at ten to three, and is there honey still for tea?"'

Tom gave her a puzzled look.

'Rupert Brooke,' Kate told him. 'Poetry! Don't they teach you anything at your school?'

The sun came out and in the ten minutes it took for them to reach the scenic village of Holcombe, and join up with the other scouts and guides, the rain had evaporated from the rustic wooden benches and tables in the garden of the thatched tea house.

There was a sign offering two scones plus a portion of strawberry jam and clotted cream, and a small pot of tea, for a shilling. The lady who ran the tea house came to take their order and suggested they should have one large pot of tea instead of two small ones if they were together. Tom said 'Yes' and at the same time Kate said 'No' which didn't please Tom.

'Well I can see you're not married, m'dears, but as you're sitting together a big pot will be a lot easier,' said the lady in charge.

Tom had never had a proper cream tea before and thought the combination of scone, cream and strawberry jam tasted scrumptious.

'Mummy and I always have a cream tea in the cafeteria on the top floor of the new Peter Jones store in Sloane Square when we go shopping in town. Do you know it?' asked Kate.

'No,' replied Tom. 'But I went to Harrods once.' He didn't add that he and his mother had walked out after only ten minutes because everything was so expensive.

Kate returned to her favourite subject – dancing. She wanted to know more about the dances in the Fred Astaire-Ginger Rogers film 'Follow the Fleet' that Tom had seen and said she was definitely going to see it when she got home. Then she said something that really did please Tom. She repeated her offer for him to come over to Crystal Palace where she lived and they could see it together if he wanted. She hadn't forgotten!

Of course, Tom said he wanted to see it again anyway as it was so good.

When they had finished their cream tea she told him she had better rejoin the other guides or 'they'll all start to talk, you know what girls are like.'

Although he had lost her for the rest of the afternoon Tom felt a warm glow. She wanted to see him when the scout and guide camp was over, that was absolutely certain. And people were beginning to 'talk' about the two of them. He liked the thought of that.

Friday August 16th 1929
Amusement Park, Littlehampton, Sussex.

The last evening they were on holiday in Littlehampton Flo took Tom to the Fun Fair near the sea front. He went on several of the rides and had a go on the shooting gallery. You got ten .177 airgun pellets for a three pence piece but although Tom loved it he didn't win anything. Then Flo saw Tom staring at the dodgem cars racing round and round the rink and banging into each other, sparks flying from the overhead electrical contact poles. Tom couldn't take his eyes off those dodgems.

At the end of each session a number of children and their dads would rush forward to claim a car and Flo could see from Tom's face that he desperately wanted to join them. She looked in her purse, there were still a few shillings left.

So Flo asked Tom if he'd like to have a go on the dodgems? She saw his big brown eyes looking up at her and he said 'But I haven't got a dad.' It was one of those unexpected things that children say sometimes but it cut Flo to the quick. She didn't let it show.

'Come on, I'll take you, didn't you know I can drive?' Flo said as quick as a flash. So they grabbed the next available dodgem car, paid their sixpence and off they went hurtling round the steel floored rink banging and bouncing off the other cars as they went. It was hard work for Flo and she found all the bumps unsettling. But whenever she sneaked a look at Tom's face she could tell he was thoroughly enjoying it and by the end he was laughing out loud every time they bumped into somebody else.

'Shall we have another go, Tom?' Flo asked. 'This time you could drive.' Tom's face was a picture of pleasure when he heard that and they quickly changed places before somebody else took the car. When the man came round to collect the sixpences he looked at Tom and said 'A bit young to be driving, ain't he missus?' Then he thought for a moment and said 'I'll just go and fetch a cushion for him so he can reach the steering wheel easier like.'

Tom soon got the hang of it and before long he was driving head on into everybody on either side. He was simply loving it. So much so that Flo dipped into her purse again for another sixpence and let him have a last go even though she thought it a bit of an extravagance she couldn't really afford.

On the walk back to the boarding house Tom talked non-stop about the dodgems and nothing else and Flo knew she had done the right thing to spend that one shilling and sixpence. She was still a bit upset though about how Tom had said 'But I haven't got a dad.'

2: The day von Ribbentrop went paddling in Bognor.

Flo was born in Dunston Road, Battersea, in south London, during the 'last hoorah' of Queen Victoria's golden reign. Flo's father was a railway worker and she had one sister, Ada, a few years older than herself. They lived in a small soot stained two-up, two-down terraced house that had seen better days. But like all the terraced houses in the road, the front doorstep was stained brilliant white once a week. It was what Flo's mum called 'keeping up standards.' It was important to keep up standards in late Victorian working-class Battersea. Once you dropped little things like that, it was a short slide into the gutter that was never far away.

The house in Dunston Road had a good roof and was dry and cosy. Not all were. Flo's mum always said that if you had a good roof over your head then you hadn't much to worry about.

Flo remembered playing in the street as a child, there was little traffic to worry about in those days. The streets belonged to the people then, or rather the children whose playgrounds they were. Someone always had a stub of chalk to draw on the road so they could play hopscotch. About the only traffic was the baker's van that brought fresh baked bread every morning. And the milkman's cart that carried the milk in metal churns from where it was measured and poured directly into jugs that people brought with them. But what Flo remembered most was the Italian ice cream seller who came round on warm summer afternoons, usually Sundays, with his tricycle that had a cold cabinet fixed to the front. If Flo's dad was around, she and Ada would never go short of a penny wafer of cool delicious Italian ice cream that was like nothing else she had ever tasted, then or since.

Another thing Flo remembered was trips to nearby Battersea Park. It was the nearest thing you got to the countryside in Battersea in those days, free train passes for railways workers and their families were still some years off.

Flo left school at fourteen, like her sister, and went to work in a grocer's shop in Queenstown Road that had dark wood-panelled walls and marble shelves. She loved the smell of smoked bacon, strong cheeses, ground coffee and other provisions that pervaded the place.

Then came the Great War and the Zeppelins.

They weren't a serious threat, not like the German bombers and doodle-bugs in the Second World War. But a big bomb did drop on the Chelsea Pensioners' home, properly called the Royal Hospital, just over the other side of the river. The explosion was so great it even rattled the window panes in Dunston Road.

Flo's father didn't have to go off to the Great War, as a railway worker it was considered duty enough to keep the trains running. But in about the second year of the War her mum died from TB. At least she was spared the long lingering decline spent coughing herself to death every day: Flo's mum passed away quickly, so it seemed, only about a week after Flo and her sister knew that something was seriously wrong. Or perhaps her mum just kept it from the family for as long as possible, not wishing to trouble them, she'd seemed pale and tired for some time.

Flo never knew why but after her mother died her father decided they should all move to his sister's house near Kingston Upon Thames. Flo's aunt was old and lived alone in a huge house which she owned in Park Road by Dinton Field between Kingston Hill and Ham Cross. It was quite something for ordinary people to live in a house they owned in those days, somehow she'd 'inherited' it, Flo never discovered who from. The aunt had been a showgirl in the music hall in her younger days. She never had any children and there was never any talk of a husband. She was a bit of a mystery really, dad's sister, and one didn't ask too many questions. She gave the impression of having a stern disposition but once you got to know her you soon discovered she had a heart of gold. Though she still wasn't someone you'd want to cross in a hurry.

Flo went to work in Bentalls, a large department store in the middle of Kingston, which she liked. Despite the War, life wasn't unpleasant. Richmond Park was only a short walk away from the house and Flo spent many happy hours exploring it either with Ada or on her own. A woman could do that sort of thing alone in those days.

In the winter of 1918, Flo's dad died in the Great Spanish Flu Pandemic that swept Europe after the Great War. It took more lives than the Great War itself and that was saying something. This meant that the only family she had left was her aunt and her sister. But through her work at the department store, Flo had met Sid, a sales assistant like herself.

Sid was a pleasant enough character and he made Flo laugh, she enjoyed his company. Although she never once saw him drinking, she knew he liked his beer because she often smelt it on his breath. Sid was popular with the other assistants at Bentalls and Flo found his interest flattering. He lived with his parents with whom he 'never got on', he often said he wanted to move out. So when Sid eventually proposed marriage, it seemed to Flo to be the logical thing. She was fond of him in her way and knew she was expected to get married before long.

Anyway, she had nobody else to compare Sid to, nobody else had ever shown her any attention in that way.

The wedding was a small affair at St. Luke's Church near to where she lived. Flo's aunt arranged it all and this was the first time that Flo met Ada's gentleman friend, Stan, a policeman from north London. Apart from them and a few of her own friends from where she worked, most of the people who came to the wedding, and the short reception in the church hall afterwards, were from Sid's side. They all seemed quite a lively bunch and like Sid they enjoyed their drink. Afterwards the newlyweds went for a week's honeymoon in Bognor Regis.

Sid found rooms for them to live in Staunton Road, not too far from her aunt's house. There were three upstairs rooms, the downstairs was occupied by another couple. But while they didn't have their own front door, they at least didn't have to share a bathroom and w.c. They had their own facilities on their floor between the living room and a bedroom with endless hot water courtesy of the latest New Improved Ascot gas boiler.

About a year after they were married, Flo fell pregnant. Sid seemed quite pleased at the prospect of fatherhood, even though it meant they would have only one wage to live on. But Sid never seemed to show his real feelings. He never argued or criticised or disagreed or showed too much enthusiasm. He just gave his charming little smile and said everything would be fine.

They called the baby Tom, after Sid's father, and Flo thought he was the most beautiful baby boy in the world. She liked those first months when Tom was a baby, she had time to look after him properly and do the shopping at leisure and still prepare a good meal for Sid when he came home after work. But as time went by, Sid began getting back late most evenings and he was often out most of Sunday afternoon when Flo would have preferred that they went for a walk in Richmond Park with the baby. But she didn't complain, Sid always paid the rent regular, not like some husbands, and gave her enough money to live on though she often had to remind him about it. She didn't even mind too much that Sid was hardly ever around. Even when he returned late after being out with his friends at the pub he was careful not to wake the baby coming up the stairs. Anyway, Tom was her life and she was never happier than when she was with him alone.

Flo always remembered the first time she took Tom round to visit her aunt in the big house in Park Road. The aunt nodded approval and served tea from a fine china pot. She seemed to ask a lot of questions about how Sid was getting on and gave her a ten pound note to open a Post Office Savings Bank account for Tom. Flo noticed her aunt was beginning to look frail.

One day, when Tom was about 18-months old, Sid never came home.

The next morning she went to a telephone box and rang the Supervisor at Bentalls in the department where Sid worked. But he hadn't turned up there either. He didn't turn up the next evening at home or clock in for work the following day. Flo was worried. She realised she didn't even know the addresses of any of Sid's friends and his parents had moved away shortly after the marriage. So she sent a telegram to her sister Ada who lived at Rayners Lane in north London. Ada had married Stan the policeman and they were both very concerned.

Ada came over the next day. Stan had contacted Kingston Police Station and they had promised to make discrete enquiries. Ada gave Flo what reassurance she could but it didn't look good.

The next day a policeman from Kingston called on Flo. Nobody answering Sid's description had come to their attention or been brought to any of the receiving hospitals. But they managed to locate the pub where Sid drank and talked to a few people who knew him. Nobody knew for certain but they thought he might have got into trouble with moneylenders or the bookies or some such. Flo was worried that she might be held responsible for her husband's debts but the policeman looked around the poorly furnished room and told her not to worry. Nobody would be bothering her for these few sticks, he thought.

As the days and weeks went by it dawned on Flo that Sid really wasn't coming back at all. She was glad that she had ten pounds saved that she'd put by for some eventuality such as this: at least it would pay the rent for the foreseeable future. But that and the other ten pounds in Tom's Post Office Savings Bank were all that they had in the world. In those days there was no universal Income Support and Child Benefit like now, the Welfare State was still twenty-five years off. And there weren't many ways you could earn a living when you had a toddler to look after.

Stan had suggested taking out a court paternity order on Sid forcing him to pay her maintenance money. But she had no idea where to find him and court orders sounded expensive.

But Flo was lucky, she was on nodding terms with the lady that managed the bagwash laundry at the top of her road. Some of the customers would pay to have their laundry ironed and Flo could do it at home. It wasn't much but it helped to stretch her meagre savings.

Every penny had to count so Flo would go with Tom in the pram to Kingston Market on a Saturday evening. Street markets stayed open until late on Saturdays in those distant days. Before they packed up, the stallholders sold off some of the left-over vegetables, unsold fish and scraps of meat at knock-down prices. Some weeks there was no money even for that and Flo had to make do with picking up discarded vegetables and trimmings from the meat that were left out with the rubbish when the market folk had packed up and gone home.

About three months after Sid disappeared a letter arrived through the post. All it contained were two one-pound notes. The post mark was smudged and unreadable but Flo knew immediately who had sent it. A month later another letter arrived, this time with a one pound note in it. The post mark seemed to suggest it was mailed in Portsmouth. Flo wondered if she should try and trace Sid. But what good would it do? He had abandoned them both; she knew he wasn't going to come back. Two months passed and another letter arrived with a single brown ten-shilling note in it. No more came after that.

Flo's aunt, the one who had lived in the large house in Park Road, had sold up and moved to a retirement home on the south coast shortly after Sid had left. Flo thought she should visit her but there was no way she could afford the train fares when struggling to make ends meet with a small child. So she wrote long letters instead. Mostly, they were about Tom: the first time he walked, his first words or their trips together to nearby Richmond Park.

If it was a fine day, Flo would pack their lunch and they would try to make it all the way to the Pen Ponds where Tom loved to feed the Ducks, Geese and Swans with stale bread. Tears would come to Flo's eyes as she watched her 'little man' standing by the Pond, holding out the crust, and along would waddle some fat Canada Goose and you could tell by Tom's face that he didn't know whether to laugh or run.

Bringing up the child single-handed and providing for them both was a full time job but Flo wanted nothing else.

She never tired of his company though sometimes she wondered if she should remarry so there would be a man in Tom's life. But she knew no man ever looked at her now. Even though she wasn't even thirty, she looked more like late middle-aged with every passing season. The same old clothes, constant hard work and the ever present worry about money took their toll.

Flo was never lonely though, certainly not once Tom began to talk and understand what she said.

Ada and Stan came over from north London when they could, the only visitors Flo and Tom ever had. They helped out with some things, buying items of clothing that Tom needed but Flo couldn't afford. You couldn't always get everything you wanted second-hand at jumble sales. Ada and Stan always made a fuss of their nephew and before long they had a child of their own: a daughter they called Doreen. One summer when Tom was three years old he and his mother went to stay with Ada and Stan for a few days at their house in Rayners Lane in north London. It was Flo and Tom's first holiday together and the child seemed full of excitement and wonder for his new surroundings. He got on well with Ada and Stan's new baby too.

About this time Flo received a letter from the nursing home in Worthing saying her aunt had died.

She wanted dearly to go to the funeral but she couldn't take Tom all that way there and back in a day. It was winter and would mean lots of standing around in a windy cemetery and at draughty stations and bus stops. She would have had to catch a train at 7 o'clock in the morning to be sure of getting to the cemetery at Worthing by ten in the morning. And the plain honest truth of it was she simply couldn't afford the rail and bus fares involved. So she sent some flowers instead even though she felt a little guilty.

A couple of months later a letter arrived from a firm of solicitors. It said that the aunt had left her two hundred pounds in her will. Flo was overjoyed, not for herself but for the difference it would make for Tom. Her savings were long since gone and she was living hand to mouth: taking in the ironing from the bagwash laundry was her only source of income and a meagre one at that. She was paid just two pence an item so she had to iron a lot of shirts and blouses just to pay the rent alone. She was at it six days a week, sometimes seven. Several things needed buying, mostly necessities for Tom, and until the bequest from her aunt arrived she didn't know where the money was coming from. For the first time it was all beginning to get her down.

Two hundred pounds was a small fortune in the 1920s but Flo knew it was going to have to last a very long time. She wasn't going to be blessed with money like that again in a hurry and she knew that children got more expensive the older they became. So although it was a great relief to know she had money in the Post Office Savings Bank, she still had to watch every penny and work late into the night with the smoothing iron after Tom had gone to sleep.

When Tom was five, he started at the church school attached to St. Luke's. It meant that she could take on a cleaning job for a few hours each morning which brought in a few extra shillings. The people she cleaned for were out at business during the day so in the school holidays she could take Tom along with her, though it was a bit of a strain keeping one eye on him all the time to make sure he didn't break anything.

One summer's day, she took Tom on a cheap day excursion down to Bognor Regis. It was the only seaside resort she knew. On the walk to the front from the station they passed the hotel where she and Sid had spent their honeymoon. Flo felt a pang of disappointment about Sid, about how things were going to be but never were.

Tom loved the beach, running around in the sun on the sand and splashing about in the sparkling water. Flo bought him a bucket and spade and they built a small paddling pool in the sand with sand pie turrets along the walls. Tom was in a world of his own. They had rock salmon and chips in a café on the front followed by ice cream before they caught the train back to Kingston. It wasn't as good as the ice cream she remembered from the Italian ice cream seller when she was a child. But Flo thought it was the happiest day of her life and Tom had loved every moment.

About a week after this, Tom caught the Chicken Pox. Flo was at home nursing him constantly for a couple of weeks. This meant she couldn't go and do her cleaning jobs so she lost her wages, the people she cleaned for were quite understanding but they didn't offer to make good the money. Ada had told Flo that there wasn't much Doctors could do for Chicken Pox and Doctors had to be paid for each visit or consultation in the bad old days before the NHS. So Flo didn't call one at first. But when the itching came out, she couldn't bear to see Tom suffer and she paid for the doctor to see him. He prescribed a milky liquid which Flo had to dab onto the spots with cotton wool, it seemed to give some relief.

When Tom left the Infants and started at Junior School, Flo gave up the cleaning jobs and began working part-time in the bagwash laundry in King's Road. But she still needed to take in the ironing as well.

The next year, they both went on their first real holiday. Ada and Stan were going down to Littlehampton for a week at Whitsun and they asked Flo and Tom to come too. They all stayed at a little boarding house near the front. The weather was fine and every day they went to the beach where Stan built all manner of things in the sand for Tom and Doreen and helped them find little sand crabs and shrimps in the pools of seawater that collected at the end of the breakwaters. The two children got on well together, they played together nicely, which pleased Flo. It was all so different to suburban Kingston and they had the time of their lives. Tom loved the little fun fair on the sea front and kept wanting to have goes riding on the giraffes and in the aeroplanes on the merry-go-round which turned to the accompaniment of flashing lights and loud music. Flo realised how important it was for children to get away from the Smoke, as London was called, and spend a few days in the fresh air and sunshine of the coast and countryside. It was a real tonic.

Another day they caught a river boat at Littlehampton and went on a trip to nearby Arundel Castle where Tom was fascinated by all the old swords and muskets and suits of armour. They climbed to the top of a tower and Stan told them stories about sieges and battles in the olden days which made it all come to life. Stan was good like that, in fact he was 'one of the best' all round. Ada had chosen well. For the first time in her life, Flo felt bitter towards Sid. Why couldn't he have stayed around and been more of a father to Tom? A child needed male influence of some kind, a mother couldn't be expected to provide everything. Stan was wonderful with Tom and she was very grateful to him. But Tom wasn't Stan's son and they saw him only occasionally.

When it was time to go home, they had one last visit to the fun fair and then started the long walk through the town with their suitcases for the train back to London. Flo had bought a cheap suitcase from Woolworths specially for the holiday and she hoped that this was the first time of many it would be needed.

Even though Stan was always willing to put his hand in his pocket for everything, Flo insisted on paying her own way most of the time. The holiday was worth every penny but it set Flo back quite a bit, she had to forgo things like buying a new pair of shoes that she needed for quite a while.

One day in a second hand shop she paid three pounds, a small fortune to her, for a second-hand radio or wireless as people called them back then. She was in two minds about buying it at first but reasoned it would be good for 'Tom's education' and took the plunge. It was an impulse purchase that brought them hours of interest and pleasure. They always listened to 'Children's Hour' on it together and in winter they would sit on the old brown sofa in the living room and snuggle up together under a quilt to listen to popular music on the BBC and even programmes from America using the shortwave bands. Flo used to hold Tom close to her and usually he would eventually fall asleep in her lap.

If she had a few coppers to spare, she would buy crumpets as a treat. These she toasted on the end of a long fork in front of the gas fire and they would eat them dripping with butter or margarine. When he was older, Tom enjoyed listening to the Dick Barton and Sexton Blake serials on the wireless and he sometimes brought his mates round to listen too. He got on well with the other children in the street, though there were the usual fights and accidents. But Flo was always there to give him a hug and tend to his grazed knuckles and knees with iodine, cotton wool and plasters.

When the time came, Tom joined the local Cub Scout troop. He never missed a meeting if he could help it. Flo had managed to pick up most of the uniform cheaply second-hand at the jumble sales held at St Luke's. She was right to have looked after that £200 carefully, children really did become more expensive as they grew up. And even though they were poor compared to most of the other childrens' families, Flo didn't want Tom to miss out on any of the things the others had if she could help it.

It wasn't always possible, though. Once Tom asked his mum for a pair of roller skates, all the other lads in the street had them. Flo had just paid the gas bill and even so didn't have money to buy new things just like that except for birthdays or Christmas. She tried explaining this to Tom but he didn't want to know. All the others were having fun with roller skates and he wanted a pair too. Tom flew into a rage and turned on the tears but Flo was firm with him even though it broke her heart. Eventually one of the other mothers in Staunton Road who knew of Flo's circumstances found a pair of skates that her child had grown out of and gave them to Flo on 'extended loan'. She had seen Tom watching the other kids on their skates and could see he was longing for a pair. Neighbours were like that in the old days, they looked out for each other. Wasn't that what going to St Luke's Church on Sundays was all about?

Tom went to his first Cub Scout Summer Camp for a week at their site at Seasalter in Kent. It was all a great adventure to him though Flo didn't know what to do with herself the week he was away, she missed him dreadfully. When the coach that brought them back arrived outside the Scout Hall, Flo had been waiting for at least an hour in case it had arrived early. There was a great gathering of mothers waiting around the coach. Suddenly, Tom came racing through the crowd towards his mother and threw his arms round her and held her in a bear-like hug. He'd obviously missed her a lot too.

Looking back, the thing that Flo always remembered most about those years was their summer holidays. They always went with Stan and Ada down to Littlehampton. The children loved it there so much, why go anywhere else? Tom would start to get excited weeks before the holiday and would count the days until they left. But one year, Ada and Stan didn't go to Littlehampton: they went to stay for their holidays with Stan's brother up in Yorkshire. So Flo decided that she and Tom would still go to Littlehampton together for a week's holiday.

They saw other children catching small fish and shore crabs from the jetty where the river meets the sea and Flo bought Tom a four penny fishing line consisting of twine wrapped round a square wooden frame with a double hook and heavy lead weight at the end. Tom soon got to know the other children who were fishing and he spent most of the week with them catching sprats or shore crabs, scraping limpets off the rocks to use as bait and discussing where the best places were to lower the lines.

The last evening they were at Littlehampton Flo took Tom to the Fun Fair near the sea front. He went on several of the rides and had a go on the shooting gallery. You got ten .177

airgun pellets for a three pence piece but although Tom loved it he didn't win anything. Then Flo saw Tom staring at the dodgem cars racing round and round the rink and banging into each other, sparks flying from the overhead electrical contact poles. Tom couldn't take his eyes off those dodgems.

At the end of each session a number of children and their dads would rush forward to claim a car and Flo could see from Tom's face that he desperately wanted to join them. She looked in her purse, there were still a few shillings left.

So Flo asked Tom if he'd like to have a go on the dodgems? She saw his big brown eyes looking up at her and he said 'But I haven't got a dad.' It was one of those unexpected things that children say sometimes but it cut Flo to the quick. She didn't let it show.

'Come on, I'll take you, didn't you know I can drive?' Flo said as quick as a flash. So they grabbed the next available dodgem car, paid their sixpence and off they went hurtling round the steel floored rink banging and bouncing off the other cars as they went. It was hard work for Flo and she found all the bumps unsettling. But whenever she sneaked a look at Tom's face she could tell he was thoroughly enjoying it and by the end he was laughing out loud every time they bumped into someone else.

'Shall we have another go, Tom?' Flo asked. 'This time you can drive.'

Tom's face was a picture of pleasure when he heard that and they quickly changed places before somebody else took the car. When the man came round to collect the sixpences he looked at Tom and said 'A bit young to be driving, ain't he missus?' Then he thought for a moment and said 'I'll just go and fetch a cushion for him so he can reach the steering wheel easier like.'

Tom soon got the hang of it and before long he was driving head on into everybody on either side. He was simply loving it. So much so that Flo dipped into her purse again for another sixpence and let him have a last go even though she thought it a bit of an extravagance she couldn't really afford.

On the walk back to the boarding house Tom talked non-stop about the dodgems and nothing else and Flo knew she had done the right thing to spend that one shilling and sixpence. She was still a bit upset though about how Tom had said 'But I haven't got a dad.'

When Tom was about ten, Ada and Stan bought Tom a bicycle as a birthday present. It wasn't new of course but Stan bought it from a proper second-hand bicycle shop that checked them over before they sold them. Stan brought it all the way over to Kingston on the train one Sunday. First he taught Tom how to ride it. Then he showed him how to fix the brakes and he gave him a special tool that you used for taking off the wheels. Stan also gave Tom a puncture repair kit in a tin and told him how to fix punctures and pump the tyre up again afterwards. Stan stressed that it was important to look after the bike. What he really meant was that as he wasn't going to be around much to fix things, Tom must learn to do it all by himself.

It was the best present Tom had ever had and he spent hours cleaning and oiling it and making adjustments. 'Fiddling with that bike' was what Flo called it and if he was missing she knew she could always find him in the shed in the alleyway at the side of the house where the bike was kept. The shed belonged to the couple who rented downstairs but they let Tom keep it there just as Flo had kept Tom's pushchair in it when he was small. Flo got on fine with the people downstairs but they kept themselves to themselves, you had to when you were sharing the same house with other people and didn't have your own front door.

Tom used to go on long rides with his friends to catch tadpoles and tiddlers in the ponds in Richmond Park, and sometimes to Bushey Park just over Kingston Bridge. His best friend came from round the corner near where the local Kingstonian Football Club used to have its original ground. He was called Sid, just like Tom's father, and Flo used to think it funny to hear her son talking about 'Sid'. Once Tom had asked why he didn't have a dad like most of the other children. Flo decided there was no point in not telling him the truth and said that he had gone away when Tom was very young and she didn't know where he was. But she made a point of adding that it wasn't Tom's fault, his dad had got into debt owing a lot of money and had to go away to avoid trouble. Tom listened to his mother but never said a word. One afternoon Flo came across Tom in her bedroom looking at the only picture she had of Sid: a photo of them taken on their wedding day. Other than that, Tom never showed any interest in his father again. In the aftermath of the bloodbath of the Great War, there were many children just a little older than Tom who had no fathers, though many of their mothers did remarry so they had stepdads.

The Great Depression of 1930 didn't affect Flo and Tom too much. When you haven't got much, you don't have much to lose. People still needed to have their laundry done and people still needed their clothes ironed. Flo only charged pennies for her ironing, so there was no point anyone trying to make a saving there if things were tight.

Eventually, when he was about 11, Flo began working almost full time at the bagwash laundry. Tom would go off to the big school in Richmond Road with some of his mates so she'd start at 9 o'clock and work through her lunch hour so she could leave at about quarter to four when Tom came home. It was a bit difficult in school holidays having to leave him home alone but she was only down the road in the laundry if he needed her. From then on, she didn't have to take so much ironing home to do. She would always prepare a cooked tea for Tom. One of his favourites was beef stew made with braising steak, carrots, and onions. Or she did bacon and bubble and squeak (a mixture of mashed potatoes and left-over greens that were fried together). Flo brought bacon off-cuts cheap from the Co-op store in King's Road and always picked out the best pieces for Tom, the bits that were lean and didn't have too much fat on them. Most weeks she did their real favourite, steak and kidney pie, which she made in a pie dish with a little china chimney in the middle to let the steam escape when it was cooking. She had learnt how to make the steak and kidney pie from her mother just before she died. Whenever she rolled out the pastry, she thought of her mother and how sad it was that Tom had no grandparents and what a fuss her mother would have made of him. But at least he had a wonderful aunt and uncle in Ada and Stan, when she saw them Flo always thanked them for all the kindness they showed Tom.

Flo usually bought a couple of pints of brown shrimps for their Sunday tea. There wasn't much meat to them, and you had to eat them with lots of brown bread and butter, but Tom would spend ages peeling the shells from the little shrimps. Often he'd make a little pile of shelled shrimps and then give it all to his mum before starting on another pile for himself. Shrimps were a lot smaller and fiddlier than the prawns that you buy in the shops today, but prawns were a lot more expensive. Flo would also make a salad to go with the shrimps from lettuce, tomatoes and spring onions which they ate with salad cream. The sophisticated delights of real mayonnaise still lay many years ahead in the future.

On Friday evenings, they had fish and chips from the shop at the top of the road for their tea, it was a big treat that Tom looked forward to. If Flo had a bit of money left after paying the rent they had a small cod and chips each and Tom could have a pickled gherkin or pickled onion, but not both. If cash was a bit short, like there were 'bills coming up', they would save a few coppers by having rock salmon and chips instead. Sometimes when money was really tight they would have one rock salmon and chips between them and a pennyworth of 'crackling'. This was all the bits of batter that fell off the fish when it was frying and collected at the bottom of the fryer. It was scooped out of the oil and left to drain and then sold for a penny a bag. Today it would be considered a 'heart-attack special' and you'd probably have to put a health warning on the bag, but with plenty of salt, vinegar and pepper it was a tasty way to make the fish and chips stretch further. Flo always made sure Tom ate an apple after his tea, it helped to counteract all the greasiness, and she knew fresh fruit was important for good health.

Tom became interested in football which he played in the road or up the local park with the other lads. Sometimes one of the other boy's dads took them to see the local team play: the Kingstonian football ground was just round the corner. Once a man from up the road came storming round to Flo, Tom had kicked the ball through his greenhouse window. She paid the man immediately for the new glass, even though she had to draw money out of the Post Office the next day to cover the rent. Tom was crying and thought she was going to be angry with him, but Flo just gave him a hug and told him accidents like that happened sometimes. Even so, it was rock salmon and crackling for them every Friday for a month.

There were a few times that Flo really did get angry with Tom though it wasn't often. Once, he played truant for the day with a couple of his mates, they went off to Hampton Court Palace Park to make a camp. But one of the Park Keepers saw them and phoned the School Board Inspector who came round and collared them. Flo shouted at Tom, what did he think he was doing not going to school? He'd be thrown out of the school if he wasn't careful, then he wouldn't learn nothing and wouldn't get a job. What would people think? Didn't he care about all the worry it caused her, wasn't life difficult enough as it was? Tom said he was sorry and promised he wouldn't do it again. The school made him make up the lost time several times over in Saturday morning detentions. Once it was finished with they didn't talk about it again.

Another time she discovered that Tom had left the electric fire on in his bedroom all day while he was at school. What made it worse, she had an electricity bill to pay and was having to rob Peter to pay Paul to make up the last few shillings. She had a go at Tom about that, wasting electricity when it was so expensive. The electric fire really burned it up when it was cold. Tom mumbled something about leaving it on to keep the burglars away. Later she smiled about that excuse, Tom knew she sometimes left the electric light on for that reason when they were out. Afterwards she felt a bit guilty about having such a go at Tom. So from then on when he occasionally left the electric fire or light on in his room, she turned it off for him and said nothing.

In 1935 Tom actually saw the King. It was Jubilee Year and King George V and Queen Mary went on a special tour of the country. One of the tours went through Kingston and Tom and Flo stood on the pavement in the Market Place and watched the big open car drive slowly by. The King waved back to the crowds while the Queen gave a regal smile. Flo thought the King looked tired but he still looked like a King what with his distinguished grey beard and robes. But she wasn't surprised when he died shortly after. When the sixth George was crowned they had a big street party round the corner and all the local children were invited. They put up trestle tables along the middle of the road and stretched red, white and blue buntings from one side to the other. For tea they had sausage rolls (which were more roll than sausage), cheese and pickle sandwiches, corned beef rolls, jam sandwiches and Madeira cake with red glace cherries in it, all washed down with jugs of lemonade and sugary tea. Afterwards they sang 'God save the King' and a neighbour who knew some conjuring entertained the children with tricks. Tom sat with the older youths drinking ginger beer and had quite a time.

That same year Tom left school. He was quite a bright lad but it never occurred to Flo for him to continue with his full-time education after he'd reached school leaving age even though he passed most of the exams in his Matriculation. He got a job as a Trainee Motor Mechanic in the workshops of a big garage on Kingston Hill. Tom had always been good with his hands and interested in fixing things and taking them apart to see how they worked. Mind you, Flo hadn't been too pleased once when she came home from work in the school holidays to find Tom had taken the carriage clock on the mantelpiece to bits. It never worked the same again after that.

With his first pay packet, Tom bought his mum a box of chocolates and a potted plant. When he gave them to her he said: 'Things are going to be easier for you from now on, Mum. I know you've had to scrimp a bit to look after us, well, now I'm going to start looking after us too.' Those words made Flo very happy and from then on the potted plant always took pride of place on the table in front of the living room window where it could catch the sun.

To begin with he was only sweeping up and running errands for the mechanics, but quite apart from anything else the extra money really did came in useful. He wanted to give Flo most of his wages but she insisted that one pound a week would be enough. It was about this time that Tom began saying that he wanted to become a proper Automotive Engineer one day and began talking about going to night school for an engineering qualification. So they began putting by a few shillings each week so that eventually he'd have enough to pay for the course. Flo wasn't exactly sure what an Engineer did, but she never asked Tom in case he thought she was ignorant.

The following year of 1937 Tom was entitled to one week's holiday with pay even though this didn't become law until the following year. As a benevolent employer who cared about the people he employed Mr. Nichols, the owner-manager of the garage where Tom worked, had anticipated the Holidays with Pay Act by one year. So it was decided that Stan, Ada and Doreen and Flo and Tom could afford to stay somewhere a bit more classy for their summer break. Their choice fell upon the Royal Hotel in Bognor Regis right on the seafront mainly because the bedrooms had balconies facing the sea and a three-course evening dinner was included.

The summer of 1937 was famous for its high rainfall but they managed to pick a slot of fine weather the second week in August so most days were spent relaxing and playing games on the beach.

It became usual for them to leave their deck chairs in mid-afternoon and go for an ice cream in a small beachside café. Tom and Doreen always chose a knickerbocker glory with its layers of different ice cream, fruit, fruit syrup and jelly: a relatively new transatlantic introduction in the 1930s that was proving very popular.

One day they entered the beachside café as usual and took their places at a table next to a group of people speaking loudly in a foreign language. Stan gave them a wary policeman's look – in those days anybody foreign or slightly different was always viewed with suspicion by members of the constabulary. There were five men wearing expensive-looking suits, a well-dressed woman and a girl with long blonde partly-platted hair in her mid-teens. She was also enjoying a knickerbocker glory and when she saw Tom also had one she smiled at him.

The man who was obviously the big shot in the group was the kind who missed nothing and suddenly stopped talking: he had noticed his daughter's reaction. Tom looked straight at the middle-aged man with thinning fair hair and noticed he was wearing a small round red, white and black badge with a swastika in the buttonhole of the left lapel of his jacket.

The man gave a slight smile and addressed Tom who was sitting quite close to him. He spoke reasonably good English.

'Hello, young man, are you enjoying your stay in Bognor Regis?' he asked.

'Yes, sir,' replied Tom remembering his manners. 'So long as the sun keeps shining and it doesn't rain.'

'Ah, the English weather,' replied the man. 'When is it not raining in England?

'One day you must come to Germany for your holiday, the summers are always hot and sunny. Specially when Adolf Hitler is speaking outdoors, the sun always shines then. One-hundred-percent guaranteed! The people even call it "Hitler weather."'

'Yes, I'd like that,' answered Tom still trying to be polite. 'Maybe I'll come and visit Germany one day.'

'Yes you must, I'm sure you would like it. Specially if my daughter was to show you round, you'd like that too I'm sure?' said the man rising from his seat to leave and placing his hand affectionately on the head of his daughter next to him who gave Tom another smile.

'Thank you, sir,' replied Tom sensing the man was important and not someone to be trifled with.

As he swept by the table where Tom, Stan, Ada, Flo and Doreen were sitting he half raised his right arm in some sort of greeting. His final words to Tom were: 'Contact me if you decide to come, young man.'

One of his side kicks lingered a moment longer to settle the bill and as he passed Tom he silently placed a small card on the table in front of him. Once the last German had left Stan reached out and took the card.

'Well, I'll be blowed, that was only von Ribbentrop the ruddy German Ambassador. I thought it was,' said Stan. And then turning to the Manager of the beach café: 'Do you know who you've just had in here?'

'Yes I know who he is,' answered the Manager. 'One of 'itler's mates. He's on 'oliday 'ere with his family. They're renting one of Gray's Bathing Huts on the beach, comes in here every day. His money's as good as anyone else's.'

'Blow me, ruddy Ribbentrop,' repeated Stan taking another look at the visiting card. 'Wait till I get back to the station and tell the lads, they won't believe me. Von Ribbentrop and his family down in Bognor for a paddle!'

Then turning to Tom he added: 'Well young man, I think the German Ambassador and his daughter took a shine to you, I dunno what your mum thinks?' and they all laughed.

Tom never did get to visit Germany as a tourist but almost did a few years later in another capacity. And nine years after his family holiday in Bognor Regis, von Ribbentrop received the death sentence at Nuremburg and danced for half an hour on the end of a rope because the U.S. executioner was ordered to botch the job or so people said.

Shortly after their return from holiday Flo became aware of the threat of war that all the papers seemed to be going on about. It still didn't seem real to her, just something that happened in the papers. Surely those politicians were too sensible to start fighting each other again, whatever their differences were? What about all those young men who were gassed and crippled in the last war, you sometimes saw them in the streets selling matches or playing a flute to earn a few coppers from passers-by, some with terrible deformities. Flo was relieved when she read about the Prime Minister, Mr. Chamberlain, flying off to Munich and working out an agreement with the Germans. She hadn't liked the way all the Reservists had been called up, and how sandbags began to appear outside the Barracks of the East Surrey Regiment in King's Road just along from the Co-op store. It was all getting too close to home for comfort.

Flo soon forgot about it once the papers switched to talking about other things.

That year they had a really nice Christmas. Ada and Stan asked them to come and stay from Christmas Eve until the day after Boxing Day, there being no public transport on either of the days in-between as usual. Stan's brother and his family were coming down from Yorkshire to stay too so Christmas that year was a big affair. They had a large roast capon for Christmas dinner, it was the first time Flo and Tom had ever tasted chicken because it was an expensive luxury in the days before battery hen farming. They both loved the taste and that of the cold roast gammon they had later that afternoon for tea with lots of different pickles including a jar of large black pickled walnuts which were Tom's favourite.

They listened to the King's Christmas Broadcast on the radio and in the evening they all played a new board game called Monopoly that Stan had bought. There was plenty of drink including bottles of pale ale, port, whisky and ginger beer. Flo hadn't had a drink for years, tea was her tipple, and she realised she quite liked the sweet heady taste of the port. Tom tried a few drinks too, he was 17 now, and enjoyed a Pale Ale followed by a whisky chaser. Flo felt a flash of caution as she suddenly remembered what it had done to Tom's father, but everybody was laughing and having lots of fun so Flo guessed it would be alright. Even though they were now older, Tom still got on well with Doreen. Together with Stan's brother's boys they all went into the front room for a time to teach each other all the card tricks they knew.

It was at Christmas that Stan and Ada talked to Flo about going somewhere other than Bognor or Littlehampton for their summer holidays the following year. The Sergeant in the Police Station where Stan was based had been to Bournemouth and came back with glowing reports of how wonderful it was. 'Just like the south of France, there's even palm trees,' was how he described it to Stan, though it was highly unlikely that Stan's Sergeant had ever been anywhere near the Mediterranean to know. So Stan suggested they should all go to Bournemouth for a change. Flo wondered to herself what was wrong with Bognor or Littlehampton and whether Bournemouth would be too expensive. But Stan was one of those people who always considered other people – he knew Flo would be concerned about the cost so he quickly pointed out that now Tom and Doreen had left school they could go in early July before the school holidays began when rates at the smaller hotels were much cheaper. And he reminded her that everyone was now allowed one week's paid holiday a year so that would help with the cost too.

When July came, Tom was sorry to leave his mates who lived in the same street but thought that a visit to a glitzy, ritzy seaside resort like Bournemouth would be quite something. The weather was exceptionally warm and they were all amazed at the size of the town and what it had to offer. There were public pleasure grounds, a two mile long promenade, tree-clad cliffs with chines running through them and an endless choice of entertainment in smart modern theatres and dance pavilions overlooking the front. And yes, there were Palm trees though some of them looked as if surviving the British winter had been a bit of a struggle.

One evening they took a sea cruise along the coast which went round Poole Harbour and on to Swanage in a large boat. It had a saloon bar where you could buy a drink and enjoy it leaning over the deck rail watching the twinkling lights along the coast as twilight fell. Stan persuaded Flo to have a Port and lemon, a highly popular 'cocktail' among working class women at the time. Another day they took a coach trip to Corfe Castle and the Blue Pool and had a cream tea on the way back. Some evenings they went to see a show, which Tom thoroughly enjoyed, specially the ones that included the latest popular songs and lots of leggy dancing girls. He thought it funny how you did things on holiday you could do where you lived but never did. Bognor and Littlehampton had nothing to offer like this.

Most days they just sat in deckchairs on the beach and read newspapers and magazines and talked and dozed. The weather was so good during that last summer of peace you had to take advantage of it when you could: there was just a gentle sea breeze to stop it getting too hot in the sun. The beaches were crowded, but not uncomfortably so, and Flo sat in a light coloured cotton frock and just enjoyed doing nothing – she could quite get used to this life, she decided!

Flo noticed that in between turning the pages of his Autocar magazine, Tom sometimes watched the girls on the beach playing hand ball in their one piece bathing suits. That was only to be expected, Flo thought to herself, after all Tom was eighteen now and was well on his way to becoming a man though he would always be her 'Little Tom'.

Tom and Doreen got to know a brother and sister of their own age whom they met on the beach. They came from Wimbledon, the next big town up from Kingston. Tom and the girl seemed to really hit it off together and they went for long walks along the promenade and explored the cool leafy chines behind the beach.

It was at Bournemouth that Flo met Connie for the first time. She had noticed her sitting alone in a deckchair near to them on the beach and thought how smart and sophisticated she looked. She was a few years older than Flo but appeared at least ten years younger and was quite attractive for someone on the wrong side of forty. She obviously hadn't had children to look after and support and clearly took some trouble with her appearance and her hair.

Several times a day Flo or Ada used to go up to one of the kiosks on the promenade to buy cups of tea and sandwiches and cake. At first they bought pressed beef sandwiches but soon discovered they sold crab sandwiches in brown bread which they all preferred and had them every lunch time from then on. They were the most expensive sandwiches on the menu but after all, thought Flo, you're only on holiday once a year.

On one occasion when Flo was up at the kiosk on the promenade she noticed the well-dressed woman from the beach was in the queue in front of her. Whilst taking money from her purse she dropped some of the coins and Flo helped her to pick them up. The woman thanked her and on the way back to the beach they fell into conversation. She told Flo her name was Connie and she came from Surbiton, just down the road from Kingston. She was staying in a big hotel in Bournemouth for the week with Eddie. Flo noticed that Connie never described Eddie as her husband but that was none of her business. Eddie was evidently a businessman and spent the daytime playing golf with business friends, which is why Connie came down to the beach each day on her own. She didn't seem to mind.

She saw Connie on the beach in the same spot each day and usually had a long chat. Flo explained that Tom was her son and Connie said what a handsome young man he was and before long all the girls would be running after him. Flo felt proud of Tom who was indeed a nice looking lad but wasn't too sure how he was going to handle all those girls running after him.

When Connie learned that Flo had to bring him up single-handed on what she earned working at the laundry she said with sincerity: 'He's a credit to you, Flo.' That was the first time anyone had ever paid her a compliment for the way she brought Tom up.

Connie evidently worked as head waitress in the Tudor restaurant in the Bentalls department store in Kingston where she was in charge of all the other girls. Flo was a little surprised, she thought that Connie would have a job that was more glamorous than that like being a Buyer in the women's wear department.

On the Friday before the Saturday that they were due to return home, Flo said goodbye to Connie. The latter gave Flo her phone number in Surbiton and said to ring her some time. Perhaps they could meet after work for a bite to eat and go and see a film. Connie liked seeing all the latest films, specially the American ones. Flo said that would be nice, but she thought to herself that it wouldn't be very practical really. She always liked to be at home when Tom finished work at the garage and that included many Saturdays. He always came home hungry and she always had his tea waiting for him. So although she thought she might phone Connie one day, she never did. Anyway, when they got home to Staunton Road there were other things to think about. The papers were full of war talk again. Flo had come to dread listening to the news on the wireless.

When it finally happened, that Sunday in early September, Flo felt very worried. She knew that sooner or later lots of young men would be going off to fight and if the Great War was anything to go by a lot wouldn't be coming back. She knew Tom could be called up, he was already nineteen, but she hoped that as he was employed at the motor works it might be considered a reserved occupation. Then, like Flo's father who had worked on the railways in the last Great War, perhaps Tom wouldn't have to go off and fight. Anyway, lots of people were saying it would all be over by Christmas so maybe the question wouldn't arise after all. Flo noticed that the sandbags were back outside the army barracks next to the Co-op store.

But it wasn't all over by Christmas. They began building military camps in Richmond and Bushey Parks and military trucks and cars became a familiar sight on the streets of Kingston. Tom told Flo that they were now servicing and repairing lots of army vehicles at the garage where he worked and this made her hope even more that Tom's job would count as war work and he wouldn't be called up. He had been attending evening classes every Tuesday for about eighteen months to study for his automotive engineering qualification. Maybe that would also count towards Tom not having to go off to war, Flo hoped.

Meanwhile, Tom had become friends with a girl called Gloria who lived just off the Richmond Road: she was a Confidential Secretary at the Hawker Aircraft works in Kingston and many of the letters she typed were top secret. They went to dances together and visited the cinema once a week. Tom had even been to her house for Sunday tea to meet her parents and a couple of weeks later Flo told Tom to invite her to their place for Sunday tea. From the way she looked at Tom, Flo could see that Gloria was quite taken with her son. But he was never home late, Gloria's parents insisted she was back by a certain time and Tom always walked her home by then. No doubt they stopped for a kiss and a cuddle, thought Flo, but what's the harm in that if they liked each other? You were only young once. Hadn't she and Sid done the same when they'd first met all those years ago?

During the first part of the War, what they called the Phoney War, not much changed for Flo and Tom. They were issued with Ration Books and more men and women in khaki appeared in the streets. One or two of the older lads up the road who Flo knew by sight were called up.

Tom began to take an interest in the progress of the War. Not that there was much progress, it seemed more of a stalemate. He read all the war reports in the papers and put up a big map on his bedroom wall with the front line drawn across it in red crayon. He also knew all the ranks and regiments in the Army. Tom said he was hoping to go into the Royal Engineers. Flo hoped he would join the East Surrey Regiment so he would be just round the corner and naively asked if any Royal Engineers were stationed there?

Then a few months after his next birthday his call-up papers came. Tom seemed excited and went off for an appointment with the Selection Board at the Guildhall in Kingston. He was a bit quiet when he came back, there were no places in the Royal Engineers and he had been posted to an ordinary infantry regiment with orders to report to their base in Farnborough the following week.

3: Don't spend all your money on the dodgems.

For Flo, the war only really began when Tom went off to join the Army. When he left his job at the garage for the duration they were sorry to see him go. There was a shortage of mechanics now that all the young men were being called up and they said they would keep his job open for him. Everyone still thought the war would be over by Christmas, but 'Christmas' now meant Christmas 1940.

The Friday before he left, Flo took Tom for a goodbye meal at a really smart restaurant in Kingston. The money didn't matter, she didn't know how long it would be until she saw him again. Tom's enthusiasm for the Army had been rekindled after the initial disappointment of not getting into the Royal Engineers. They had a most enjoyable meal with Scotch Broth with a dash of whisky to start followed by saddle of lamb with mint sauce and trifle to follow. It was the first time they'd eaten together at a fancy restaurant like that and Flo wondered why she had never thought of it before. It was the money she supposed. Things had been a little easier the last few years but old habits of having to watch the pennies died hard. She gathered that Tom had been to the restaurant before with Gloria.

Tom was full of all the latest war news and how some of his mates were getting on who had joined up right at the start. 'Don't worry, Mum, everything's going to be O.K.' said Tom. 'We'll soon have Jerry on the run, whether or not the Yanks come in on our side.' Flo wasn't so sure, she knew how long the last war had dragged on, and on one of her rare visits to the cinema she had seen newsreels of all those German troops in steel helmets at one of their march pasts. They looked quite formidable to her.

The Sunday before Tom left, Flo trimmed his hair. She had always cut Tom's hair to save the cost of going to the barbers. But this time when she had finished she picked up a lock of Tom's hair without his knowing and later put it in an old silver snuff box that had belonged to her father. Then she put it away in her 'jewellery box', a collection of cheap beads and trinkets. She remembered how when he was a young lad Tom loved playing with these things and called them his 'Pirate's Treasure'.

The night before he left, Tom went out with Gloria. He came back quite late, Flo was beginning to get a little worried. She'd washed and ironed the clothes that Tom was going to take with him and packed them in the little suitcase she'd bought years before for their holidays in Littlehampton. She slipped a couple of packets of biscuits into the case too, which she told him about, and a pad of writing paper and envelopes and some stamps, which she didn't. The next day, she walked with him down to Kingston Station to see him off. She bought a penny platform ticket so she could go right up onto the platform and stay with Tom till the last possible moment. Tom had been given a travel pass.

As the train began to arrive she hugged him tightly and kissed him hard on the cheek.

'Look after yourself, Mum,' said Tom as he stepped aboard. 'I'll send you some money soon as we get paid.' Flo waved and watched the train leave until it disappeared from view round the bend towards Norbiton, Tom had to change at Clapham Junction for Farnborough where he was to report to the barracks. As Flo walked back alone along King's Road to her home, she felt a little bit sad and a bit excited too. It would seem strange without Tom around. She would have lots of spare time on her hands. Flo had bought a paper as she left the

Station, she thought she might as well keep up-to-date on the War from now on. Flo had rarely bought a paper before, relying instead on the news on the wireless. She bought the Daily Telegraph because it seemed to have lots of maps and long articles with news from the front in it. When she got home, she made a pot of tea and sat by the table in front of the large sash window to read it: the table with the pot plant on it that Tom had bought her with his first pay packet. She also smoked a few cigarettes, which she always did when she needed to calm her nerves. Everybody seemed to be smoking like chimneys these days.

Flo sat there reading the paper from beginning to end until the light began to fade. A few months before Tom's call up the Germans had made their lightning strike westwards driving the British Expeditionary Force back to Dunkirk. Mr. Chamberlain, the Prime Minister, resigned and Winston Churchill took over. The War had begun in earnest but Flo still wasn't convinced by Tom's optimism about soon having Jerry on the run.

Tom wrote to her every week and he always included a postal order for one pound and five shillings in the envelope. His basic training had been tough but he didn't seem to mind. They were a good bunch of lads in his unit and the Sergeant wasn't all that bad either. The one he seemed to mention most in his letters was someone called Peter who came from up Richmond way.

After a couple of months, Tom received his first weekend leave. He arrived home late in the evening, Flo had been looking out her bedroom window for him for several hours before he came. She thought he looked wonderful in his khaki uniform, it seemed to fit perfectly and he obviously felt completely at ease in it. He looked a bit thinner, not that he had been overweight before. He'd brought her a whole pound of tea as a present: where he got that she couldn't imagine, it was getting scarce what with all the convoy ships being sunk by U-boats and Flo regularly had to reuse old tea leaves for a second cup.

She had a large cod and chips waiting in the oven which he devoured hungrily. Then he had a cup of tea and a cigarette, Tom had taken up smoking too. He was full of stories about his life in the Army. 'The food's not bad, Mum, and there's plenty of it. But it's not a patch on your cooking,' he said. That pleased her.

The thing he enjoyed most of all was the rifle practice, he was evidently quite a good shot and had been chosen for an inter-regimental shooting competition. There were rumours that they were going to be moved to another place now that the invasion scare was on, probably down to the south coast. 'Maybe it will be Littlehampton, Mum,' Tom said with a smile. 'That'll be nice, dear,' replied Flo. 'Just mind you don't spend all your money on the dodgems.' They both laughed.

The next morning Tom slept late and after a big breakfast of eggs and bacon that used up most of Flo's ration for the month he went off to Kingston to buy some things he needed. That evening he saw Gloria, they went for a meal together at a café and then on to a dance afterwards at the Kingston Empire. But Tom didn't say much about it when he came back. On the Sunday he and Flo went for a walk up in Richmond Park and got as far as the Pen Ponds before Tom realised they had better be getting back as he had a train to catch. Before he left, Flo gave him a present: a new Bravington Renown watch that she'd bought at the jewellers in Kingston Market. Then she walked with him down to the Station and he was gone again. The time seemed to have passed so quickly, what with arriving late Friday and having to leave Sunday afternoon to get back to Farnborough before his pass was up. It was a bit easier saying goodbye to Tom this time, specially as he seemed to have settled in nicely to Army life.

Flo bought the Sunday Telegraph and went home to read about the War, the news didn't look too good to her. She brewed some of the tea Tom had brought her, which tasted just like a pre-War blend, and smoked a couple of cigarettes.

The following Friday the woman who managed the bagwash laundry where Flo worked had some bad news. Business had fallen off at the laundry, what with so many men away in the services. The long and the short of it was, the owner had decided to close the laundry down for the duration. They'd stay open for the following week to hand back the washing that was already accepted but that would be it. But the Manageress had managed to squeeze an extra week's wages out of the owner for Flo.

The evening of the day she left the laundry, Flo sat down to read the 'Situations Vacant' in the local paper, the Surrey Comet. The first thing she saw was a large advertisement with a picture of three RAF Pilots staring out of the page and the headline: 'Help Them Defend Britain! Women Workers Needed For Immediate Start!' Evidently they were desperate for women assemblers on the shop floor at the Hawker Aircraft works in Canbury Park Road. Flo suddenly felt excited. It would be different from anything she had ever done before but they promised to train you - and the wages they were offering were a lot more than working in the laundry ever brought in.

She would also be doing her bit for the war effort or, to be more exact, to shorten the War and hasten the day when Tom would come back safely. So at 8.30 the next morning Flo took her place in the queue of new applicants outside the Personnel Office at Hawkers. She needn't have worried whether they would accept her or not, they hardly looked at the letter of reference the Manageress at the laundry had written for her. She was told she could start on Monday.

Her training began right away, basically she had to stand at a bench and bolt metal parts together using a pneumatic wrench. It hissed and made a lot of noise but Flo soon got the hang of it. She always remembered the Instructor's last words about the life of some young pilot depending on her bolting those parts together properly.

There were subsidised hot meals at the canteen and on the third day Flo was queuing for her lunch when she heard a familiar voice behind her.

'The tea isn't half as good here as in Bournemouth, is it Flo?'

She turned round to see Connie standing there, the woman she'd met on holiday at the beach the summer before last. Connie had been at Hawkers since they had started taking on extra workers in the autumn of 1939.

'The work's a lot easier here than at Bentalls,' whispered Connie. 'Popping rivets into bits of tin. The money's better too - and you're not running round on your feet all day like with waitressing. Don't want to spoil my legs with varicose veins if I can help it.'

Flo told her how she'd been laid off at the laundry just the week previously. And rather guiltily, she explained how she had meant to phone Connie but then the War intervened soon after the holiday and everything had gone topsy-turvy.

'And how's that handsome son of your's?' asked Connie. 'One of them fighter pilot aces I wouldn't be a bit surprised.' Flo had to admit he was only a Private in the Army. 'Well, that lad will do well wherever he ends up,' replied Connie reassuringly.

Over the weeks, Flo and Connie became regular friends. The assembly line that Connie worked on went to lunch five minutes earlier than Flo and Connie always kept a place at her table for her. After work on a Friday when they'd been paid they would go over to the Canbury Arms, opposite the factory, for a drink and a meal of spam fritters and mash or corn beef hash. It was always crowded at the Canbury Arms on Fridays and they had even opened a bar upstairs to cope with the extra customers.

Flo would always have a small stout, there were less shortages of beer in those early war years. Connie always seemed to know everybody, and after they'd finished their drinks several of them would go off to the 'flicks', as cinemas were called, of which there were four in Kingston at the time. Connie persuaded Flo to come along too, of course there was no reason why she shouldn't now that she had nobody to go home for after work.

Flo was quite flattered by the way Connie always sought her out. When she thought about it, she'd never had any real friends before, only Sid and her sister and brother-in-law Ada and Stan. She'd never had any time for friends, Tom had filled her life completely and she'd had to work all the hours God sent to support the both of them.

Flo began to enjoy her new found social life, she really looked forward to Fridays when they went to see the latest movies. Even work on the assembly line was fun, everyone was always joking and the loudspeakers blared out dance band music all day long while they worked. But Flo couldn't really understand what Connie saw in her as a friend, they were as different as chalk and cheese. Connie was outward-going and always ready for a good time. She was still attractive and had her hair permed regularly, wore stylish clothes and smoked De Rezke filter cigarettes. Flo had led such a sheltered life by comparison: she wore the same clothes year in and year out, it never occurred to her to do otherwise, and always bought the cheapest cigarettes going. Perhaps Connie wanted the company of another woman of her own age, most of the others in her group were still in their early twenties. Whatever the reason, Connie seemed to take Flo under her wing.

But weekends when she wasn't working overtime always went slowly for Flo, except for the five or six times each year when Tom came home on a weekend pass. So to keep herself busy Flo became a part-time Land Girl. They had dug up one of the playing fields in Park Road next to where Flo's aunt had lived in the big house. It was divided up into allotments to grow vegetables as part of the 'Dig for Victory' campaign. Flo took on half an allotment with a view to growing her own food. It would keep her occupied weekends and evenings when she wasn't working and was another way that Flo could help the war effort. Any surplus veg she gave away to old people living in her road who were most grateful. It all helped to fill the nation's larder. She planted lots of potatoes as she'd heard there was going to be a shortage next year, Doenitz's U-boats were torpedoing our merchant ships at an alarming rate and all food was getting scarce. She also planted onions which for some unexplained reason had been in short supply ever since the War began. Then there were carrots, leeks and cabbages and a few lettuce and tomato plants. Flo also grew a row of French beans which she thought very exotic and daring, she would have grown runner beans but she couldn't find any sticks for them to climb up.

From her allotment, Flo could see the little bedroom window at the back of her aunt's old house where she had lived over twenty years before. What would her aunt think of her if she could see her now, thought Flo?

Tom's girlfriend, Gloria, who worked in the office at Hawkers, belonged to what was called the white collar staff who took their lunch break an hour later than the blue collar workers on the shop floor. But sometimes their afternoon tea breaks in the canteen coincided and Gloria always came over to Flo for a quick chat.

During one of these she told Flo that while Tom didn't really want her to go out with other blokes while he was away, he had said it was unrealistic to expect she wouldn't as the War could go on for years and years. Nobody knew what was in store for them and there was always a chance that he wouldn't come back from the War at all. There was no point in hurting each other unnecessarily, so he'd got her to agree that while the War lasted they should only be friends. But he still wrote to her and saw her when he came home on leave. Flo could see Gloria wasn't really happy with the arrangement, she was very keen on Tom and hoped they'd get back together again properly when the War was over. But as the months went by Flo noticed her going off to the Canbury Arms after work with one of the young draughtsmen that worked at Hawkers. You couldn't blame her for that though, thought Flo, not after what Tom had said to her.

But what really upset Flo and sent a chill through her heart was what Tom had told Gloria about there being a chance that he wouldn't come back from the War. The fact that he was thinking along those lines really frightened Flo for the first time. When she told Connie about her fears, she told her not to worry.

'I reckon he's a sensible lad, your Tom, he's got his head screwed on right over this,' Connie told her. 'There's too many of them "Dear John" letters flying around these days and you can't fight a war with a broken heart. And of course he's bound to think of the worst happening sometimes. They all do.'

'I bet he comes back and marries that Gloria in the end, I wouldn't be a bit surprised, Flo. This war won't go on for ever, you know.'

Flo felt reassured, it was good to have a friend like Connie who you could share your fears with and calm your nerves, rather than bottling them all up inside.

At least Tom hadn't been posted overseas, she thought to herself. A lot of our boys who were taken prisoner after the fall of Norway were having a really tough time by all accounts. Or he could have been sent to fight in North Africa, war itself was bad enough but trying to fight in all that heat didn't bear thinking about.

Tom's unit spent most of the time guarding the coast in Sussex in readiness for the invasion, which the Germans called Operation Sea Lion, that was expected to come at any time. All leave was cancelled for long periods at the height of the invasion scares. Eventually he was stationed down at Selsey Bill, one of the key targets where the Germans were expected to make landfall when the invasion came.

There was one Christmas that Flo would always remember, the last time the whole family were to spend the festive season together - 1941. Tom had a whole week's leave and it was decided to have a real family Christmas despite the War. Stan had a few day's off from his police duties too so it was agreed that he and Ada and Doreen would come and spend Christmas at Flo's. They'd have to stay Christmas Eve, Christmas Day and Boxing Day nights as there was no public transport to get back to north London over Christmas. It would all be a bit of a squeeze but everyone was getting used to that in wartime.

Flo was very excited but was soon worrying about what to get for the Christmas dinner: the food shortages were really severe for any kind of meat by then. Roast Spam was alright for normal Sundays but you couldn't serve that up to the family on Christmas Day. Connie could tell Flo was concerned and came to the rescue. She managed to get Flo a leg of pork through Eddie, her gentleman friend. Flo wondered how Eddie had obtained such a rare luxury in wartime. She didn't say it, as she didn't want to offend Connie or appear ungrateful, but Flo wouldn't have wanted anything dodgy from the Black Market. Connie knew what Flo was thinking and said Eddie's family were all vegetarians and they had lots of spare meat coupons from their ration books. The leg of pork wasn't quite big enough for five people on its own but with plenty of sage and onion stuffing and some chipolata sausages it would do fine.

Tom, who by then had been promoted to Corporal, arrived a few days before Christmas and Flo managed to get time off from her work at Hawkers. Tom noticed she was looking a little older but he knew she had a strong constitution and always took everything in her stride. He slept a lot but they went to see a variety show at the Empire Theatre in Kingston and took some long walks in Hampton Court Palace gardens: the weather was quite mild for the time of year. She remembered all the times they'd gone there together when he was a child. It was just like old times and Flo wished it could go on and on for ever and ever. Well, it will, she told herself, once this blessed war is over. Once or twice Tom went out for a short while on his own, Flo wondered if he was going to see Gloria. But he never mentioned her name so she never asked.

When the others arrived just after lunchtime on Christmas Eve, everybody began to have a great time, war or no war. There was so much news to catch up on, you could only say so much in letters.

Stan and Tom hadn't seen each other for ages and they hit it off right away. As soldier and policeman they seemed to have a lot in common. They even went for a quick drink together at the Richmond Park pub in King's Road where the East Surrey Regiment squaddies went. It had to be a quick one though as beer was strictly limited by then. But Stan had brought over some bottles of pale ale, a bottle of sloe gin for the ladies and a half bottle of whisky for later. Heaven knows where that came from.

That evening they listened to the news on the wireless and then sat around drinking tea and talking about old times. Mostly that meant the holidays they'd spent together, especially that last one they'd enjoyed in Bournemouth over two years before. Stan had even brought along some photos he'd taken which he passed round. They all agreed that had been the best ever holiday and promised themselves they'd all go back together again once the War was over.

Stan said he wished he could have snapped a photo of von Ribbentrop paddling in the sea at Bognor the year they ran into him there in the ice cream parlour, he'd get a few quid from one of the newspapers for it if he had. Tom said he'd heard they'd laid mines along Bognor beach and the Promenade was covered in barbed wire 'just in case Jerry thinks it's a soft spot for an invasion.' Stan reminded them how Ribbentrop invited Tom to visit Germany. Tom told them he probably would be visiting Germany before too long but not at Ribbentrop's invitation!

They all had a good laugh over that but then Stan became serious and said people believed it was Ribbentrop telling Hitler that the British wouldn't fight that encouraged him to invade Poland which started the whole blinkin' War.

Doreen had an important announcement to make: she had just become engaged to a lad in the R.A.F. He hadn't got Christmas leave but Doreen passed round a photo of him in uniform. Everyone congratulated her and Flo asked when the wedding would be but she said it was too early to know.

The next morning they opened their presents in Flo's living room. Tom had bought her a thick woollen cardigan, she wondered how many clothing coupons that must have cost. Flo had bought Tom a Dunhill cigarette lighter and a hot water bottle. There was quite a shortage of hot water bottles, you couldn't get one for love nor money. But quite by chance she'd been in Bentalls and discovered they'd had an unexpected delivery so she joined the queue and bought one. It had cost a bit, but she was earning good money now at Hawkers and, anyway, if it kept Tom warm at night Flo would have bought it whatever the cost.

Stan and Ada gave Flo a Mother of Pearl picture frame and a bottle of port wine. Nobody was in any doubt about whose photo Flo would be putting in the picture frame and the bottle of port was quite something as by Christmas 1941 none of it arrived on the convoys even though Portugal was a neutral country. In return Flo gave her sister a pair of leather gloves and her brother-in-law a dozen packets of his favourite Senior Service cigarettes: tobacco and cigarettes weren't on ration but often they were in short supply and a devil of a job to find. Later they went to the Christmas morning service at nearby St. Luke's Church followed by a drink at the Grey Horse in Richmond Road which allowed Flo to get on with preparing the food.

They had their Christmas dinner early, it was a grand affair. Flo made a point of telling everyone she had grown all the vegetables herself on the allotment. That included the potatoes, some of which were boiled and some roasted, mashed parsnips, casseroled leeks and cabbage. The gravy was perfect, Tom said he'd never tasted gravy so good.

The pork was nice and tender and had a flavour most of them had almost forgotten. Stan wanted to know where Flo had obtained such a nice joint, the policeman's curiosity in him was aroused. She explained it was from Connie's gentleman friend, Eddie, whose whole family were vegetarians so they didn't use their meat coupons. Stan gave his wife a knowing look and asked no more questions. Flo had also made a Christmas Pudding. Not like the ones you could make before the War with lots of sultanas and nuts. But she had followed the recipe on a Ministry of Food leaflet that advised putting grated carrot and bits of chopped up apple in it and nobody appeared to notice the shortage of dried fruit.

They listened to the King's Christmas broadcast which introduced a serious note to the occasion. But they all agreed that now the Yanks were in the War after the attack on Pearl Harbour they had more reason than ever to hope it would 'all be over by next Christmas'.

They never seemed to stop talking, that last wartime Christmas they all spent together. Stan had so many interesting and funny stories to tell about things that cropped up in his police work, and a few macabre ones too which he toned down for present company. He was a great story teller with a good sense of humour was Stan. Tom had a few good tales to tell too, like the time they captured the crew of a sunken German E-boat who landed in Pagham Harbour in a huge rubber dinghy. They didn't have a compass on that starless night and stupidly thought they had arrived back on the French coast. It took a few rounds of .303 rifle shot over their heads to convince them which side of the English Channel they were really on and force them to give themselves up.

As the evening wore on, Stan got out the bottles of pale ale, the sloe gin for the ladies and the whisky. Tom produced a bottle of Schnaps that he had liberated from one the German E-boat crew. The couple who lived downstairs from Flo were invited up for the evening and the proceedings took on something of the semblance of a party. They even sang some of the favourite wartime songs that Vera Lynn and Ann Shelton had made popular. Ada always led the singing. Flo liked the one called 'Yours' which she'd heard Vera Lynn singing on the wireless.

On Boxing Day everybody got up late, except Flo who rose early as usual to prepare vegetable soup and an enormous Spam and Leek Pie made with powdered eggs for later in the day. They all went up to Richmond Park for a walk. It was a sunny day and still quite mild, if you half-closed your eyes you could even imagine it was spring already. Large parts of the Park were occupied by the Army and were fenced off but they still managed to reach the Pen Ponds by a round-about route.

Flo almost felt they were all on holiday again, sitting there together on a bench in the sunshine. Stan had brought his camera and took a photo of them with the Upper Pond in the background. Flo stuck close to Tom the whole morning, she didn't let him out of her sight for a minute. Several times he took her by the arm as they strolled along through the Park.

There were lots of different kinds of ducks and geese wintering on the ponds and they swooped low over the visitors. They were still expecting pieces of bread, thought Flo, like in the days before the War began. But nobody had scraps to throw away that winter, the birds had to forage for pond insects and worms as best they could. Flo remembered Tom's face when he had first seen all the birds the first time she had taken him there more than twenty years before. Then the sky clouded over and it began to get colder so they started to make their way back. The hot vegetable soup and the Spam and Leek Pie went down a treat when they returned and nothing was left. That evening they tucked into Welsh Rarebit made with a nice piece of mature Cheddar that Ada and Stan had brought over.

The next day, Ada and Stan and Doreen left for Rayners Lane first thing in the morning. Stan was due on duty for the afternoon shift. Before they left, everybody agreed it had been a wonderful Christmas break, a welcome respite from the work and worry of wartime. No air raids either and so much good food, how did Flo manage it when everything was in such short supply everyone asked?

A couple of days later on it was Tom's turn to leave. Flo had had him all to herself for those last two precious days, she was so happy. Before he left, Tom made her promise always to go down the public air raid shelter in nearby Latchmere Lane the minute the warning siren sounded. Like a lot of people she had become complacent and didn't bother half the time, unless it was a really big raid.

'I don't want to come back one weekend and find you missing, Mum,' said Tom.

As usual, Flo walked with Tom to Kingston Station when it was time for him to return for duty. Tom could see that Flo was a bit low as they were walking along King's Road.

'Cheer up, Mum,' he told her. 'Things are going to change for the better this year. The Second Front's coming and though there'll be a hell of a shindig when it does, the Germans can't fight us, the Yanks and the Ruskies all at the same time. Then this rotten War will be over once and for all and I won't have to go off and leave you like this.

'I'll train to be a proper Motor Engineer after the War and get an apprenticeship. It's well-paid work and more and more people will be wanting cars once the War's over. I'll see you never want for anything, Mum, you see.'

They hugged on the platform as the train pulled in and Flo waved until the last carriage disappeared round the bend towards Norbiton. Then she bought a copy of the Daily Telegraph and went home to make a cup of tea and read about the War from cover to cover.

Connie had a great Christmas too. In the Staff Canteen she told Flo that while Eddie was tied up on Christmas Day she and Eddie had gone away on Boxing Day to spend a couple of days at a posh hotel on the Thames near Henley. It was one of the few that hadn't been requisitioned by the Armed Services. Eddie had given her an expensive diamond brooch in the shape of a flying bird. How many weeks wages that must have cost, thought Flo? What ever did Eddie do for a living to be able to afford things like that, she wondered? But of course, she didn't ask and Connie never said.

Flo told Connie what Tom had said about the Second Front and it being the beginning of the end for the Germans. 'He's quite right, that lad of yours,' replied Connie. 'I really reckon that once we get over there it will all be over by next Christmas, and probably quite a long time before that. Imagine the Victory party we'll have then!'

Connie persuaded Flo to join her and a group of girls from Hawkers who were going to a Saturday night dance at Surbiton Assembly Rooms. 'Me go dancing?' Flo had said when Connie first asked her. 'But I'm not looking for a boyfriend. Not at my age.'

Connie laughed. 'We're not going there to get married,' she replied. 'We're going there just to have a good time. Have a few giggles and a few drinks, that's all Flo. Come on, why don't you come too? Everybody needs cheering up once in a while these days what with this blooming War.'

So Flo decided to go. It was all in aid of the Kingston Hurricane Fighter Fund, all the half crowns from the entrance money were going towards the cost of a new fighter plane. Once she was there Flo felt reassured. Although they were mainly younger girls at the dance, there was still a sprinkling of middle aged women like her there too.

Inside the hall, everyone was laughing and showing off. They took over a table near to the entrance and all of them chipped in for some drinks. They mostly drank a punch of some sort, nobody knew what was in it but it certainly lived up to its name.

At first the girls all sat there smoking and sipping their drinks but one by one they were invited to dance. There were quite a few servicemen in uniform present and they weren't shy about making the first move. The girls usually returned to the table after each dance but after a while there were quite long periods when everyone at the table was on the dance floor except for Flo and a girl from the Costing Department who was lame in one leg. Even Connie was joining in the dancing, but nobody asked Flo.

That neither surprised nor bothered her, she hadn't expected anyone would ask her to dance. Ever since Sid had left her she'd never really thought about finding another man. Tom was the only man in her life and he was enough for her, even when he was away for long periods guarding the coastal defences down at Selsey Bill. So she just sat there enjoying the music of the dance band, sipping her punch and smoking cigarettes.

Then she noticed an older, somewhat distinguished officer in a light blue uniform looking at her. Eventually he walked over and asked her politely if she would care to dance. Flo was surprised but she didn't say no. She'd hardly ever danced before but on the crowded dance floor there wasn't room to do much more than just hold your partner and shuffle round taking care not to tread on anybody's toes.

The guy turned out to be a Staff Officer in the Royal Canadian Air Force. He wore rimless glasses just like the bandleader Glen Miller and had swept back hair with a high forehead. They made small talk as they danced, he was very polite - the sort of man you immediately felt at ease with. After a couple of dances he asked if she would like a drink and they went and sat at a little table together on the other side of the hall. He spoke softly, but Flo could tell he was well educated and he had a gentle smile on his face as he talked.

He asked Flo where she worked and she told him about the Hawker Aircraft works and what she did there. 'You better not tell me too much about that - careless talk costs lives!' he joked, repeating the slogan from the famous wartime poster of the time. She told him all about Tom and he seemed interested.

It turned out his name was Rick and although he didn't say it, he must have been in his late forties. He was an accountant from Winnipeg where he had a wife and two sons still at school. The mention of his family dispelled any slight fears Flo had about his motives, somebody with ungentlemanly designs wouldn't mention that he was married surely? He told Flo all about his home town and his two boys and other relatives in Canada. She told him about her friend Connie, and the nice times they had together going to the cinema. They spent some time discussing the latest films and discovered they both had the same favourite actor, Clark Gable, fresh from his latest success in 'Gone with the Wind' shot just before the War started.

Then after about an hour and a half or so Rick looked at his watch and said that unfortunately he had to leave as his furlough ended at midnight and he had to be back at his base in Bushey Park. As he was leaving he said: 'I'd like to thank you, Flo, for letting a home-sick stranger monopolise your time for so long. I've enjoyed talking to you greatly and I feel more at home in England now.' Flo mumbled something about the pleasure being all hers and they parted.

It was like that in wartime, people met and did and said things they would never do or say in peacetime. Flo felt a slight pang of disappointment as he walked away. She never saw him again of course but she was surprised and flattered that a complete stranger seemed to have enjoyed her company so much, even though it was for just an hour or two. For the rest of her life, whenever she heard Canada mentioned she always thought of Rick the air force officer whom she had met briefly one night in wartime and hoped he was among those who survived the bloodshed.

Of course, when she got back to the other girls they pulled her leg about it. 'You're a sly one, you are,' said one of them called Winnie. 'We all know who you'll be sitting in the back row of the Regal with next Saturday night,' joked another. And they all laughed and Flo became quite embarrassed and said it wasn't at all like that. Then Connie came to her rescue and told them to leave her alone. Of course Flo could have men friends if she wanted, she was a very nice person and there was no reason why she shouldn't. Flo didn't really mind, she just lit another cigarette and sipped her punch and hid behind a smile.

The War seemed to go on for ever and ever and there were times when the imminent threat of invasion meant all weekend leave was cancelled. Selsey Bill was in a restricted coastal zone which civilians from outside the area couldn't visit so when Tom only had a twelve hour pass they always arranged to meet in nearby Chichester. On one such visit Flo was travelling down by train when German daylight raiders appeared overhead and the train had to shelter for a time in a tunnel near Arundel until the danger passed. There was no heating on the train but Flo had taken a Thermos of tea which warmed her up. She'd allowed plenty of time for delays and eventually managed to get there without being too late.

Tom was waiting for her at Chichester Railway Station wearing his army great coat and they walked along South Street chatting. Flo liked the way he took her by the arm as they walked. Although everything was rationed and there were many shortages, the streets were still crowded with busy shoppers, just like in the days before the War. They went into the Cathedral Close and sat on a stone bench in the Cloisters, it was more peaceful there. It was a cold day and the sky was a leaden grey but Flo didn't seem to notice: when she was with Tom for a few precious hours the sun always seemed to be shining. He told her about what his unit had been up to - mainly endless hours of watching the English Channel, the boredom occasionally broken when they had to search the beaches for the body of some unfortunate airman or sailor washed up after engaging the enemy out at sea.

His platoon had been attached to the Coastguard Lookout on the shore at the bottom of West Street in Selsey. They were billeted in a row of cottages next to the Lookout which Tom said was comfortable enough. Evidently he'd become friendly with a girl called Vera who lived in the cottage where he was staying: she was the daughter of one of the Coast Guards and helped out with the cows on a nearby farm. They often went to dances at the Marine Hotel on the sea front, or the Pavilion in the High Street, and took long walks across the Saltings as far as Bracklesham - but they had to be careful not to wander onto the beach as it was mined. Flo noticed that Tom didn't mention Gloria any more.

It was getting a bit chilly on the bench so they went inside the Cathedral and sat there for a few moments. Flo fell silent for a while, Tom knew she was asking a favour from the boss man upstairs and had a pretty shrewd idea it had something to do with him coming back from the War in one piece. Then they walked back to South Street where they went into the Crypt Tea Rooms that had toasted muffins and brambleberry jam on the menu. Flo told Tom all about life at the Hawker works and what she'd been up to with Connie. Tom was glad his mum was keeping occupied and had made a good friend, he thought she seemed to be happy with her life despite his absence and the War.

Then Tom turned a bit serious and almost whispered in a secretive way: 'Look Mum, we're not supposed to talk about it but everyone does. You know all this talk about a Second Front, well, between you and me I don't think it's too far off. If we're ever to end this War we've got to cross the Channel and start fighting the Jerries on their own ground.

'There's a rumour going round that when that time comes, our unit will be going over, not necessarily in the first wave but shortly after. All this hanging about waiting is getting everybody down - we want to be over there and finish the job.'

Flo felt slightly anxious when she heard that, she was hoping he'd be kept away from the actual fighting. She lit another cigarette and offered Tom one. Then he continued.

'Well what I'm saying is, when that time comes I might not be able to write for a while. And if I do there's a chance that the mail might not get out of the battle zone very quickly. So what I mean is, don't worry if my letters stop for a while, that's the reason why. And don't worry Mum, everything's going to be alright.'

Eventually, Tom looked at the Bravington Renown watch that Flo had given him when he first went off to the War.

'I'm afraid we better be getting back to the Station, don't want you to miss your train to London. No telling when the next one might be.'

When they reached the Railway Station, Tom's friend Peter was waiting for him, he'd also had a twelve hour pass and had come into Chichester. He was the lad who came from Richmond and was Tom's best mate. They hoped to hitch a lift on a military transport back to Selsey or, failing that, they could catch a bus from the bus station opposite. They saw Flo onto the train which to everyone's amazement actually arrived on time.

Everybody was working flat out at the Hawker works during the spring of 1944. You just knew something big was coming up, they were turning out Hurricanes faster than ever before. Everyone was expected to work as much overtime as they could. Those with families grumbled but Flo didn't mind, she had only herself to think about. Whilst most of the other women lived for the weekends and evenings and almost had to drag themselves to work, Flo positively looked forward to going in. Sometimes Flo couldn't believe the amount of money there was in her pay packet what with all the overtime. It was far more than she could spend on herself so what was left over went straight into her Post Office Savings Bank every week.

Despite going to the pub and the pictures with Connie and the other girls in her group, Flo didn't have much to do on her time off other than work her allotment. Of course, she had to spend time queuing for food and hunting around to find shops that had things that weren't on ration, specially cigarettes. But mostly it meant going to the butcher, bakers or grocery store where she was registered to draw her ration and waiting patiently in the queue. Flo seemed to spend most of Saturday morning queuing outside the butchers on the corner of

Wyndham Road opposite the Roman Catholic Church in King's Road. But she didn't mind because she liked listening to the other women gossiping in the queue, it broke the boredom of her lonely weekends.

Saturday was also the day that Tom's weekly letter usually arrived, that was something she really looked forward to and became quite disappointed if it was delayed a day or two. She usually wrote her letter to him on Sunday afternoon and posted it on the way to work the next morning.

One afternoon Flo was sitting in her living room reading the Daily Telegraph when there was a terrible explosion. It shook the whole house and rattled the windows until she thought they were going to break. The blast was so great that even the potted plant on the table began to totter as if it was going to topple over. Looking out the window the sky seemed to darken for a moment as a great cloud of dust swept by and Flo heard debris raining down on the roof above her, it was really quite frightening. Then came the sound of bells ringing on emergency vehicles. There wasn't an air raid on at the time so she guessed it must have been one of those new pilotless flying bombs that had landed and exploded.

Flo went down the stairs and opened the front door. She looked up towards King's Road and saw an Auxiliary Fire Service pump speed by, people were running in the direction of the Richmond Park pub and there was a lot of shouting. She followed them up the street and as she approached the crossroad with Park Road she could see that houses had collapsed into the road and fire was raging in several places. By the time Flo reached the crossroads two fire appliances were dealing with the flames but round the corner the devastation was even worse. Civilians and people in all sorts of ARP, AFS and London Fire Service uniforms were clawing at the wreckage of homes and shops. A policeman was shouting instructions, trying to get ordinary people who had come to help to work in groups searching for survivors and keeping them away from the buildings that looked likely to collapse.

Flo joined one of the groups pulling bricks and lumps of concrete away from the side of a maisonette where voices had been heard. As she looked down at the rubble, Flo noticed she was still wearing her carpet slippers. Everybody was working like demons shifting the fallen masonry. Then the Heavy Rescue Squad arrived and everything began to take on some semblance of proper order.

There was obviously going to be quite a few casualties. Some were being carried away on stretchers or doors that had been blown off in the blast. Flo saw an old woman with blood dripping from her head being helped away. She must have been eighty if she was a day. Flo concentrated on the rubble of the collapsed maisonette. She never knew she had the strength to lift some of the bits of debris, it took several people to lift some of the larger pieces.

It was Flo who found the first child, a little girl of about seven years old. She saw her arm first among the rubble and had lifted her clear even before the others came over to help. She looked so peaceful, lying there in Flo's arms, almost as if she was asleep. The child was completely unmarked but it was clear she was already dead. As a man from the Heavy Rescue Squad took the body from her he whispered to Flo: 'It was the blast, she wouldn't have known a thing, love.' It was horrible to think that only half an hour before she was alive and well, playing nicely with a brother or sister no doubt.

Flo continued helping with the rubble even though there were now lots of rescuers on the scene. They pulled out an older woman and two younger women from the ruins before Flo finished. Only a little boy was still alive. Eventually, one of the policemen took Flo by the arm. 'Come on, Ma, you've done enough, you can leave it to the professionals from now on.' He led her over to a makeshift canteen where she was handed a cup of strong sweet tea. As he left her, the policeman said: 'Look after those hands when you get home, you'll need to put some Dettol on those cuts.' Flo looked at her hands for the first time and realised they were raw and bleeding from grappling with the rubble. She finished the tea and slowly made her way home down King's Road.

Not long before she would never have believed she was capable of doing anything like that. It was quite surprising the things people did, and the strength they found to do them, in time of war. But she couldn't get the thought of that little girl she had found out of her mind. How horrible this war was to do things like that to innocent children. And that little boy who survived, how do you explain to him that his mother has gone forever? And she thought of Tom, no longer a child but a man, but always 'Little Tom' to her, even though he was over 6 feet tall.

The next day she went into work as usual. Connie was amazed when Flo told her what had happened and insisted she went up to the First Aid Room to get her cuts cleaned and dressed properly. 'You're a real hero, Flo,' she said in the canteen at lunchtime. 'I don't think I could have done what you did. Not for a minute. You deserve a ruddy George Medal, if you ask me.'

Tom and Flo met just before he went over to France. It was the fifth spring of War and his unit was back in the barracks at Farnborough. There was no real leave coming up but Tom wrote to say he had an afternoon pass the next Sunday. Not enough time for him to get up to Kingston and back, specially with the uncertainty of the trains and the constant alerts caused by the so-called 'Little Blitz': the last German bombing offensive on Southern England that lasted from January to May 1944. So they arranged that Flo should go down to Farnborough in order to meet for a few hours and make the most of the available time.

Flo started off early, it was a bright morning and there was warmth in the Sun. As the train crawled slowly out of the London suburbs, Flo noticed that the yellow daffodils were out everywhere. They were such an uplifting sight after the long grey winter and the constant struggle with food and fuel shortages. Once she arrived at Farnborough Station, she followed the instructions in Tom's letter and walked south along the main road until she reached the Barracks. There was a tall red-brick wall surrounding it and as Flo passed the main gate she noticed an assortment of multi-storey Victorian buildings inside. A few yards further on there was a small public garden set back from the road with a couple of benches in it, just as Tom had described. Flo was about half an hour early, so she poured herself a cup of tea from the Thermos she had brought with her, lit a cigarette and waited. After a while, another woman arrived and sat on the other bench. She was obviously waiting for someone from the Barracks too.

Eventually Tom turned the corner in his smart khaki uniform now displaying three stripes and with a smile on his face. She gave him a quick hug and they sat down on the bench. 'How you keeping, Mum? You look a bit thinner, sure you've been eating properly?'

'Don't you worry about me, dear,' replied Flo. 'You know me, never had a single day's illness in my life.

'But what's all this, you promoted to Sergeant, you never told me.'

'Thought I'd surprise you, Mum,' Tom replied. 'I'll probably be a General before this War's over.' They both laughed and Flo secretly wondered whether being a Sergeant meant there was less chance of him being killed?

Tom gave her something wrapped up in greaseproof paper inside a brown paper bag. She could tell from the aroma, without even having to look at it, that it was a piece of mature Stilton cheese, her favourite.

'Had to twist a few arms to get that, I can tell you Mum.' Then they went for a walk in a nearby park where the daffodils were out in force, everywhere was ablaze with their golden heads.

'I think we're going over soon, like I mentioned before,' Tom said in a hushed voice. 'Lots of troops and transports have been moving down from the north. They're bivouacked on commons all around here. Can't be long now.'

'You will be careful, won't you Tom, don't do anything silly,' said Flo holding his arm and staring at him with a worried look in her eye.

'I know you've got a job to do but you will take care of yourself, won't you? I don't know why they let this War start in the first place, someone must have seen it coming and could have done something to stop it.'

Tom smiled. 'I've told you not to worry, Mum. I'm not the only one going over, you know. And we have been training for years, we know what we're doing.

'I'll be coming back alright, you'll see. Someone's got to take care of you in your old age,' he joked.

She replied: 'Yes, dear, but I'm bound to worry, I can't help it.'

Flo told Tom all about her work at Hawkers and how Connie was getting on. And then she told him about the flying bomb that had fallen at the junction of King's Road and Park Road and had killed eight people. There were lots of other soldiers walking with relatives and girlfriends in the park but they managed to find somewhere to sit and Flo poured them both a cup of tea from her Thermos.

'There's nothing like your tea, Mum,' said Tom.

'We drink gallons of the stuff but none of them can make a brew like you do.' Then Tom said he knew a little tea house back towards Farnborough and they slowly walked in the direction of the town.

They managed to get the last table and ordered a pot of tea and toast and plum jam. There were no scones on the menu in the Spring of 1944, just another little 'shortage' that everyone was used to by now. The jam was quite passable for wartime but the margarine wasn't a patch on the butter from the local dairy they sometimes had when they could afford it in the old days.

Tom mentioned Vera a few times in the conversation, the daughter of the Coast Guard down at Selsey Bill where he had been billeted. Flo sensed he was quite keen on her. While he was paying the bill at the tea house, she noticed a letter in his wallet with a Selsey postmark. It must be serious, Flo thought, and hoped she was a nice girl and Tom wouldn't get hurt. If they were right for each other, then that's all that mattered, she decided.

They slowly walked back down the main road towards the Barracks. Flo knew she wouldn't be seeing Tom again for quite some time if what he said about the coming invasion of mainland Europe was right. He'd suggested they walk straight to the Railway Station to save her the walk back, but every minute with Tom was precious now and she wanted to delay their parting for as long as possible. So holding his arm more tightly than ever she insisted on seeing him back to the Barracks.

She saw the Main Gate growing larger as they approached it and knew it was now only a matter of seconds that they had left together. She didn't want to embarrass Tom by becoming too emotional when they said goodbye, she knew other soldiers would notice and she knew what squaddies were like. So she just gave him one last hug and kissed him quickly on his cheek. For a fraction of a second as Flo stood there with her arms round him, and feeling him close to her, she felt Tom was just a little boy again who she was saying goodnight to like years ago.

'Just you take care, my love,' were her last words to him.

As she turned to go Tom said: 'You look after yourself too, Mum. I'll be thinking of you every day.'

Then she walked away as briskly as she could so Tom wouldn't notice the tears beginning to well up in her eyes. But after she'd walked about ten yards she stole a glance back and just saw him about to disappear into one of the buildings inside the gate. But just before he did he turned and looking back towards her gave her a big smile and a wave.

Flo walked back to the Station with a heavy heart. But once she was on the platform waiting for the train, she lit a cigarette to steady herself and began to think. It was all for the best really, like Tom had said. We couldn't go on like this for ever, better to get the War over and done with and then everyone could get back to a more normal life. So as the train crawled back to London, she was quite hopeful that what was coming was for the best. And she began to look forward to having a piece of the Stilton that Tom had given her when she got home.

4: The War Office regrets to inform you

One day not long after, Flo was working at her bench at the Hawker works listening with the others to Worker's Playtime on BBC radio that was relayed over the Tannoy system. Every now and then, when a popular song that they knew the words to came on, they would all sing along. It helped to relieve the boredom of the repetitive work.

That day they were all singing the words to 'Yes, My Darling Daughter' when suddenly the music stopped. A scraping noise was heard from the loudspeakers and then they heard the familiar voice of the BBC news reader Alvar Lidell speaking: 'Ladies and gentlemen. It has just been announced from Downing Street that Allied Forces have successfully landed on the Normandy coast in France and have secured a beach head. Fierce fighting is taking place but already Allied Forces are moving inland. The Prime Minister will be making a special broadcast to the Nation later today.'

Everybody had stopped working at the first sound of the announcement. Even before the last words had faded, a tremendous cheer spontaneously went up from the workshop floor. People began clapping and standing up and hugging each other. Flo joined in but even as she hugged the woman at the next bench she was thinking: 'Has Tom's regiment gone over there yet? Is he in action even now?'

Before long, the General Manager of Hawkers was on the Tannoy appealing for everyone to settle down and get back to work. 'We're going to need those extra aircraft more than ever now,' he reminded them. And paraphrasing one of Mr. Churchill's famous speeches he added: 'So let's go to it!'

That lunchtime the Canbury Arms was packed with people celebrating. It was almost as if final victory had been won. Flo was squeezed into a corner next to Connie, they'd managed to get a pale ale and the last of the cheese and pickle rolls.

'Bloody disgusting, I call it,' said Connie. Flo could tell she was annoyed as she didn't use proper swear words unless she was really angry.

'Celebrating as if the bloody war was over already. Don't they know there's men fighting and dying over there as we speak.' Even as the words left her lips, Connie realised her mistake and she looked at Flo and touched her hand. 'Sorry, dear. Wasn't thinking, I know you must be thinking about Tom at a time like this.'

Flo forced a smile. 'No, you're quite right as usual, Connie. There's nothing to celebrate yet. The real fighting's only just beginning.' Flo worked an extra half shift that evening so she missed the Prime Minister's broadcast. But when she left Hawkers at eight-thirty she went straight to the Station where she could be sure of getting the very latest edition of the Evening News. Then she went home and after a quick meal she made a pot of tea, sat by the sash window overlooking the garden and read the paper by the fading light. Almost every page was full of the landings in Normandy but reading between the lines it was clear there was very little real information. Certainly there was no mention of whether Tom's Regiment had gone across yet.

Just as Tom had predicted, there was a long gap in his letters. At least it indicated that Tom must be over in France. And then, a few weeks later, came a short note from him. It simply said 'Dear Mum, Landed safely on the other side. Things beginning to warm up. Keep smiling. Love, Tom.' Over the next few months other letters arrived. They were a bit longer but the censorship meant that Tom couldn't say too much. But she could tell that he must be in the thick of it. Flo read the paper and listened to the BBC News every day.

At the Hawker works, everybody was saying it was only a matter of time now. It would probably all be over by Christmas.

It was a sunny Thursday evening in October in that fifth summer of war. Flo came home from work at her usual time and began to climb the stairs to her rooms. She half noticed that the door to the kitchen of the couple who lived downstairs was slightly ajar but thought nothing of it. She was thinking of doing a poached egg for her tea. She didn't cook much now there was just herself and anyway she usually had a proper cooked meal in the Hawkers canteen at lunchtime.

Flo was halfway up when the kitchen door fully opened and the lady from downstairs called to her in a subdued voice from the hallway. A telegram had arrived for Flo about an hour before and the woman handed it to her. Flo wondered who it could be from and wondered if it was some urgent message from Ada. She thanked the woman and climbed the rest of the stairs. She entered her living room. Already deep within her a panicky feeling began to arise and dark fears began to surface. Flo's shaking hands seemed to take an unbearably long time to open the telegram. She took only a couple of seconds to read it.

'The War Office regrets to inform you that your son, Sergeant Thomas Harman, 174927786, was killed in action Friday August 4th 1944. Letter to follow.'

Flo gasped and felt an electric-like shock in the pit of her stomach. She felt the panic spreading up her whole body and down to her knees and her legs. She steadied herself against the old sideboard as she read and re-read the telegram hoping to find there was some dreadful mistake. Then she turned it over to read the back, desperately looking for some indication that would mean everything was alright. But the telegram was clearly addressed to her. It contained Tom's name. There was no mistake.

Flo gave a loud cry that came from the very depths of her soul and broke into tears of bitter anguish. And whilst she sobbed she prayed. 'Oh Tom, dear Tom! Don't let it be true! Please Lord, don't take my Tom away from me. . . don't let him be dead. Please Lord, all I've got in the world is him!' And she pleaded quickly, as if because his death had only just occurred it could still quickly be reversed.

The half closed door to the living room swung open and the lady from downstairs came in. 'What is it dear, what's happened,' she asked. But she knew what had happened and had known ever since that moment when one of those telegraph boys on a bicycle they called 'Angels of Death' had delivered the telegram. 'It's Tom,' sobbed Flo, 'They say he's dead.' And she handed the lady downstairs the piece of thin paper with the short cold words.

The woman wrapped her arms round Flo and searched for something to say to console her neighbour. 'Oh, my dear, I'm so sorry, so sorry.' And after a few moments she too re-read the telegram to make sure there was no mistake. She made Flo sit down on the small sofa in the living room and asked if there was anybody she could call. Flo asked her to call Connie. The woman quickly went to find her husband, who had been standing at the bottom of the stairs all along, and told him to go to the phone box next to the Co-op and ring the number that Flo somehow managed to find.

Not many people had phones in 1944. But Eddie, Connie's gentleman friend, had arranged for hers to be installed so he could visit her at short notice whenever his other responsibilities allowed. Barely twenty minutes after the call was made, Connie arrived at the door in a taxi.

Flo was sitting quietly on the sofa when she arrived, the telegram lay on the table that stood in front of the window overlooking the garden. Outside, the warm double-summertime evening sun was still shining brightly, almost as if to mock Flo in her agony of grief. Connie held Flo close to her and neither said a word for several minutes. She could feel Flo shaking from top to toe. Then Flo spoke.

'He's gone, Connie. Tom's dead, my beloved boy…'

Connie knew that there were no words of consolation that anyone could give now or ever in the future. 'Poor, poor, Flo. That lovely lad. This damned, damned War!' was all that she could say as she held her hand tight on the small sofa.

A little while later Connie made a pot of strong tea. Flo asked for a cigarette and drew hard on it, as if the smoke from the tobacco would somehow make everything alright. Her tear-stained eyes looked dazed. Slowly they began to talk. Connie read the telegram. What made it worst was not knowing the details, other than the stark statement of fact. There was no one you could ask either.

'Someone will write, Flo. You'll hear the details soon enough. His Commanding Officer most likely, or one of the officers in charge of his platoon.'

Flo suddenly asked what the funeral arrangements would be? Connie had to tell her that it was military practice to bury soldiers killed in action in war cemeteries near to where they fell. So there wouldn't be any funeral to worry about. She wasn't sure whether this was some small relief or if it made matters worse.

'Do you think he suffered, Connie. I hope he didn't suffer,' Flo said eventually. Connie tried to comfort her and said that in modern warfare if you were hit then it was usually all over in a second. Of course, she really had no way of knowing but she had to say something to console her. Then Flo went on about the body of the child she had found after the flying bomb landed up the road and how the body was unmarked, almost as if the child was asleep. She hoped Tom was like that.

They sat together smoking and drinking tea in the living room for several hours. Later Connie, who always wore a crucifix, suggested they pray for Tom and for strength for Flo in her terrible hour of need. Like Connie, Flo was a believer too. Although she didn't go to church very often she had always prayed every day, mostly for Tom. Connie said the prayers out loud, they both sat there with their hands pressed together.

'Dear Lord, take into your loving care the soul of Flo's dear son Tom who has died fighting for his country. Have mercy on him, Holy Father, for he was a good son and was loved so very much. And please comfort his mother Flo at this terrible time who devoted her whole life to him, for he was all she had. Comfort her in her grief and bring her the peace of understanding that it was not all in vain. Holy Father, hear our prayer.' Flo added her Amen and silently added a prayer of her own whilst Connie crossed herself.

It was ten o'clock though it had seemed like hours and hours since that awful moment when she had first read the telegram. Suddenly Flo said that she wanted to phone her sister Ada to tell her the news and asked Connie to come with her down to the phone box in King's Road. Connie suggested it could wait until the morning but she could see that Flo badly wanted to tell her sister. Slowly they walked along the black-out darkened street to the telephone kiosk where Connie waited outside. When she emerged from the red box Connie could see fresh tears in Flo's eyes.

Connie made another cup of tea and they both smoked another cigarette. She offered to make some toast but Flo couldn't eat. Then she suggested that Flo should try and get some sleep, Connie insisted on staying the night and would sleep on the sofa in the living room. So Flo went up to her bedroom to spend the first sleepless night of many. How could she ever sleep after losing Tom? As she walked along the corridor to her room, Flo went into Tom's bedroom and took one of his jackets from the old wardrobe. It was the one she thought he always looked best in. She took it to bed with her and hugged it and remembered how she had sometimes slept with Tom in her bed when he was ill as a small child. And she held the collar to her lips. 'Oh Tom, Tom, why did you have to leave me?' Connie listened in the corridor and heard Flo sobbing quietly, but she could do nothing. Time was the only possible healer and it was going to take a great deal of that.

The next day, Flo insisted on going into work at the Hawker works as usual. She had to keep going, she told Connie, she couldn't just sit alone within the four walls. The word soon got round the shop floor and there was no singing or laughter that day. Some of the other women who knew her came over and briefly expressed their sympathy and said if there was anything they could do she had only to ask. But other than a quick squeeze of her arm or a peck on the cheek there was nothing that they could do.

Flo worked like an automaton that day. When she got home that evening Ada was waiting in her living room. She had arrived an hour before her, the lady downstairs had let her in. An hour before her, thought Flo. Just like the telegram had arrived an hour before her the day before.

Ada seemed as distraught as Flo. She held her in her arms for a long time. Then Flo showed her the telegram and they drank tea and smoked cigarettes. Ada insisted that Flo eat something and made them both cheese on toast. 'You've got to eat something, Flo. You can't live on tea and fags, love,' she said. Then she half whispered: 'Tom would want you to eat something now.' That did the trick and Flo ate for the first time since hearing the dreadful news. But as she ate, she could only think of the cheese that Tom had given her that last time she had met him in Farnborough. Ada stayed the night and was a great comfort. Flo even dozed for a couple of hours but then there was that feeling of waking up as normal and then the sudden sickening realisation of how everything had changed.

The next day was Saturday and Flo didn't have to go to work. Ada told her that Stan and her wanted Flo to come and stay with them for a few days. But Flo said No. Everybody had been so good but now she must be alone. So as soon as lunch was over Ada left after making her sister promise to phone each day and giving her some coppers so there could be no excuse. When Ada had gone, Flo felt so completely alone. Of course she had lived on her own ever since Tom had gone off to the War but now the rooms felt hollow and empty.

Later in the afternoon Flo went for a short walk in Canbury Park Gardens down by the river. She felt she had to get out of the house or her brain would explode. But all she could think about were the times she had gone there with Tom, as a baby, as a child, as a man. On the way back she passed the secondary school in Richmond Road that Tom had attended and where he had begun to go for his evening classes in Automotive Engineering. It was all such a waste, she thought, such a waste of a life that was now over when it should only have just been beginning in earnest.

A few minutes after she had returned to her rooms, the lady downstairs came up and gave her a small freshly baked loaf of bread, two eggs and a couple of ounces of margarine. And she told her that if there was ever anything they could do, or if she just wanted to come down and talk, well they were only one flight of stairs away. Flo thanked her profusely and thought how kind everybody was. She spent Saturday evening alone, smoking and drinking tea and listening to the war reports on the radio for solace. They made her feel closer to Tom. Then she actually felt hungry for the first time and made some scrambled eggs on toast for herself.

But that night, her first alone, was awful for Flo. She lay in bed in the dark thinking only of Tom and all their happy times together and then shuddered with the heartbreak of knowing she would never see him again. She thought of all those things she planned they would do when he came back after the War was over. And she shed the bitterest tears a woman can. That night a few stray Luftwaffe bombers came, the first for many months. She heard them whining overhead through the open bedroom window, and she wished that one would drop a bomb on her and end the agony, even though she knew it was wrong to think that way. But when they came, the explosions were always few and far away.

The next day was Sunday so Flo decided to go to church at the morning service at Saint Luke's. It seemed the right thing to do, specially as there was no funeral service she could go to. The Church was quite well attended and she noticed once or twice the Vicar looking her way. But Flo found little solace in the service.

That Sunday afternoon she was sitting at the open window in her living room looking at the sunlight falling on the few flowers in the garden, and watching the leaves on the trees beyond swaying in the light breeze, when there were two knocks on the downstairs door. Two knocks meant it was for her, one for the people downstairs: a well used code in shared houses. It was the Vicar from St Luke's, a kindly old Welsh man with grey hair whom Flo had spoken to a few times over the years when Tom had attended Sunday School and gone on Summer Camp with the Scouts. She invited him in and put the kettle on for a cup of tea. Flo knew he had come to comfort her and in her desolation of spirit was willing to listen to anyone who might offer some meaning to it all. After giving her his deepest sympathy on the loss of Tom, he began to speak slowly and with deliberation as if considering every word with care.

'I'm sorry to intrude on your grief, my dear. But I'm a Vicar and we're allowed to intrude on people's grief at times like this, you know.' And he gave a gentle smile. That and his forthright manner made Flo warm towards him.

'I know you and Tom didn't attend the Church too often but I feel that I know you both. I remember him at the Sunday School and I used to think what a well brought up lad he was. Your son was a credit to you, Mrs. Harman, and all the more because you did it single-handed. I know it must have been very difficult for you at times.'

The old man thought for a while, as if looking back into the past, and then continued.

'Such a likeable lad he was. Although it's easy for me to say, I can understand a little of what you're going through now. You see, I lost my only son too in the last War, he died at the Somme. So what I want you to know is this.

'You must be wondering what the point of it all is, Mrs. Harman. All that love and devotion that you gave him and the hard work in bringing him up. Perhaps you think it was all wasted time and effort, all for nothing, as he departed this life with hardly a third of his allotted span spent and with what should have been his most fruitful years still to come.

'Well I tell you, my dear, if you're thinking that way you are most mistaken. Absolutely mistaken. For you see, it isn't really how long someone lives that counts or how few the years they are with us. It's what those few years were like that matters most. All his life he knew he was loved. You made him feel safe when he was afraid and you were his comfort in all his trials.

'He never went cold or hungry with you around. You nursed him through his sicknesses, helped him bear his disappointments. I'll wager you never let the wind blow on his face. And more than that, you showed him something of the beauty of this world too. I used to see you together on my walks round Richmond Park and I used to think there were no two happier souls in the world than these.

'Just imagine what life would have been like for him if you hadn't been there to do all that. Or what all those years would have been like for you if he hadn't been there for you. Don't tell me it was all for nothing.

'So remember always: it isn't how many years you were together that counts, it's what the years you did have together were like that's important.

'War is an abomination created by Man out of pride, greed and hate. God gives and God takes away: it is not within our gift to devise the meaning of all things within His plan.'

He spoke for a little longer but this was the substance of his message. As they drank the tea, they discussed times before the War. And the Vicar asked if there was anything the Church could do to help in any small way. Before he left, he told her that she could come and talk to him at any time if it would help. But in his heart he knew that she would not come, experience had taught him that most choose to bear their grief alone.

Flo thanked him and he left. She poured herself a cup of cold tea and lit a Players Navy Cut. What did the expense of cigarettes matter now? She remembered the old phrase 'tea and sympathy'. But for the first time since receiving the dreadful news she felt a little comforted, a small numbing of the pain. For a while that evening the terrible anguish of it all seemed to lift slightly. What the Vicar had said left its mark on her mind and although the heartache returned when she awoke the next morning, it was tempered to some small measure by the feeling that their life together had not been completely wasted after all.

In all her years that lay ahead, that crumb of comfort alone made the difference between holding on and letting go.

A couple of weeks later, Flo had another visit that she would always remember. It was Tom's friend Peter, the lad from Richmond who was in the same platoon. He had been wounded at the same time that Tom had been killed and was back in Blighty on medical leave.

Peter was graven-faced when he called on Flo, not knowing what to expect. He told her of the last few hours of Tom's life. They had been advancing on a heavily defended German strong point, crouching behind a Mk. 4 Churchill tank for cover. As they were moving forward, a hand-launched Panzerfaust anti-tank shell scored a direct hit on the tracked vehicle and everybody within a few yards of it had been killed or injured.

Flo pressed Peter if the end had really been quick? She wanted to know if Tom had suffered at the end and stressed that she wanted to know even if he had. Peter reassured her that Tom would have known nothing from the second the shell struck. He had been on the side where it had exploded on impact with the tank and had been killed instantly.

Tom and the others who died had been temporarily buried in marked graves in a local churchyard, as was military custom. Eventually they would be transferred to their final resting place in a proper military cemetery that would be set up somewhere in the area. Peter handed over Tom's belongings in a kit bag with his name and service number stencilled on the outside and also a letter from his commanding officer praising his courage and sacrifice.

The minute he had left, Flo lifted the kit bag over to the table by the window and opened it. Her heart beat quickly as she felt inside for the contents. There was underwear, woollen socks and a spare shirt. She noticed the thick pullover that she had given him for Christmas a few years before. There were some army magazines and a couple of cheap thriller novels by Andrew Andrews and a half-eaten bar of NAAFI chocolate.

There was also a large stiff brown envelope containing Tom's Bravington Renown watch, the end of the leather strap torn away and the face cracked, and the remains of his wallet.

It was badly damaged and most of the contents must have been scattered. But a couple of photographs had survived. One was of a young blonde woman who Flo had never seen before, taken in a garden against a flint stone wall with a hint of the sea in the background. The other was of Flo and Tom, taken on the promenade at Bournemouth during that last lovely summer holiday before the War.

Through her red-rimmed eyes she looked closely at Tom, with his tanned face and white open-neck shirt with rolled up sleeves. Both hands were thrust deep into the pockets of his white cotton trousers and he leaned back casually on the promenade railings. Oh, if only she could go back in time for just a few minutes to that wonderful week when they were all together and Tom was by her side, smiling and young and so full of life.

For Flo, the War really ended the day she heard of Tom's death.

Although she continued to work at the Hawker aircraft works, her heart wasn't in her war work any more. She had really only been doing it for Tom, and she felt a little ashamed when she realised it. After all, there were other mothers' sons to think of. But she never went down to the allotments again to 'Dig for Victory'. She wrote a letter to the Allotment Department at the Council explaining. Then she arranged with another allotment holder up the road to give her tools to a poorly off pensioner who relied on the produce that he grew to feed himself.

Connie was a brick and a tower of strength during those days. Every Friday evening they went for a meal or a drink together in Kingston after work. Despite her grief, Flo still looked forward to Friday evenings, it was the only social occasion in her life. That and the occasional visit from Ada and Stan when they could get over from north London.

Flo made a point of not talking about Tom all the time, she didn't want to try people's patience when so many others were dying.

One Saturday afternoon when she had nothing to do, Flo was rummaging about at the top of a cupboard in the living room when she found a photograph album. Tom had bought it for her birthday just before War was declared. She'd never got round to putting anything into it before, but now she collected together what few precious photos she had of Tom and carefully stuck them all into it. There were two taken when the photographer had visited Tom's school when he was 9 and 10 years old, she could ill afford them at the time but was glad now she had managed to.

There was one head-and-shoulders photograph of Tom in his army uniform taken shortly after he had been called up. That was probably her favourite, he looked so handsome he could have passed for a film star. Most of the others had been taken by Stan when they were all on holiday together or had gone for walks in Richmond Park on Sunday visits. One was of Tom sitting astride the bike Stan had bought for him, you could see the pleasure of ownership on his face.

There were also the photos returned with Tom's wallet: the one of Flo and him at Bournemouth and the one of the young blonde woman standing against the flint stone wall. She put that in the album too, she didn't really know who the woman was but she obviously meant something to Tom. Most likely she was the girl that Tom had met at Selsey Bill when he was stationed there, the one he had briefly told her about. Flo tried to think of her name but the grief had muddled her memory and she couldn't recall it.

Finally, Flo took the wedding photo of herself and Sid out of the picture frame that she kept on her bedside table and stuck it on the first page of the album. Sid didn't really deserve to be there, she thought, what with the way he had deserted her and Tom. But he was part of her life and after all he was Tom's father.

When it was finished, she wrapped the album in a tartan woollen scarf so it wouldn't fade in the light and placed it in the centre of the table by the sash window, right next to the potted plant Tom had bought her with his first week's wages. And there it remained until the day she died.

After the War when things were more back to normal, Flo had copies made of the photo of Tom in uniform. She gave one each to Connie and Ada. One she put in the picture frame beside her bed. Another she put in another frame and kept it on the mantlepiece in the living room. The last one she covered in transparent paper and always carried around in her handbag.

There was one other possession that had been returned with Tom's personal effects: a black address book. One of the ways Flo kept herself going in the early days of her grief was to inform everybody in the address book, anyone who was a friend or knew him, of Tom's death.

Flo did this by letter and almost without fail she received back a reply of sympathy which she found comforting and kept them all. The Manager of Kingston Hill Motors, where Tom had worked, wrote a particularly moving letter on behalf of himself and everybody who worked there, saying how much Tom's cheerful presence would always be missed and remembered.

There were a few entries in the address book that were just telephone numbers and of these there was one that Flo simply could not place. The entry read 'Kate – CRYstal Palace 2157'. She had no knowledge of Tom knowing anyone of that name or any connection with Crystal Palace in south London. It was a complete mystery.

One evening she walked down to the telephone box that stood near the boarded-up bagwash laundry in King's Road with a handful of coppers and dialled the number. A woman's voice answered.

'Hello, could I speak to Kate please,' Flo asked.

'Speaking,' replied the voice.

'Oh, you don't know me, I'm Mrs. Harman, Tom's mother. I found your number in his address book.'

'Ah, yes, Tom...' the voice answered guardedly.

'I'm afraid I have some bad news, I'm telling everybody he knew. Tom was killed in action a little while ago during the advance on Germany.'

'Oh no, not Tom!' said the voice at the other end of the line. 'I'm so, so sorry, Mrs. Harman. He was such a sweet guy...Tom. Oh this f-f-frightful war, why does it have to take all the best men? Poor Tom...I'm so sorry!'

Flo sensed the voice was faltering with emotion and there was a hesitancy on the word 'frightful' that made Flo sure she would have used a stronger word if she had not been talking to a stranger.

'Did you know him well, dear?' asked Flo.

'For a time,' came the reply. 'I hadn't seen him for some while. But he was such a sweet boy...we were close for a time.' And then remembering the formalities of such an occasion she added: 'I'm so sorry for your loss, Mrs. Harman.'

The woman seemed to be taking the news badly, she was clearly experiencing some distress.

'Thank you, dear,' said Flo. 'I hope you didn't mind me phoning and telling you, I'm so sorry to bring upsetting news.'

'No, I'm glad you have told me, I would have wanted to know, Mrs. Harman. We've all known losses in this War and after a while we get used to them. But this one is hard to take.'

'Thank you,' replied Flo who was slightly uplifted to find a kindred spirit in her grief, albeit a complete stranger.

'I'm getting married in a fortnight. My husband is an officer in the RAF and we've been posted to India. I'm so glad you rang when you did,' the woman said sadly.

'I wish you every happiness, dear,' replied Flo.

'Poor Tom!' the woman repeated one last time. 'Thank you for letting me know.'

With that the call ended and although Flo was to come across her again many years later, the full story of Kate and Tom's relationship would remain a closed book to her for ever.

The late summer turned to autumn. The only thing that approached being a pleasure in Flo's life, other than her Friday evenings out with Connie, was to sit by the open window in the living room and look at the album and smoke cigarettes and drink cups of tea. Before long, she knew every detail in every picture in the album. And in her mind she remembered everything that had happened on the days the photos had been taken. She never tired of that album and never a day went by that she didn't look at it, just as never a single minute passed when she didn't think of Tom.

That first Christmas without Tom, Flo spent with Ada and Stan. She kept a brave face but all the time she was thinking of previous festive seasons that they had all spent together. Doreen and her husband called round, it was the first time she had seen her since Tom's death and they spent a long time talking together. Flo realised for the first time how fond Doreen had been of her cousin. They had a quiet time but it was good for the family to all be together again. All except Tom, of course.

Flo was never more comforted than when in the company of anyone who had known her son. It was that Christmas that Ada and Stan gave Flo the green coat that she afterwards always seemed to wear whatever the weather. It wasn't new, what was in wartime? But it was of excellent pre-War quality, Ada had bought it from a rather well-to-do lady in Rayners Lane.

When VE Day and VJ Day came in 1945, and peace returned to Britain, it was a hollow victory for Flo. Of course she was glad that the fighting was over, though Stalin and the Russians were beginning to look as big a threat as Hitler and the Germans had ever been. Some people were even talking of the possibility of another war, mostly people who were hoping to retain their well-paid jobs at Hawkers now the Second World War had ended.

The radio and the papers were full of the Victory Celebrations and shortly afterwards the streets of Kingston were full of young men in ill-fitting demob suits. She had forgotten how few young men in civvies there had been in the streets since Mr. Chamberlain's fateful declaration. The General Election of 1945 caused quite a stir, what with the unexpected Labour landslide victory. Flo voted Labour as she had always done, she had always thought they would look after the interests of ordinary working people much more than the Tories. Not that Flo was particularly short of anything at that time, the pay at Hawkers for war workers had been good and she put quite a bit each week into her Post Office Savings Bank. Flo sensed the job at Hawkers wouldn't last for much longer and there could well be rainy days ahead. Even with her burden of unabated grief, Flo knew that financial hardship and even destitution wouldn't help matters.

It didn't take long for the lay-offs to start once the War was over. Most of the women were only classified as temporary workers, strictly for the duration. The men coming back from the front needed employment, specially those with families to support. After all their sacrifices, who could deny them first call on what jobs there were available, reasoned Flo? So when she received her notice she was disappointed but not angry. Not so Connie, who ranted on about how women had helped to win the War but now it was over they were being thrown on the scrapheap. But Connie wasn't really too worried, she had other plans.

'Listen to me, Flo,' she said seriously during one of their Friday evenings in the Kardomah Café near Kingston Market.

'We've got to think ahead, nobody knows what tomorrow is going to bring. I've been contacted by my old Catering Director at the Bentalls cafeteria where I used to work before the War. And guess what, he wants me to come back as Manageress. What do you think of that, Flo?'

Flo agreed it was very nice when people you knew offered you a good job just when you needed one.

'Well I've accepted. Apart from anything else, it's the only thing I know. I'll be responsible for all the girls but I think I can still handle them O.K.' Flo noticed how Connie had picked up all the American slang from the films they saw, like 'O.K.' and she often used 'Babe' and 'Doll'.

'Now listen carefully, Flo. I'm going to need some reliable new waitresses. The Catering Director wants to get rid of some of the old hags and harridans he's had to put up with during the War because of the labour shortage. I think it would suit you down to the ground.'

'Me?' asked Flo somewhat taken aback. 'But I've never done any waitressing. I wouldn't know a soup spoon from a fish fork.'

'Don't worry about all that Flo,' replied Connie. 'I can soon teach you the ropes. You learnt how to make fighter aircraft, didn't you? Learning how to waitress is a piece of cake compared to that. You'll be doing Silver Service in no time. The only question is, would you mind being on your feet all day?'

Flo said that she'd never ever had a sitting-down job in her life, she did all her work standing up at Hawkers. When she'd worked as an Assistant at Bentalls years ago there was no sitting down allowed and when she worked at the bagwash laundry before the War she was on her feet all the time.

'Right, then you can start Monday week. Apart from anything else, a change of scene will do you good,' said Connie.

Flo was flustered by the unexpected offer of employment. 'But won't I need to be interviewed by the Catering Director or somebody?' she stuttered.

'Listen, Doll,' replied Connie almost confidentially. 'As far as the waitresses go, I am the Catering Director.'

Flo finished at Hawkers and turned up bright and early on her first day at the Tudor Cafeteria in Bentalls. She could vaguely remember the staff entrance from the days when she had worked there before Tom was born. So many, many years ago now it seemed. The cafeteria was on the top floor and even though it was looking a little run down after the War years, it still retained something of its original elegance. It was certainly a lot posher than Workshop No. 3 at Hawkers. She was fitted with a uniform and spent the first morning receiving instruction on waitressing with the other new girls - from none other than Connie.

Flo soon realised that learning to be a waitress was no big deal.

The basic pay wasn't all that good though, nothing like as good as building aircraft. But they all knew that high wartime wages wouldn't last for ever. And you could always pick up a few extra bob or two by doing overtime at the private functions that were frequently held in the cafeteria in the evenings or weekends if you weren't doing anything special. And Flo, of course, was never doing anything special in her evenings or weekends now Tom was gone.

Then there were tips. Connie explained that waitressing was really all about tips. A cheery smile and a helpful manner with the diners could make all the difference to what you made in a week. Naturally, you occasionally came up against a customer who could be really difficult, usually to make himself look big in front of his girlfriend. Or some old battleaxe with a double barrelled name who thought she was the Queen of Sheba. But when that happened you must never answer back, Connie told the girls. You just called her and she would sort it out. That was why she was paid a bit more than the other girls, to handle unpleasant people like that.

Sometimes there were perks too, like being allowed to take home some of the left-over food that would otherwise be wasted. Rationing was quite strict for a long time after the War so it counted for a lot. But Connie impressed on the girls never to take anything without express permission, otherwise it would be considered stealing and that meant instant dismissal.

In some ways, those immediate post-War years were even greyer than during the War itself. There were so many shortages and the shops and houses all looked in need of a good lick of paint. Eventually things did begin to get back to normal but everything seemed a bit run down for a good few years to come. The glitter and excitement of the streets of pre-War Kingston seemed a long time returning.

One fine summer day, Flo was passing Kingston Railway Station when she noticed a poster advertising cheap day excursions to the south coast. One was for Littlehampton the following Sunday. Now the War was over people were beginning to go for holidays and days out again, the other waitresses at Bentalls were always talking about going away to Brighton, Weymouth or even Torquay – specially since a week's annual holiday with pay had come in just before the War started. Flo felt she would like to see the sea again, she hadn't left London since before the War except for those few visits to see Tom down in Chichester and Farnborough. Peacetime Sundays were very quiet and uneventful in Kingston now that Tom was gone.

Flo bought a ticket and the following Sunday caught the 8.30am excursion train. It was a sunny day but not too hot. The countryside looked beautiful from the train window on the way down but half way she began to wonder if she had done the right thing. Soon she would see all those familiar places where she and Tom had spent such wonderful days before the War. She began to worry it would all be too emotionally draining? Or would she feel some comfort from the remembered surroundings and recapture a little of the happiness from when Tom and her were there together?

The train chugged past Arundel Castle and Flo felt a lump in her throat as she looked at its tall walls and turrets on the side of the valley. There was the tower where Stan had got young Tom all excited with tales about sieges and knights in armour in the olden days.

Suddenly Flo felt a great sadness: 'Why wasn't Tom here today to share nice days out like this now the War is over?' But the feeling passed and soon the train arrived at Littlehampton. Clutching her shopping bag containing the flask of tea and sandwiches made with cold ham left over from Bentall's cafeteria, Flo began the long walk through the town to the front. As she passed the little shops in the High Street she tried to remember how many times they had been to Littlehampton. It must have been half a dozen at least. Flo specially remembered the time she and Tom had once come without Stan and Ada. Now she was coming without Tom.

The bed and breakfast signs were back in many of the windows and here and there exterior decorators were giving outside walls a well needed coat of paint. She hurried on past a large square with gardens and a colourful display of flowers until she arrived at last at the sea front. Immediately she made for the spot by one of the breakwaters where she remembered they had always sat when they visited the beach. The tide was out and the beach was full of bathers, she never remembered seeing this many before. And there were children playing in the little pools of trapped water at the end of the breakwater, hunting for shrimps and tiny crabs, just as Tom had done in exactly the same place when he was their age. Every now and then one of them would squeal with delight at discovering some small creature from the sandy waters.

Flo looked out to sea and saw a few fishing boats making for their moorings on the quayside next to the river. She remembered how Tom had fished there for shore crabs and small fry along with the other children. The sun glittered on the sea and everything looked bright and it lifted Flo's spirit for the first time in many a long month.

She sat in one of the shelters on the Promenade overlooking the beach and poured a cup of tea. Flo was feeling a little hungry after the early start but it was still too early to eat her sandwiches so she lit a cigarette and found it particularly satisfying. She felt contented and for the first time since her great loss experienced a few moments that approached tranquility.

An older retired couple were also sitting in the shelter and the woman, who saw Flo watching the children on the beach, smiled at her. 'So nice to see the little 'uns enjoying themselves again,' she said to Flo. 'It makes you realise the War's really over.' Flo agreed and they both commented on how lovely the weather was, a perfect summer's day in fact, with just enough of a breeze to stop things getting too warm.

She decided to take a stroll over towards the quayside and passed through the little amusement park. The music from the merry-go-rounds and the rattle of the dodgem cars brought back long cherished memories. A day at Littlehampton was never complete for Tom without a visit there in the evening. The bright lights, loud music and aromatic odours from the hot dog stalls had an irresistible appeal to tiny eyes, ears and nostrils.

Down by the river, young lads in short trousers were fishing for crabs, dabs and elvers with the same fascination that Tom had shown. Flo sat watching them from a nearby bench and for the first time in a while felt tears welling up. To distract her thoughts she poured another cup of tea from the Thermos and lit a cigarette to steady herself. Then she walked over to where one of the newly arrived fishing boats was unloading its catch. A crowd had collected and a blue-jerseyed fisherman with a wrinkled leathery brown face was selling herrings from a large wicker basket. Flo bought a large one for three pence and hoped the double wrapping of newspaper would mask the fishy smell in the railway carriage on the journey home.

Then she headed back to the beach by the breakwater and hired a deckchair. She sat there alone in the brilliant sunshine and watched the families enjoying themselves on the sands. Some of the older boys were playing cricket with makeshift stumps fashioned out of driftwood. It suddenly dawned on Flo that although she was remembering Tom at the age when they came on holiday here, he would just be old enough to have children of his own by now had he lived. That really made her think, time had gone by so quickly since Tom joined the Army and even more so since the War had ended.

Flo decided she was ready to eat her sandwich, the sea air had sharpened her appetite. All afternoon she sat there in the deckchair, watching the children and their parents play on the sands and listening to the chatter. Later, as she walked back to the railway station, Flo decided it had been a very nice day out indeed. Even though the thought struck her that the only people she had spoken to the entire time was the retired couple in the wind shelter and the deck chair attendant.

The following spring, the couple who had lived downstairs ever since Flo had lived in Staunton Road moved out. They went down to Newlyn in Cornwall to run a small bed and breakfast boarding house. It saddened Flo a bit, although they had always kept themselves to themselves they had been nice neighbours. And of course, they had known Tom for many years so in a way it was another break with the past that increasingly meant so much to Flo.

Before they left the woman called on Flo, she was obviously a bit concerned about something. She explained that they were having a clear out and had come across Tom's old bike that he kept in their shed. Flo had forgotten all about it and the couple hadn't wanted to risk distressing Flo by raising the matter before. The woman said that her husband thought it was still in working order, all it needed was cleaning and oiling and the tyres pumping up.

Later on, Flo went down to the shed to see the bike. It had stood untouched for the past seven years, exactly where Tom had left it. Flo held the grips on the handlebars and moved it backwards and forwards a little. She was no expert but the wheels still seemed to turn perfectly. Then she thought, the last person to hold those handlebars was Tom and she felt close to him for a moment. Next she looked inside the leather saddle bag. There were a few spanners, some loose tyre valve caps, a puncture repair kit and a faded copy of the Daily Sketch.

She remembered how thrilled Tom had been when Stan had given the bike to him on his birthday all those years ago. It had given him a lot of pleasure and he was still using it occasionally, with the saddle and handlebars raised to their maximum height, right up until his call-up even though it was a bit small for him by then. She was glad that it had given Tom so much enjoyment in his short life, specially when he was younger. How sad that he was no longer here to enjoy things like that. If he had come back from the War, Flo thought, he would probably have an old motorbike to roar about on and tinker with by now.

Flo was on nodding terms with a woman who lived up the road who had lost her husband in the War. Flo had often noticed her son playing in the road with the other lads, he never seemed to have cap guns or roller skates like the rest of them who had dads and he certainly didn't have a bike. He was a tall lad for his age and always looked at the others who had these things with a longing look.

Flo went round and knocked at the door and spoke to the lad's mother. She told her she was welcome to the bike if she wanted it, though she couldn't be certain everything worked properly. The woman's face lit up at the thought of her son getting a bike, she had obviously felt bad about not being able to afford one. She asked how much it would cost but Flo said she wanted nothing for it, just a good home. So next day the mother and the boy came and wheeled the bike away and Flo seemed to notice something of the same gleam in his eyes as there had been in Tom's when he had first seen it. Before they took it, Flo removed the folded up newspaper from the saddle bag. The woman thanked her for the bike and the following evening the boy came round to Flo's house and gave her a small box of Cadbury's chocolates that must have cost a couple of week's sweet ration at least. He told her the bike worked fine.

Flo read the old copy of the Daily Sketch because Tom must have read it years ago and it was another link with him when he was alive. Then she put it with all the other letters and things of Tom's that she kept in the large shoe box in the living room cupboard.

The couple downstairs finally left a week later. The woman came to say goodbye to Flo and said they would keep in touch and that if she ever thought of having a holiday in Cornwall to come and stay. But except for a Christmas card for four or five years, Flo never heard or saw again from the woman who had given her the fateful telegram about Tom's death and had been so kind in the aftermath of her great tragedy.

Flo was very content working as a waitress in the Tudor cafeteria at Bentalls. It was hard work fetching and carrying all day but Flo's strong constitution let her take it in her stride. She enjoyed seeing Connie each day too who was always cheerful and such good fun. Connie's support and the memory of the Vicar's words about Tom when he died sustained Flo through many dark periods.

One Friday evening when they were having a quick meal in a cafe in Kingston before going to the cinema, Connie asked Flo if she would like to spend a week in Bournemouth with her. It appeared that she and Eddie had rented a bungalow for a holiday together in June but due to sudden business commitments Eddie wasn't going to be able to make it. The bungalow was paid for so Connie suggested they could go together instead. Flo jumped at the chance.

June came and they travelled down by train in one of the super-luxury Pullman carriages of the Bournemouth Belle one Saturday. They had lunch in the dining car and Connie ordered a taxi at Bournemouth Station which she insisted on paying for. It seemed an extravagance to Flo who had only ever travelled by bus or train, or walked, and had only been in a taxi once before in her life. But she enjoyed the ride and Bournemouth looked at its best in the bright sunshine with so many tall trees everywhere and the rhododendron bushes in full bloom. The bungalow was very comfortable and only a ten minute walk from the front along one of the wooded chines that ran through the cliffs down to the shore. They had a wonderful time and visited the beach most days and went for walks along the Promenade and into Bournemouth town centre where Connie seemed to do endless shopping. Flo was surprised that Connie had so much money to spend, she hardly seemed to take any notice of the price labels and appeared to know her way round all the smart stores and shops.

A couple of afternoons they went on coach trips: once to Beaulieu Abbey and another to Rhinefield House in the New Forest which Flo thought was the most beautiful countryside she had ever seen. She had never been anywhere else that you could look in any direction and not see a single house: just miles of yellow gorse, Scots pines, oak trees and wild ponies grazing on the open lawns and glades. The coach even stopped at a thatched tea house where they had a pot of Earl Grey tea and chocolate éclairs with real cream inside.

Connie didn't like cooking on holiday and each evening they went into the centre of town by bus. Connie seemed familiar with all the places to eat and they had nice meals in fish restaurants and chop houses that she always insisted on paying for. When Flo objected, Connie told her not to worry as Eddie was paying which was no less than he deserved considering how he had let her down in the first place.

They went to the cinema and took in a show and even went for a boat trip along the coast to Weymouth and back. Flo enjoyed every minute of it all and realised how much more life had to offer. For the first time since she could remember, five minutes or so actually passed in her waking life without her thinking of Tom, such were the distractions and the pleasures of Bournemouth and Connie's company. It really brought Flo out of herself.

But one afternoon, while walking along the Promenade, they came to the spot where during that last summer before the War she had spent long days on the beach with Tom. Indeed, the same spot where Connie and her had first met. Connie commented on the fact and she could tell from looking at Flo, who had gone quiet, that she was seeing Tom on that beach.

That evening, tired by the long walk, they decided to stay at the bungalow and not go out. They bought two large cod and chips on the way home and Connie went into an off-licence and treated them to a bottle of the best Vintage port to be had anywhere in Bournemouth.

After their meal they sat on the comfortable sofas in the lounge and had several large glasses of the Douro Valley's finest which made Flo quite tipsy. She smoked some Senior Service as her favourite brand was temporarily unobtainable and Connie puffed away on her usual cork-tipped variety. Then Connie suddenly became serious.

'You still think of him a lot, don't you Flo,' she said.

'Tom you mean?' replied Flo. 'Yes I always do, Connie. You see...he meant everything in the world to me, he was all I had and I still miss him terribly.'

'You're a believer, aren't you Flo?' Connie asked. 'You know there's more to life than this vale of tears. You'll be together with him again one day.'

'Oh, I know he's not gone forever, Connie. But it's still so very hard to live life without seeing him and I think of all the things he's missed out on by dying so young,' replied Flo.

'Look, Flo, I've been thinking of mentioning this for some time. I think it might help,' said Connie.

'Sometimes I go to a little church in Kingston over in Villiers Road. It's different to other churches, you see it's a spiritualist church. I don't go there very often but when we get back we could go there together if you like. There might be some message for you, Flo.'

Flo thought for a minute. She'd never considered anything like that before but she immediately felt excited by the idea.

'Yes, I think I'd like that very much, Connie.'

'I had a great loss too when I was younger,' Connie continued.

'I've never mentioned it before but it was the usual story. We were going to be married but he was killed in a road accident. I never really came to terms with losing Rafe, that was his name, so I've always known how you feel about Tom you see, Flo. I couldn't marry anybody else after knowing him.'

'I often wondered why you never married,' replied Flo. 'It's always surprised me that you and Eddie have never thought about it. I know he's often away on business but you seem to get on so well and you've known each other for such a long time.'

Connie looked at Flo with a fond smile, her friend could be so naive sometimes.

'Maybe we will some day, Flo. Maybe we will.'

5: Is there anybody there?

Flo returned from the holiday in Bournemouth feeling as if she had been reborn. It had all been so enjoyable and the sun had shone unrelenting every day. Most of all, she was excited about what Connie had said about the spiritualist church and whether there really could be a way of getting a message from Tom.

Connie didn't mention it to her again on their return to Kingston. She didn't want to push Flo into anything, it had to come from Flo herself. Sure enough, a couple of weeks later, Flo asked Connie about the spiritualist church and they arranged to go to a meeting the following Thursday evening after work.

Flo didn't know what to expect but she was reassured when they entered the little church opposite the recreation ground in Villiers Road. It was quite full and everybody looked normal and seemed to know each other. The Minister didn't wear a cassock like at St Luke's but he seemed nice enough and came over specially to welcome Connie who hadn't been there for a while.

Everybody took their seats and there was a short service to begin with, just like in any church. Then the Minister introduced the visiting clairvoyant who was evidently quite well known in spiritualist circles and had a very good reputation which is why the little church was full.

He was about 60 with white hair, a little overweight but with a lovely smile that immediately set you at your ease. And he spoke with the strong and confident manner of someone who was long used to public speaking. He thanked them for coming and explained for the sake of any newcomers that contact with the other side was perfectly in accord with God's purpose. It demonstrated survival after the end of life in the earthly realm and that we have nothing to fear from death, which is merely like passing from one room into another. What's more, it helped people to complete unfinished business with loved ones who had passed over.

The clairvoyant then became quiet and trance-like and asked if there was anybody there? His first message came quickly, it was for a middle aged woman who had lost her father. The clairvoyant revealed that she had only just found his gold pocket watch that had fallen behind a chest of drawers. The woman replied excitedly that she had indeed found it in that very place only the week before, she had been searching for it for months. The clairvoyant told her that it wasn't her who found it, her father had guided her hand. He went on to say there had been differences in her family, with her sister, and her father wanted her to heal the rift.

Several other contacts were made, including one from a small child who had died of consumption and wanted her mother to know she was at peace: 'No more coughing, Mum.' Another involved someone's sister in the realm of spirit who knew her surviving sibling and her husband were thinking of emigrating to New Zealand and advised them to go ahead as it would be a good move.

Flo noticed that some of the messages seemed to fall on stony ground: there would be nobody in the audience who responded and sometimes a contact would start well but falter as names and events were mentioned that the person could not place. Later, Connie explained that the gift of the clairvoyant was not infallible, they made mistakes like everyone else. Messages could be misinterpreted and some times several spirit voices crowded in on the clairvoyant's mind to confuse.

Flo sat there absolutely absorbed by it all but regretting there was no message for her. Connie knew what she was thinking and touched her sleeve and whispered that you didn't always make contact the first time.

Almost immediately, the clairvoyant asked if there was anybody present called Flo. Several women raised their hands or called out to the white haired medium: it had been a popular enough name at the turn of the century. Flo felt a stab of angst and remained motionless. But the clairvoyant pointed to the back of the hall, right towards where she and Connie were sitting, and asked if there was anybody over there by that name. Flo hesitantly put her hand up.

The next sentence from the clairvoyant struck Flo like a flash of lightning.

'You had a son called Tom, didn't you?' Flo gasped and answered that she did. Connie shifted nervously in her chair beside her.

The clairvoyant was concentrating deeply and gave a one-thousand yard stare as he spoke.

'There's a strong image of a young man coming to me, a man in army uniform with a black beret.' The clairvoyant paused and Flo wondered if that was all.

But the speaker continued. 'I can see Sergeant's stripes. He's telling me he wants you to know all is well with him. He's saying "Don't worry Mum, everything's going to be alright."'

Flo gasped again, how many times Tom had used those exact words!

'He's sorry he left you all on your own. But he's saying he still looks after you from the other side and you're not to forget it. And he's glad you had such a good holiday recently in a place that you had both been to together. He's saying "You really needed that holiday, Mum."'

'That's right. I've just come back from Bournemouth,' Flo blurted out.

The clairvoyant fell silent for a moment. Then he said: 'Is there anything you want to ask him?'

Flo half rose from her seat and said she wanted to know if he had suffered at the end. The medium repeated the words as they came to him. 'All over in a second. Just a blinding flash and it was all finished. Don't worry yourself on that score, Mum.' Flo fell back in her seat.

The white haired man fell momentarily silent again and then added: 'He's fading now but as he goes he's saying that you'll see him again...in this world and the next.'

There was a further pause, the clairvoyant seemed to be concentrating even harder. 'There's another person here for you,' he added. 'An older woman who passed over many years ago.

'She was a lot fonder of you and baby Tom than you realised, she's telling me. She was an aunt and she says that she understands why you couldn't come to her funeral, there was no need to feel guilty about it.'

Then he moved on to another message for somebody at the front of the audience.

Flo sat there inwardly trembling with emotion: a mixture of elation and sadness, relief and anguish, belief and incredulity. Connie put her arm round her shoulders.

The meeting ended twenty minutes later and half the audience went to a room behind the church for biscuits and a cup of tea. Flo and Connie joined them and Flo lit a cigarette which she drew on ardently. She kept looking at the clairvoyant who was also standing there drinking tea with his back to her, surrounded by a coterie of people that included the Minister.

'I've got to ask him something, Connie,' Flo said after she finished the cigarette and she pushed quickly through the crowd towards the clairvoyant. He seemed to know she was coming and turned purposefully to greet her with the warmest smile that Flo could imagine.

'I'm sorry to interrupt you, sir,' said Flo. 'But I must know. What did my son Tom mean when he said I'll see him again in this world and the next?'

The clairvoyant gave a polite shrug and chose his words. 'I'm sorry, my dear, but it's not given to us to know everything. All I know are the words that came to me and I simply repeated what I heard.

'Perhaps your son means you will find a lost photo of him, something like that.' He touched her gently on the elbow and whispered quietly: 'Be assured, in the fullness of time the answer will present itself.'

Flo thanked him copiously for his help and slipped back through the crowd to where Connie was standing. And so they left the little church opposite the recreation ground and made their way on foot through the quiet back streets of Kingston.

As they parted Flo said: 'Thank you so much for bringing me, Connie. It was such a wonderful experience. I would never have thought of coming myself if it wasn't for you.'

Flo never went back to the spiritualist church again. There was no need.

Everything had been said, the only question answered: Flo now knew for certain that Tom would always be with her. For a while she still wondered what the last words had meant, the bit about seeing him again in this world. But she gradually forgot about them as the months went by and Flo's daily life reclaimed her. It was a fairly routine round of waitress work in the Tudor cafeteria at Bentalls, going out with Connie on Friday evenings, Saturday morning shopping in Kingston Market and occasional Sunday visits from Ada and Stan.

Life was gradually recovering from the austerity of the immediate post-War years and returning to normal. But Flo hardly noticed and time hung heavily on her hands most weekends.

It was during this period that she became involved with the childrens' charity, the NSPCC. She had read articles from time to time in the newspapers: dreadful cases about child cruelty. Flo couldn't understand how anyone lucky enough to have children could treat them so badly. Every week she sent the Society a postal order for two shillings to help them continue their work and she regularly collected for them on Saturdays in Kingston Market on flag days. But it still left her with lots of spare time.

One Saturday there was no shopping to do and no flag day for the NSPCC. She felt like getting right away from Kingston and taking a train ride somewhere. Suddenly the thought struck her that she would like to visit Farnborough and return to the barracks where she had seen Tom for the very last time.

An hour and a half later she arrived at the railway station in that garrison town about lunch time. Nothing had changed much in the intervening years and she walked down the familiar road towards the barracks. On the way she noticed that the little café where Tom and her had taken tea was still there.

When she came to the barrack gates, she walked slowly past, looking inside at the spot where she had caught her last glimpse of Tom walking away from her. There were sentries at the gate and a red-capped military policeman who smiled as she passed by. A few yards past the gate she came to the small public garden where she had sat with Tom. It was really only a recess in the wall of the barracks next to the road with a few flower beds, some shrubs and two benches.

Flo took out her Thermos and poured a cup of tea adding the milk from a small bottle. It never did to put tea already mixed with milk in a Thermos she had once been told and had never thought to question the received wisdom. She began to eat her Double Gloucester cheese and pickle sandwich, more leftovers from the Bentalls restaurant, and threw a few crusts to the sparrows that gathered on the pavement around her. Flo finished her tea and smoked a cigarette. The day was warm and she found it very pleasant sitting there.

A few squaddies passed by in uniform and she was transported back to the last occasion when she had come there to meet Tom during the War for the very last time. It had been a cold spring day. She tried to remember what they had talked about and recall exactly how the conversation went. After about an hour, she walked back past the barracks gate and took another long look inside as she went. The military policeman smiled again and remarked what a pleasant day it was for the time of year. Flo enjoyed her day out and most importantly she had felt particularly close to Tom sitting in the small garden near the gate.

That visit to Pinehurst Barracks in Farnborough was the first of many dozens that continued down the years. After a while, the military policemen at the gate got to know her well enough to always pass the time of day. Even some of the people who lived in the houses opposite got onto speaking terms with her as they walked their dogs or headed for the park round the corner with their children. Flo became something of a local character, perhaps an oddity. At some stage she must have told someone about Tom and the reason for her visits for it eventually became common knowledge among the military policemen who guarded the barracks and the residents who lived opposite.

Stan and Ada visited Flo in Kingston about once a month. Ada worried about her sister and knew that she had never laid Tom to rest: she was holding on to him and refusing to allow him to die and pass on in the normal way of things. Otherwise Flo seemed to be getting by alright, even though she didn't have too many friends. She was glad that Flo at least had one good friend in Connie and a job she seemed to like which kept her occupied and paid the rent. And Flo was hardly ever troubled by illness or complained about anything – even though she didn't earn very much and still wore the same green coat that Ada had given her as a Christmas present during the War. Worldly goods held no fascination for Flo.

Anyway, there was nothing more that someone like Flo could expect from life, reasoned Ada. She was too old to remarry and start a family and was clearly set in her ways. Although she was still only in her late forties, Flo had looked and dressed like a much older woman for years, though an energetic one at that. No, Ada decided, her sister wasn't doing too badly bearing in mind how her husband had deserted her years before and the tragedy of losing her only son in the War.

But when Ada heard Flo mention she was regularly visiting Farnborough where she had last seen Tom, her concerns about her sister resurfaced.

On the way home from Kingston on the train one Sunday, she voiced her worries to her husband. Stan didn't think it was anything to get too concerned about. But he did agree that Flo's continuing obsession with Tom wasn't quite right. They wondered if there was anything they could do or say to help her come to terms with Tom's passing and move on.

It was just as well that Flo hadn't told Ada about her trip to the spiritualist church!

As the Piccadilly Line train rattled through Acton Town on their way back to Rayners Lane, Stan had an idea. Like most of the old-time coppers in those days, he had a wise head on his shoulders when it came to human nature that owed nothing to fanciful theories about psychology and profiling.

'Perhaps the problem all along has been that there was no funeral service and no grave for her to visit,' suggested Stan. 'Perhaps that's the reason she's still holding on to Tom and can't let him die and rest in peace.'

That seemed to make sense to Ada and she agreed it could be the cause of the problem. Quietly she marvelled at her husband's powers of deduction.

'But of course there *is* a grave somewhere, isn't there,' Stan continued. 'Those who were killed in action were all given a proper burial, there must be one over there in Holland or Germany. Maybe if Flo saw it, just the once, it would put things in proper perspective and help her to come to terms with things.'

'That makes a lot of sense, Stan,' Ada said. 'But maybe it's the feeling that Tom's still around that keeps her going. She might go to pieces if she lost that.'

'I wouldn't think so, Ada,' replied Stan. 'Leave it to me, I'll see what I can find out.'

But Stan forgot all about it by the next day. There was a long strike going on at a west London engineering works and the picketing was getting out of hand. Political agitators were trying to exploit the situation and the papers were full of it. All local police leave was cancelled and Stan had no time to think about anything else. Ada knew better than to bother her husband when there was a big flap on like that. But when the strike was eventually settled, Ada didn't take long to remind him.

Stan approached the problem with all the diligence of his colleagues in the Criminal Investigation Department. He wrote to the Imperial War Graves Commission giving all the details about Tom that he knew. It took a couple of weeks but they eventually replied giving the war cemetery, row number and plot number where he was buried. Included with the letter was a small printed leaflet advertising coach tours to some of the major war cemeteries. These were organised by an independent travel company in cooperation with a well-known organisation for ex-servicemen and their families.

Stan contacted the travel company and discovered that later that autumn they were planning a pilgrimage that included the large cemetery where Tom had eventually been laid to rest. But they would have to make up their minds fairly sharpish as seats on the coach were strictly limited.

They arranged to visit Flo the following Sunday. They were having tea sitting at the table in front of the window looking out onto the garden, Flo's favourite spot in the whole house. The window was open and Flo had prepared a cold salmon salad followed by great doorsteps of Russian cake, all courtesy of 'Bentalls Friday Teatime Tasties'.

When they'd finished, Stan broached the subject of Tom's grave with his customary tact. As he spoke, Flo's eyes visibly widened. Yes, she was very interested. Yes, very interested indeed. Stan said they could help her with the cost but Flo said that was alright as she could pay for it out of her savings. And so it was arranged that Stan would make the booking for all three of them the following day.

All that week Flo thought of nothing else. One evening she was hurrying back from work, her mind miles away, when she almost collided with a young woman with a child in a pushchair. Before she had time to apologise, she recognised who it was.

'It's Gloria, isn't it?' she asked the mother. It must have been all of eight years since she had last laid eyes on Tom's former girlfriend but there was no mistaking her blue eyes and jet black hair sleek as a raven's wing.

The woman recognised Flo immediately. She knew that Tom had been killed in the War and had given her condolences to Flo at the time when they both worked at Hawkers.

'It cast a shadow over my life for a long time after,' Gloria told Flo wistfully. 'I was very fond of him, you know.' As she spoke she stared at her child in the pushchair.

'I know, my dear,' replied Flo. 'I never understood why you two drifted apart. Lots of people did in the War, I suppose. It was such a topsy-turvy time. But how are you doing now?

What a fine little chap you have there.' And Flo bent down to smile at Gloria's chubby two-year old.

'Yes, I'm very settled now. My husband's in accountancy and we have a house in Worcester Park. We've just been to visit my mother.'

Flo looked again at the child in the pushchair. Was this what Tom's son would have looked like if he'd lived to have one of his own with Gloria? Then Gloria touched Flo's arm gently and said: 'I know it must have been a terrible loss for you, Mrs. Harman.'

'It is, my dear. He was such a special person. But I'm glad to see everything turned out right for you. I often wondered what became of you after I stopped working at Hawkers.'

As they parted, Flo fumbled in her purse for a shilling. 'Get the little one an ice cream on me, dear.' Flo knew it was the sort of thing that grandmothers did: another of life's little pleasures that had been denied her by Tom's death.

'That's very kind of you, I'm sure,' Gloria replied. And with a final 'Take care!' she was off down Fife Road towards Kingston Bus Station to catch the 213 to Worcester Park. Flo walked on and then turned and watched Gloria disappear in the distance. She realised that she had lost so much more than Tom when that blessed shell had hit the tank he was taking cover behind.

The meeting saddened Flo for a few days after. But soon her thoughts turned to the prospect of seeing Tom's grave. There seemed so much to do, not least of all obtaining a passport, there had never been any question of Flo going abroad before. She even bought a map of the Low Countries from W.H. Smiths to see exactly where they were going.

Weeks passed and the day came. Flo packed everything she needed into the small suitcase that she had bought when she and Tom had gone on their first holiday all those years ago. Wearing her green coat, despite the mild weather, she caught the train and at Victoria Station she crossed the road to meet Stan and Ada at the Coach Station opposite.

The people on the coach travelling to the war cemetery were a mixed crowd. A few were ex-servicemen themselves, going out of respect for fallen comrades and quietly giving thanks that they had been spared. Others were relatives, mostly wives and parents of those killed on active service.

The sea crossing was a little choppy and the sky overcast but when they landed in Calais the wind dropped and the sun came out. France looked so different to the Kent countryside they had been driving through only a couple of hours before. The coach motored on along straight tree-lined highways that Tom must have seen. Eventually they arrived at a small hotel on the outskirts of Brussels where they were to stay the night.

The evening meal consisted of clear onion soup, which Flo found strange but quite nice, and a meat casserole with olives and other unusual looking vegetables in it. One joker at the next table suggested the meat was probably horse. That didn't put Flo off who thought it tasted very nice whatever it was, though Ada seemed a bit suspicious and left most of hers. Afterwards they went for a walk round the town square and then for a drink in the hotel's bar. They made friends with some of the other British people in the party and Flo discovered one couple's son had been in the same regiment as Tom. The couple who managed the hotel and served behind the bar were Hungarian. When she told them she would like a glass of port, a lengthy discussion ensued trying to identify the drink. Several people joined in and the manager took the trouble to find a bottle of local fortified wine that resembled Flo's favourite alcoholic tipple.

It was all a great adventure for Flo. She decided that she could quite grow to like foreign holidays, she had heard some of the other waitresses and shop girls at Bentalls talk about going to Spain and Italy.

They crossed the border into Holland the next morning and the countryside changed again. Flo fell silent as the coach sped along the motorway. This land was where Tom had spent his very last days on Earth, this landscape Tom's last living view of the world.

In the early evening, they approached the Dutch town outside which the War Cemetery lay. The coach drove slowly and reverently past the concrete triumphal arches at its entrance but it was too late to go inside that day.

'Dear Tom, always so near but yet so far,' thought Flo.

The hotel evening meal consisted of some spicy boiled sausage which Flo thought very tasty, though once again Ada was not so sure as she detected more than a hint of garlic. That night Flo hardly slept a wink. It was strange that she should be reunited with Tom's earthly remains in such unfamiliar surroundings.

First thing after breakfast, the coach took them to a large flower store. Flo chose a wreath of white carnations and asparagus fern, Stan and Ada were careful not to buy anything that upstaged hers. There was a special desk where they could write their tributes on the cards that were attached to the wreaths. Flo wrote 'To my beloved Tom, Always on my mind, Forever in my heart'.

As the coach made its way slowly to the war cemetery, there was none of the idle chatter that had accompanied the rest of the journey. Everybody was silent and deep in thought about their loved ones lost in a war that cost over a third of a million British lives. At a respectful, almost funereal, pace the coach passed through the triumphal arches and drove along the central avenue between perfectly kept lawns and flower beds. The coach parked near a small chapel and everybody disembarked, each clutching a printed sheet containing a map of the cemetery with the plot, row and grave number of the deceased marked clearly in blue pencil.

Stan took the lead through the endless rows of identical white grave stones that stretched all around them in military formation. It didn't take long to find Tom's grave, Stan held Flo's arm as he guided her forward and whispered in a hushed voice 'Here we are, Flo'.

Flo stood before the white stone and read the brief inscription. There was just Tom's name, rank, service number, regiment and the date he died. She looked at the lush green grass beneath which Tom's body lay and slowly bent to place her wreath. They stood still and silent for a few minutes and then Stan passed their simpler wreath of golden lilies to Ada who placed it beside the white carnations. It was Flo who broke the silence.

'Everything's kept so nicely here, they've gone to a great deal of trouble,' she commented.

'It's a very pleasant setting, Flo,' Ada replied. 'It must be a great comfort to know Tom's at peace in such a lovely place.'

They began to read the inscriptions on the adjacent graves and Flo wondered if any had died at the same time as Tom.

'No doubt others who died with him are here somewhere,' Stan suggested. Then he mentioned that he had brought his camera and would Flo like him to take a photo of the grave and Flo said she would like that more than anything else. Stan took two photos just in case one didn't come out. Then they walked deep in thought back to some benches near the coach.

But Flo was thinking to herself: 'It's all very nice and I'm glad I came. But I don't feel that Tom is here, I feel closest to him back in Kingston and Farnborough.' But she didn't say anything to Stan and Ada in case they thought she was being ungrateful and their thoughtfulness in arranging the visit wasn't appreciated.

As they sat on the bench, a few tears rolled down Flo's cheeks. Ada comforted her when she saw and Flo said: 'It's so very good of you both to bring me here. I do appreciate it so very much, you know.' Then Flo said she was just going back to the grave on her own for a few minutes and off she went. She knew she would never return there again.

Four days later after visiting some major World War Two battlefields and another larger war cemetery they were all back home. The following day was grey but dry. Flo went off with her Thermos and sandwiches to Farnborough as usual.

A couple of weeks later Stan sent Flo a letter which had a photo enclosed, it was one of the photos he had taken of Tom's grave. Flo looked at it and thought how identical all the grave stones had been: somehow that seemed to reduce the hundreds of different human beings they stood for into one single person. But then she supposed that all are equal in death.

As she looked at the photo she spotted something unusual lying on the top of Tom's stone. She peered closer. It was hard to tell exactly as it was so small, but it looked like a wrist watch.

Flo put on her reading glasses and looked at it even closer. Indeed, not only did it look like a wrist watch, it looked remarkably similar to Tom's Bravington Renown. Except that the watch in the photo didn't have a torn strap and cracked crystal like the one that had been returned to her shortly after Tom died.

Flo was certain it hadn't been there when she had stood in front of the grave, she would certainly have noticed something like that. And if she hadn't Stan and Ada certainly would. Quite apart from anything else, since its return she had always kept Tom's watch in the old shoe box in her kitchen cupboard.

Immediately, Flo reached for the precious box and opened it. Sure enough there was Tom's Bravington Renown with part of the strap missing and the crystal broken.

Next time Flo visited Stan and Ada at Rayners Lane she asked to see the other photo of the gravestone that Stan had taken either a few seconds before or after the one he had sent to her. Stan and Flo thought the request a bit strange but fetched the other photo for Flo to look at. Exactly as she was expecting, there was no watch on the stone in that photo. Flo knew instinctively and without shadow of doubt that the wrist watch was a sign from across the void for her and her alone. And she knew with certainty who had sent it.

Years came and went and nothing changed. Flo's life consisted of the same old job of waitressing at the Bentalls Tudor Cafeteria, the regular Friday evenings out with Connie and repetitive day trips to Littlehampton, Bognor Regis and Bournemouth which she had visited with Tom. She even looked the same, never growing noticeably older nor different in appearance in any way.

Sometimes even Flo, a creature of habit if ever there was one, began to tire at the similitude: the same endless routine of her daily life with no prospect of change. And there were times now when she began to feel lonely, usually on Sunday afternoons when she didn't go to Farnborough because of the weather and there was nothing to do except look at her few precious photos of Tom. Sometimes she began to wonder at the point of it all.

Then she would remind herself she had the memory of her wonderful son, someone only she could lay claim to, and this made her feel special. So she would make another pot of tea and sit smoking cigarettes by the table in front of the window whilst looking through her shoe box of happy memories and the dark thoughts would soon pass.

One Friday evening she was having a meal after work with Connie in the Railway Hotel, a large pub that stood opposite Kingston railway station. There was just the two of them and Flo had sensed that Connie had something on her mind, she was a bit on edge which wasn't like her at all.

'There's some news I want to tell you, Flo,' Connie said eventually.

'I'll be fifty-five before too long and I'm going to retire shortly. Don't tell anybody yet but I wanted you to be the first to know. Eddie has been on at me for some time to stop working and retire. So I'm going to hand my notice in and move to a nice little flat down in Brighton overlooking the front and the sea. Eddie has arranged everything and, frankly Flo, I'm ready to put my feet up.'

Then to lighten the conversation she added with a little laugh: 'Not all of us have your iron constitution you know, Flo.'

'But I don't want you to worry about anything. I'll put in a very good word for you with the new manageress at Bentalls, you know that.'

Flo felt anxious at the news but took pains not to show it. Connie was her best friend, her only friend with the exception of relatives. She looked forward to seeing her every working day and going for meals out and visits to the cinema. They were the only social life she had.

'I'll be coming back to Kingston regularly to do my shopping and see my old friends. And as you know, Flo, I've no better friend in the world than you so we'll still meet regularly.

'Eddie even wants me to learn to drive and says he's going to buy me a little car. It's only an hour's drive from Brighton by road. Think of it, Flo, me learning to drive a car at my time of life. And I'll be expecting you to come down and stay with me some weekends. You'll love it down in Brighton.'

This cheered Flo up a little. It would be a nice change going somewhere different like Brighton.

'Well, it's a bit of a surprise, Connie,' replied Flo. 'I never thought of you as being near retirement age. But it'll be nice to go and live in Brighton and I'm sure you'll love it. It's an opportunity you can't afford to miss. And of course I'll love coming to visit you.'

Connie looked relieved when Flo said that. 'I'm so glad you're pleased, Flo. Good friends like you are hard to find and there's no need for my retiring down to Sussex to make any difference to us.'

But as Flo walked home alone later that evening, she felt more than a little sad that Connie was going. Whatever they planned, she certainly wouldn't be able to see her nearly so often. And Flo didn't like change, specially when it was someone going away who had known Tom. Someone to whom she could talk about Tom and who understood. Those who remembered her beloved son were a dwindling band now, some eleven years after he was taken from her.

A couple of months went by and Flo secretly hoped that Connie would change her mind about moving to Brighton. But Connie did leave in July. Before she left, she had a going away party in the upstairs bar at the Canbury Arms pub in Canbury Park Road. Lots of people came to say goodbye including some people who still worked for the Hawker aircraft works where she and Flo had spent the War years. That upstairs room had hardly changed and it brought back bitter-sweet memories to Flo. Happy lunch hours spent with a glass of warm beer and a spam sandwich before Tom died; and the agonising time when she struggled to keep going and keep up appearances afterwards.

There was no question of Flo retiring early or anything like that. Her wages and tips from working at the Bentalls cafeteria were enough for her to get by on but she still had to watch every shilling if not every penny. She only had the Old Age Pension from the State to look forward to and knew that would hardly be enough to make ends meet. So every week for years now she had still tried to put a little money by in her Post Office Savings Bank for when she would have to stop working.

Connie moving away was partly compensated for by Flo being invited to join Stan and Ada that Summer on a touring holiday of the West Country. It was the first real holiday she'd had for quite some time. They had bought a Morris Traveller car so they picked Flo and her suitcase up from her front door. The idea of a car calling to take her on holiday seemed very grand to Flo.

She had never been on a long car drive before and enjoyed watching the countryside race by and the relaxed and carefree conversation with Stan and Ada. The journey along the A30 took them past Camberley where there were several large Army barracks. Ada glanced in the sun visor mirror and saw that Flo was looking at them and the sentries on guard outside and knew exactly what she was thinking but said nothing. They stopped in Winchester and visited the Cathedral which Flo thought very impressive and they had lunch in a nice old pub that stood within the Cathedral Close. Then they continued through the New Forest, which brought back happy memories to Flo of the time she had visited it with Connie when they stayed in Bournemouth just after the War.

The thought suddenly hit her that she had never been further west than Bournemouth before in all her life. Flo was fascinated at how the countryside changed as they passed through Hampshire and Dorset and Devon but still remained essentially English. They stopped for afternoon tea in the charming old county town of Dorchester which Ada explained was the setting for many Thomas Hardy novels. After a walk up the High Street to stretch their legs they drove straight on to Sidmouth where they were booked into a little guest house for a couple of nights.

The weather was warm and they went for long walks along the red cliffs either side of the town. One afternoon on the way back they paused to sit on a bench in some Gardens at the top of a zig-zag path that led down to a sandy beach on the western side of Sidmouth. There were lots of children playing on the beach, running in and out of the water and squealing with delight, while fathers with rolled up trousers made sandcastles and poured water from buckets in vain attempts to fill the moats around them.

Flo was sitting next to her sister and she said softly: 'I can imagine Tom would have brought his children to a nice place like this, Ada.'

'Indeed he would, my dear. And you can be sure of one thing, he'd have brought you along too. But you're here anyway with us, Flo. The family's still together.'

The tour continued with one-night stays at Budleigh Salterton and Dawlish and then across Dartmoor, where Stan took photographs of them with Becky Falls in the background. Eventually they arrived at Bude on the north coast where they spent the last three nights.

As they drove home along the A4 trunk road, Flo felt refreshed and happier than she had known for years. The sea air had blown away the cobwebs from her monochrome existence and put colour in her cheeks. For a while it had also taken her mind off Connie's leaving.

A week after Flo's return from holiday the new Manageress of the cafeteria was introduced to the staff by the Catering Director of Bentalls. Evidently, she had previously held the same position in the cafeteria of one of the big stores in central London. She was tall and thin, wore her hair in a bun and looked very businesslike standing erect with her hands clasped loosely in front of her whilst the Director spoke. Her name was Mrs. Wright and Flo thought she might say something but other than giving a kind of smile she made no response.

Things carried on as normal at the cafeteria for the next few weeks. Mrs. Wright seemed a woman of few words, she only spoke to give instructions or reply to questions from customers or the management. Flo decided she was a bit of a cold fish.

'I must stop comparing her with Connie,' thought Flo. 'She's a different person after all and it takes all sorts.'

Then Flo heard that a couple of the girls were leaving, one of whom had been there quite some time. Flo heard them grumbling about Mrs Wright being too strict about something and saying they didn't have to stay there and be spoken to like that. They were quickly replaced by a couple of waitresses who seemed to have worked for the new Manageress before.

One day Flo asked Mrs. Wright if it was alright if she left a bit early as she had an appointment to have her eyes tested for some new reading glasses. The Manageress umm-ed and ahh-ed and told her that she'd have to make up the time by working Saturday morning.

'Your friend Connie isn't in charge here now, you know,' she added which Flo thought was quite unnecessary. So she worked the whole Saturday morning for nothing just for taking an hour off on Thursday afternoon. But Flo didn't mind too much, she had nothing to do most weekends anyway.

Flo told Connie about it in her next letter and her reply came almost by return of post. Connie told her not to worry 'just keep your head down and do your job well like you always do and eventually she will see how lucky she is to have someone like you working for her.'

One afternoon just before she was due to leave work, Flo noticed there was some food left over in the kitchens. It was the store's policy never to use leftover cooked fish the following day and there were several large pieces of cooked plaice that hadn't been ordered. Flo was particularly fond of plaice so just before she left she approached Mrs. Wright and politely asked if she could take one of the left-over pieces home.

Mrs. Wright seemed to think about it for a moment and then gave a big grin and nodded her approval. Flo thanked her and went back to the kitchen where she took the largest piece of plaice and put it in her shopping bag. Then she changed, visited the ladies and headed down to the staff exit at the side of the store.

Old Jim, the elderly security guard, was standing behind his wooden desk next to the staff clocking-in machines. He was a kindly soul and always had a friendly word for the staff whenever they arrived or left. But as she was leaving Flo noticed that today he had a serious look on his face. He called to her as she was walking out.

'Could I just check your bag, dear,' he asked her. One of Jim's jobs was to occasionally check any bags that staff were carrying out which was quite normal at department stores to prevent pilfering. Mind you, Old Jim had never stopped Flo since she could remember and he seemed a bit embarrassed.

He found the fish wrapped up in paper and asked if it was her's. Flo replied it was left-overs and that Mrs. Wright had given her permission. Jim asked her to wait a minute and made a phone call. Flo wondered what it was all about, it wasn't like Jim to check up on things like this.

A few minutes later Mrs. Wright and the Catering Director came along looking very po-faced. The Director asked her if she had taken the fish and Flo repeated that Mrs. Wright had given her permission. It was all getting a bit embarrassing for Flo, other members of the staff were leaving and they were gawping and wondering what was going on.

Mrs. Wright breathed out sharply. 'I said nothing of the sort,' she replied.

'But Mrs. Wright, I asked you only ten minutes ago, you remember, don't you?' answered Flo.

The Catering Director realised it was all a bit public and said they should go to his office on the top floor. Once there, Mrs. Wright really let off steam.

'I really won't put up with pilfering by any member of my staff. I've seen what it leads to when I was working up in

London, it can cost the store quite literally hundreds of pounds each year. We're not a charity you know.'

Flo protested and repeated that she had spoken to her before taking the fish and would never take anything without getting permission first. She was getting quite upset.

Mr. Evans, the Catering Director, was clearly embarrassed by the whole business. Flo thought that surely he at least would believe her, he knew she wouldn't steal anything from the store.

'Now, now, calm down Flo and we'll discuss this sensibly,' he said. 'You say Mrs. Wright said you could take the fish, now think carefully. What were her exact words?'

'Well, she didn't exactly say anything,' Flo had to admit. 'But she nodded her head when I asked her. There was no doubt in my mind.'

'Ah,' said Mr. Evans. 'So Mrs. Wright didn't actually say you could take the fish?'

'There's no question about it, Mr. Evans,' Mrs. Wright said most emphatically. 'She never asked me at all. And it is always my policy to instantly dismiss anybody caught stealing the store's property. If you tolerate it once it sends a signal to all the other staff and before you know it they're all at it.

'There can be no exceptions I'm afraid, Mr. Evans.'

The Catering Director was obviously uncomfortable about this.

'I'm sorry Flo, but you have admitted that Mrs. Wright didn't actually say you could take the item in question. I think it would be better for everyone if you just left quietly.'

Flo grew very distressed and flustered. She mumbled something about it being an honest mistake and she even offered to pay for the plaice there and then. But it was all in vain, she was dismissed on the spot and Old Jim was called up to escort Flo from the premises. It was all most humiliating. The security man tried to console her saying that it would probably all be sorted out in the morning. Flo was in a complete daze as she made her way home. So much so, that whilst crossing the street at the top of King's Road, she almost walked into a large black car that was turning the corner and she heard the driver call her a 'Stupid old cow!' through the open side window. That added to her unsettled state of mind.

Before she reached home something strange and inexplicable happened that, whilst not connected with her dismissal, added a further element of surreal nightmare to the day's events.

As she turned the corner into Staunton Road where she lived, she noticed a woman she had never seen before standing on the pavement opposite her house. The woman slowly turned and stared up the road. And there was no doubt she was looking straight at Flo. Almost effortlessly, as if her feet were not touching the ground, she seemed to float towards Flo. As she got nearer, the woman's eyes appeared piercing and cold in a way that Flo, in her present agitated state, found particularly disturbing.

The apparition glided even closer and Flo could see that its lips were moving but no words seemed to issue from her mouth. Flo looked around desperately but there was nobody else in the street to help her even though it was broad daylight.

Suddenly the figure reached out to touch her. Flo was panicking by now and brusquely pushed her back and shouted at her to go away and leave her alone. Stranger still, Flo couldn't hear her own words even though she was conscious of what she was saying, just a noise like rushing water in her ears. Finally, Flo broke away and with one superhuman effort ran across the road, still shouting at the top of her voice. After fumbling with the keys to open the front door she quickly entered the hallway and slammed the door closed behind her. The experience had been most unreal, she had never experienced anything like it before. Whatever was the ghoulish apparition and what was it doing waiting for her in her road?

After a cup of tea and a couple of cigarettes to steady her nerves, Flo looked out her bedroom window to check that the woman was gone. To her great relief she was nowhere to be seen. But there was a young man in a grey double-breasted suit standing on the opposite side of the road leaning against a lamp post. And he was looking up at her.

At first Flo thought it was the tallyman, the person who lent money to cash strapped people and then collected the repayments in inflated instalments. Flo had never had anything to do with tallymen who exploited vulnerable people and could then turn nasty if someone had difficulty repaying. But as she looked at him more closely she saw it wasn't the tallyman at all. Then she heard words that materialised in her mind without sound and seemed to come from far, far away. It was only a whisper and only the once.

'She only wanted to help, Mum.'

Just then a red Post Office van sped by obscuring the young man from view and when it had passed he was gone. Flo understood the message and knew who had given it alright. But for the life of her she couldn't see how that fearsome phantom could possibly have been there to help her.

Flo ran down the stairs and out of her front door as fast as her legs would carry her. Her eyes scoured the street to left and right but it wasn't the weird woman she was looking for. She was searching for Tom. She ran down the street to King's Road but the pavements were near enough deserted. Then she hurried to the other end of Staunton Road as far as where the air raid shelter used to be in the recreation ground. Only a few mothers pushing their children on swings were to be seen. Then physically and emotionally exhausted she slowly made her way home.

'Oh, why couldn't he have waited?' she asked herself. Just a few precious minutes together again would have meant the world to her. Then she remembered what the clairvoyant at the Spiritualist Church had told her years before, he had been true to his word: 'You'll see him again…in this world and the next.'

The following morning Flo went down to the public telephone kiosk by the Co-op and phoned Connie in Brighton and told her all about losing her job. Connie was incensed.

'Mistake? That was no mistake, Flo. That bitch set you up deliberately. She wants to get her own cronies in to work for her, that's what it's all about. I'm coming up tomorrow, Flo, and I'm going to see Evans and give him a piece of my mind. I always knew that man was spineless.'

Flo pleaded with her not to do that as she didn't want any more trouble. But Connie insisted she was still going to write to the Catering Manager and protest at how badly Flo had been treated.

Then Flo told her about the incident with the strange woman in the street though she didn't tell her about the figure in the grey double-breasted suit. Connie told her to forget all about her. 'Mad as a Hatter, probably. The streets are full of them these days.'

The day after Flo phoned her, Connie, who had passed the driving test first time, drove up from Brighton in her sporty Singer Gazelle, ordered Flo to pack her bag and drove her back to stay with her in Brighton for a few days. They spent a lot of time walking along the Promenade and had lunch at a nice fish restaurant on the corner of Regency Square. Connie was careful not to order plaice. One afternoon they drove out to the gardens at Sheffield Park which were in full bloom. Connie kept reminding Flo that she had done nothing to be ashamed of, the shame belonged to those people who had treated her so badly and was their's alone.

By the end of her few days at Brighton, Flo was more settled in her mind. How lucky she was to have such a good friend as Connie. Without her to talk to she would have just stewed about it for weeks all on her own.

A week later, Flo received an envelope by registered post containing her National Insurance cards and a letter of dismissal from Mr. Evans. In it he said that he regretted having to make the decision but he had to back his departmental managers on questions of discipline. However, he did include a cheque for a week's wages in lieu of notice.

Connie wrote her letter to the Bentalls Catering Director but only received a standard reply in return. About six months later, Connie heard from one of her old contacts at the store that Mrs. Wright had left the cafeteria. She was so unpopular with the waitresses that most of them found other jobs and their replacements didn't stay long either. There was so much coming and going, and they were so short staffed at times because of it, that service in the Tudor cafeteria began to go downhill and customers started complaining. What's more, takings at the tills started to drop. Eventually the directors had stepped in and replaced Mrs. Wright. They even contacted Connie to see if there was any chance she would come back and manage the cafeteria. Connie wrote back that she was now fully retired but recommended that Flo would make an excellent Manageress. Flo and Connie both had a good laugh over that.

But when things settled down after her dismissal, Flo felt far from laughing. She was 56 years old and in no position to think about retiring. She knew that even when she became entitled to the State Pension at 60, it was a paltry amount to live on even by her modest standards. And she certainly hadn't saved up enough half-crowns and ten bob notes for her old age to cover the difference.

Flo had long realised that she would have to continue working well past 60 to make ends meet. Not that it bothered her, she liked getting out of the house and mixing with other people at work. But for the present she was out of a job and without the prospect of finding a new one.

Flo had no problem about signing on at the Labour Exchange and applying for the dole. Not like some older people who thought that taking unemployment benefit was accepting charity rather than it being your entitlement. The little bit of dole money she received wasn't enough to live on by a long chalk and she had to dip into her savings to pay the rent when what she really needed to do was to build them up further. Even though there were lots of jobs about, the Labour Exchange didn't seem to have much to offer Flo. She had no special skills other than waitressing.

If she had been experienced as a secretary or shorthand typist then there were lots of vacancies going. Another problem was that not many employers were keen to take on an older woman only four years away from retirement. Her age was definitely against her. She did get a couple of interviews for waitressing jobs in the canteens of large companies. But when they asked for references from her previous employer, Flo couldn't supply any of course.

Three months after her dismissal, Flo still hadn't found work. She had tried applying for jobs as a shop assistant but even there they wanted people with recent experience in retailing. The Labour Exchange seemed to give up on Flo but she wasn't going to give up on herself. She couldn't afford to. Every morning, to get herself out the house as much as anything, she used to walk round all the newsagent and confectioners' shops in the area looking at the advertising cards that people placed in their windows. Sometimes some of them were for jobs but mostly for cleaners. Of course, Flo could have taken up cleaning again but the pay was very poor, it was lonely work and endlessly cleaning other people's houses was quite depressing. She'd done it when she was young but that was a long time ago. Surely she was capable of better things now?

One morning she was hurrying along King's Road when the thought suddenly came to her to see if there were any new cards for jobs in the window of the Co-op round the corner. On the way she had to pass the old bagwash laundry where she had worked before the War, the premises had been empty and boarded up for years. She noticed that the outside had been freshly painted and new lettering boldly announced the opening of a new bagwash laundry. Flo's eyes were suddenly drawn to a notice stuck in the window that said 'Assistant Wanted'. Immediately she went inside.

The Manager was an older man in a waistcoat who seemed very preoccupied. Flo asked about the notice in the window and the Manager explained that he was looking for someone to handle the dry cleaning side of the business.

'Not to actually do the dry cleaning, you understand,' he added quickly. 'We don't do that here. Everything is collected and delivered by van once a day. What I need is someone to deal with the dry cleaning customers and keep track of each garment. Checking them in and checking them out and sorting out any queries, that's all really. But it needs someone who never gets in a muddle. If we lose track of a garment, we don't only have to pay for it but we lose a regular customer.'

Flo assured him that it was all well within her capabilities.

'Do you have any experience in the business?' the harassed Manager enquired.

'Why yes,' said Flo. 'I worked in this very laundry some years ago. I must have been here for nearly 10 years and only left when the shop closed at the beginning of the War.' Flo mentioned the name of the woman who ran the shop in those days but it meant nothing to the new Manager. But he was obviously impressed by what Flo had told him.

'Well, handling the dry cleaning is basically the same as handling the bag wash, I suppose. In it comes and out it goes. You've just got to keep tabs on what's what, who's whose and what stage it's at.'

The man offered her the job on the spot. 'Start tomorrow,' he almost pleaded. To Flo's great relief, there was no mention of references. Flo was thrilled at her stroke of luck and immediately went home and made a cup of tea and smoked a couple of Kensitas in quick succession. It was all such a relief to get a job at long last. The money was a few shillings a week more than the basic she had earned waitressing but of course there would be no chance of tips or working special events to boost her earnings. Still, she was fortunate to get a job at all at her time of life. What a stroke of luck that she had taken it into her head to check the cards at the Co-op on that day of all days. The card had only been put in the window that morning and the job was sure to have been taken by that afternoon if not before.

Suddenly words from long ago came into Flo's head. They were something that Tom had said to her the last time they had met, sitting in that park in Farnborough.

'Someone's got to take care of you in your old age.'

Flo was suddenly certain that luck had played no part in finding her new job.

She started at nine the next morning and the Manager showed her round, not that there was much to show. The front of the laundry had been refurbished since she had worked there 15 years or so before but the back room was almost untouched. There was even the old Victorian chair with the brass-studded leather upholstery that Tom used to sit in sometimes after school and read a comic whilst waiting for her to finish work. There was a pang of sadness and longing as Flo pictured him sitting in the chair, head buried in the previous week's issue of the Hotspur or the Eagle. Suddenly she felt tears begin to well-up in her eyes which she knew would never do so she hurried to the front of the shop and began getting her part of the counter organised.

Flo got on well with the dry cleaning and lost no time in working out a ring binder system whereby she could tell exactly what stage each garment was at, who it belonged to and when it would be ready. The Manager was very complimentary when Flo explained it to him and knew he'd made the right decision.

She got to know the regular customers quite well and enjoyed the friendly banter with the women who came into the laundry. But there wasn't the same camaraderie that she had enjoyed at Bentalls, or at the Hawker aircraft works come to that. Still she made the most of it and stayed there for over seven years until about 1963.

Flo had been to the Citizens Advice Bureau and discovered that by not taking her pension at 60 she would eventually qualify for a higher Old Age Pension. In the time she worked at the laundry, Flo also managed to save some of her wages to augment her 'retirement nest egg'. But she saved a lot less than she hoped and the price of everything just seemed to shoot up during those years.

One day, the Manager, with whom she got on well, called her into the back room at the end of the day.

'Sorry, Flo, but we're both going to be out of a job at the end of the month. The owner has decided to close down the bagwash laundry and dry cleaners and change it into one of those self-service launderettes.

'Everything's got to be do-it-yourself these days, you see Flo. And you don't need people like us to run a launderette - whether for the damp wash or the dry cleaning. Yes, they've even got a do-it-yourself machine that lets people do their own dry cleaning. All that's needed is someone to open the shop up, empty the coin boxes and lock up in the evening.

'Well, the owner can do that himself and save on our wages. It's cheaper for customers too, so they're all happy. Of course, their clothes aren't quite so well cleaned as doing it the old way, but nobody cares about quality these days, it's all about saving pennies.

'People like us just aren't needed any more, Flo.'

The last day at the bagwash laundry was quite emotional for Flo. Specially leaving that tiny back room that she had first entered over 30 years before. The old brass studded leather chair was still there. When she thought she was alone, Flo ran her hand over the leather where Tom's back had once rested and said to herself: 'Dear Tom! How I wish we could be together again like before – just one more time.'

Just then the Manager came into the back room and saw her touching the chair.

'You can have that if you like, Flo. Take it away with you if it's not too heavy. The owner wants me to clear *all* the unwanted old stuff out of here. Not just you and me!'

They shut up the laundry for the last time and Flo slowly carried the upright leather-backed chair home with her. The very chair Tom had sat on, she kept telling herself. Somehow it seemed to lift the disappointment of the occasion. She placed it in front of the table in front of the sash window that overlooked the garden in her living room, sat down on it and had a cup of tea and a cigarette. Flo noticed that the potted plant that took pride of place on the table was putting out new shoots. She remembered how proud Tom had been when he gave it to her as a present out of his first week's wages.

Suddenly she felt a little bit lighter in spirit. A new chapter in her life was about to begin. She could give up work and start drawing her 'enhanced pension'. And although her life savings weren't as much as she hoped, she told herself she would get by. After all, she was nearly sixty-four now. She had worked hard every day of her life since she had left school in Battersea at the age of fourteen. Didn't she deserve her retirement like everybody else?

6: The voodoo witch doctor's dance of death.

But Flo's retirement didn't work out quite as she expected. Time hung heavily on her hands and her enhanced pension and savings weren't quite enough to pay the bills comfortably. The price of everything continued to rise by a few pence almost every month. All the newspapers were going on about 'inflation'. So Flo began to do cleaning a few mornings a week for business people in the bigger houses overlooking the Recreation Ground at the top of Staunton Road. It was lonely work but it brought in a few much needed pounds.

She also worked two days a week in a charity shop in Richmond Road that had been opened by the NSPCC. There was no pay of course, but she enjoyed the company of the other women who gave their time there - and they always had first call on everything donated.

However, the next few years brought several cruel blows for Flo. First her brother-in-law, Stan, died suddenly of a heart attack. Ada blamed it on all the stressful years he'd spent in the police force. At his funeral at the Breakspear Crematorium at Ruislip, Flo thought what a good man he had been and how kind he had been to her. She remembered in particular that second hand bicycle that Stan had got for Tom and how he had carried it all the way over to Kingston on the train and had showed Tom how to use it. And once again she remembered that look of sheer pleasure on Tom's face when he had seen it for the first time.

Then almost two years later, Ada died of cancer. Flo knew her sister had been ill with something for some time but Ada protected Flo from the truth until just before the end. Just like their mother had done before her.

But the greatest blow of all came in 1966 when Connie died, also of cancer. Flo visited her several times during her illness which Connie dismissed at first as 'women's trouble'. But there was no disguising it at the end when she spent the last few weeks of her life in a top nursing home in Hove.

The last time she saw Connie it was obvious even to Flo that she didn't have long for this world. Flo held her hand and thanked her earnestly for her friendship and for taking her under her wing during the bad times.

'I could never have survived without you, Connie,' she told her.

'And you gave me so much, Flo, more than you'll ever know. You were the most sincere friend I ever had…completely without guile. Maybe too much so for your own good. With you I could always relax and be myself.'

It didn't escape Flo's notice that her friend was using the past tense now.

Connie gestured towards the bedside cabinet and told Flo to look inside for a small black box. When opened she saw that it contained a beautiful jewelled broach in the shape of a spray of flowers. There were three stems made from white gold each one inset with rubies, emeralds or sapphires. The imprint on the satin liner read 'Mappin and Webb'.

'It's very beautiful, Connie,' Flo told her dying friend.

'Now listen to me, Flo, this is for you. I won't be leaving any money, Eddie paid all the bills so I never needed any. This is worth a few hundred pounds, maybe more, and I want you to have it. Keep it safe and if you ever feel the need then sell it, you know, if times get hard.'

'No, Connie, I can't take it, it's yours!' protested Flo.

'Think about it, Flo – what good is it to me now? Its only worth is in knowing that it could give you a bit of security in the future. Nobody knows what the future holds.'

Flo thanked her friend again and again.

'Just think, Connie, how different it might have been if before the War in Bournemouth I'd gone for the teas five minutes later. We might never have met and got to know each other then.'

'Do you remember that week we spent in Bournemouth together after the War...after Tom died?' Flo continued. 'I think that was the most wonderful week of my life. It was as if I'd died and come back to life.'

'Happy days,' whispered Connie. 'And I remember the New Forest ablaze in a sea of yellow gorse as far as the eye could see...'

Flo sensed Connie was tiring now.

'I'll give your Tom a big kiss and a hug for you when I see him, Flo, and tell him all the news. Though I'm sure he knows it all already since he's sure to have been keeping his eye on you all along...'

Flo rose from her seat beside Connie's bed and bent over and kissed her on the cheek and gently stroked her hair with her hand. As she left, Flo noticed that Connie had closed her eyes and was drifting into deep and distant slumber.

With her eternal optimism Flo still hoped she would see her dearest friend at least one more time. But Connie died the next day and a week later Flo attended the funeral in a large cemetery on the east side of Brighton. On the way down by train, Flo recalled how years before she had been unable to attend her aunt's funeral just along the coast at Worthing. And she remembered how years later at the little spiritualist church that Connie had taken her to the message had come through that her aunt understood and absolved her of any feeling of guilt.

Flo was astonished at how many people attended the funeral, at how many friends Connie had. Some of them she remembered from Hawkers and Bentalls and she spoke for a while with them.

After the service, Eddie came across to her and thanked her for coming. Then he gave Flo his business card and told her that if ever she needed his help to contact him. That touched Flo as she had never met Eddie before but suspected his was fulfilling a promise to Connie.

'You know, Eddie, I always hoped you two would marry one day,' Flo told him and immediately wondered if she had overstepped the mark. But keeping his ring finger thrust deep in his jacket pocket Eddie smiled and gave her a sidelong look.

'Connie always said you were priceless, Flo,' he replied. 'I think I know what she meant.'

Of course, Flo never did have any contact with Eddie again. Though she did receive a card at Christmas from him for a couple of years and then they stopped.

Another year passed, a grey empty year for Flo: there was only her work to occupy her now, that and her regular visits to the Pinehurst Barracks at Farnborough.

The only person who had any special meaning, the last remaining link to her life with Tom, was her niece Doreen.

Doreen was married with a family of her own and lived in north London. But she used to drive over to visit Flo every month or two and spend Sunday afternoon with her. In summer, it became their habit to go and have tea at Pembroke Lodge in Richmond Park which was always Doreen's treat.

The cosmic watershed that changed Flo's life forever came one afternoon when she was 67 years old.

It was Sunday the fourteenth of May and Flo had been down to Farnborough that morning. As she travelled back on the train, she felt distinctly weary - something she had began to feel more and more of late. It was a terrible thing to survive all your friends and almost all your family. Perhaps she was beginning to feel her age at last, the cast iron constitution beginning to corrode a little around the edges? Walking slowly back from the Station to her house, Flo decided she should give up at least one of her cleaning jobs and was wondering which one it should be.

As she approached her front door on that warm spring afternoon, Flo half noticed a white car parked in the road a few houses up with two people sitting in it. She didn't think any more about it and went upstairs and put the kettle on and spooned some tea into the pot. The kettle had just begun to boil when her front door bell rang.

Long before, the landlord of the house had made a separate entrance for Flo's upstairs flat so that the downstairs one could be let as 'self-contained'. But Flo's door bell rarely rang, except when the gasman came to read the meter or to fix the Ascot geyser in the bathroom or when Doreen came on one of her visits. She certainly wasn't expecting Doreen that Sunday.

Flo went down the stairs and opened the door. Two people were standing there, a middle-aged woman and a young man. Flo's eyes went straight to the young man.

It was Tom.

Flo was stunned. Her mind couldn't grasp what was happening or take any of it in. Tom stood there smiling at her, making no attempt to move. The woman broke the silence but not the tension.

'You're Flo, aren't you,' she said. 'Look, do you think we could come inside?'

Flo heard herself say 'Yes' but her mind was still trying to make some sense of it all. She led the two callers up the steep staircase and half-way up looked back to make sure she wasn't imagining it. But no, they were both still there. She could still see Tom's smiling face.

Flo led them into the living room and turned to face them. Tom still just stood there. Flo felt the emotion rising within her. Why didn't he rush forward and put his arms around her and hold her close? Why didn't he say anything? Flo couldn't contain herself any longer, something inside her seemed to erupt.

'Oh Tom, dearest Tom! You've come back after all these years!' and she stretched her arms out towards him. Then the woman intervened.

'It's not Tom, Flo. It's Tom's son. Your grandson.'

Emotion flowed through Flo's body in waves but gradually the realisation sunk in. Of course it couldn't be Tom. The young man looked exactly the same age as when Flo had last seen her son, Tom would have been more than twenty years older now, middle-aged in fact. That was why he hadn't rushed forward to greet her.

The young man stepped towards Flo and spoke for the first time.

'I'm Ray and it's nice to meet you after all this time.' Then he added 'Grandma.' So saying he took her right hand in both of his and shook it gently.

The woman suggested they should all sit down and then she began to explain. Flo fumbled for a cigarette and Ray, quick as a flash, pulled out a Zippo lighter and lit it for her.

'I'm Vera, Ray's mother. I don't know if Tom ever mentioned me. There's no reason why you should remember, it was all such a long time ago and we never did meet. But during the War, your Tom was billeted in our cottage down at Selsey where he was stationed. My father was with the coastguards.'

Vera stopped and asked Flo if she was alright and if she was going too fast? Flo said not to worry and to please continue.

'Well...Tom and I became very close. I don't know if he ever told you about me?' she repeated.

'In fact, we were going to marry after the War. Ray knows all about it, of course.

'We were together for a couple of years and you know what it was like in wartime. We were both young and didn't know how much time we would have together. Then Tom's Regiment went over to France a little after the D-Day landings.

'We still wrote to each other and a couple of months went by. Then I discovered I was pregnant by Tom. Of course, I wrote and told him. But strangely no letter came back.

'My parents weren't best pleased, you know how it was in those days, specially in out of the way country places. But they rallied round. But still no letter came from Tom. We began to think it was the old, old story.

'In the event I had twins, Ray has a brother called Jeffrey. My dad wrote to the War Ministry to trace Tom and back came a letter saying that he'd been killed in action. The news hit me hard as you can well imagine. But in a way, there was some solace and relief that at least Tom hadn't abandoned us. I couldn't believe he would ever have done anything like that.'

Suddenly Ray chimed in, he had something he considered important to add: 'By the way, I'm your oldest grandson, Grandma. Fifteen minutes older than Jeffrey, he's always late for *everything*!'

'I never knew any of this,' said Flo still struggling to take it all in. 'Please do tell me all.'

Suddenly, as she was speaking, Flo thought she'd seen Vera's face before: there was a small flash of recognition. Wasn't it a much younger version of her that was in one of the photos that had been in Tom's wallet when he died?

Before Vera could continue, Ray, who had noticed the electric kettle and teapot said: 'I think we all need a fix of Tetley's finest before we go any further, don't you?' Everyone agreed, so Ray quickly refilled the kettle, let it boil and made tea for them all whilst Vera continued.

'It was difficult to begin with in a small village like Selsey. The War wasn't even over when I had the twins. There was a lot of prejudice and tongues wagged. But we kept ourselves to ourselves and discovered who our true friends were. And many there were...and my mum and dad were marvellous. Your gran and grandad are very good to both of you, aren't they Ray?

'Then a few years after the War ended, I met and married Ray and Jeffrey's second dad, Frank. We've never called him stepdad, I've always hated that word. He came to work for my father in the Coastguard Service, that's how I met him.

'He's a fine man, Frank. Never given any of us any reason to complain. And always treated Ray and Jeffrey like his own – it's no small thing taking on another man's kids. He's got his own fishing boat down in Selsey now, he supplies restaurants and fish shops round and about.'

Flo lit another cigarette and noticed that Ray smoked too.

'Tell me,' Flo interrupted. She was beginning to compose herself after the shock. 'Do you have any other children, Vera?'

'Frank and I did have a daughter after we were married but she died of diphtheria,' Vera reflected sadly.

'Now there's something I have to explain to you, Flo. Because if it hasn't already crossed your mind it will before long. And that's the question of why I never tried to find you after the War.'

Flo hadn't thought about it at all. But now that she did, she thought what a difference it would have made to her life, knowing that Tom had sons and perhaps seeing them occasionally.

'It was quite a struggle managing to begin with, I can tell you, despite all my mum and dad's help. And Selsey was such a quiet and isolated place in those days, specially where we live on the edge of the Saltings. Not like now with hundreds of holidaymakers streaming in and out the village all day long.

Well, I just lived for Ray and Jeffrey and making some sort of life for them and myself.

'I thought about you from time to time, believe me Flo. But I didn't have your address and didn't know how to go about tracing you. You weren't in the phone book and Kingston is a big place. Though if I'd really tried I suppose I could have found you earlier. Perhaps I should have put an advert in your local paper? But then I met my husband Frank. His parents were very wary about me to begin with, just as you might imagine.

'I didn't want anything getting in the way between Frank and me. Don't take this the wrong way, Flo, but I didn't want a third grannie turning up, reminding everybody. Looking back, I was probably far too sensitive. Frank turned out to be twenty-two carat and always took my side - even if it meant putting his mother in her place occasionally.'

Then Vera paused and added more quietly: 'I'm sorry, Flo. I should have tried a little harder. But I did try once years later. I was reading an old letter from Tom which mentioned the name of the road in Kingston where you both lived. That set me on the trail and one day I came up to Kingston by train by myself .

'I'd written to Kingston Library to get them to check the Electoral Roll and found you were still living in the same street and discovered your house number. Well, I turned up one afternoon and called at your door but there was no answer. So I waited around for about an hour. I knew roughly what you looked like because you're in one of the few photos I have of Tom, one that was taken when you were both on holiday together at the seaside somewhere just before the War.

'Eventually I saw you coming along the road, at least I was pretty sure it was you. But when I approached you and tried to speak to you, you got very agitated for some reason and rushed away as if you were terrified. I knew for sure it was you because you went into the house I knew you lived in.

'To begin with I thought you must have recognised me somehow and didn't want to know. Or maybe you'd turned crazy like one of those women who stand on the corner of the street and shout at the traffic. Either way, it put me off trying again for some time.'

'Oh my dear,' Flo exclaimed. 'I remember that occasion well. It would be about ten years ago, the very day I lost my job at Bentalls in very distressing circumstances. I was very upset and confused about everything.'

'I'm sorry, Flo,' Vera said again. 'I really should have done more to make contact sooner.'

'Don't worry, dear,' Flo replied. 'I was like a widowed mother myself remember. I'm sure you had your reasons like you've told. But I'm so glad you've made contact now, that's what's important.'

'It was Ray's decision really,' continued Vera looking at her son. 'The last couple of years he's been asking more and more about his first father. He's always known Frank came along later because he's just old enough to remember when there was just the three of us.'

'What about you, Grandma?' Ray interrupted. 'What happened to you after my dad died?'

Flo told them how she was absolutely devastated by Tom's death. But she tried to put a bit of gloss on all the years she had spent alone, she didn't want them to think that she was some sad old woman of no consequence whose life had no meaning. She told them proudly about her war work making the fighter planes that won the Battle of Britain at the Hawker works and the years spent waitressing in the Tudor restaurant of Kingston's top department store. How late in life she had run a dry cleaners single-handed. And she told them about all her friends, the closest of whom was Connie, though truth be told she wasn't only the closest one but the only one. And she mentioned that she'd had her family: her sister Ada and her husband Stan, alas all now departed.

She told them how she had travelled to Holland and visited Tom's grave. And of all the wonderful holidays she had over the years in Bournemouth and the West Country. And how even now at the grand old age of 67 she was still doing work to help the NSPCC.

Vera asked her if she had ever thought of remarrying. Flo told a white lie and said that she had been friendly with a very nice Canadian Air Force Officer once but things hadn't worked out that way.

But Vera wasn't altogether taken in. She only had to look around at the room to see how empty the old woman's life had been since Tom's death. And she felt guilty.

'And what of you, Ray?' asked Flo. 'What do you do? It's going to take some time getting used to the fact that I've got two grandsons, and grown up ones at that.'

'I'm a motor mechanic at Rowes, the big Ford Dealers up at Chichester,' came the reply.

'Well blow me down,' replied Flo. 'Do you know, that's exactly what your dad did before his call up. He was training to be an engineer at a garage on Kingston Hill. What an amazing coincidence. But do you live at home still, with your mum? Are you courting yet?'

'He's supposed to be living at home,' interrupted Vera. 'But he's hardly ever there, certainly never Saturday nights.'

'You know how it is, Grandma,' Ray explained with a sparkle in his eye. 'I go out with my mates and have a few ciders. And we meet a few young ladies on holiday at Bunn's Caravan site. Well, you know how you shouldn't drive home when you've had a few drinks - so I just put my head down for the night wherever I can.'

Ray winked and laughed and even Flo, the most unworldly of grandmothers, knew exactly what he meant.

'That seat you're sitting on,' said Flo pointing to the brass-studded leather chair she had taken from the laundry the day it closed. 'Your dad used to sit in that seat reading his comics when he was a child, waiting for me to finish work.'

Ray became serious and turned round to look at the old Victorian chair.

'I've got a few photos of him if you'd like to see them,' Flo suggested. And she uncovered the album on the table in which she kept her few precious photographs and went through the handful of pictures one by one.

Ray spent a long time looking at each and asking where they were taken and who else was in them. Vera also took a long quiet look at them all. Then Flo brewed some fresh tea and, apologising that she had no cake because she didn't know they were coming, opened a packet of Garibaldi biscuits.

Eventually the time came for them to leave.

'Look, Flo,' said Vera. 'We've found you now and we're not going to lose you. I'm going to give you our address and phone number. And before long we're expecting you to come and stay with us down at Selsey. You'll love it down by the sea now that summer's coming.'

'Oh, I'd like that very much,' answered Flo.

As Ray and Vera left they both kissed her on the cheek. Flo came down to see them off in the Ford Anglia that Ray was driving.

'I'll write soon, Flo. We'll be expecting you to come and visit,' were Vera's parting words.

'Bye, Grandma,' said Ray giving her a big smile. Flo waved and watched the little white car head off down Staunton Road and turn right into King's Road.

Slowly she returned to her flat. She cleared all the cups and plates away and noticed the light was beginning to fade outside. Then she poured herself a glass of British sherry, and wished she hadn't been so miserly and had bought a bottle of real Spanish sherry instead. And she sat by the table by the window and lit cigarette after cigarette and collected her thoughts.

'Me a grandmother all these years and never knew it,' she reflected. 'Who would have believed it. And him such a fine lad, just like his father.' But he was different, which was only to be expected, even though he was Tom's spitting image. And Vera seemed such a nice woman too. Flo felt happy that her son had found true love, even if for such a brief time, and had gone to his grave knowing the physical expression of love that made manhood complete.

Then Flo noticed something strange. She was seated on one of the old kitchen chairs round the table when her attention was drawn to the brass-studded leather chair that Ray had been sitting in. On the padded leather seat there was a circular depression that she had never seen before. Suddenly she felt Tom was very close. Of course, she had often felt him close before but never as close as he felt then. And words came to her that she could understand clearly even though they were devoid of sound.

'Everything's gonna be lots better now, Mum.' Then the words came again only more distant the second time as if they were drifting away. Then there was silence. Flo's eyes refocused on the upholstered seat of the brass-studded leather chair. It was perfectly flat like it always was when nobody was sitting in it. The depression had vanished as quickly as it had appeared.

Flo hardly slept a wink that night, just like the night after she found out about Tom's death. But this time it was excitement not grief that kept her mind working overtime. She slept a little before dawn came and awoke wondering if it had all been a dream. So she went down to the living room and found the scrap of paper with Vera's name and address and phone number on it. There was no mistake.

Flo wanted to rush out and tell someone about her good fortune. Not about feeling Tom's presence maybe but certainly about Ray and Vera's visit. But there was no one left to tell. Connie was gone, Ada was gone and Stan was gone. There was only Doreen, to whom she wrote a brief letter explaining what had happened.

A few days went by and Flo had a horrible feeling. What if they didn't contact her again? What if they'd only come to satisfy their curiosity or Vera had thought better of it in case it caused problems with her husband's family? But towards the end of the week a post card arrived that simply said 'WISH YOU WERE HERE' signed 'Ray'. Flo looked at the pictures on the front of the post card. There was a bustling little high street with flint stone walled shops, a windmill, a lifeboat station perched on stilts some way from the shore and a beach with lobster pots in the foreground and folk sitting in deck chairs looking out to sea. Selsey looked like a very nice place, Flo decided, and she thought that Tom must have been familiar with all these scenes when he was stationed there. How strange she had never thought of going down there some time over the years on one of her journeys into Tom's past.

The following week a short letter arrived from Vera inviting Flo to come and stay with them for a few days. She gave the date when they would be expecting her and said she was to phone the day before to say what time her train would arrive at Chichester Station.

When the big day came, Flo was all a flutter with excitement. She packed everything she would need into the little cardboard suitcase she had bought before the War when she and Tom had gone on their first holiday together. She remembered how Tom had insisted on carrying it for his mum, even though it was almost as big as himself and a bit of a struggle. Dear Tom. Little could she have known then that one day she would be using it to visit his sons.

On the train, Flo remembered the times nearly twenty-five years before when she had made the same journey in wartime to meet Tom. She recognised Arundel Castle as the train sped by and the long tunnel where the train had sheltered from the German bombers during a raid.

Flo got off the train at Chichester and entered the Booking Hall. She saw Ray immediately, he was wearing a smart blue suit and tie. He was standing in exactly the same spot that Tom used to stand when she had come to visit him when he was stationed in Selsey. And suddenly Flo remembered the words of the clairvoyant, spoken so many years before at the little spiritualist church in Kingston: 'You'll see him again...in this world and the next.' Here surely was another example of what the white haired seer had meant.

As soon as he saw her, Ray switched on his winning smile. He really was what Connie used to call in her later years 'a 1940s Charmer'.

'Hello, Grandma. Ticket Inspectors didn't catch you with the other fare dodgers then?' he quipped in his breezy style.

It took a couple of seconds before Flo understood Ray's little joke. He kissed her on the cheek and took the suitcase. Just like Tom did.

Ray's car was waiting in the station car park. Soon they were wending along winding country roads flanked by sturdy oak trees and flint stone wall buildings just like in the post card.

'Is this the main road into Selsey?' Flo asked.

'It's the *only* road into Selsey,' replied Ray. 'Just one road in and one road out. Unless you fancy a long hike across the Saltings. That's what they call the sea marshes round here, Grandma. You wouldn't want to try that in daylight let alone on a dark night.'

So this was the way that Tom would have come to Selsey all those years ago, thought Flo. It really was a journey back in time into Tom's past.

Eventually they entered the village. Flo noticed that the High Street was lined with old-fashioned shops that probably hadn't changed much since before the War. There were butchers, bakers, fishmongers, greengrocers, an ironmongers and several general grocers selling provisions. The shoppers seemed mostly of her generation, retired couples with a sprinkling of young housewives and even a few early holidaymakers. The great annual invasion of caravanners was still a couple of months off and Selsey was looking its chocolate-box best. Just like on the postcard, in fact. Ray turned down a side street and then drove along an unmade track that ran parallel with the sea. He stopped the car in front of a Victorian coastguard's cottage that stood at the end of a row.

'The Grand Hotel's full up this time of year, Grandma,' Ray joked. 'So you'll have to rough it in our spare bedroom.'

They walked through the front garden, where a few hollyhocks, some sea kale and a tamarisk hedge struggled for survival among the crab and lobster pots, and entered the cottage. Vera was waiting to welcome her. She sat Flo in a large armchair of uncertain vintage and immediately put the kettle on.

'Frank apologises for not being here but he's working down at the Fish Sheds. Just brought in a catch this morning but he'll be here later,' she said. Then Vera shouted loudly through the window that opened onto the small back garden.

'Jeffrey! Come in *now* please and say Hello. Our guest has arrived.'

The back door opened and in walked a slightly-built lad with fair hair and clear blue eyes.

'This is Ray's brother.' Then turning to her younger son, Vera said: 'Jeffrey, this is your long-lost grandma.'

Jeffrey came over and sat next to Flo, looked her up and down quizzically and said 'Hello'. And so they all fell into easy conversation, Flo remarking what a delightful spot Selsey was and how lucky they were to live right next to the sea. They talked about Ray's job at the Ford dealers up in Chichester and how he eventually wanted to be a mechanic with a motor racing team at nearby Goodwood. Jeffrey was working for a bank in Chichester but was planning to go on to a polytechnic before long to study computers. Anything except following in Frank's footsteps and going to sea in all weathers chasing fickle shoals of smelly fish!

Jeffrey told Flo that he thought all businesses would use computers one day, how the 'hardware' would get smaller and smaller, and how they would do all sorts of different jobs. He was obviously very keen on computers, decided Flo who only had the vaguest idea of what a computer was but didn't want to show her ignorance.

Jeffrey poured the tea and offered his new grandma the first cup. Meanwhile Vera produced some sandwiches she had made earlier from ham carved from the bone by one of the grocers in the High Street. Flo thought how delicious the ham tasted, so much nicer than anything they served in the Tudor cafeteria at Bentalls when she worked there.

When they had finished lunch, Vera said to Ray: 'Go on, I know you're itching to get off to Goodwood. He likes to hang around with the oily rags at the motor racing track, Flo. But you be back for this evening mind, we're taking Flo to the Sundowner's and everyone's going. No exceptions!' There was an authoritarian tone in her voice that told Flo that in this house Vera's word was law and not to be trifled with. Jeffrey was excused too, to return to the back garden where he was tinkering about with an old BSA motorcycle that one of his uncles had given him.

Once they were alone, Vera showed Flo to a small bedroom with just enough room for a single bed and a chest of drawers and left her to unpack and freshen up before taking a walk along the shore.

As they walked towards Selsey Bill, the sun sparkled on the sea and Vera pointed out the silhouette of the Isle of Wight on the horizon. The coastline leading up to the Bill was lined with large houses of the grand sort whose back gardens came right down almost to the beach. One very large house even had an ancient seawater swimming pool projecting from its grounds that was refilled by the tide twice a day. 'What a truly heavenly spot this is,' thought Flo.

Vera spoke of Tom and how happy they had been in their two short years together. She told Flo about their plans to marry when the War was over. Tom had felt strongly that it would be wrong to do so before then, before they could settle down properly.

'He was very proud of you, Flo,' Vera said just as they reached the furthest point of the Bill. 'He was always talking about you. He knew how hard you had to struggle to bring him up alone and how you always gave him the best of everything you had. You meant the world to him.'

Flo felt very happy when she heard that. But it was still followed by more than a flicker of regret that they would never share a moment together again in this world.

'We made plans for after the War,' Vera continued. 'You know how people do at times like that - something to look forward to and keep you going. Sweet dreams of life to come.'

'Eventually, when Tom qualified as a motor engineer he wanted to find a job in a garage down here away from the Smoke. And he even talked of having his own small garage one day, he knew everyone would want cars after the War was over. And his plans included you, Flo. He wanted to get somewhere big to live, somewhere big enough for you to live with us too. He thought you'd like it down here, he had your retirement all worked out.' Vera gave a little laugh and Flo thought how different her life would have been, how wonderful if it had all come about that way. If only Tom had survived the War.

'I almost met you once, you know Flo. One time when you came down to Chi to visit him. He wanted me to come with him and introduce me to you. But I knew how precious your few hours together were and thought you'd best spend it just the two of you. I knew he'd be going over to France before long and would be away for some time. So I told him there would be opportunities enough for us to meet later.'

'Well you weren't wrong there, dear,' Flo laughed. 'It was just later than expected.'

From Selsey Bill, they could see along Fisherman's Beach and Vera pointed out the fishing boats anchored off the shore. And there was the lifeboat station, perched on stilts over the sea reached by a long walkway, just like on the post card.

'Frank moors his old rust bucket there, just past Pontins holiday camp. His shed, where they cut and gut the fish ready for sale, is just opposite.'

They stood there for a moment longer, looking across the bay past Pagham Lagoon to Bognor Regis in the distance where reflected sunlight flashed from the windscreens of unseen cars as they glided along the Esplanade.

As they walked back along the shoreline, Flo wondered why Tom hadn't told her about his plans to marry Vera. Or maybe he had told her but she hadn't been listening, not wanting to recognise that one day there would be another woman in his life. They walked on past the burnt-out ruins of the old Marine Hotel until eventually they reached the cottage where Frank was waiting for them. Vera introduced him to Flo and he welcomed her warmly. Frank made them a pot of tea and toasted some crumpets, the sea air had sharpened their appetites. And so Flo finished the most enjoyable afternoon she could remember for some time, sitting in a deckchair in the garden in good company, enjoying hot crumpets spread with generous helpings of local farmhouse butter and apricot jam.

The Sundowner's Club was a large mock-Tudor beam building with a thatched roof opposite the Marine Beach where the main road literally ran into the sea. It looked like it must have been quite a substantial residence for someone of importance before the War. They all drove there in Frank's van, Flo sat between Vera and Frank on the front bench seat while Ray and Jeffrey crouched in the back and complained they would smell of fish and none of the girls would want to dance with them.

'They'll be queuing to dance with you two,' Frank wound them up. 'That's prime smoked haddock been in there.'

The Club had a cavernous barn-like interior and it was filling up fast. They sat at a large table and Flo noticed everyone was spruced up and flaunting their trendiest finery. The boys were wearing smart single-breasted suits with pastel-coloured polyester shirts and thin ties and their hair slicked down with Brylcreem or Silvikrin. Most of the girls were wearing mini-skirts.

All the older people seemed to know Frank and Vera and the atmosphere was very convivial. Ray went to the bar to get the drinks having persuaded Flo to try a glass of local Sussex cider.

'Don't you get yer gran sozzled,' Vera shouted across to him. But alas too late as Ray had already told the barman to slip a double vodka in Flo's pint of cider.

There was a real buzz about the place and they decided they'd better order some food before the kitchen got really busy. Jeffrey explained to Flo that everything came in a basket and that you ate it with your fingers. There were no knives or forks, it was the 'cool' thing to do when eating out.

'Makes the washing up easier for the gaffers too,' added Frank cynically. There was a choice of Chicken and Chips in the Basket, Hamburger and Chips in the Basket or Scampi and Chips in the Basket.

Flo had heard about Hamburgers but had never tried one. 'Now's your chance, Grandma,' Ray urged her. 'I knew you'd be up for something trendy. And the really great thing about burgers is you can be absolutely sure they're not made of fish.' This was another friendly dig at Frank, the family would live on fish if he had his way. Everybody laughed but Frank just smiled.

The Hamburger and Chips in the Basket came with all the trimmings: fried onions, pickled gherkin, a wedge of tomato and a big slippery blob of tomato sauce. Flo was a bit self-conscious about eating a meal with her hands at first but she liked the taste of the Hamburger combined with the onions and the ketchup. Everyone laughed when at Flo's second bite the concealed gherkin shot across the table.

'Steady, Grandma, you'll have someone's eye out with that gherkin if yer not careful,' warned Ray. They all hooted with laughter including Flo who soon had tears streaming down her face. The Hamburger and chips soon gave her quite a thirst which she quenched with yet another generous draught from the large glass of cider.

Just then the band, who called themselves 'Elvey Preslis and the Hound Dogs', began to play. They were a local rock group who unashamedly aped Elvis Presley and his band and played only songs popularised by the 'King'. Soon a number of dancers were on the floor, mostly youngsters, rocking and writhing to the beat of the band and the seductive tones of 'Elvey'.

'They must have ruddy ants in their pants,' Frank commented. Flo, who had never heard this well worn phrase before, thought it very funny and couldn't stop laughing at the thought. Then she had another long drink, she found the sweet fruity cider very refreshing - it was getting warm in the Club and what with all the excitement and laughing Flo felt quite thirsty and was glad Ray had ordered her a whole pint.

'C'mon Grandma, let's 'ave a dance,' demanded Ray. 'Reckon you must have been a right little raver in your day. One of them Charleston flappers I wouldn't be surprised!' Normally Flo would have been mortified by such an invitation. She hadn't danced a step since the wartime dances that were held at the Hawker Works Social Club and she even felt awkward then. But the Sussex Wild Boar Cider that Ray had bought her, amply fortified by two shots of 'Stalin's Revenge', had softened her inhibitions and she was enjoying herself.

'But I can't dance,' Flo protested mildly.

'Neither can anyone else on the dance floor,' replied Ray. 'And the singer's tone deaf but that doesn't stop him from singing. Come along, Grandma.' And so to the sound of 'You Ain't Nothing but a Hound Dog' Ray led Flo over towards where the other dancers were shimmying and shaking. Once he had found a spare square yard on the crowded floor, Ray suddenly seemed to become double-jointed as his knees, hips, ankles and shoulders began to bend and twist in every direction in perfect time with the rhythm.

Meanwhile Flo began by trying to copy what the other female dancers were doing. But unbeknown to her, she had consumed a full pint of Selsey's most lethal cocktail which increasingly had the effect of loosening every joint in her body. And so she embarked on a highly esoteric dance of her own making that was a cross between some kind of wartime jitterbugging and a voodoo witch doctor's dance of death.

Slowly, Ray manoeuvred himself and his gyrating gran to the centre of the dance floor, which he considered his rightful place. The dancers either side soon became aware that some strange metamorphosis to Rock and Roll was taking place in Selsey. The other dancers slowed down, pulled back and watched spellbound as the youthful snake-hipped Ray and his groovy super-gran danced to the beat of their own drums.

By the time the band slipped seamlessly into the next number, 'Blue Suede Shoes', everybody in the Sundowner's Club had stopped dancing, drinking and even breathing to watch the spectacle - and several pony-tailed teenagers were clapping them on in tune with the music. When the finale came, everyone was clapping, cheering and whistling. And the applause continued at full volume as Ray led Flo from the floor and her career as a show dancer ended as quickly as it had begun.

'Better than flippin' Top of the Pops,' shouted Frank as they approached the table.

Ray guided Flo back to her seat, thanked her for the dance and ran his hand down the inside of his jacket to smooth his tie. After directing Jeffrey to 'Get gran another cider but better make it a half' he turned and disappeared in the direction of a gaggle of mini-skirted girls who welcomed him like the returning hero he was.

Before Jeffrey and the cider arrived, a silver bucket filled with ice and a bottle of pink Peralada sparkling wine masquerading as Moet & Chandon Champagne appeared with a card saying 'With the complements (sic) of the Management'. And for the rest of the evening Flo sat with the others who spoke of nothing else but her debut as a 1960's dance diva and she chain-smoked and sipped the cold sweet bubbly and enjoyed her fifteen minutes of fame.

Flo awoke the next morning in her bedroom at Frank and Vera's cottage. The sun was shining through the window and she could hear the sound of the waves breaking on the sea wall not far away.

It was two hours later than the time Flo usually got up but there was no hurry. Although she couldn't remember the journey back from the Sundowner's Club, she could recall Vera saying that on Sunday mornings everybody had a lie in. So Flo dozed for another half hour and went over the events of the previous evening in her mind. Had she made a complete fool of herself, she wondered? On the contrary, she decided, everyone had seemed most impressed by her bold attempt at modern dance. Despite all the cider and bubbly that had passed her lips the evening before, Flo felt fresh as a daisy and still somewhat exhilarated by the previous night's performance.

As she lay there, with the rays of the morning sun falling gently on her face, Flo felt that a new period of her life was beginning. Now she had got to know Ray and Vera better, and met Frank and Jeffrey, she felt like a different person. She knew that life was never going to be quite the same again. And Flo realised what a difference indeed it made to be part of a family and have nice people around you who cared.

During their years together, Tom had been Flo's family and was all she ever wanted. Although you would never call her extrovert, Flo wasn't shy either. But she hadn't made friends easily, Connie of course was the only one. Stan and Ada were her family too and they had been very good to her and Tom. But they weren't family she had seen every day because they lived so far away on the other side of London.

To be fair, trying to make ends meet and bringing up Tom on her own had taken up all her nervous energy before the War. She hadn't any spare time for making friends and socialising. But for the first time, Flo began to realise how much she had missed, specially after the War when she was alone. And then Flo thought of Tom and knew that she had never been alone and realised that it couldn't have been any other way for her.

How wonderful it would be, how completely perfect, if only Tom could be present in this house now with all these wonderful people that she had met. But she thought how lucky she had been to have a son like Tom, even if their time together was not meant to be for long.

And she knew she wouldn't have wanted to change anything about her life, not for all the gold in Ghana.

Then Flo heard someone moving about in the living room so she got up and dressed and made herself ready. It was Vera making a start on the Sunday roast. She asked Flo if she had slept well and put the kettle on to make tea. She explained that they didn't usually have a big breakfast on Sundays because they always had a big roast for lunch. Vera offered Flo a bowl of milk and Kellogs Rice Crispies, something Flo had seen in the shops but had never tried before. She discovered she quite liked their light crunchy taste.

Flo helped Vera with the Sunday roast by peeling the potatoes and scraping the carrots. The joint consisted of the biggest leg of pork she had ever seen. Vera made criss-cross cuts in the skin and then rubbed salt into it because 'everyone likes lots of pork crackling!' Then she peeled a couple of enormous Bramley apples to make apple sauce with.

An hour later everything was roasting away in the oven and Flo and Vera were just finishing another cuppa. Suddenly the kitchen door opened and Jeffrey walked in. Flo could see from his greasy hands that he'd been working on the motor bike.

'Now, young Jeff,' said Vera. 'I want you to go down to the Fish Sheds and choose three of the biggest crabs you can find for our tea. Mind you give 'em a good tap first to make sure they're not empty. And wash those hands before you leave.'

Then she added aside: 'Perhaps you'd like to accompany Jeffrey for a stroll down to the East Beach, Flo? He'll show you what's what in our village as you go.'

'Get your coat then, Grandma,' said Jeffrey who was slowly getting used to the idea that he now had three grandmothers. And so they left the cottage and walked past the tamarisks and hollyhocks competing with the crab and lobster pots in the front garden. It was a mild bracing day with just the hint of a breeze and enough warmth in the sun to offer the promise of a fine afternoon to come.

As he rehooked the garden gate Jeffrey looked at the pots and said: 'You wouldn't think we'd be needing to buy crabs. But dad only ever seems to catch haddock and herrings.'

They walked along the unmade track just beyond the cottage and headed towards the tarmac road. The tide had gone out revealing large stretches of sand on which numerous squawking gulls gathered and fought over tiny shore crabs, small shrimps and fish fry trapped in the sand pools. As they walked up the main road, Flo noticed that it was lined with large red brick houses with nice front gardens. A few of them had been converted into guest houses, others into convalescent or retirement homes for elderly folk.

'You couldn't do better than end your days in one of those,' thought Flo.

Jeffrey kept up a constant commentary on who lived where, what each building was used for and where each side road led to. Flo decided that nobody would ever want for conversation in Jeff's company and wondered if he had Irish blood.

Eventually, they reached the High Street. Except for a couple of newsagents, all the other shops were closed as you would expect on a Sunday in the 1960s. But Flo could see they were all well-kept and even included a haberdashers, milliners and several ladies outfitters: shops that much to her regret had long since disappeared one-by-one from the shopping centre of

Kingston. Jeffrey continued to ramble on about where was the best place to buy what and led Flo along the entire length of the High Street.

Then they turned right and passed through an area where new bungalows were sprouting up on the last remaining open land between the High Street and the sea. It was just as well Flo was a good walker, but the fact that her guide was a good talker helped the distance slip by unnoticed. His running commentary made Selsey sound an even more interesting place than it looked at first sight.

Finally, they arrived at the Fish Sheds just before the East Beach. The Sheds were a run-down assortment of ramshackle tin and timber huts that looked as if they had been thrown together in a storm. This was where the local fishermen prepared and sold their catch. There were empty fish boxes and crab pots everywhere. And next to most sheds were large rusty vats for boiling the crabs and lobsters. The ground was littered with broken cockle shells and bits of crab claws that had a not unpleasant air of putrefaction about them. You had to watch your step though, steel wires from winches used to haul the fishing boats up the beach were everywhere waiting to trip the unwary. And over the whole area hung the evocative seaside aroma of fresh fish, creosote, boiling crabs, rotting seaweed and spilt diesel oil.

Jeffrey led Flo towards one of the sheds where he bought three fat crabs still hot from the boiler, dutifully tapping them with his knuckles as his mother's bidding. Flo was amazed at how cheap they were, less than half the price that you paid at the fish stalls in Kingston Market: prices that Flo had hardly ever felt able to afford except on rare occasions before the War when she had bought one as a special treat for Tom and herself for Sunday tea.

Besides the crabs, Jeffrey bought two little tubs of cockles and he led Flo to a wooden bench overlooking the beach. Here they sat and ate the plump salty molluscs over which he had shaken a little vinegar. Flo was fond of cockles which she could remember her mother buying from a horse-drawn cart that came round the streets of Battersea on Sunday mornings when she was a child. As Jeffrey ate, he continued to talk: about how the Emsworth cockles were reckoned the best around here and how in Roman times a fort stood about a mile out to sea from the point where they now sat when it was all still land. It showed how fast the coast was falling into the sea but, according to Jeff, all that would stop when they finished building the concrete sea walls and lines of wooden groynes.

'Let's visit dad's shed and see if we can cadge a lift back in the van,' said Jeffrey and he led Flo along the path that linked the East Beach and Fishermen's Beach and led to another cluster of huts. They entered one and sure enough there was Frank, standing among boxes and baskets of herrings mixed with ice chips. Frank looked worried and was deep in conversation with another fisherman but he broke off to welcome Flo with a cheery smile.

It turned out that they'd landed a bumper catch of herrings the previous day. They'd been bought by a pickling company down in Portsmouth who wanted them supplied cleaned and boned by Tuesday morning.

'That gives us tomorrow to get this lot filleted. And I'm three women filleters short. One's ill, one's too far-gone pregnant and one's decided to take a holiday, now of all times,' moaned Frank.

'I pay good enough money for the work but no one wants to get their hands dirty these days,' he complained. 'When I was a boy, the women would drop everything and come running once they heard there was a boat in and the chance to earn a few extra coppers. Now hardly anyone knows one end of a herring from the other.'

'Really? But there's nothing to it, is there Frank,' said Flo. 'I have a herring for my tea every Friday, have ever since I can remember, and I've never had a bone stuck in my throat. Even a townie like me knows how to fillet a herring.'

It went quiet for a few seconds. Then Frank picked up a well-worn knife with a wooden handle and handed it to Flo with a herring. 'Go on then Flo. Show us how townies do it,' he challenged.

Flo went over to a large wooden table and placed the fish on the slab. She cut off its tail and head and then neatly slit it open along the belly. She scraped its insides clean having put the roe to one side, opened the fish out and pressed the inside flat against the surface. Then she pressed all along the backbone and lifted the bones clean away from the flesh.

'There you are,' said Flo. 'Not so much as a whisker left on that.'

Frank picked up the fish and examined it from both sides. He looked at Jeffrey in amazement and then back at the fish. 'Well I'll be blowed, not bad at all.' Then half-joking he asked: 'What you doing tomorrow, Flo?' and they all laughed.

'We'd better be getting back Dad or we'll be late for lunch,' said Jeffrey. Nobody was ever late for Vera's Sunday roasts so Frank locked up his shed, and they all piled into the front bench seat of his old Bedford van and headed homeward.

7: Flo attacks an S.S. Panzergrenadier with a broken brolly.

Flo hadn't enjoyed a proper roast joint for lunch since the days that she worked in the cafeteria in Bentalls. Or was it in the canteen at the Hawker works during the War? Either way it was a long time ago. There wasn't much point in cooking a roast for one, so Flo usually had a lamb chop or a couple of beef sausages for her lunch on Sundays.

Everybody was seated round the table when Vera brought in the enormous joint of pork for Frank to carve. Then in came the vegetable dishes with boiled and roast potatoes, roast parsnips, carrots, mashed swede, Brussel sprouts and roast onions. And of course the gravy.

'Roast wouldn't be the same without mum's gravy,' said Jeffrey. 'Not like that bilge water you get with pub grub roasts.'

Ray was looking a bit subdued. He hadn't come home until nine in the morning and had slept until long after mid-day. But when Flo sat next to him he bucked up and turned on his best Ronald Coleman 1940's Charmer smile.

'That was some dainty dancing you got up to over at the Sundowner's yesterday, Grandma. You're a real natural! I hear Ginger Rogers has really got the wind up!' he teased her.

'I made a right spectacle of myself, you mean,' answered Flo. 'That cider went straight to my head.'

'You did fine!' everybody told her. Ray began laughing at the thought of the previous evening's revels. And then they all tucked into the roast which was served complete with the crispest crackling and the tangiest apple sauce Flo had ever tasted.

'Frank went to see the doctor once about losing some weight,' Vera said to Flo. 'So the doctor tells him what to eat and what not to. But he sees Frank's face drop like an anchor so he says "You can still have roast chicken, though just don't eat the skin."

'And you know what Frank said?' asked Vera. Ray and Jeffrey knew exactly what Frank had said and began sniggering at this oft told family tale.

'Frank says "O.K. I won't eat the chicken skin. But pork crackling's still alright, isn't it Doctor?"'

They all hollered with laughter, including Flo.

'I keep telling you, I was only winding him up,' Frank protested lamely.

The walk and the sea air had given Flo quite an appetite and she didn't say no to seconds when they were offered. After they'd finished dinner Frank spoke to Vera in a loud voice.

'I dunno how we're going to fillet thirty boxes of herring tomorrow for that pickling order. Half my regular women are off so we're three filleters short.'

'Well, I'm off to Chichester to take Flo round the shops tomorrow. So for once I can't help,' replied Vera, sensing what Frank was angling for.

'Wish I had a few like Flo 'ere,' said Frank enthusiastically. 'Do you know, Vera, she filleted a fish so fast this morning she should be in the bloomin' Guinness Book of Records.'

'Well, Flo's not down here to fillet fish,' said Vera. 'She's our guest.'

'I'd be happy to help out if you wanted, Frank,' chirped up Flo. At that point the jaws of the trap snapped firmly shut. So after some feigned 'Oh I can't possibly ask you to do that' and 'Are you sure, Flo?' it was arranged that Flo would help with the filleting the next day so Vera said she might as well come along too.

After lunch, Frank had a nap on the sofa and Ray fell asleep in the armchair. It was a pleasantly warm afternoon so Vera, Flo and Jeffrey went into the back garden to sit in the sun in deck chairs that had 'B.R.U.D.C.' stencilled on them indicating that three of Bognor Regis Urban District Council's deck chairs had gone AWOL. Jeffrey began reading the Sunday Express but soon he nodded off too.

'Now you're sure you don't mind about this filleting business tomorrow?' Vera checked. 'It's a ruddy cheek if you ask me, inviting you down here and Frank setting you to work cutting up herrings.'

Flo said that she'd be delighted to help out, specially after all the hospitality they'd shown her. Then there was a lull in the conversation and a few minutes later Flo noticed that Vera was also having a nap.

It was so peaceful sitting there in the sunshine. The very same garden that Tom must have sat out in on warm Sunday afternoons when he wasn't on duty more than twenty years before. And she hadn't eaten such a wonderful Sunday lunch since she was a child. Mind you, she always tried to do a roast of some sort for Tom on Sundays when they were together, though her slender means didn't run to joints of beef or pork. But she did manage a rolled neck of lamb with stuffing most weeks or sometimes she bought some belly of pork rolled up to look like it was a joint. And she could only afford those cheap cuts by waiting until just before Kingston Market closed on Saturday evening and buying the left-overs at knock down prices. Then Flo nodded off for forty winks herself.

They had a late tea and once again Vera excelled herself. The crabs were delicious and packed with meat. More than enough to go round, specially as Ray had slipped away to meet his mates. Vera also made a lovely crisp salad with cos lettuce, tomatoes, radishes and spring onions. And she cut up the remaining boiled potatoes from lunch and mixed them with salad cream to make a potato salad. Afterwards they watched 'Sunday Night at the London Palladium' on the television and Frank brought out the bottles of stout and the sherry. It was real Spanish sherry of course with a nice almondy taste to it, not the cheap syrupy stuff they called British or Cyprus Sherry. And as she sipped the seductive brown liquid and smoked her third cigarette of the evening, Flo thought again how very lucky she was to have found such a nice family.

It was an early start the next morning. The sun was still struggling to add warmth to the land when Frank's van, also carrying Vera and Flo, shuddered to a halt outside the fish shed. Two women were already waiting there to be let in and Frank lost no time in opening up. Once inside, he unlocked the refrigerated storage chamber and wheeled out the boxes of fish. When they saw the mountain of wooden boxes, they all blanched slightly at the task ahead of them.

Frank broke the silence. 'Well, as the wise old Chinaman said "The journey of a thousand miles begins with one short step."'

So saying, Frank manhandled the first fish box onto a bench and handed out the small sharp knives. Then he went and turned on the wireless and pop music from Radio Caroline flooded the shed. Frank knew that when it comes to doing monotonous work, nothing keeps the workers going like non-stop pop. Soon hands were darting in and out of the boxes and the knives glinted as they flashed backwards and forwards on the work bench.

'Don't forget to put the herring roes in the bucket,' Frank added. 'They's what pays your wages!'

Some of the women started singing along with the pop songs. Just like at the Hawker Aircraft works during the War, thought Flo. Only then it was Vera Lynn, Anne Shelton, the Andrews Sisters and Bing Crosby songs whereas now it was the Beatles, Elvis Presley, Roy Orbison and the Rolling Stones.

Flo found it easy work and within no time she was filling the boxes with fillets even faster than the regulars.

Frank joined in too, it was all hands to the pumps. 'Careful no one cuts themselves,' he shouted out. 'The customers don't want any pickled fingers turning up in their jars.'

There were two fifteen-minute tea breaks and a half-hour stop for lunch. Other than that they were at it flat out without a pause. Gradually the empty wooden boxes started to outnumber the full ones. And by the time in the late afternoon when the lorry with 'Pompey Picklers – The Perfect Way to Get Pickled' painted on the side had arrived, the job was finished and everyone including Flo was enjoying a much deserved mug of tea and a fag outside the fish shed. There were two men on the lorry and they lost no time in loading the boxes of herring fillets into the back. When they had finished, the driver went inside to do the paperwork with Frank.

While they were still standing outside, one of the other women who Flo had got to know said to her: ''Ere Flo. I reckon that bloke over there has taken a fancy to you. 'E's been giving you the glad eye all the time he's been loading those crates.'

Everyone laughed in a friendly sort of a way and Flo looked over towards the man who was lifting the last two boxes over the tailgate. Even as she looked he cast a glance her way. It was more a furtive, even fearful look that showed in the eyes of the driver's mate. He was a wizened old man who looked well past pension age but there was something very familiar about him. But for a moment Flo just couldn't place him. She racked her brains and looked again just as he was lifting himself into the cab of the van. He shot her another worried look and slammed the door closed quickly.

In that instant Flo realised who it was. It was Sid, her husband who had walked out on her more than forty years before. He'd been a young man still in his twenties then and now looked more like eighty. But there was no mistaking him, she was certain it was Sid beyond shadow of a doubt.

Flo caught her breath, not knowing what to do. Just then the other man came out of the shed, climbed into the driver's seat and started the engine. Flo walked forward as fast as she could without attracting attention, stood beside the passenger door and looked up through the lorry's side window just as it was moving off. There was Sid with a look on his face like he'd just seen the ghost of Ghengis Khan, just wanting to get away as quick as possible. Flo didn't know whether to shout his name or shake her fist or wave or what. In the event she did nothing.

On the way home in Frank's van, Vera noticed that Flo was rather quiet and asked if she was alright. Of course, Flo said she was fine and forced herself to join in the idle banter. Frank said that they'd go out for a meal at his club that evening as a reward for all their hard work.

So after a thorough wash to get rid of the scales and the smell of the fish, Flo put on the smartest dress she had brought with her and the three of them headed off for Frank's club.

The Thatched House Hotel was located on the sea front not too far from Frank and Vera's cottage. It was a large rambling place but even by the 1960s it was past its glory days. The Hotel had been built before the Great War but its heyday had been in the 1920s and 1930s when it had acquired the status of a slightly exclusive club for local businessmen, tradesmen and regulars from London who drove down for long weekends, many of an extra-curricular nature. Now it accepted anybody with a few pounds to spend but still retained some of its former charm and had a friendly bustling feel about it. There was certainly no shortage of members.

After a drink at the bar, they went into the brightly painted restaurant with a large panoramic window that looked out over a lawn. Flo noticed that instead of grass the lawn consisted entirely of thrift, or sea pinks, and the pale reddish flowers were just coming into bloom. At the end of the lawn was a thatch covered lych-gate that framed a view of the sea beyond.

Flo asked Frank to order for her. Everything on the menu was a mystery to her, she couldn't remember ever eating in such a smart restaurant as this before. They all had the same, a coarse Ardennes pate on thin slices of toast to begin with. Flo enjoyed the pate which was made personally by the chef, it was much tastier than the little glass pots of meat paste they sold back home at the Co-op in Kingston.

'That was lovely,' Flo told Frank. 'I can't wait to see what you ordered next. The menu's all Greek to me.'

'Mousaka,' replied Frank. 'And that's exactly what it is - Greek.'

They all laughed at Flo's unintended joke. Vera explained that they'd had it before in a Greek restaurant down by the Docks in Pompey.

The mention of Pompey made Flo think of Sid again and the sign on the van that had read 'Pompey Picklers'.

'Where is Pompey, exactly?' asked Flo.

'Why Portsmouth of course, Flo,' Frank replied. 'Everyone calls Portsmouth *Pompey* around here. Except when their football team misses a goal at Fratton Park and they call them something else!' And they all laughed again.

When she heard the word Portsmouth, something from the distant past stirred in Flo's memory and eventually the penny dropped. *Portsmouth.* That was the post mark on the envelopes containing the few pitiful pound notes she'd received from Sid immediately after he abandoned her and Tom. So he hadn't strayed far in all these years.

Flo stayed an extra day in Selsey to make up for the time she had spent filleting fish. Vera took her shopping in Chichester and bought her a lovely navy blue jacket in Morants, the big department store in West Street. Flo wanted to pay for it but Vera insisted it was her treat. Of course, it wasn't the type of jacket that Flo would have bought for herself. And of course, that was exactly why Vera had bought it for her. Then they had a crab and watercress sandwich in the same tea rooms near the Cathedral Close where Tom had taken her during the War.

The next day, Flo packed her little suitcase and thanked Vera and Frank for all their kindness. 'And if you ever need an extra pair of hands to help out with the filleting, just let me know,' she told Frank jokingly. Frank gave her a knowing wink, making sure that Vera didn't see. Ray gave his grandma a lift to Chichester Station in the white Ford Anglia on his way to work and waited with her until the train arrived.

'Don't want you catching the wrong train and ending up in Portsmouth or Penzance,' he joked. Then he gave her a peck on the cheek and waved her goodbye. All the way home, Flo kept thinking of only one thing.

Portsmouth.

It took a while for Flo to settle back into the usual rhythm of her routine life. While safe and familiar to her, Kingston and the flat in Staunton Road now seemed lifeless and dull compared to Selsey and the exciting time she had spent down there. But soon the memories of her beloved Tom, and the years they had spent there together, reasserted themselves and she felt at home once more. But Flo knew she would never feel quite the same again, not after being part of Frank and Vera's happy family for a few days. She began to think once again of everything she had missed down the years by not being part of a proper normal family. How different it might all have been, she thought, if she'd married someone who hadn't walked out on her like Sid.

Tom might even have survived the War if Sid had stayed around and been a proper father, she reasoned. Perhaps he could have encouraged Tom with his ambition to become an engineer and helped him to get into the Royal Engineers like he really wanted instead of the infantry. And if he had, perhaps Tom would still be alive today. For the first time, she began to feel angry and resentful about how Sid had left them all alone to fend for themselves.

How better life could have been if only Sid had been a better sort!

Flo had never asked for much out of life but she remembered how hard it had been bringing up Tom all on her own and all the years of loneliness that had followed his tragic death.

Slowly, a great undertaking began to form in Flo's mind. During the following week she thought about it more and more as she went about her daily chores. So one afternoon, after she'd finished her shopping in Kingston Market, she went round to the Public Library opposite the Fairfield Recreation Ground and made for the Reference Section. There she found what she was looking for: a set of Post Office Telephone Directories that covered the whole of the country. Flo lost no time in finding the Portsmouth book and with a slightly trembling hand she looked up 'Pompey Picklers'. Her hand shook because in her heart she knew that once she found the address there would be no turning back.

There it was, printed in bold type, and Flo jotted down the address in pencil on the back of an old envelope. Then she enquired at the desk if they had a street atlas of Portsmouth. The Assistant Librarian was very helpful. They hadn't a street atlas as such but she thought there was a street map in the Town Guide to Portsmouth and Southsea that was included in the collection of holiday brochures they had. Sure enough, the Assistant Librarian's hunch proved right and before long Flo was sitting at a large wooden table with the unfolded map spread out in front of her.

She had no trouble in locating the road in which the bottling plant of Pompey Picklers could be found. The only question was, how to get there from the nearest railway station? Flo drew a little map on the envelope which she folded and put in her handbag. Then she headed back to Staunton Road wondering whether she would have the gumption to go through with it.

Flo decided to go to Portsmouth the following Friday. Why wait and leave it festering in her mind? Anyway, it was her pension day so she could draw the money and pay for the return train ticket out of that. The day came and suddenly Flo began to wonder if it was such a good idea after all. But then she looked around at the flat which hardly anybody else but her ever entered, with its meagre collection of worn out furniture and the door on the landing that led to Tom's empty bedroom. And Flo experienced an emotion quite strange to her, a feeling of bitterness, and she resolved that she *must* go.

Even though there were patches of blue sky between the hurrying clouds, Flo took her umbrella. The weather forecast on the radio that morning had warned of occasional showers.

On the long railway journey down to Portsmouth, Flo began to wonder what she would say to Sid. She thought of a few easily remembered choice phrases if she should need them but knew that the emotion of the moment would bring forth the right words. As the train stopped at Chichester station she became concerned that Vera or Frank or Ray would see her and wonder why she was there. They would think it strange. While the train remained in the station, she shrank back in her seat, and pressed herself against the carriage wall next to the window, in case anybody saw her. But soon the train was moving off again towards Portsmouth and the anxiety passed.

Portsmouth and Southsea Station was a big hustling, bustling place with people and porters hurrying by in all directions. Flo had intended finding a bus going towards the pickling factory but she spotted a taxi cab rank immediately outside the station and decided the importance of the occasion outweighed the expense. The driver knew exactly where to go and sped off through the city traffic, weaving in and out of the cars and lorries as if his cab had a charmed life. It seemed only minutes before he was pulling up a few yards from the entrance to an old red brick building with a big blue weather-beaten sign announcing 'Pompey Picklers of Perfection'.

Flo paid off the cabby and walked straight in through the main door. The receptionist, an older woman in a hand-knitted cardigan, sat behind a desk with sliding glass panels. After each enquiry, she would push the glass screen firmly shut and withdraw into her solitude until the next interruption. Flo tapped firmly on the glass panel which immediately slid open. Flo told the receptionist in an authoritative way that she wanted to see Sid Harman.

'He's gone to lunch, dear,' said the lady in the crystal box. And then looking at the clock she added: 'I saw him leave about ten minutes ago.'

Flo leaned towards the receptionist as if she was imparting confidential information. 'I'm in a bit of a hurry and I've got an important message for him. Could you be awfully kind and tell me where he goes for his lunch?'

'Where everybody else does on a Friday, I expect,' she replied with a chuckle. Then she added in a conspiratorial whisper: 'The Jolly Roger, love. Turn right out the door and left at the end of the road. You can't miss it.'

Flo was out the door in an instant and hardly two minutes later was entering the Public Bar of the Jolly Roger. It was a cheery beery pub that hadn't changed much since the General Strike of 1926, the kind where everybody spoke in a loud voice and laughed twice as lustily as normal. It reminded Flo of the downstairs bar at the Canbury Arms in Kingston during the War. She quickly looked about her, people were standing and sitting around in small groups engrossed in conversation. For a moment she thought she must have missed him for Sid was nowhere to be seen. Then she heard a distant toilet flush and the door of the Gents opened and Sid emerged. He took a seat on a stool in a corner of the bar with two standing companions, re-lit a hand-rolled cigarette and began to drink from a straight-sided beer glass.

Flo moved slowly but purposefully towards her quarry, clutching the rolled up umbrella in her right hand. Suddenly she became aware that Sid was staring straight at her, wide eyed and with a look of mounting shock-horror erupting across his face. Flo approached him slowly, pushing one of his drinking companions aside.

'Yes it's me Sid, your wife Flo. Been a long time hasn't it?' she said loudly so all could hear.

'What a good-for-nothing rotter you turned out to be, walking out on me and little Tom. You remember him, don't you? He was your son!'

You could have heard a pin drop in the Public Bar of the Jolly Roger after that, everybody stopped talking and turned to watch. Sid leaned back further on his stool, his unblinking eyes transfixed in growing terror at what was about to unfold.

'I didn't mind for myself. I was well rid of you, what with yer drinking and gambling. But little Tom, he needed a father. You let him down real bad, Sid!

'You didn't care less whether he lived or starved, did you? Just a couple of measly quid through the post for a week or two and not even a card on his birthday.'

Flo's voice was growing louder and more confident now.

'Want to know what happened to yer son, Sid? Well, he grew up to be a fine young man. God knows how with such a useless waster like you for a father.

'He tried to get into the Royal Engineers in the War but he didn't make it. No father to help him, see? Ended up in the infantry instead – shipped off to fight the Germans and that's how he died. Yer son's life over just when it really should have been beginning.

'Oh, Sid, if only you'd been around for him it might have been so different. You could have taught him things I couldn't. *He might still be alive today!*'

Flo was beginning to get really angry now, all the bottled up sufferings and disappointments of the past forty-five years welled up inside her and began to pour out in a rising torrent of rage. But most of all it was everything that Tom had missed out on during his short life that drove her on. In her increasingly distraught state, this man who now cowered before her became the sole cause of the unbearable separation from her beloved son that had blighted her life for so long.

For the first time, Sid took his eyes off Flo and looked about him. At least thirty pairs of eyes stared back and Sid slunk even further down on the wooden stool.

'How could you do such a thing to your own flesh and blood, you beast?' Flo yelled even louder. Then she snapped. Cringing before her she saw not Sid but some faceless German soldier who had just fired the fatal rocket from his Panzerfaust at the advancing tank which Tom's platoon was using for cover. Instinctively, she brought the handle of the rolled up umbrella down on his head. Again and again the blows rained down and Sid toppled backwards off the stool and onto the floor, his arms raised above his head in a futile act of protection.

The cheap plastic handle broke. But the woman, who before and after that moment in time would never harm a fly or knock the skin off a rice pudding continued to pummel the cowering SS Panzergrenadier with her broken brolly.

Eventually Flo felt gentle hands reach out from behind to restrain her arms and somebody was speaking in a firm but sympathetic voice.

'That's enough of that, mother. I don't allow that sort of behaviour in my pub and you should know better at your age. Why, I'll lose my licence at this rate.'

Flo turned round and saw the kindly but serious face of the publican and his equally determined looking wife. Flo tried one more blow but as she looked forward she just caught sight of Sid's right foot disappearing out the back door, gone without a word spoken.

The restraining arms began to guide Flo back towards the front doors through which she had entered.

'C'mon mother, best be on your way. I'm sure you had your reasons but you've had yer say and now it's time to leave,' the publican insisted.

Then his wife joined in: 'Yes, go home and have a cup of tea, dearie. I'm sure he's simply not worth it.'

The distance from the site of the scuffle to the front door seemed to stretch for eternity as the publican and his wife gently escorted Flo out. But halfway across the floor a woman with heavily peroxided hair, bright red lipstick and a King Size cigarette shouted: 'Good on yer, luv. You showed him proper!'

A murmur of agreement russled through the assembled lunchtime drinkers, a bit of a cheer went up and some even began to clap. Flo paused for a minute, straightened her clothing and lifted her head high before resuming her onward progress unaided to the pub door. Outside, the publican looked both ways up the street.

'There you are, he's long gone now. You go home and have a lie down and forget all about 'im,' he suggested.

And so ended the second occasion in seven days when Flo had become the centre of attention in a crowded room.

Flo felt somewhat elated as she walked back towards the main road. She experienced a great relief that after all these years Sid hadn't entirely got away with it. The way the people in the pub had applauded her stand buoyed her up. And she was sure Connie was looking down and saying 'Good for you, Flo. You told him alright!'

But soon her only thought was to get as far away from it all as possible, her normal tremulous timidity was beginning to return. What if the police had been called and were looking for her? Or worse still, what if somebody recognised her and word got back to Frank and Vera?

How Flo found her way back to the railway station on foot in her highly strung state she never knew. But find her way she did. There was just time to buy a tea in a paper cup and clamber aboard the 14.25 London train before the whistle blew and the engine and carriages lurched forward along the line. As the suburbs of Portsmouth began to slip by, Flo started to sip her tea and lit a Kensitas which really tasted good. And all the way back to the metropolis, Flo went over in her mind the events in the Jolly Roger again and again. She was so engrossed trying to remember every word she had said that she didn't notice the odd looks from the other passengers in the railway compartment – each one wondering who was this strange looking old woman with the distant stare and sticking up hair? And why was she clutching a broken brolly that was of no use to anyone as if it was her most prized possession?

A week later a letter arrived with a Selsey post mark. Flo immediately began to feel worried. And it didn't get any better when she opened the envelope and read the letter from Frank: it simply asked her to ring him as soon as possible.

Vera and Frank must have found out about the fracas at the Jolly Roger and must be displeased to say the least, she thought. After all, Pompey Picklers was an important customer for Frank's fish. Perhaps they had cancelled the contract because of the trouble that Flo had caused and Frank was angry. So it was with some trepidation that Flo made her way to the public phone box near the Co-op store.

Vera answered the phone, she seemed just as friendly as ever. Frank was out in his boat fishing for herring and wouldn't be back until tomorrow.

'I'll tell you why Frank wanted you to phone though,' said Vera. Flo felt a sharp stabbing pain in the pit of her stomach. She had really gone and done it, she thought. Vera was going to give her a real telling off and probably wouldn't want to see her again after the way she had showed herself up.

'Frank wants to know if you could come down tomorrow and help with the filleting?' Vera continued. 'He's been badly let down again by some of his regulars.'

Flo felt elated with relief.

'I think he's got a cheek even asking you, Flo, specially at such short notice. So don't worry about not coming if you don't want, I wouldn't if I was in your shoes...'

But of course Flo was only too pleased to come and said so. Frank's boat was expected back in the late afternoon so Vera told Flo to arrive whenever she liked after lunch. Bring enough clothes for a couple of day's stay, Vera told her. She explained that Flo could either catch a number 51 bus to Selsey from Chichester or better still take a cab. Frank would pay for everything.

Flo walked back from the telephone kiosk feeling a lot happier than she had on the way going there. It was a great weight lifted from her mind. She was even going to stay with Vera and Frank again down in Selsey. And not least of all, she was going to see her own grandson Ray once more - the living image of her beloved son Tom.

It was a warm spring evening and Flo felt an excitement in the air as she walked back along King's Road. So she popped into the Co-op and bought a half bottle of their own brand of Spanish sherry and a packet of twenty Craven A cork tipped cigarettes: she preferred cork tips if she could afford them because they didn't stick to your lips. As she made her way back to her home the unmistakable aroma of fried fish wafted along the road from the chip shop on the next corner. Flo was feeling hungry, she had lost her appetite completely before making the phone call to Vera and now it was starting to return. So she joined the queue and bought a small portion of rock salmon and chips.

Back in her flat, Flo tucked into her meal on the table in front of the open sash cord window that looked out over the back gardens. It was well past dusk but Flo didn't put the light on. Instead she switched on her black and white television, bought from a second-hand shop in Kingston, and turned the sound down low. Flo found that having it on even when she wasn't watching it made the flat seem less empty and the bluish glow from the screen filled the room with a subdued but pleasant light. Then Flo looked out through the open window as the last of the light faded in the sky and poured herself a glass of sherry and lit one of her cigarettes.

How much more enjoyable life was now, she thought. She felt like a different person. Who would have guessed just a few months ago that she would go down to Portsmouth and give Sid a telling off and win the approval of complete strangers? Or that she had amazed everybody in her new-found family with her rock and roll antics at the Sundowner's Club?

She must continue to be more adventurous, Flo told herself. She quite liked it.

So the next day, Flo started her journey to the coast early. But she had decided not to go by train. The previous week, while passing Kingston Bus Station, she had noticed from the timetables on display that she could catch a Green Line coach from there that went all the way to Guildford. She also picked up a route map for Southdown Buses. From this Flo worked out that from Guildford Bus Station she could catch a bus to Haslemere and from there she could catch another bus all the way to Chichester. Once she reached the Cathedral city itself, she knew that there was a regular bus service from there to Selsey.

Of course, it meant catching four different buses and making three changes. But time was something Flo had plenty of and it all seemed in keeping with her new spirit of advanture. A more fulfilling world was beginning to beckon and she must embrace it and eschew the mundane stick-in-the-mud ways of her former existence.

By 8 o'clock in the morning she was aboard a three-quarters empty Green Line coach accelerating down the A3 road towards Guildford. Flo enjoyed watching the countryside and the small towns and villages pass by. It was so much nicer than travelling by train, almost like travelling by car with your own chauffeur, she thought. As they were passing the Wisley Hut Hotel, one of the other passengers asked her for a light for her cigarette. Flo obliged and fell into conversation with the woman who looked a few years younger than herself. She turned out to be an Anglo-Italian from the Norbiton area of Kingston, not far from where Flo lived.

In the course of the conversation the woman let slip that she was going to visit her son in Guildford. She and her husband ran an Italian delicatessen and sandwich bar in Park Road. Her name was Gina and she told Flo that there had once been quite a thriving Italian community living in Norbiton. They had mainly inhabited the rabbit warren of streets that sprawled across the area where the Cambridge Council Estate now stood but few lived in the area now.

In reply Flo told her travelling companion all about her son Tom and how he had died in the War.

When they parted at Guildford Bus Station, Gina told Flo to call in at the delicatessen any day and she would show her how to bake a real Italian pizza with mozarella and pimentoes and anchovies and capers. Flo had never heard of any of these things. But as she waited for the Southdown bus for Haslemere to arrive she congratulated herself on having made the acquaintance of such an interesting person - and a foreign one at that - who had asked her to call on her.

'So travel really does broaden the mind even aboard a Greenline bus,' thought Flo, as she climbed aboard the next one. The bit of the journey that Flo liked most was the ride from Haslemere to Chichester. It was a windy country road that went through sleepy villages with names like Fernhurst and Easebourne and one lovely old country town called Midhurst. There were tall oak trees lining the road and thatched cottages with a blaze of colourful flowers in their front gardens and village shops that still had toffee pane windows. And each village had its flint clad church, surrounded by ancient tomb stones that leaned over at all angles, and a perfectly mowed and rolled cricket green.

How lucky people were who lived in such beautiful surroundings, thought Flo. Or those who lived in towns but had cars and could leave their homes behind each weekend and explore these peaceful country lanes. She was sure that if Tom had lived he would have taken her out for Sunday afternoon drives to lovely places like this.

It was almost lunchtime when Flo got to Chichester so she sat on a bench outside the Bus Station and ate the corn beef and pickle sandwich she'd brought with her. Then, ignoring Vera's offer to catch a taxi as too extravagant, she caught the last bus on her marathon journey to Selsey.

Flo walked down the long road that led to Vera and Frank's cottage and was glad of the exercise after sitting on buses since early morning. Only Jeffrey was in when she arrived but he immediately made her at home. Vera had just popped up to the shops but before long Jeff had produced a cup of fresh tea and some chocolate biscuits for Flo. Then they sat together in the garden to wait for Vera's return.

'You certainly know how to make a nice cup of tea, dear,' Flo told Jeffrey who replied that it was just a matter of getting the water really boiling and letting it brew for at least three minutes. Jeffrey obviously had hidden depths, thought Flo, there was more to him than first met the eye. Soon Vera arrived back, full of apologies for not being there sooner, and joined Flo in the garden for a cuppa and a natter.

Later, about six o'clock, Ray arrived home from work and made a quick fuss of Flo. 'Real glutton for punishment you are, Grandma, coming back for another session of herring hell. You'll have all the cats in Kingston following you up the street when you get home.' Flo laughed.

Shortly after their evening meal the phone rang, it was Frank calling from his shed to say he'd just landed and the fish were ready for filleting. Ray was imposed upon to drive them over to the Fishermen's Beach in the Ford Anglia. At first he was full of excuses: 'But I've just got in from work, Mum!' he moaned. But when Vera asked him if he really wanted his grandma to walk all the way over to Frank's Shed after such a long journey he gave in without a murmur.

Vera, Flo, Frank and three other women who turned up spent the next eight or nine hours hard at it cutting, gutting and filleting the countless crates of herring. It was well into the early hours when the work was finished.

As the last of the fish were being boxed, Flo began to panic. Was Sid going to turn up again with the van from Pompey Picklers, she wondered? That might be embarrassing. But she was relieved when she found out that these herrings were going to a fish wholesaler in Bognor.

Most of the next day was spent filleting plaice which were destined for local hotels and restaurants along the Sussex coast. It was harder work filleting the plaice, much harder than herring. But by six o'clock the last of Frank's catch was devoid of skin and bone. Flo went outside to drink a mug of tea and smoke a well-earned 'gasper' among the crab pots overlooking the beach while Frank shovelled ice chips over the boxes of filleted fish inside.

Vera was doing some paperwork and asked him for the receipt for the herrings that had been picked up previously by the Bognor wholesaler. Frank pulled the crumpled piece of paper from his shirt's top pocket and handed it to her complete with dried-on fish scales.

'Oh, I didn't tell yer,' said Frank. 'Yer know that bloke who always comes with the Pompey van driver to help with the loading?'

'You mean that weasel-faced character who makes my flesh creep?' asked Vera.

'Well, he won't be giving you the creeps any more, my dear,' continued Frank. 'I heard on the grapevine he did a runner last week. Some sort of lunchtime punch-up with some woman at their local pub would you believe? He never turned up for work next day and when someone went round to his digs his landlady said he'd done a midnight flit.

'We've all seen the last of him.'

8: The faceless spectre in the shadows at Ray's wedding.

Flo stayed a couple more days with Frank and Vera and loved every minute of her new found life. She pottered around Selsey exploring the shops, helped Vera with the shopping and even cooked a meal for everybody one evening. It was her speciality, a big steak and kidney pie: she had made it exactly the same way for Tom when they were together. Everybody thought it was absolutely marvelous and wanted seconds, which pleased Flo no end. When everybody had finished eating Ray called for a round of applause for Flo's amazing pie and joked 'You did say snake and kidney pie, didn't you, Grandma? I never knew snakes tasted so delish!'

Without anything being agreed, Flo's visits to Selsey started to take on a regular pattern. Every couple of weeks she would go down to help Frank and Vera with the filleting for two or three days. At first she resisted Frank's attempts to pay her for the work. But Vera told her she couldn't go on doing it for nothing now that it was becoming a frequent occurance.

Frank also paid her train fares. He told Flo she was the fastest filleter he'd ever had and worth two of his other regulars. After a few months Frank even paid for Flo to have the telephone laid on at her flat and gave her the money for the standing charge each quarter. When she protested he was being too generous, Frank told her that he wanted to be able to get hold of her at short notice and anyway he could charge it as a business expense for tax. Flo was excited about being on the phone but she promised herself that she wasn't going to run up big bills. This meant that she only used the phone when Frank or Vera rang her.

Flo wondered if it was all Frank and Vera's way of being kind to her but if it was they never let on. What she earned from the filleting was big money for Flo and she was able to give up all her cleaning jobs. It was all cash in hand at ten shillings an hour, more than twice the rate for cleaning. And because it never occurred to Flo that she should declare it as earnings, there was no tax to pay. So she could get along very nicely with what she earned from the filleting and her Old Age Pension.

It still left Flo with lots of spare time on her hands. One day she was coming back from Sucklings the bakers in Park Road when she passed the Italian delicatessen shop and sandwich bar. She remembered it was the one owned by the husband of the Italian woman she had met on the bus going to Guildford.

Flo remembered the promise she had made to herself, the one about being more adventurous. So she pushed past the line of people queuing to collect their lunch and sat down at one of the small tables inside. She noticed two older men of distinctly Mediterranean appearance behind the counter battling with mountains of sliced bread and all sorts of unfamiliar fillings.

Without raising his eyes, one of them shouted across and asked what she would like. Flo ordered a cheese sandwich but, even as she was saying it, realised that there was no sign of anything remotely resembling Cheddar in sight.

'You want Gorgonzola, Gruyere or cream cheese?' demanded the man with a pronounced accent.

This momentarily threw Flo into confusion. Fears quickly arose of having to eat some strong-smelling variety so she settled for the cream cheese.

'One cream cheese and chives. You want coffee?' the Italian asked.

Flo wondered whether she would like the chives, which she had never heard of before, but remembered once again her pledge to be more bold and not so mundane.

In the event her fears were unfounded. As she sat at the white plastic-topped table eating her sandwich she decided that chives went nicely with cream cheese, whatever they were. But it was the coffee that really impressed her. It certainly didn't taste like the instant coffee that she sometimes made at home from powder that came in a round cardboard Co-op carton. This was rich with flavour and tasted as good as the delicious smell she had noticed whenever she passed the coffee roasters shop near the Apple Market in Kingston.

Just then Gina, the Italian woman Flo had met, came in from the back of the shop. When she saw Flo her face lit up.

'Ah, the lady from the bus, you found us! How are you?' she asked. So saying she shook Flo warmly by the hand like a long-lost sister.

Flo said she was keeping very well, thank you, and told Gina she had just returned from visiting her family in Selsey again.

Gina introduced Flo to her husband, Luigi, and his brother Gianni. Luigi stopped sandwich making and wiped his hand on his white apron before politely shaking hands. Gianni's face broke into a charming smile and he slightly bowed his head as he shook hands and said 'A pleasure to meet you,' in a soft Neapolitan voice.

Once Flo had finished her sandwich Gina led her into the back kitchen which was full of the smell of freshly baked bread. She sat Flo on a chair and they chatted about this and that whilst Gina kneaded a great ball of stiff pizza dough. Once the pizza bases had been rolled out, the conversation turned to food. Gina showed Flo how she layered the thin slices of cheese, tomato and salami on the circles of dough and then decorated them with tomato paste, capers, basil, anchovies and olives. Then she slid them into a large old-fashioned oven and slammed the iron door closed. Soon the aroma of cooked cheese and herbs filled the tiny kitchen.

How these Italians can talk, thought Flo, and how friendly they are. Why, she had only met Gina once on a bus journey but she was already treating her as if she had known her for years. Gianni came into the kitchen a few times to collect more salami or loaves of sliced bread. Each time he smiled politely at Flo and nodded.

Eventually, when the pizzas were baked, Gina took one and wrapped it in greaseproof paper and pushed it into Flo's shopping bag. And despite Flo's protests, she wouldn't accept a penny's payment for it.

That evening Flo ate most of the pizza for her tea and thought she had never tasted anything quite so tasty in her life. It contained a whole barrage of amazing new aromas and flavours. In some ways it was similar to Welsh Rarebit, Flo decided. She often made this herself - even adding a few slices of tomato and a dash of Coleman's mustard on occasions. But Welsh Rarebit was a poor substitute for this Mediterranean masterpiece.

The next week, after one of her working visits to Selsey, Flo dropped in to see Gina again. To repay the favour of the pizza, she had brought with her a parcel of fresh filleted plaice. Gina was delighted. She said there was so much of it that she insisted Flo should come to dinner with them the following evening to help them to do it justice.

The next day was a Saturday and Flo went to Sainsbury in the centre of Kingston to buy a bottle of good Italian wine. Of course, she had no idea what to buy, even though she read all the descriptions. So she chose a Dolcetto d'Alba, the most expensive bottle that she could afford.

At 7 o'clock that evening Flo arrived clutching the precious bottle of wine wrapped in tissue paper. Gina and Luigi lived in rooms immediately above the delicatessen shop and Luigi's brother Gianni lived in a couple of rooms on the top floor. It was Gianni who opened the front door and guided Flo up the steep flight of stairs to the front parlour. There, surrounded by ornate Italian furniture and bric-a-brac, Flo was relieved of the wine and ushered into a comfortable armchair.

Luigi poured Flo a glass of dark red wine and soon all four fell into easy conversation. It transpired that they had come to Britain just after the last War and the brothers had worked as waiters in Soho for many years. They had moved to Norbiton about ten years previously to run the small cafe and delicatessen shop. Flo gathered that Gianni's wife had died some years before. Both Luigi and Gianni were convinced that Italian food was on the verge of a major upsurge in popularity in Britain and when that day came they would make their fortunes. The brothers joked how they would be driving Maserati cars, have big houses on the St George's Estate in Weybridge where the Beatles lived and would drink only the finest wines.

'They've been saying that for ten years,' commented Gina. 'But Gianni still only drives a Fiat 500 Topolino, how you say "old crock", and we still only have to order three kilos of Milano salami a week. Round here I think they're just as happy with a fish paste sandwich as one of our Parma Ham and Beefsteak Tomato Specials.'

Flo thought guiltily about the dozens of little pots of Shippams fish paste she used to buy for Sunday tea before the War when Tom was still with her and still bought occasionally for herself.

Gina disappeared into the kitchen to check on the meal and the two men began to examine the bottle of wine Flo had brought. They read and re-read the label and held it up to the light approvingly. And they told Flo that she obviously knew a thing or two about how to choose really excellent Italian wine: something that was rare among the English who usually only seemed to know of Chianti, Soave or Frascati. This pleased Flo no end though she had only chosen it because of the pretty label and the price.

Then they all sat down at an enormous round table with a large tureen of steaming soup in the middle. Gina ladled out enormous bowls of minestrone which were a meal in themselves. Then in came the plaice that had been rolled and baked in a dish in the oven along with olives, tomatoes, capers and mushrooms that had been sliced paper thin. Flo could also taste wine and garlic in the sauce and thoroughly enjoyed it.

Afterwards, they sat in well-upholstered chairs and Luigi poured Flo a glass of some golden Italian dessert wine and everyone lit a cigarette. Soon Flo's new Italian friends were talking of days long ago in the Old Country and long lost relatives and the price of olive oil and whether it was better to visit Italy in the spring or the autumn.

Flo told them all about Selsey and what a wonderful place it was and they all agreed that the fish caught in the waters around the coast of Britain was the best they had ever tasted. Of course, before long Flo was telling them all about Tom and her one and only trip abroad to visit his grave. Of her husband, she only said that he had 'passed on'. She gave them an amusing account of her rock-and-roll exhibition at the Sundowner's Club. And she told them all about Connie who had been her true friend through bad times and good and had died far too soon - and about the great time they had together on holiday in Bournemouth, only the way she told it she made it seem as if they had gone there regularly and not just the once.

It was Gianni of the permanent smile who humorously chided Flo for never having remarried as she would surely make someone an excellent wife. What was the matter with Englishmen, he joked, that not one of them had successfully courted her? Was it the warm English beer and their diet of greasy chips and saveloy sausages made from unmentionable pig's parts that had robbed them of all interest in romance?

They all laughed. Then Flo explained that looking after Tom had taken all her time and energy: he alone was the one she lived for. In an attempt to make her life sound a little more exciting, she referred once again to the Canadian Air Force Officer she had met at the dance during the War. And once more she put a spin on the story to make it sound like she had known him for longer and there was more to it than there was.

'You see, I am right,' Gianni butted in. 'It takes bloody foreigners, like Canadians and Italians, to really appreciate the ladies of England.' And they all laughed together again.

It was past midnight when Flo said she must make a move. She had thoroughly enjoyed herself in the company of this wonderful Italian family who had made her so welcome and were so full of the joy of life. Gina kissed her on both cheeks, Luigi shook her hand and thanked her again for the excellent fish and bottle of wine and Gianni said he would walk her home.

'Unfortunately it is no longer safe for a woman to walk the streets after dark late at night, not even in Kingston,' he insisted with thinly-veiled regret.

The easy conversation continued to flow between Gianni and Flo as they walked down Park Road and turned left along King's Road. This was where the Flying Bomb had fallen in the war and Flo remembered herself scrabbling in the rubble where now newly-built houses stood. She told Gianni about the incident and then began to regret doing so for she remembered that at that time Gianni would have been on the other side. But Gianni was unperturbed and only replied: 'War is a terrible thing, Flo. A crime against the people of all nations.'

As they walked the last stretch along Staunton Road, Gianni fell silent for a moment. Then he cleared his throat.

'Tell me, Flo. Do you like the musical films?' he asked. Flo replied that she often used to enjoy them when she went to the cinema in Kingston with Connie but hadn't seen one in years.

Gianni needed no further prompting. 'Ah, then you must come and see "The Sound of Music" which is playing in the West End again. Perhaps we could go together?' Flo said she would like that: the red wine before dinner, the white wine during dinner and the dessert wine afterwards had blunted her reservations about spending an evening in the company of a man. So it was arranged that Gianni would pick Flo up early the next Saturday evening. The greying but distinguished-looking Italian, somewhere in his late 60s, bowed his head slightly, kissed Flo's hand and wished her pleasant dreams.

As the day approached, Flo began to look forward to the prospect of an evening spent in the company of such a charming and knowledgeable person. At the appointed hour the door bell rang in the upstairs flat in Staunton Road and Flo came hurrying down the stairs wearing the smart new jacket that Vera had bought for her in Chichester. Gianni opened the door of his little red Fiat 500 car for Flo to enter and soon they were speeding off along Kingston Vale heading towards the bright lights of the metropolis.

The centre of London with its colourful neon signs, milling crowds of smartly dressed people and enormous palatial cinemas was like foreign territory to Flo.

She remembered coming to the centre of London when Tom was a young lad to see the 'sights': Buckingham Palace, the Houses of Parliament and feeding the pigeons in Trafalgar Square followed by tea in Lyons Corner House. Another time they had come up one bitterly cold day in January to visit the Boys' Own Exhibition somewhere near Victoria Station.

Then there was that awful time when Tom had ear-ache for over a week and the local doctor had sent them to the Ear, Nose and Throat Hospital in Golden Square, Soho, to see a specialist. Afterwards poor Tom was in such pain, because of all the proding and poking, that she spent her last two shillings on a taxi to take them back to Waterloo Station so she could get him home quickly.

The little Fiat 500 buzzed through the congested streets and despite the heavy traffic and road crossings heaving with Saturday night pleasure-seekers, Gianni knew exactly where to park. They walked along crowded pavements towards the cinema and passed the statue of Eros in Piccadilly Circus. As they continued down Coventry Street Flo was pleased to see that the Lyons Corner House, where she and Tom had enjoyed an iced bun and milkshake so many years ago, was still there.

They entered the imposing foyer of the Odeon Leicester Square and as they approached the box office to buy the tickets, Flo began to scrabble in her bag for her purse. Gianni saw this and asked Flo to allow him to pay. But Flo said she couldn't possibly and continued to struggle with her purse, whereupon Gianni's demeanour became serious and he told her that among Italians it was not permitted for an escorted lady to pay for herself. So Flo stopped her rummaging, smiled and thanked Gianni, having realised that any other course would seriously offend.

The film was very spectacular and Gianni clearly enjoyed it, as in some of the livelier songs Flo could hear him singing along to the soundtrack. At the end, as the crowd flowed out of the auditorium and into the foyer, Gianni suggested they should go to a little pasta restaurant that he knew nearby and Flo readily agreed. It was now late into the evening and she was feeling hunger pangs, having had nothing to eat since an early lunch.

Gianni led the way through a maze of streets behind Leicester Square, full of people going this way and that, until they reached Soho proper. In Dean Street they entered an Italian restaurant where Gianni was welcomed by the owner with a great display of bear hugs and much waving of arms. Flo was introduced as a 'friend of the family' and they were led to a secluded table for two near to the bar. Here Gianni declined the menu and ordered a carafe of red wine.

'Now, Flo,' he said once they had settled. 'May I recommend the ravioli, the speciality of the house, made fresh every day on the premises by the wife of Roberto, my friend the owner. I tell you, Flo, nowhere in this country will you find better ravioli, not even at the banquets of the Italian Embassy itself, and people who know come from all over London to eat it here.'

Flo had no idea what ravioli was, though she vaguely remembered seeing the name on Heinz tins on shelves in the Co-op store. But after such a build up it would have been cavalier to refuse and she enthusiastically agreed as if she regularly ate it whenever the opportunity arose. The steaming ravioli arrived with a green salad of young spinach and sorrel leaves which Gianni anointed with a dressing of oil with some ceremony. Of course, the envelopes of minced meat in pasta, with a piquant herb and tomato sauce, proved every bit as delicious as Gianni had promised.

After dinner, over coffee and the remains of the wine, the Italian continued to enthuse on the virtues of the land of his birth. Eventually, Flo asked him why he had left such a beautiful country?

Gianni's face clouded over. 'Flo,' he replied. 'You have no idea how terrible things were after the War. There was hardly any jobs and people with crazy ideas began to take over all the important positions. If they didn't like you, there would be no work for you.'

Intrigued, Flo asked who these crazy people were?

'Political people who had had a hard time before the War and wanted to take revenge on their fellow countrymen. Life became impossible, even though Luigi and I had served in the

British Army for the last two years of the War fighting against the Germans. At one stage these crazy Rossoa looked like taking over the whole country.

'Before the War things had been O.K. You knew where you were, everybody had work and life was good. Until Musso became charmed by that troublemaker in Berlin and took us into the War on his side.

'The act of an imbecile, I tell you Flo. Things are much better now, the crazies are still there but people are wise to them, they are no longer so powerful I think. But back then it was different, a man had to eat and provide for his wife and family and there was no way of telling how things could go. So we came to Britain, which we were allowed to do as we had fought for the British Army, and found work in the restaurants of Soho.

'We would do anything, help out in the kitchens, be waiters, do the washing up and even the cleaning. It doesn't matter what you do, all work is noble. It gives a man dignity, without a job he is nothing. That is why we came to England, it was the right thing to do at the time. We felt safe, we could work, even though the hours were long we knew we would not go hungry.

'We go back for holidays now, we have been many times, of course. My son went back some years ago and has, what you call it...a butcher shop...in the covered market in Florence. I am too old to find work there now, but I tell you Flo...'

Here Gianni's serious face melted instantly to a smile.

'I tell you, I wish for nothing more than to spend my last years back in Italia, sitting on a...how you say...veran-dah overhung with the grape vines, with the warm sun on my face and a view across the vineyards and olive groves to the distant mountains – and to just listen to the grapes and the olives as they grow.' Then his face changed from a smile to a laugh as he cupped his hand to his ear.

Flo agreed it all sounded very nice. 'I hope very much you do that, Gianni. After working hard all your life, you deserve it.'

'That right, Flo. You understand,' replied Gianni. 'A man should deserve that after a lifetime of work. Why not?'

Flo's eye caught the clock on the wall behind the little bar, it was a quarter past midnight. At first she began to feel uneasy, but then why should she worry? Gianni had a car, they were not relying on last trains or buses to get home. And she was thoroughly enjoying herself. So instead she asked Gianni if he had ever tasted pickled walnuts? The Italian frowned.

'You are serious, Flo? They pickle the walnuts in England? But they must pickle them for years before the shells become soft enough to eat.'

Flo laughed and explained that the walnuts were pickled when their shells were still green and soft. 'They are a great delicacy, to be eaten with cheese or cold meat. My son Tom loved them and when I could afford one, I always bought a jar at Christmas.'

Gianni wanted to know what region of Britain they traditionally came from. Flo explained it wasn't like that, you just bought them in jars labelled 'Crosse and Blackwell'. But she could remember as a girl when you could buy the green walnuts at greengrocers at a certain time of the year, just as you still could with Seville oranges for marmalade, and make them yourself. Her aunt in Kingston, with whom she had lived after her mother died, regularly made them and told her the recipe.

'And you know the recipe for these pickled walnuts, Flo?' asked Gianni pretending to get excited. 'Then we could make our fortunes with this recipe. We could open a bottling plant in Italy, where everybody appreciates good food, and where walnut trees grow everywhere yet there are no pickled walnuts.

'People would say "All the time we have been cracking the walnuts when really we should have been pickling them like cucumbers!" Why, Flo, after a few years we would have more money than we could hope to spend!'

Flo was getting to know Gianni and she knew he was pulling her leg so she began to laugh.

'Tell me, Flo, what is the secret recipe handed down through generations in your family?' Gianni continued.

'Well, you pick the walnuts in the early summer when the shells are still soft...then you prick them all over with a fork. After that, you soak them in brine for three days...then soak them in fresh brine for another three days...you do this three times in all. Last you have to spread them out to dry in the sun until they turn black...'

'To dry in the sun?' interrupted Gianni pretending disbelief. 'But how could you possibly make pickled walnuts that way - there is no sun in England! They would rot in the rain before they would dry...' And they both laughed and laughed.

'Oh you are funny,' she told Gianni. 'I haven't laughed so much for years.'

'But it is so important to laugh,' replied the elderly Italian. 'When people laugh it means they have forgotten their worries. That is why in Italy people laugh all the time.'

Later, after more hugging and waving of arms and some loud conversation in Italian with the Manager, they left the restaurant and Gianni drove Flo home. It was past two o'clock in the morning when they arrived in Staunton Road and Flo thanked Gianni for a wonderful evening. Again he took her hand and kissed it and thanked Flo for being such an excellent companion.

As she entered her living room, she noticed how late it was from the clock on the mantlepiece above the gas fire. She had never been this late coming home, except perhaps in wartime when she worked at the Hawker factory and they introduced round-the-clock shifts to increase the production of aircraft.

Flo didn't feel very sleepy so she made herself a cup of tea and decided to have one last cigarette before she turned in. She ran over the events of the evening in her mind, what a nice man Gianni was.

Then her thoughts turned back to those grey days in the War when she worked at Hawkers. She remembered her feeling of complete desolation at the time, when Tom's death was a freshly open wound, before she got used to the reality of it.

Of course, she still felt the great emptiness in her life. She had never stopped grieving for her beloved Tom, now as always the person she poured all the love she had into. Not a waking moment had passed since she received that fateful telegram in which she hadn't thought of him. How much she missed her dear dead son. How much she wanted to see him once again.

She didn't even need to look at the few photos she possessed of him to see his likeness: in her mind's eye his image never faded. She could remember him as a young boy in short trousers, then as a teenager in his greasy garage overalls and finally as a man in his smart khaki Army uniform with three sargeant's stripes. She could see him in this room now, doing his school homework at this very table or tucking into their weekly treat of fish and chips from the shop on the corner.

What a pity, she thought, that she couldn't have done more for him then, more things to make his short life happier. But she knew in her heart she had done the best she could at the time, she had been so poor she had nothing more to give.

Then she thought of dear Connie, she alone had made life just about bearable in those awful first months. What a wonderful friend she had been, how lucky she was to have known her, how sad that she had lost Connie too. Connie should have lived longer, much longer, to enjoy her full term in this earthly life.

These sad broken-hearted thoughts began to exhaust her so Flo resisted the idea of smoking another cigarette and went to bed. Next day she made the pilgrimage to Farnborough.

Over the following months Flo was a frequent visitor to the Italian delicatessen in Park Road and the rooms above it. There was always some good reason, like it was Gina's birthday and would she join them for a little birthday celebration? Or there was some special film on the television, would she care to watch it with them? Or they were going to visit the gardens at Hampton Court, would Flo accompany them? Of course, she would. And of course Gianni was always there and his face would always light up with his 150-watt smile whenever he saw her.

Flo thought she must repay them for their kind hospitality and invited them all round for Sunday lunch. She bought the largest leg of English lamb she could find in Kingston Market and when she was in Sainsburys she saw some Crosse and Blackwell pickled walnuts on a shelf and bought two jars.

She had to borrow two kitchen chairs from the young couple downstairs who were only too happy to oblige. The roast lamb with mint sauce and all the trimmings was a great success, her three Italian friends thoroughly enjoyed the traditional British roast which for them was a rare luxury. And Gianni was overwhelmed by the gift of a jar of pickled walnuts and kept everybody amused for almost a quarter of an hour with his humorous commentary on this improbable British delicacy.

After this occasion Gina and Luigi began to withdraw into the background and it was mostly just Gianni she saw. He used to take her out on Sundays in his little red car to visit beauty spots like Newlands Corner near Guildford where the view extended for miles or to Ockham Mill where they would walk beside the canal and then go for tea in the old world village of Ripley.

Even Flo, who could be naive at the very best of times, realised that Gianni must be interested in her because she was a woman. Though what he saw in her, she being of pensionable age, she simply could not understand. She began to worry a little in case Gianni should ever show any physical interest in her and want more than just their platonic friendship. Flo would find that embarrassing, it was something she never thought about or wanted: now only a distant memory of a short interlude nearly three-quarters of a lifetime ago. But Gianni was always the perfect gentleman and never did or hinted at anything that gave her cause for concern. She decided that her fears had been groundless, after all Gianni was advanced in years now and probably had no interest in things like that.

However, his attention to her never seemed to wane. Hardly a week went by without them going out together, for a meal, to see a film or for a drive in the country.

Frank and Vera were very interested in Flo's new 'fancy man' and invited them both down to Selsey for lunch.

And so, one fine Sunday in high summer, they started off early and motored south to the Sussex coast in Gianni's car. Flo guided Gianni the last quarter mile or so round the backstreets of Selsey until they arrived at the row of old coastguard's cottages.

Everybody was there to greet them, even Ray had exerted himself and had risen early and shaved and put on a new white shirt. That was quite an effort for him after the booze fuelled jollifications of the previous night. But Vera had made it clear that everybody was to be on best behaviour for Flo's new gentleman friend.

After much shaking of hands they all sat down in the front room and Gianni said how honoured he was to meet the family of his 'dear friend Flo'. Never lost for words, he spoke with Frank about fish, with Ray about cars, with Vera about cooking and was even able to give Jeffrey some tips about what to look for when buying a new motorbike, which was Jeffrey's next goal.

Frank brought out a litre bottle of red wine and poured everyone a glass, there was just enough left to use in the gravy for the roast beef that Vera was preparing. Frank apologised for the fact that the wine was French, not Italian, and they all laughed. But Gianni graciously admitted that whilst Italian wine was best for everyday drinking, French was preferable for special occasions. And this was indeed a special occasion. From the laughter and smiles on everyone's faces, Flo knew that her charming Italian *beau* was winning them all round.

After their lunch, Ray and Jeffrey made their excuses and slipped away, their duty done. Being low tide Frank, Vera, Gianni and Flo took a slow stroll along the Marine Beach towards Selsey Bill. Here they paused and Frank pointed out his fish shed in the distance. He also explained with local pride that the view of the area beyond, known as Pagham Harbour, had inspired the song 'A Sleepy Lagoon' which was used to introduce the ever popular 'Desert Island Discs' programme on BBC radio. Gianni seemed suitably impressed.

They bought ice cream cones from a van that had parked beside the recreation field behind the Bill and sat on a section of the old sea wall to eat them in the warm sunshine. Later they had tea and slices of Dundee cake back at Vera's.

Eventually it was time for Flo and Gianni to set off back to the Smoke in the little Fiat allowing for the long traffic jams on roads from the coast that were usual on summer Sunday evenings before Britain replaced winding lanes with dual carriageways and arterial roads with motorways and every one-shop village was given its own bypass.

Flo didn't visit Frank and Vera's again for a couple of weeks but it was a special occasion when she did: Ray's 24th birthday. They celebrated it by all going out for dinner to the Old Cross, then the smartest restaurant in Chichester. It was there that Flo met Linda for the first time, the girl whom Ray was later to marry. Flo was fascinated by her Bee-Hive hair style, something very fashionable at the time having been made popular by the singer Dusty Springfield.

Flo sat next to Linda at the dinner party and took an instant liking to her, specially when she told her she was a shop assistant at Morants, the big department store opposite the Cathedral. Flo was able to tell her what life was like when she was a shop girl at Bentalls just after the Great War. Linda couldn't believe how strict things were in those days, like only being allowed to go to the Ladies 'to powder your nose' in your own lunch break.

'Like to see them try that at Morants,' Linda threatened. 'They'd have half the staff parading up and down outside in protest. Some of those girls spend half the morning in the Ladies if they've been out on the sherbets the night before. Everyone covers for each other, see.'

'Not you though, eh, Lin,' chimed in Ray. 'You'll sit there all evening nursing a bitter lemon when you've got work the next morning. Proper conscientious she is, Grandma.'

But from Linda's giggle it was clear that she would be knocking back the sherbets with the best of them, work or no work the next day.

During the dessert course, Frank annoyed Vera by talking to another Selsey trawlerman who happened to be sitting at the next table. Flo could hear Frank complaining about the poor catches they were getting recently and his friend was agreeing.

'We had a good few years after the War but it's been going down hill ever since,' the latter added.

'Don't tell me you're talking about fish again and on Ray's birthday!' Vera shouted across the table. 'You can pack that up for a start, don't you get enough of it six days a week?'

Frank mumbled something about it being his living and what paid the rent but only half-heartedly because he knew he was out of order. To change the subject Vera decided it was time for everyone to give Ray their presents. Ray's face brightened when he heard this and he joked about having the pantechnicon parked outside ready to take everything away. Linda gave another little squeal just as she did at all Ray's little jokes.

Jeffrey started off with a set of Swank cufflinks the size of milk bottle tops. Vera followed with a top of the range Philips electric shaver. Frank gave a car radio for the Ford Cortina that Ray had just bought and added 'You're the car mechanic so don't ask me how to fit it, mate.'

Then Linda brought out a large parcel from underneath the table. Ray ripped away the wrapping paper to reveal a genuine cashmere sweater. It had obviously cost her a small fortune and for once Ray was speechless.

'And don't let me catch you wearing it whilst you're working on that greasy car or I'll skin you alive!' said Linda sounding as if she really meant it.

Finally it was Flo's turn. Everyone was expecting her to produce a pair of woolly socks or a pack of monogrammed hankies. So you could have heard a feather hit the carpet when Flo piped up and said: 'I want you to know I went all the way up to Soho to get this for you.'

Ray's eyes nearly popped out on stalks when he saw the bag it came in – 'Colonel Custard's Trading Company of Carnaby Street'. Inside was a purple shirt with a frilly front and a black velvet bootlace tie.

'Wow, you're the coolest gran that ever was. It's bloody gorgeous!' said Ray as his hand stroked the purple frills. 'Even I've never bought anything in Carnaby Street.'

'Well, I hope you like it,' added Flo. 'I asked the man in the shop with a pony tail about it but he wasn't much help. He was too busy puffing away on a strange cigarette and his eyes didn't seem to have any irises.'

Everyone around the table roared with laughter which in Linda's case developed into uncontrollable hiccups and they had to ask the waiter for a glass of water.

The following morning was a Sunday so everybody had a lie in. Everybody except Vera who had the Sunday roast to get ready. She was peeling the potatoes on the kitchen table when Flo joined her.

'Can't sleep, Flo?' asked Vera. Flo admitted she hadn't been sleeping too well just recently.

'Anything wrong?' enquired Vera. 'I thought you looked a bit peaky ever since you arrived in spite of the celebrations.'

'I've something on my mind, Vera,' replied Flo. 'Something's happened with Gianni.'

'Don't tell me he's done a runner, Flo?' enquired Vera.

'On the contrary, he wants to marry me. At my age!' Flo seemed quite upset by the prospect.

Vera stopped scraping the potatoes and looked straight at Flo with a bemused expression.

'Well what's so terrible about that, in Heaven's name? Most women would give their right arm to get an offer like that from such a nice man. And although I've only met him the once, he does seem a nice man, really nice, unless you tell me otherwise.

'If it's your age you're worried about, well, it's never too late to find the chance of happiness and there's no virtue in a lonely old age.' Then she added quickly: 'Though either way you'll always have us, of course, Flo.'

'It's not just that, Vera,' replied Flo. 'He wants me to go and live in Naples with him. You know, in Italy. That's where he and Luigi and Gina want to retire to once they've sold the café.'

'I know where Naples is, Flo, though I've never been lucky enough to go there myself,' replied Vera.

'This just goes on getting better and better the way I look at it. Not only does this latter-day Valentino want to spend the rest of his life making you happy, he wants to take you away from the grey skies and sooty streets of London to live in warm sunshine beside the Mediterranean.

'I know it may come as a bit of a shock when it happens late in life, Flo. But it looks more like a rather pleasant surprise to me. We all have to grab our opportunities when we can 'cause Lady Luck doesn't come knocking too often in my experience.'

'But that's just it,' replied Flo. 'I don't want to live under a baking hot sun with a lot of foreigners. They may be very nice foreigners, but they're not *my* people, Vera.

'Kingston has been my home for nigh on half a century and it's *my* home. I wouldn't swap it for all the sunflowers and vineyards and avenues lined with palm trees that Italy or anywhere else has to offer. And anyway, my family's here, it took half a lifetime to find you and I'm not going to turn my back on you now. Blood's thicker than water, Vera.'

'Yes I know,' answered Vera sensing she was fighting a rearguard action for a lost cause. 'But these days Italy's only a couple of hours away by air and fares are coming down all the time. You can get a return flight from Gatwick for not much more than fifteen quid. You could come and visit us whenever you want, you're always welcome, you know that.'

What Flo said next stopped Vera in her tracks. But although it gave her cause for concern, it really only confirmed a strong suspicion that she had always pushed to the back of her mind whenever Flo had given hint of it.

'Apart from anything else, I couldn't leave Tom.'

It was probably only a few seconds but the silence that followed Flo's statement seemed like an eternity. Vera chose her words carefully.

'But Flo, Tom's been dead these twenty years or more, you know that. He's not even buried in this country.'

'Oh, that stone slab in an army cemetery in Holland doesn't mean a thing to me,' said Flo. 'His poor body has probably wasted away to nothing by now anyway. It's where Tom spent his life that means everything in the world.

'You're the only living soul other than my sister Ada that I've ever told this to, Vera. But I often go back to that army barracks down at Farnborough where Tom was last stationed in the War, the place where I saw him last.

'And when I stand just outside the barracks entrance, I sometimes get the feeling that he's just around the corner waiting for me, and suddenly his smiling face is going to come into view and I can put my arms round him and hug him again…'

Flo never finished the sentence as her voice began to break up while she fought back the emotion.

'You know, Vera, everywhere I walk in Kingston I remember Tom and me being there together. Whenever I pass the shoe shop opposite the War Memorial I see Tom and me going in there to get his first pair of grown up shoes for the big school.

'And when I pass Woolworths in the Market Place I remember that time he lost his gloves during the bitterest winter for years. And he was frightened to tell me because he thought I'd be angry, or because he knew I didn't have the money to replace lost gloves. But when I saw his frozen little fingers when he came home from school, almost blue they were, I knew he'd lost them. He'd been hiding it for days. But I couldn't be angry with him, I loved him so much.

'The next day I took the last two shilling piece in the house out of the electric money and took him to Woolworths where I bought him the warmest, woolliest gloves a florin could buy.

'Happy times too, Vera, like whenever I pass the Station I see us going off on our day trips to Littlehampton on what Tom used to call our "one-day holidays". Him carrying the sandwiches and a bottle of pop in a string bag and me with his towel and trunks packed into my handbag.

'Everywhere is so full of wonderful memories of Tom. Not least our home where we lived together so many years. Not much to it maybe but it was *our* home. Each day I sit at the same table in front of the window where we had our dinners, or on the old sofa where we listened on the radio to episodes of 'Biggles' and 'Dick Barton, Special Agent' just before he went to bed.

'Oh, why did he have to go, Vera? Why Tom? He was such a good boy and he was all that I had in the world, he meant everything to me...'

Vera put her arm round Flo and placed her left hand on her shoulder to comfort her. She realised in that instant that smiling Gianni so full of life didn't stand a chance against Flo's dead son.

'I know, dear, I understand,' she told her. 'Remember, I loved him also. Not for as long as you but I understand. And I tell you, Flo, you meant the whole world to him too. He loved you deeply though he probably didn't tell you very often, that's the way kids are.

'He knew well enough all the sacrifices you'd made for him, all the hardship you'd gone through to give him the best you could.

'After the War once he'd opened that little garage down here he vowed that you wouldn't have to work another day ever again, Flo. He was going to bring you down here to live by the sea with a three-mornings-a-week charlady to do all the housework whilst you sat in a deckchair on the beach reading 'Woman's Weekly' and the 'Picturegoer' all day long.'

Flo's face lit up and her eyes sparkled. 'Was he really going to do that for me?' she asked.

'Yes, Flo, but things never worked out that way – he was one of millions who never returned from that War and we just have to accept it,' continued Vera who had decided the time to speak her mind was now or never.

'We all have to move on and learn to let go. We have to accept that Tom has gone and let him rest in peace. But he can't rest in peace, Flo, you won't let him die. Surely it's time to let him pass on? Keep your happy memories by all means but live for the present, live for the future, don't dwell constantly in the past.'

'There, I've said it,' thought Vera.

Flo wasn't offended in the least because she knew in her heart it was the truth.

'But I can't let him die just like that, Vera, I need him so and he knows it. That's why I feel him round me most of the time, I know he's there looking after me. Even if I don't leave my home all day I never feel lonely, I know he's always with me somewhere in the background.'

Vera now realised that Flo was never going to move on but would spend all her days reliving the past with her ever-present dead son. In fact the past had become the present for Flo. The forward passage of her life had surely stopped for all time the day she received that awful telegram in the autumn of 1944, even as a clock stops at the exact moment the building it's a part of is struck by lightning or an earthquake.

'I understand, Flo,' she repeated again sympathetically. 'But you must tell Gianni your decision as soon as you get back to London, it's only fair to him. No sense in letting it drag on.'

'I will, Vera, I will,' replied Flo, relieved and gladdened that for the first time somebody really understood her life and how much Tom still meant to her. Even Connie had never known that.

Just then Ray's head appeared round the kitchen door. 'Any chance of a fry up, Mum?' he enquired. 'You can leave out the fried bread if you're really pushed.'

'Sunday lunch is running late, son, on account of me and your gran having a chinwag. So you'd best forget about the fry up and make yourself a bacon sandwich to tide you over.'

Flo stayed on in Selsey for a couple of days to help with filleting the fish. But as soon as she arrived back home she phoned Gianni and said she wanted to see him.

Late the following afternoon he called and they drove to the Pen Ponds car park in Richmond Park. On the walk down to the Ponds Flo explained as best she could why she wasn't able to marry him and go to live in Naples. Her whole family was here in England, she couldn't just pull up her roots and leave everything behind. But she didn't mention anything about 'leaving Tom'.

Gianni didn't try to persuade her otherwise but simply accepted her decision like the gentleman he was. But he was clearly disappointed.

'It was a lovely dream, Flo. But dreams don't always come true, not like in the Hollywood movies,' was his reply. Then they sat on a bench by one of the Ponds and each smoked a cigarette to release the tension.

Flo looked out over the water at the Canada Geese and the gulls fighting for crusts of bread thrown by children. As they flapped and squawked and hovered in the air, Flo remembered the time she had brought Tom here when he was just a few weeks old. She remembered the look of wonder on his little face as he stared up at the flock of circling birds for the very first time.

She knew in her heart she had made the right decision, how could she leave all these wonderful memories? It would have been nothing less than a betrayal of Tom. And she was glad that she had told Vera everything about how she felt, spilled the beans so to speak, and that Vera had understood all.

As they drove back to where Flo lived Gianni asked her if they could still be friends. 'Of course we can,' she replied.

Once home alone, Flo made a cup of tea and smoked another cigarette. It was like a great weight had been lifted from her mind: she could continue to live her life alone, the way she wanted. Though not really alone of course, she did have her family down in Selsey. And Tom was always with her.

A couple of weeks later Flo decided to pay the Italian delicatessen in Park Road a visit, she thought it would be rude not to. After all, Gianni had said that he wanted to stay friends. She noticed there was an estate agent's sign outside saying 'Shop and flat for sale'.

Flo entered the shop and saw Luigi was serving someone with a sandwich to take out. He looked slightly taken aback when he saw her. Flo thought she would try something different and asked for a smoked salmon sandwich and a cup of Italian high-roast coffee. She was a bit surprised when he asked her whether it was to go or whether she wanted to eat it there. Flo sat on one of the stools and placed the food on the narrow shelf-like table that ran round the wall. Luigi continued to avoid eye contact and said nothing while he busied himself tidying up the containers behind the glass counter that held all the different sandwich fillings. Finally she broke the silence and asked Luigi how Gianni was? He gave her a quick glance and simply replied: 'Gianni, him fine. He's out now, you want me to give him a message?'

'Just say I was passing and dropped in,' asked Flo and left shortly after.

A couple of weeks later she tried again and visited the delicatessen in the middle of the afternoon when she thought it wouldn't be busy. Gina was the only one serving behind the counter this time. She sort of smiled when she saw Flo but only asked her what she would like?

Flo ordered a piece of cake that tasted as if it was soaked in alcohol and which she ate with a fork. Gina busied herself serving a succession of customers whilst Flo ate the cake hoping for a break in orders so she could enquire after Gianni. When the break came Flo glanced across at Gina who was staring straight at her. She had a malevolent expression on her face - but it was her eyes that said everything. They had a cold piercing look of barely concealed anger, as if she was just about managing to hold back from a torrent of caustic verbal abuse. Flo gulped down the remnants of the cake and left without another word spoken.

A couple of months later she purposely made a detour past the shop and noticed that the fascia was freshly painted and sported a new Italian name above the window.

Nine months or so after that Flo received an envelope with a Naples postmark. Inside was a printed card which if Flo could have read Italian she would have known was a wedding announcement. Beneath it Gianni had written a few lines in English saying he was marrying an old flame from long ago and wished Flo well.

At least *he* didn't hold anything against her, she thought. Flo never saw or heard from any of them again.

Flo spent the following Christmas down at Selsey and that Christmas Eve they were all in the Fisherman's Joy at the bottom of East Street, Frank's favourite pub. He'd been buying rounds of Gale's Ale for his trawler men and port and lemons for the ladies who did the filleting, as he always did during the festive season. Flo noticed that there were fewer folk present than the previous year and asked Frank why.

'Had to cut back, Flo. We're just not catching the fish, you see. I reckon we're lucky to haul in half the cod we did ten years ago and not much better for herrings. Wouldn't you say so, Jack?'

Jack was the owner of another Selsey trawler and one of Frank's best mates.

'I'd say less than that, Frank. And although the price has gone up a bit there's not the money in it like there was.

'The only skipper round here in danger of getting rich is Captain Birds Eye.' Everybody chuckled. Jack turned to Flo and started to explain.

'Yer see, missus, it was the War. During the War there was hardly any fishing in the Channel for obvious reasons and not much more in the North Sea come to that. So the fish, they just bred and bred, there was no one to catch them, yer see. The sea was heaving with them.

'So when peacetime came we were in clover, you'd only have to throw the net over the side a few times and you'd have all the fish you wanted. And big fellers they were too, because they'd been allowed to grow, left alone beneath the waves for all those years. I tell yer, you could almost walk from here to Boo-loin on fish without getting your boots wet.'

One of Jack's crew chimed in. 'Even so, there'd still be fish a plenty if those ruddy Spanish trawlers would stay away. They fish well within our waters bold as brass, they do. Some days you can even see them from the Bill.

'Ever since they turned up the fish have been scarcer than bacon butties at a bar mitzva. And the ruddy Government does nothing about it! What've we got a Navy for if it's not to see off poxy poachers like them?'

'Careful Jim, ladies present,' Jack reminded him.

'If I had my way we'd best sink a couple of those blinkin' Spaniards, they wouldn't come here no more if they had to swim all the way back to Spain!'

'You can't do that, Jim,' interrupted Frank. 'You'll start a bleedin' war with Franco if yer did!'

'Death to the Spaniards!' shouted Jim, his courage fortified by his fifth pint of Gale's Old Ale. Others roared their agreement and even those that didn't agree thought the prospect of a gunboat war with the 'despicable spics' hilariously funny and rocked with laughter. Which is exactly how it should be in pubs on Christmas Eve and how it certainly was in the Fisherman's Joy at Selsey two hours short of Christmas Day 1968.

'Quiet now! Quiet now!' Vera piped up. 'Ray's got something important he wants you all to hear. Ray, where are you?'

'Oh...right,' mumbled Ray taken unawares and struggling to find his feet.

'Well, I've decided it's high time I entered the Shangri-la of wedded bliss about which I have heard so much...So next spring I'll be taking the long walk down the aisle at St. Peter's. And since I'd look pretty daft walking down there on my own, I've asked Lin to join me...'

A great cheer went up from around the bar and all thought of revenge on the dastardly dagos was instantly forgotten. Franco's navy could stand down. Dozens of arms shot out to shake Ray's hand and the smoke-filled room resonated with the sound of 'Congratulations, young feller!' and 'Good luck, Ray!' from a crowd that included many married veterans who had long ago discovered that marriage was rarely a bed of roses but knew this wasn't the time to mention it.

'More drinks all round, barman!' yelled Frank and there was no shortage of ready takers. Meanwhile, in a quieter corner of the pub, Linda was already deep in conversation with every female under twenty-five discussing arrangements for bride's maids, the three-tier cake and...The Wedding Dress.

Come the New Year and the weather took a turn for the worse. Every day tall white-capped breakers lashed the Bill and it was a brave Selsey dog owner who took his pet for a walk along the wind-swept, pebble-strewn promenade of East Beach. Most of the time it was far too rough for the local trawlers to leave their moorings and over the best part of seven weeks Frank hardly got in more than a dozen full day's fishing.

So although Vera phoned Flo every week to see how she was, there was no question of her coming down for filleting.

Towards the end of January, Flo received the invitation to Ray and Linda's wedding and was surprised to see it was set for Saturday the eighth of March.

'That's quick,' thought Flo. 'Young people certainly don't hang about these days.'

As the big day approached, Flo travelled to Selsey on the Wednesday before to help with the last-minute arrangements. The reception was to be held at the famous Sundowner's Club at the bottom of Hillfield Road. Flo was busy non-stop in Vera's cottage kitchen baking home-made pies and sausage rolls and filling vol-au-vents with peeled prawns and a new concoction called Seafood Sauce. This was two-thirds salad cream, one-third tomato ketchup and a good shake of Worcester Sauce. There was no Marks and Spencer's Party Food in those days and everything had to be prepared by hand unless you could afford baker shop prices.

St. Peter's was packed at 3pm on the Saturday and hot-house flowers of every description bedecked each window ledge and recess in the Church. Both Ray and Lin's families were well-known and long-established in the district - and the bride and bridegroom had many friends who would never say No to a free booze up. As Ray entered the Church by a side door more than five-minutes behind schedule, with his best man Jeffrey in tow, Vera was heard to hiss: 'It's the bride who's supposed to keep everyone waiting not you!'

Flo took a sideways look at Ray who was the smartest she'd ever seen him. He was dressed in a charcoal grey suit, polished winkle-picker shoes and was wearing the purple shirt with the frilly front and bootlace tie that she'd bought him for his last birthday. She was thrilled that he liked it that much to wear on his wedding day. Ray saw her looking and winked.

Then an old phantom stepped out of the recesses of Flo's mind as her long departed but immortal son reasserted himself.

'I should be sitting here at Tom's wedding,' she told herself. 'He should have had his day like this and all the love and joy that comes after.' Then she comforted herself with the thought that he wouldn't be far away, not on the day when his eldest son was getting married.

Flo felt a gentle nudge from Vera who was sitting beside her.

'Why the long face, Flo?' she asked gently.

'No reason, Vera,' Flo replied trying to hide her true thoughts and feelings. 'Weddings can make you feel a bit weepy, you know.'

But Vera knew, Vera knew.

After the wedding ceremony Ray and Lin emerged from the church door and passed through a Guard of Honour made up of two lines of car mechanics from where Ray worked. Each was holding up a section of exhaust pipe instead of the usual sword which everybody thought a nice touch.

Then came the ceremony of the wedding photographs that seemed to take longer than the wedding service itself. There were various shots of the bride and groom together, shots of them with close relatives and several that included as many guests as the photographer could cram in with his widest angle lens. There were endless delays as people had to be hunted down and recalled from the Church toilets.

While she was waiting outside, Flo looked across the road. A number of people, mostly passers-by, had stopped in the hope of catching a glimpse of the newly-weds. Flo's glance fell upon a lone character standing in the doorway of a car dealer's showroom. The face was completely in shadow but she could see he was in army uniform. Flo noticed he was wearing a distinctively shaped black beret just as Tom's regiment had during the War.

Just then, Flo's gaze was distracted as the assembled throng parted to let Ray and Lin through to the wedding car. As they passed by, a shower of multi-coloured confetti fell on them almost concealing them in the flitter-flutter of its descent. The vicar looked skyward hoping the forecast was for dry weather - so sparing the ever complaining verger the task of scooping up buckets of papier-mache.

As the limousine drove away, Flo's eyes returned to the figure in the doorway. It was still there and for a moment Flo had the weirdest sensation. Although the area of the face was still in darkness she had the distinct feeling it was looking straight at her.

Just then Vera grabbed her arm: 'Come on, Flo, we're getting a lift to the reception but we'll have to hurry!'

This broke her train of thought and the moment passed. So whether a few seconds further reflection would have resulted in Flo recognising her paranormal minder must remain speculative but highly probable.

Now that all the wedding photos were safely in the can, one of which duly appeared in the Chichester Observer, everybody headed for the Sundowner's Club that had been decorated with silver-coated cardboard wedding bells and lucky horse shoes. Flo sat with Frank and Vera and Lin's parents, drinking a large schooner of sherry and chain smoking like everyone else. She was pleased to see that the pies, sausage rolls and vol-au-vents were disappearing as fast as the waiter could bring them in.

'Makes me think of our Big Day, Vera,' Frank reminisced wistfully. And then turning to Lin's parents: 'We held the reception at the old Marine Hotel that stood t'other side of the road from here. Pity it burnt down a few years back, brought a touch of class to the neighbourhood that old Hotel did.'

'Certainly did, quite a few rich and famous stayed there in its time, not always with the right partners though if you follow my drift,' replied Linda's dad. 'But that fire was an insurance job if ever there was one.'

Once everybody had had a chance to eat and chat and the speeches were over the band started up. It was a local group from Bognor, Raving Roger and the Rockettes, and whilst many of those present hoped for their sake they hadn't given up the day job they were adequate to the occasion.

Earlier, Ray had explained that their first choice of band had been Jack Boot and the Goose Steppers but they were booked up. 'Just as well,' grunted Frank who had spent three years dodging German torpedoes whilst on convoy duty in World War Two.

As the music hotted up and the drink flowed some guests wondered if Flo was up for an action replay of her now famous boogie-woogie whirling dervish dance that she'd performed the last time she was at the Sundowner's. But such voyeurs of the follies and foibles of others were to be disappointed: the few dances that Flo had, including one with Ray, were performed at a temperate pace no matter how animated Raving Roger and his Rockettes became.

At one stage in the evening, fortunately when Lin's parents were off circulating, Flo commented to Vera: 'I do believe Lin's putting on a bit of weight, you know. She'll have to watch that if she wants to keep her figure.'

Vera and Frank's eyes met furtively and the former quickly replied: 'Don't let anybody hear you say that, Flo. It might upset Lin.'

The Sundowner's had an extension to its licence to stay open until 1a.m. When the party finally broke up there was a bit of a scene when Vera realised that Frank, who had been delegated to drive the newly married couple to the Royal Norfolk Hotel in neighbouring Bognor Regis for their wedding night, had consumed so much Boddington's IPA Ale that he was incapable of opening the car's door let alone driving it. In those days of carefree motoring it was considered nothing special to down five pints and drive, beer being only about 2.5% alcohol then instead of the 5% of today's 'domestic disturbance' lagers. But not being able to open the car door was pushing it even by 1969 standards.

So it was left to one of Lin's teetotal uncles to drive the happy couple to the Royal Norfolk. There they spent the night in the hotel's best suite which, unknown to them and quite possibly to the Hotel Manager, was the self-same bedroom that Joachim von Ribbentrop, the German Ambassador to the Court of St James, and his wife Annlies, had occupied for their family summer holiday in Bognor some 32 years previously.

The next morning, after Sunday lunch at the hotel, the couple left in Ray's Ford Cortina for a week's honeymoon at Lulworth Cove.

Spring came early to the West Sussex coast that year as if to compensate for the harsh winter weather. Trawling for herring and cod resumed, though Frank and the other Selsey fisherman continued to grumble about the smaller catches and the incursions of Spanish trawlers now joined by Russian factory ships. But before long Flo was once again travelling regularly to Selsey to help with the filleting.

One Sunday afternoon she accompanied Frank and Vera to have tea with Ray and Lin in the tiny 'cottage' they had moved into facing the East Beach. They had to drive along a dirt road almost as far as the point where the Pagham Marshes began.

As Flo gazed at the newly wed's new home she saw straight away that it was an old railway carriage that had been rendered with cement at the front and extended slightly at the rear. But the distinctive size and shape of the windows, rounded top and bottom, made it clear that Ray and Lin's new home had once given service as rolling stock of the Southern Railway Company.

Frank explained there were quite a few of them about, converted into holiday homes in the 1920s by town folk who bought a small plot of land by the coast and wanted a cheap roof over their heads. Old railway carriages could be had for less than a week's wages, and transported for just a few pounds, and scores of them were pressed into service for this very purpose in places like Pagham and East Wittering as well as Selsey. Even today many examples survive, now extended and gentrified beyond the wildest dreams of their original owners: Roaring Twenties weekend refugees from the manic bustle of the metropolis.

Flo thought it was an ever so charming place to live, specially when she went inside and realised how roomy they could be with the compartment walls removed. Heavily pregnant Lin wasn't so easily convinced and muttered about it being 'no place to bring a kid up in' while Ray stressed that with the housing shortage so acute they were lucky to rent it for just a few pounds a week and it was only temporary anyway.

It was July when Flo answered the telephone in her living room and learned that she had become a great-grandmother, an almost unheard of event in 1960s Britain.

Flo was surprised the baby had come so early and asked if it was premature? She heard Frank mumble something in the background about 'Very premature indeed!' whilst Vera replied 'A little early, Flo. But baby's doing fine...it's a boy, by the way.'

It was after she'd put the phone down that Flo did the maths and realised it couldn't have been *that* premature and the penny dropped. Suddenly she realised why no time had been lost in organising the wedding. Even in the Swinging Sixties some veneer of respectability had to be maintained – being conceived out of wedlock was one thing but born out of wedlock still carried the stigma of 'Bastard'.

Flo went down for the christening at St Peter's in Selsey, she had been very touched when Vera had told her that Ray and Linda had decided to call the new baby Tom. Ray because he knew it would please his grandma, Linda because she just liked the name.

After the church service they adjourned to the big back room at the Fisherman's Joy where the Lambrusco flowed like wine and every table was covered with triple-decker prawn sandwiches, Scotch eggs and the latest food fad from France known as quiches.

'All bought in,' Vera whispered to Flo. 'Not so many people to cater for as the wedding so Frank and Lin's dad went halves.'

Linda brought young Tom over to Flo so she could have a closer look and hold him. He had brown eyes just like his grandfather and he stared and stared at Flo as if he recognised her. Well, that was the thought that went through Flo's head. She held him close to her, he was no heavier than a ball of fluff, and it brought back memories for Flo of when her Tom was that age and she held him the same way.

Vera knew what Flo was thinking and let her hold Tom for a few minutes more but when she showed no sign of handing him back she said: 'Come on Flo, pass the parcel. There's others want to see him and it'll be his bedtime before long.' Flo reluctantly gave up her son's namesake.

The next day the whole family went down onto the Marine Beach, close to Frank and Vera's cottage, for a barbecue. They built a kind of oven from large stones they found on the foreshore and a metal grill from an old kitchen stove. They used dry driftwood gathered from above the high water mark for fuel and after much arguement among the 'beach chefs' present managed to reduce it to dark red glowing charcoal and white ash. Then out came the rump steaks, sausages, burgers and a few herrings that Frank managed to smuggle along against almost everyone else's wishes.

When the time came to add more driftwood to the fire it crackled and spat, shooting out glowing cinders in all directions. Family and passers by ran for cover and everybody thought it all a great laugh, nobody worried too much about Health and Safety in those happy-go-lucky days.

'Didn't know you were planning a firework display too,' Frank joked.

As the summer sun went down, and with everybody's appetite well satisfied, out came the crates of Pale Ale, cider and Babycham and a sing-song began which everybody joined in that could be heard all the way from Pagham Lagoon to Bracklesham Bay. They started with the old time favourites like 'Roll out the Barrel' and 'Yes, We have no Bananas' and quickly progressed to the latest hits by Elvis such as 'Are you lonesome tonight?' and 'It's Now or Never'. Everybody had a brilliant day, including Flo who took a liking to the Babychams and found herself singing at the top of her voice to songs she didn't even know the words to.

Little did Flo know that it would be the last big social occasion she would enjoy in the company of the loving family she had discovered so late in life - and who always welcomed her with open arms like the greatest grandma of all on the third planet out from the Sun.

Flo watched baby Tom growing up over the coming months with special interest and affection. But despite those big brown eyes, and the big smile he always gave Flo whenever he saw her, baby Tom was not *her* Tom and he was not going to grow up with the appearance and personality of his dead grandfather.

'Why should he?' Flo eventually reasoned. The blood line and gene pool that linked him to her Tom were already twice removed.

That September Frank and Vera decided to go on a two-week touring holiday of the West Country and they invited Flo along. The plan was to break the journey in Devon and then push on into Cornwall. It was decided that after all the trauma and hard work of Ray's wedding, the 'premature' birth and the christening they deserved a break. So Vera made reservations at several top-notch hotels chosen from the AA Guide Book and insisted Frank hire a decent car to take them around.

'We're certainly not squeezing into that noxious old fish van,' she told Frank. 'They'd never let us past hotel reception if we arrived reeking of last week's pilchards!' Ray got them a nice four-door Ford Cortina in slate green for the fortnight at a special rate from the car hire department of the garage where he worked.

Flo jumped at the offer to join them. 'But are you sure you want me along?' she asked when Vera first invited her over the telephone. 'Don't you want some time to yourselves?'

'Between you and me it's going to be a bit of a busman's holiday for Frank,' Vera whispered conspiratorially.

'He wants to see if the fishing's any better in the West Country than it is down Sussex way. So I'll be glad of the company while he's off discussing fishy business and government quotas. Frank's very dissatisfied at the moment, he says he won't be able to earn a living round here for much longer.'

Flo felt a sudden flash of anxiety when she heard that. Was it a first warning shot that the comfortable routine she had settled into wasn't going to last for ever? But that was quickly overtaken by the thought of two whole weeks in the scenic West Country where the coastal views and country scenes were among the most spectacular in all England. She fondly remembered the lovely time she had touring round Devon with Ada and Stan nearly twenty years before.

'Well, I'd love to come but I must pay my way, Vera. I know hotels don't come cheap,' Flo replied.

'Don't you worry about that, dear,' answered Vera. 'Frank hasn't taken me away on a proper holiday for years. The holiday account is well in the black!' But it was agreed that Flo could pay something towards the petrol which at four shillings and sixpence (23 pence) a gallon, or 5 pence a litre, certainly wasn't going to break the Post Office Savings Bank.

Flo began making plans right away. She even bought a new suitcase for the trip, she would need lots of changes of clothes for a fortnight. The old cardboard Woolworths suitcase she'd bought for her holidays with Tom forty years before simply wasn't big enough. But she didn't throw it out, she put it on top of the small cupboard in Tom's bedroom that had served him as a wardrobe. There was no way she would part with something so full of precious memories as that.

Summer stayed late that year and the slate-green Cortina sped westward beneath unbroken skies of azure blue. As they passed the New Forest Flo saw a sign for Bournemouth at a roundabout and wistfully looked left in that direction.

Bournemouth of fond memory – both of Tom before the War and that wonderful bitter-sweet week spent with dear Connie afterwards. What a Rock she had been immediately following Tom's death. Why did they both have to die so early?

They stopped for a Ploughman's lunch at an old coaching inn in Bridport where they dined on Dorset Blue Vinny cheese, crusty bread rolls and a half pint of cider.

'You don't get cheese like this at the Co-op in Kingston,' Flo volunteered.

'And you don't get cider like this from those chemical works that pass for cider presses down our way either,' replied Frank.

As they walked past the old shops and market stalls in East Street back to the car, Flo felt she was entering a different world, one that hadn't yet succumbed to the Swinging Sixties, with its synthetic food and equally synthetic values, and was all the better for it.

It was mid-afternoon when the Cortina swung off the main road west and began the gentle descent to the sea through pine-clad heathland.

'There it is!' said Frank suddenly. 'Straight ahead, that streak of blue on the horizon. I could smell it before I could see it - just like any man who's spent half his working days on the blessed briny.'

They drove round the Square at the centre of Exmouth to get their bearings and then crawled slowly along the Esplanade admiring the clean yellow sands; the public gardens with their close-cropped lawns and tall foxgloves; and the white Georgian villas that stood at the top of the hill that ran parallel with the shore. The walls were unscathed by mindless graffiti and discarded cigarette packets were noticeably absent from the pavements. How refreshing compared to south London, thought Flo.

But Frank was looking for something more than seaside postcard scenery. Instinct took him west to the harbour where he parked behind the old Customs House.

'I'll leave you ladies to stretch your legs, I'm for a wander round the trawlers, see how things are doing,' said Frank with a wink. So off he went to engage in fishery talk with the blue jersey brigade while Vera and Flo took a stroll eastward along the broad promenade. They walked and talked as the seagulls wheeled and squawked above their heads and quite forgot about the time. Suddenly up ahead, just where the road ended, they saw a little art deco teahouse built into the cliff and decided it was time for tea and a scone with some of that clotted cream the West Country was famous for.

They took their tea and sat outside on a small terrace overlooking the beach so they could smoke. There they fell into easy conversation with an elderly couple who, it turned out, had retired to Exmouth from Croydon.

'We've never looked back since we came down here,' claimed the husband. 'Croydon's never been the same since Jerry bombed the living daylights out of the place, everything's new there now, just like a little American skyscraper city.'

He'd started so he intended to continue. 'They sacrificed Croydon just to save the Big Wigs in Whitehall from getting flattened, you know. Jerry was sending the Doodle Bugs over, you remember them flying bombs don't you? Well, Jerry had a spy who was radioing back to Berlin telling them where the blinking things were falling. But unbeknown to Hitler we discovered the spy and gave him an ultimatum. Either play ball with us and send back what we tell you or take your turn on the end of a rope.

'So they got the spy to radio that the bombs were falling 15 miles too far north and to shorten the range if they wanted to hit central London. Which Jerry did. And what lies 15 miles south of Whitehall? You guessed it - Croydon. We copped the lot!'

Flo listened with fascination. 'But that's terrible!' she exclaimed. 'All that destruction just to save a lot of civil servants in Whitehall.' And she added her own wartime experience of the dreadful day the flying bomb fell near the junction of King's Road and Park Road in Kingston.

Suddenly Vera saw Flo's attention distracted by something outside. Down by the end of the promenade a bunch of children who had been canoeing in the sea were bringing their craft on shore and storing them in a wooden shed beneath the cliff. Then they formed an orderly line and began to climb up the zig-zag path past the art deco tea house and back to their camp site in a nearby field. You could just see the Bell tents between two hedges if you craned your neck.

Vera suspected that Flo's next sentence was going to begin with 'Tom'.

'Tom came on holiday down this way with the local Scouts before the War, about their age he was. I wonder if he stayed at that place? He was my son who was killed in the War.'

'Sorry to hear that, dear,' said the retired husband expatriate from Croydon. 'But it wouldn't have been at this place before the War, they've only been coming here five or six years.'

He rubbed his chin and turned to his wife for guidance.

'I reckon it could be over Teignmouth way, Bert,' she chimed in. 'Just where the fields begin on the Dawlish side. Our local Church used to send 'em down for a fortnight's holiday in the fresh air and sunshine every year.

'Donkey Meadow…that was it! I can still remember the name all these years later. Not much wrong with my marbles, eh?' They all laughed politely as she tapped her forehead.

Flo remembered the day in 1936, the year the old King died, when Tom had come rushing back from Scouts at St. Luke's Church Hall one evening with news that the troop was going off to a summer camp for two weeks and could he go? He even had a piece of paper, an application form with all the details on it. But Flo's eyes had got no further than the cost - 5 guineas. Even though that covered all food and the cost of the coach it was far more than she could afford, living hand to mouth as they did.

She remembered how hard it had been explaining it all to Tom, crushing his enthusiasm had almost broken her heart. But he had quietly accepted probably knowing all along his mum couldn't afford it but just hoping she might.

Then she recalled how a couple of weeks later Tom came home from Scouts with a note from the Vicar asking her to call on him any afternoon at the vestry which he used as his office. Of course, she went the very next day.

The kindly Welsh Vicar immediately put Flo at her ease and poured her a cup of tea. He understood that Tom hadn't applied for a place at Scout Camp despite being quite keen to go and appreciated it was a heavy expense for many families these days. But someone who had paid for a place early on had to drop out but said there was no need to refund the money and to use the spare place as thought fit.

It was all confidential, the Vicar had insisted, just between themselves. But did she think Tom would like the place and would she let him go?

'Oh, yes please,' she had told him and then spent the next five minutes in effusive gratitude saying how delighted Tom would be when she told him. The Vicar had said he was glad that it was all settled and shook her hand as she left.

What Flo hadn't seen, and would never know, was how once the vestry door was closed the Vicar withdrew five one-pound notes from his own wallet, felt in his pocket for two florins and a shilling, and put them all in a large tin box in his desk marked 'Scout Camp Fund'.

Later that afternoon Flo, Vera and Frank checked into the Imperial Hotel, formerly a minor stately residence in the Regency style, that stands in its own grounds and gardens on Exmouth front. They had seaward facing bedrooms with a wash basin with hot and cold running water in the room and a shared bathroom just along the corridor: a standard arrangement in those pre-ensuite days.

'This must be what the inside of Buckingham Palace looks like,' thought Flo to herself. Then she stood at her window and gazed across the blue waters of Lyme Bay before unpacking her things. Her view of the hotel was reinforced by the magnificently decorated high-ceilinged restaurant where they took their evening meal. There were all sorts of things on the menu that Flo had never heard of before so as usual she took her cue from Vera and Frank and ordered the same as them. They started with Prawn Avocado, another new food sensation that was sweeping 1960s Britain, it was even rumoured to be a favourite of the Beatles, and then moved on to Chicken Kiev. Flo thought both courses were wonderful, she particularly liked the lime and honey dressing in which the prawns were smothered and the way the melted garlic butter oozed out of the chicken when she cut into it.

Being a warm evening, they sat out afterwards on the terrace of the bar and enjoyed a drink and a smoke. They all agreed, no meal was complete until you'd had a cigarette afterwards. Across the open expanse of lawn they could see the fairy lights twinkling along the front and hear the excited chatter of late-season holidaymakers, newly arrived by Wallace Arnold coach, as they made their way along the Esplanade for an evening's entertainment in the nearby Pavilion.

'Well, Frank?' said Vera. 'We know you're dying to tell us, how's the fishing around these parts? Are the silver beauties jumping nineteen to the dozen out of the sea and straight into the fish boxes?' They all laughed.

'Would that they were, my dear Vera, would that they were,' replied Frank.

'No, things are almost as bad down here as over our way. The catches are down and even though prices are up no one wants to pay 'em. Fish has always been cheap, see, and because it's getting dearer and dearer people are turning instead to cheap battery-hen chicken and burgers made from butchers' left-overs.' Flo began to feel a bit uneasy about her Chicken Kiev but she was only following Vera and Frank's lead.

'And if we go into that bloomin' Common Market with all its boo-rocracy we'll be finished once and for all.'

'Let's wait and see how they're doing down in Cornwall,' Vera consoled her husband.

Flo slept like a log on the deep pile feather bed and next morning enjoyed smoked haddock crowned with a fried egg for breakfast in the chandelier-lit restaurant. 'Must support the local fisherfolk even at breakfast, y'know,' Frank suggested to the waiter who, coming from landlocked Austria on a working holiday, just looked blank.

They took the Starcross Car Ferry across the Exe estuary and drove on through Dawlish to Teignmouth where they parked next to the Salty: the town harbour protected from the open sea by a short but broad peninsula and much favoured by fishing trawlers. Once again Frank headed off 'to test the waters' whilst Vera and Flo walked east along the seafront enjoying the morning air and the bright sunshine.

'Indian Summer, Flo,' commented Vera as they passed the small pier and watched holidaymakers with small children trailing buckets and spades hurrying forwards expectantly to where the beach began to see if the tide was in or out. Vera knew what Flo was thinking. Tom had been a blessing in both their lives in different ways and that seemed to create a conduit whereby their thought waves ran unimpeded the one to the other.

'I remember Tom telling me all about those holidays you took him on. To Littlehampton, wasn't it Flo?' And without waiting for an answer Vera continued. 'He told me he was never more excited than the night before you set off on holiday. And he told me all about the fishing for crabs and small fry by the quay where the river meets the sea. And how once you weren't best pleased when you had to fork out sixpence for another fishing line because in all the excitement of packing he'd left the one you bought him the previous year behind.'

Flo remembered it well and knew that Vera was speaking the truth, and wasn't just making it all up to please her, because only herself and Tom had known about the fishing line that was left behind.

'We had our good times, Vera,' Flo acknowledged. 'But I still wonder if perhaps I should have spent more time helping him with his studies, taken him to museums and exhibitions more often. His life might have been so much different then. Maybe I should have taken him out more to shows and the pictures, and not just on his birthday. Or gone up town to see what London had to offer or taken him away on proper holidays down here, so he could have seen all the beautiful countryside like we've seen today. Not just Bognor and Littlehampton.

'Sometimes I think, Vera, that Tom died fighting for his country but only ever saw the smallest corner of it.'

'Those things cost cash, Flo,' Vera replied sympathetically. 'Money most people didn't have in those days, specially if you were bringing up a child single handed. No, you did all you could, nobody in your position could've done more and Tom knew it.'

'I hope so,' answered Flo with some relief.

Eventually they had walked and talked as far as the most easterly seafront refreshment kiosk in Teignmouth and they decided to have their morning coffee alfresco. They sat quietly watching the sun playing on the sea as the waves rolled gently back and forth with their hypnotic sound of crash followed by swish. When they had finished Flo insisted on taking the cups back.

Vera heard Flo ask the woman serving in the kiosk whether she knew where Donkey Meadow was, the place where the scouts used to hold their summer camps. 'Donkey Meadow?' she replied half laughing. 'You'll be meaning Mule's Field. You see that path leading up behind our tea house, it's up there about 20 yards on the left. But you're going back awhile, m'dear, there's been no scout camps up there for donkey's years,' and she laughed at her unintended joke.

'Let's take a look, Flo, we've got time,' suggested Vera knowing that was exactly what Flo wanted.

So they ascended the steep sloping path and soon came to the entrance to a large field fringed with tall trees and undergrowth. They opened the gate and went inside.

'This must be it, Vera, Tom must have stayed in this very field.' Flo looked around almost in wonder as the leaves in the distant trees rustled softly on a gentle sea breeze that also made undulating patterns in the long grass.

'Bet he had a fine old time, Flo. What with the countryside up there and the sea over here,' replied Vera.

They stood for a few moments more and then began to walk back to the sea front. But just as they reached the exit to the field Flo turned to take one last look. And then she saw it.

Way over on the other side of the field, where the tall trees began, Flo could see a boy standing motionless facing their way. The figure was not much more than a grey smudge, half in and half out of the shadows. But although it was a good hundred and fifty yards away or more Flo immediately recognised its likeness, there was no mistaking that fringe of straight hair that fell over his forehead.

It was Tom. Flo knew it in her bones, just as every mother instinctively recognises her own child no matter how far or fleeting the view.

'Alright, Flo?' asked Vera turning to see what was delaying her.

'Fine, Vera,' replied Flo momentarily taking her eyes off the figure on the far side of the field. A split second later she looked back again but he was gone. But just as they reached the gate and Flo was securing the latch there was a slight gust of wind and she felt something rush by. She looked up and for a fleeting second in the corner of her eye Flo thought she saw a faint black shadow quickly disappearing down the path towards the sea.

As they walked back to rejoin Frank and the Cortina, Vera was puzzled by how quiet Flo had fallen, deep in thoughts of her own. But Vera had felt something in that field too: the rekindling of an affinity with Tom that she hadn't known for years, not ever since her father had read her the fateful lines from the Ministry of War sealing his fate for ever.

They motored on through south Devon, stopping only for a Cornish pasty lunch at a wayside 'caff' once they had crossed the Tamar and entered Cornwall. Frank soon discovered that the gaffer was a former Brixham deep-sea trawler man who had changed profession due to declining catches. A 'Refugee from Atlantis' was how he described himself and said switching to the 'caff' was the best decision he ever made.

Flo marvelled at how bakers in this most westward county could turn a humble pie into a meal in itself: meat, gravy, potato and two veg all wrapped up in the most delicious melt in the mouth pastry you could imagine.

Little more than a half hour later they were crossing the bridge between East and West Looe and heading for the Hannafore Point Hotel high up on the shoreline facing out to sea. Flo fell in love with both the town and the Hotel right away. In the course of the week that followed they explored the warren of fishermen's sheds and tenements in East Looe; looked in wonder at basking sharks caught for sport hanging from hooks by the quayside; and took a half day's boat trip to Looe Island where they were told the legend of how Joseph of Arimathea, accompanied by his great-nephew the boy Jesus, once landed on the Island on the way to trade for Cornish tin.

'And did those feet in ancient times walk upon England's pastures green?' If they did, this was where they walked said the ferryman who took them over to the Island in his converted fishing trawler, a change of use that wasn't lost on Frank.

Other days they spent lazily sitting in deckchairs beside Banjo Pier watching the kiddies engaged in the eternal Canute-like task of holding back the tide with walls of sand; visited the sub-tropical gardens in nearby Polruan; and enjoyed scallops, monster lobsters and prime West Country sirloin steak in the spacious dining room of the Hannafore Point Hotel. By now Frank had given up on sounding out the local fisherfolk because he knew what the response would be. He'd heard enough.

Next came the long drive westwards to the nethermost parts of Cornwall, along almost deserted lanes and 'A' roads that led past sleepy, peaceful villages with white walled cottages that dazzled admiring visitors with the reflected glare of the sun. Flo was surprised by the barren but still beautiful nature of the countryside, you hardly saw a soul for miles nor passed another car. It was certainly the most marvellous and enjoyable holiday she'd ever had - or would ever have if she had but known it.

The Carbis Bay Hotel in St. Ives was, if anything, even grander than the Hannafore Point in Looe. It had a sun terrace, its own private beach and the most beautiful sea views across the Bay. The sands looked pure white as far as the eye could travel. No wonder the Hotel appears in many of Rosamund Pilcher's novels and films as the 'Sands Hotel'.

In the course of the days that followed they relaxed in hired deckchairs on Porthminster beach in front of the town; and went for day drives to Land's End, St Michael's Mount and 'Frenchman's Creek' on the Helford Estuary immortalised in the writings of Daphne Dumaurier. Flo was quite amused by some of the names of the Cornish towns they passed through like Zennor, Cripplesease and Mousehole.

One day they wondered through the narrow alleyways of St. Ives fishermen's quarter with its stone cobbles and granite cottages. Many were still occupied by sea-going Cornishmen though some had already been sold for a king's ransom to 'grockles' as weekend or holiday retreats. In one small church hall they chanced upon an exhibition and sale of paintings by local artists past and present. Frank took a liking to one picture in particular: it showed St. Ives Harbour back in the early interwar years with dozens of trawlers just returned from the fishing grounds unloading limitless boxes of pilchard, skate, cod and herring on quays bustling with activity.

'I do like that!' exclaimed Frank whom it reminded of the 'good old days' when fish were plentiful, alas now long gone. Although knowing little about artistic matters, Vera and Flo also admired its use of vibrant light and colour and the draughtsmanship of the boats and toiling blue jerseys.

Frank lingered until his two holiday companions had strolled a safe distance further on and asked 'How much?' On being told it was 55 guineas Frank tried bartering with the arty type in a paint smudged smock and beret who was clearly the senior dealer. But he only managed to save five guineas 'on account of it being a genuine Herbert Truman, he's dead now so it can only go up in price.' Frank took out the fat roll of readies he always kept handy for the immediate settlement of debts and deals in that pre-credit card era and peeled off £50 in fivers and two one-pound notes to which he added four half-crown coins from his pocket.

'That's a rock solid investment,' said the arty type. 'Those London dealers are snapping up every Herbert Truman they can find.'

'Well I bought it 'cause I like the look of it,' replied Frank, slightly peeved that paintings as pleasing to the eye as this were being bought just to keep some fine art speculator in Porsches and penthouses.

The painting was wrapped in brown corrugated paper and string and Frank carried it around protectively for the rest of the day. Not wanting to seem a spendthrift and upset Vera he fudged the truth when she asked how much he had paid for it.

'A little over forty pounds,' answered Frank. 'And I reckon if I took it up to one of them fancy art galleries in London I'd get over an 'undred for it tomorrow.'

Vera was no art expert but remained unconvinced.

The next day the slate green Cortina was cruising eastwards along the Atlantic Highway, the Herbert Truman in the boot wrapped up in one of Frank's jackets. Soon they were leaving Cornwall and entering Devon where they stopped at Clovelly. Predating political correctness towards animals by twenty years they declined the offer of a donkey ride down the steep cobbled streets to the harbour and back and took a gentle stroll instead.

'Them donkeys were never meant to carry grown adults like us, shouldn't be allowed,' commented Frank and Vera and Flo agreed.

Half way down they splashed out on a lobster salad and a glass of local ale in an old pub reputed to have once been the haunt of smugglers.

'No need for smuggling these days when they can charge prices like these,' grumbled Frank.

'Aren't you going to ask the fishermen here what the catches are like?' asked Flo.

'No need, m'dear,' answered Frank. 'It's the same sad story all along these shores, no better than Sussex and that's a fact. I think fishing's had its day, nice while it lasted but time to move on.'

Frank and Vera's eyes met fleetingly and he wondered if he'd said too much.

'Just look around you, most fisherfolk here sold out to holiday-makers like us years ago. More money in it, see, and no need to face a sou'westerly head on in driving rain.'

Flo wondered what Frank intended to do, he wouldn't be retiring for another twenty years at least and needed to earn a living. But she didn't think it was her place to ask.

As they stood on the end of the harbour wall and looked back at the quaint up-and-down town they all agreed that although Clovelly may well be in Devon it was more like Cornwall than Cornwall itself.

They spent the last two nights before the homeward journey in the nearby Hartland Quay Hotel. The coastline was wild, windswept and desolate. Here you could look down on rocky outcrops that were strewn with the debris of rusting shipwrecks of years gone by, forbidding monuments to the dangers of jagged rocks and fast running currents.

While waiting for Frank and Vera to bring the suitcases along the stony path to the Hotel, Flo paused and looked out to sea. What a holiday this had been, what wonders her eyes had seen. Scenery of exquisite beauty that she would never have believed existed in Britain. She had stayed in hotels that were fit for toffs and millionaires. And she had tasted food that put anything she had ever served at her own table to shame.

What a pity Tom couldn't have enjoyed all this. What a shame it wasn't him that was driving her and Vera round the West Country in the slate-green Cortina. He would have been middle-aged by now but Flo always pictured him as the last time she ever saw him: the image of a fresh-faced lad in his early twenties etched into her eternal memory. Why, oh why, was he taken from her?

It was an open wound that all the balm in Christendom would never heal nor soothe.

Then Flo began to feel slightly guilty about Tom replacing Frank as the driver of the Cortina. He was such a nice man, the very best. He had paid for all the enjoyment this holiday had brought, her contribution of paying for the petrol was merely the widow's mite.

Flo composed herself as she heard Frank and Vera clattering up the stone clad path.

'Lovely place again, Vera!' she said looking at the Hotel behind them. 'You certainly know how to pick 'em.'

That evening they dined in the Hotel on grilled skate with capers; fresh asparagus; and potatoes and parsnips mashed together. Flo loved it all and wondered why she'd never thought of mashing potatoes and parsnips together? That at least was one bit of fancy cooking that she could have afforded, even in the hard up days before the War when Tom and her were together. But she'd never thought of it, just went on serving up the things her mother had taught her to cook when she was young, all so long ago.

After dinner they strolled along to the bar next door which was part of the Hotel and enjoyed a glass of the local North Devon cider which Frank and Vera chased down with a fine French brandy. Flo stuck with the cider.

In the course of the evening they fell into conversation with a couple of retired Royal Navy men who had served on minesweepers and who Frank hit it off with straight away. The former matelots told them that this was the very hotel that had been used as the location for the Admiral Benbow Inn in the 1950 film 'Treasure Island' in which Robert Newton played Long John Silver.

'Shot in this very bar, much of it were,' they were assured by another regular.

The mention of 'Treasure Island' took Flo back to one of Tom's birthday treats when she had taken him to see the 1930s MGM version of the same film in which Wallace Beery portrayed the peg leg pirate. How Tom had loved it, she remembered. For weeks after, all he wanted to play was pirates, she had even made him a black patch to go over one eye. Flo smiled to herself at the happy, distant memory.

All good things come to an end. The morning after next the weather broke about an hour after starting for home: the rain came down like stair rods and they abandoned a planned visit to Lynmouth. Frank took the torrential rain in his stride, a trawlerman who had sailed through Force Ten gales wasn't going to be intimidated in a modern motorcar by half an inch of water on the road.

It was late afternoon when they pulled up outside Flo's flat in Staunton Road, Kingston. Frank and Vera wouldn't stop for a tea, they still had a 70 mile drive before they reached their home. Flo thanked them again and again and told them she'd had the most enjoyable time of her life. There were kisses and hugs all round.

Once they'd left, Flo sat at the table in front of the window in her living room, watered the potted plant that Tom had given her so many years ago and reflected on the past two weeks. What an experience it had been, she thought to herself. What breathtaking scenes she had witnessed, what delightful hotels she had stayed in and what wonderful food she had enjoyed. And she had seen her beloved son again, even if only for one short moment, confirming what she had already known: that Tom was never far away from her even though they were separated by the unbridgeable void between life and death. How grey and dull life in Kingston would seem by comparison.

Then she reminded herself that she wouldn't have it any other way: it was *her* life, *her* Kingston, *her* three rooms in a soot-stained road of late Victorian houses - and most of all it was the place she had shared in body and spirit for over 45 years with her own dear Tom.

But what was this splash of colour against the grubby brown brick wall in the back garden down below? She looked closer at three giant sunflowers standing at least five feet tall radiating a reflected yellow glow in all directions. This was the work of Val and Spence, the new downstairs tenants who had moved in just before the previous Christmas. She'd been told they were Flower Power people and they wore headbands and played strange Oriental music. But they'd been good to her, bringing

Flo a small Bloomer loaf every other day during the bakers' strike. And when a light bulb needed replacing high up on the ceiling, and Flo didn't think she'd feel steady standing on a chair, up came Spence and changed the bulb without having to be asked twice.

One Sunday Flo had watched them erecting a small lean-to greenhouse made from tall wooden stakes and PVC sheeting. She'd seen the plants they put inside grow like wildfire in just a few weeks. When she had asked Spence what the plants with the five spiky leaves were called he told her they were 'Chinese Artichokes' which of course she'd never heard of.

Those three vibrant Sunflowers were most welcome examples of Flower Power, Flo decided. They certainly had the power to cheer and lift her from the slight post-holiday melancholia she felt now that the great adventure was over. It lifted further when she heard cutlery clinking in the flat below and realised that Val and Spence were home, she was not alone in the house. This was confirmed when she smelled the freshly mown hay aroma of the hand-rolled cigarettes they always smoked. Flo was living with Hippies! She bet Tom was laughing in Heaven at the thought of that!

A few weeks later Frank and Vera dropped their bomb shell.

Flo was staying with them for a long weekend down in Selsey and felt the nervous tension even before they broached the subject.

'We've got some news, Flo,' was how Frank started the conversation. 'You might have heard me going on about how the money's gone out of fishing in Blighty. Catches are still dropping like a stone and Government quotas make it so darn difficult there's no longer a living in it. Not here, at any rate.

'Besides, nobody seems to want fish any more, it's all Chinese take-aways made with cheap belly of pork and Vindaloos using any old mutton going that are all the rage now.

D'yer know, half the fish and chip shops in Bognor have closed in the past three years alone?

'I've got to earn our keep for some years yet and fishing's all I know, see. So...we're going to emigrate to Australia where things are different and start anew. One of my old crew, George Brooker, took his family over there a few years ago on one of those £10 assisted passages and he's never looked back. Modern trawler, big Estate car, bungalow by the beach with its own swimming pool, I tell you, he's got the lot!'

Flo felt a swift stab of anxiety and her mouth instantly went dry.

'Fish are still plentiful in the warm waters off Perth in Western Australia and none of this quotas nonsense neither. That's where we're hoping to go. Ray, Lin and little Tom will be coming too, they've outgrown that railway carriage on East Beach but can't find anywhere decent to live at a reasonable rent for love nor money. George says they're snapping up car mechanics in Australia like hot cakes and property prices are real cheap.'

At this point Vera intervened, knowing full well what was going through Flo's mind, something Frank had forgotten to address in his enthusiasm for all things Australian.

'Flo, we want you to come too,' she said quickly, getting straight to the point.

'We're your family now and have been for years, it's only right that we all keep together. Think of the future, Flo, none of us are getting any younger. We all need family around us when we're getting on, more than ever.'

She continued in a softer tone: 'I know you can't bear to leave Kingston with all its old memories. I quite understand all that, m'dear. I know that's the reason you didn't go to Italy with that lovely man Gianni. But this is different, Flo, we're *real* family - people mean much more than just memories and dwelling in the past.'

Vera wondered if she had gone too far with that one. It was time to play her trump card: 'And I tell you something, Flo, I know it's exactly what Tom would want for you more than anything else in the world.'

Flo's face lit up like a field of ripening corn when the sun appears from behind a cloud. 'Do you really think that's what Tom would want?'

Vera knew she had pushed the right buttons and soon heard Flo telling her: 'Yes, of course I want to come with you all to Australia. That's what Tom wants, I'm sure.'

Vera noticed the change of tense but said nothing.

So the die was cast, there was no going back for any of them now. There was much to do, Frank had to sell his boat and business and there would be visits to Australia House in London. Flo asked if they'd be going by plane or boat but they didn't know.

'Early days, Flo,' Frank kept repeating. 'Early days. Best take it one day at a time.'

The first thing Flo did when she got home was to go round to Kingston Public Library and look up where Perth was in a huge world atlas. It seemed a long way away from the rest of Australia, a one road in and one railway line out sort of a place. Then she found a travel book all about Australia which she borrowed from the Library and took home to read.

There was a whole chapter on Western Australia where Perth is located. Flo read it with a mixture of excitement and apprehension. It seemed to enjoy permanent summertime and the scenery was stunning, not like Cornwall of course but in its own particular way. There were photos of lots of delicious food like thick lamb chops, giant crabs and fish of all sorts that grew to huge sizes in the tropical waters of the Indian Ocean. No wonder Frank was keen to go.

She noticed it was separated from the rest of Australia in the east by three enormous deserts that ran from north to south and other than Perth there didn't seem to be any other big cities at all in Western Australia. In the other direction, westward, there was nothing but sea for thousands of miles until you reached the coast of Africa. She began to wonder: was it all too much for her to take on specially at her time of life? But then she reassured herself: most Australians were similar to British people, they spoke the same language even though they used a few queer words they'd made up themselves and every woman was called Sheila. And she'd have her family around her: the nicest and kindest people imaginable and one of them, Vera, had been very special indeed to Tom.

Ah yes, Tom, she thought. She'd be leaving him behind and all the lovely memories and important places they had shared together: there would be no more trips to Farnborough once she was in Australia. Flo felt in need of a cigarette and a cup of tea to steady her hand and clear her head. Once the pot had brewed and her cigarette was lit she went back to the table by the kitchen window.

'Pull yourself together, Flo,' she told herself. 'Not going would be like deserting the family for a lot of grimy old streets built in the days of the Old Queen and grey dusty roads that smell of drains and diesel fumes.'

But more than anything else, since that glimpse of Tom in the Mule's Field at Teignmouth, she had the feeling that Tom was close to her more than ever now wherever she went: looking after her since she was past her three-score-years-and-ten. She knew Tom cared about her just as much as she cared for him and it was only natural enough he'd be drawing closer as autumn years turned to winter.

Over the next couple of weeks Flo took to wandering round her three rooms and writing down what things would go with her and what things wouldn't. Her passport still had a few years to run but she'd need more than one suitcase for all the things she'd want to take. She even got out her old Tenancy

Agreement dating back from just after the Great War and read through it. There were other letters folded into it as different landlords came and went over the years but as far as she could tell she still only had to give a fortnight's notice. There at the bottom in ink that had dried half a century before was Sid's signature. As she brushed her thumb across it she wondered how different life would have been if he had stayed to raise his son and ease the burden of the years that she had borne alone on her broad shoulders.

'Why ever did he leave?' she belatedly asked herself. It couldn't have been just to escape the gambling debts, maybe he just couldn't take on the responsibility of fatherhood and being head of the family? Or maybe it was something she had done? Maybe she'd let him down as a wife in some way that escaped her notice at the time and ever since?

No, she decided, she'd not been such a bad wife as that during the short time they were together or he'd have said something. Or she'd have sensed something herself. He was just no good, a good-for-nothing alcoholic who when faced with gambling debts could only see one way out: catching a fast train to Portsmouth with his coat collar pulled up to hide his face to start a new life free from fear of the razor gang debt collectors. But how did he know they wouldn't come calling on her and little Tom instead and do all sorts of wicked things when she couldn't pay either? No, Sid was simply no good, a man with no backbone and that's all there was to it.

Things started moving fast for Frank and Vera once they'd decided it was 'Australia here we come'. Vera seemed to phone Flo every other evening with news of what was happening. There were forms to fill, all sorts of loose ends to tie up and interviews to attend at Australia House in central London. Sooner or later Flo would have to go for one herself, Frank told her.

It was just after Frank and Vera's second interview that the phone went quiet for a number of days. Then one Saturday afternoon Flo's phone rang unexpectedly.

'That's another thing I must have disconnected and remember to inform the Post Office before I leave,' thought Flo as she reached out to lift the black receiver. It was Vera, they were up in London on business to do with the move and could they call on her and sorry for the short notice.

Just over an hour later they entered Flo's living room where a pot of tea was ready to receive boiling water next to a plate of Jaffa Cakes that Flo had found in her larder. As Frank and Vera sat down Flo immediately sensed a problem of some sort. After a few strained pleasantries Vera swiftly drank half her cup of tea and got down to brass tacks.

'There's a bit of a hiccup, Flo, to do with our going to Australia and we want to discuss it with you,' she started. Flo sat back on the sofa and prepared herself for bad news.

'You see, we've just found out that they're not too keen about people over retirement age emigrating to Australia. I think they're afraid of them becoming a financial burden of some sort. We've told them that we'll always look after you but they say that's not enough. Basically, they want people of working age to help them build Australia.

'Anybody who's retired has to be able to reassure them they'll never become dependent on Australian state welfare.'

'Oh I'd never do that,' interrupted Flo. 'I'd never want to become a burden to you, the Australians or anybody else! And I'll still have my Old Age Pension. I checked that at the Post Office last Thursday, the man at the counter told me you can draw your pension anywhere in the Commonwealth once you're entitled.'

'It's not as simple as that, Flo,' replied Vera. 'They want to be sure retired people can more than adequately support themselves. And that means having a guaranteed income that's a lot more than the British Old Age Pension pays. What's more, you'd need to have at least £5,000 in savings and I think I'm right in saying you don't have that much salted away under the floorboards?' Vera smiled as she asked the question trying to lighten the atmosphere a little.

'£5,000?' asked Flo with disbelief. 'Who's got money like that whether they're retired or not?'

'Sadly, I think that's why they do it,' replied Vera back in serious mode. 'They don't really need older people and if they do come they have to have a Top Hat pension - or a good income from investments and a nice little nest egg to boot.'

'Oh dear!' Flo exclaimed. At first she was at a complete loss to know what to suggest but then she said the only thing she could think of.

'Look Vera, you must go ahead and emigrate to Australia even if it means going without me. You, Frank and Ray and Lin and the baby have still got your lives ahead of you, mine's mostly in the past now. We can always speak on the phone.'

Vera was instantly relieved.

'That's very nice of you to say that,' she replied gently taking Flo's hand. 'But we think we can do better than that.

'What we thought was, we'll go to Australia as planned. But we've discovered that anybody can come to Australia on a visitor's permit and stay three months of the year. Each and every year, that is.

'So what we were thinking is - you could come and stay with us for three months of every Australian summer, we'll pay the air fares of course. Just imagine, you'd never have to live through a British winter again - you'd get two summers every year.'

'Two summers every year,' repeated Flo with a smile despite having difficulty in getting her head round the prospect. 'That would be nice!'

'There's more, Flo,' continued Vera in deadly earnest.

'We don't want you left all on your own for the other nine months of the year. Not at your time of life, not without someone to keep an eye on you. That's where Jeffrey comes in.'

Flo really had to concentrate to keep up with the proposition that followed. Jeffrey didn't want to come to Australia with everyone else. After school he'd gone to work for the National Provincial Bank in Chichester but in the psychedelic Sixties had found banking deadly dull. Jeffrey had an almost messianic belief in the future of computers – even by that time every sizeable company had its own Computer Room and anyone with eyes to see knew it wasn't going to end there.

Soon there'd be one on every desk in every office, reasoned Jeffrey, and after that one in every home. He was absolutely sure of it, though he still couldn't quite work out what people would use them for at home.

Anyway, Jeffrey knew the whole computer thing was about to take off faster than the Apollo Moon Rocket and he intended to get in at the ground floor. So he'd decided that he was still young enough to apply to King's College London and Kingston Polytechnic to see if he could get onto one of their newly founded courses on Information Technology.

Flo listened but couldn't quite see what all this had to do with her staying in the U.K.

'The thing is,' continued Vera, 'Whether he gets into Kingston or King's College he'll need somewhere to stay.

'We know you've got a spare room, Flo, Tom's old room. Now it's completely up to you, dear, if it's not your cup of tea just say so and you'll hear no more about it. But we thought, if Jeffrey came to lodge with you it would solve the problem for him of where to stay. And Jeffrey could keep an eye on you, do the shopping when the weather's bad and help out around the flat. He's good like that, considerate and reliable - and there's not too many youngsters around you can say that about these days.'

Vera had always been quietly proud of Jeffrey, Ray would always be the life and soul of any party but it was Jeffrey who was going to make something of his life, of that she was sure.

'I know all this is a lot to take in, Flo,' continued Vera. 'So you don't have to make your mind up right away. Think about it and we can talk again.

'Of course, Jeffrey would be a *paying* lodger, he'll get a grant from the government to cover food and rent. If you don't mind, we'd need to put a lick of paint on the walls in that room and buy a modern divan bed. But we'll talk about all that later.'

On one of her recent visits Vera had opened the door to Tom's old room and looked inside. As she had expected, nothing had been touched ever since the day Tom left it to go off to war. The windows had been cleaned and the furniture dusted but nothing else, almost as if it was waiting for Tom's return more than a quarter of a century later. Vera had wondered if this would be a stumbling block to Jeffrey moving in, would Flo be able to accept the room becoming a home for the living and no longer a shrine for the dead. But there was no doubt in Flo's mind, she had always liked Jeffrey and although she had lived alone all these years the prospect of company and somebody to *do* for would be nice. For the first time since Tom had gone, Flo felt she had lived alone for too long.

'Yes, I think it's a very good idea. Of course I'm disappointed at not leaving here for good and coming with you to live in Australia. But as you say, I could still spend three months every year with you – and while Jeffrey is keeping an eye on me, well, I can be keeping an eye on him,' replied Flo with a twinkle in her eye.

'That's right, Flo,' said Frank with palpable relief. They all laughed with some amusement at the thought of the younger keeping an eye on the older who in turn was keeping an eye on the younger.

Before they left, Vera looked closely at Flo's face and into her eyes to gauge her true feelings. She noticed a look of tranquility that had been lacking for the last few weeks: ever since Flo had first agreed to leave Kingston and move to Australia for good. In that instant Vera knew that Flo was relieved that she wasn't going to spend the rest of her life in Australia, just as it had been a relief when her relationship with Gianni had ended and she didn't have to leave Kingston to go and live in Italy.

As the days passed, Flo became aware of a feeling of contentment that seemed to engulf her and she didn't quite know why. Was it the fact that she now knew for sure that she would spend all of her remaining days in her beloved Kingston filled with its fond memories? Or was it the thought of having someone young to live with her, someone roughly Tom's age when he was last with her, someone to fuss and fret over and look after - thereby fulfilling a motherly impulse forced dormant for so many years?

It had been arranged that Frank and Jeffrey would come up the following weekend to sort the bedroom. Out would go the metal frame bedstead and Tom's old wooden table and in would come a brand new divan bed and a desk. The latter would arrive in flat-pack form which Frank and Jeffrey would put together: a strange new way of buying furniture thought Flo. They would apply a couple of coats of emulsion to the walls and ceiling and spread carpet tiles and a couple of rugs on the floor.

The whole thing would be finished in a day.

9: Tom meets the Goddess Aphrodite on a charabanc in Devon.

The Wednesday afternoon before the redecoration was due to take place Flo visited Tom's room: she knew it would be the last time she would see it just as he had left it. They were going to keep the dark wooden wardrobe but Flo removed all Tom's clothes from inside it and hung them in the big wardrobe in her bedroom. There was no way she was going to let those go to a jumble sale or the rag and bone man. Then she stripped the bed of its sheets, blankets and pillow cases and transferred them to her room too: Jeffrey evidently preferred one of those new continental duvets that were becoming so popular. As she did so she paused to press her cheek against the feather pillow on which Tom's head had once rested.

Then she went to the old wooden table that had served Tom as a desk in his schooldays and later whilst studying to be an Automotive Engineer when working at Kingston Hill Motors. On the right hand corner of the desk stood a small wooden cabinet of similar vintage with three drawers in which Tom had kept pencils, rubbers, a spare cycle puncture repair kit - and a treasured metal fountain pen given to him by his Uncle Stan. Clearly Tom thought it far too valuable to take to war.

What a good uncle Stan had been, reminisced Flo. He had helped Tom in so many little ways: once again she remembered the bicycle Stan had given him and could see them now both fixing a punctured tyre in the passageway beside the house that led to the back garden. Stan and Ada only had a daughter, Doreen, and Flo often thought that in some way Stan looked on Tom as the son he never had. He certainly went out of his way to help him in ways that only a father could.

Flo was familiar with the contents of the drawers which she intended keeping as any material connection with Tom was to her as precious as gold and more valuable than diamonds. She had never removed the three drawers before - but as she did so to make it easier for her to carry she saw something wedged into the space between the bottom of the lower drawer and the desk beneath. It was an A4 school exercise book with feint ruled pages such as could be bought for sixpence in Woolworths or any stationers. Flo lifted it from its resting place without difficulty and ran her fingers across its plum coloured cover made from thin card.

There written in permanant ink, in the handwriting Flo recognised instantly, were the words 'MY BIG ADVENTURE - SCOUT CAMP IN DEVON' and underneath in smaller writing 'Saturday August 1st to Saturday August 15th 1936'.

How well Flo remembered Tom's holiday without her in 1936 and how she fretted and was filled with angst for most of the time they were apart, even though he sent her picture postcards almost every day. Then her thoughts went back to the Vicar of St. Luke's who had made the impossible dream come true. How kind it had been of him to think of Tom when that cancellation came up and offer him the free place, she thought. There were so many good people in the world, so why was there so much misery too?

Flo apprehensively opened the exercise book and could see every page was filled with Tom's best writing and took the form of a diary or journal. The first half was in ink written with his metal fountain pen no doubt - but clearly the pen had run out of ink halfway through the holiday as the second half was written in indelible pencil. Flo felt a moment of conscience and she held back for a few seconds. This was Tom's private diary, words he had never intended to share with any other person. Did she have the right to trespass into that secret world of so long ago? But could she resist and desist from reading what would surely be his innermost thoughts? It was bound to reveal new things about Tom's life - little things maybe but so important to Flo whose recent life had consisted of going over the same old momentoes time and time again.

Why, it would almost be like hearing Tom's sweet voice again talking to her for the first time in so many years.

Flo decided that they never had any secrets before so why should they now? Tom would know how important it was to her to read these words and wouldn't resent her intrusion, if intrusion it really was. She decided to read it.

Flo carefully carried the exercise book along the hallway to her living room and placed it on the kitchen table in front of the window. She made a cup of tea, she felt she was going to need one. Then she emptied the ash tray and placed her cigarettes and a book of matches next to it. She knew she was going to need a few of those too: a cigarette always calmed her nerves. Who needed Valium when there was a packet of Rothmans King-size close at hand?

Flo took a mouthful of refreshing tea and lit a cigarette. Then she reread the words written in dark ink on the plum coloured cover: 'MY BIG ADVENTURE – SCOUT CAMP IN DEVON.'

'How old did that make him at the time?' she asked herself. 'Little more than fifteen years old, almost two-thirds of the way through his life if he had but known it.' At this thought the old feelings came tumbling out: why did he have to leave her so young? Why him? What had they done to deserve it? How right people were when they said what a terrible thing it is to outlive your own child. Tom was such a good boy. She knew that God sent trials to test us but this had been too much. How had she managed to bear it all these years?

She took another mouthful of tea and drew on the cigarette for comfort. Then she opened the exercise book.

The first short entry was for Friday 24th July 1936 and read: **'School broke up today, just 8 days until the start of my expedition to Devon. Two weeks exploring all sorts of new places and having loads of fun with my mates!'**

Flo could feel the excitement that came with those words more than thirty years after they were written. Only those who spend fifty weeks a year as a city child couped up in grey suburban streets can hope to understand the exhilaration and elation that escape to coast and countryside can bring.

The next entry was for July the 26th and told how Uncle Stan and Aunt Ada had visited for Sunday tea and Stan had given him a whole ten shilling note towards his holiday pocket money. Together with the ten bob that his mum had given him and another ten bob he'd saved up himself from his pocket money he would have a whole one pound ten shillings to spend.

On Friday July the 31st Tom had spent the day packing and repacking the little cardboard suitcase and making sure nothing had been forgotten. Then it was an early night for an early start tomorrow.

Flo remembered how she had wanted to tie a piece of thin rope round the case as she was none too sure about the lock. But Tom would have none of it – it was one of the only times he had argued with her. He was concerned that his mates would laugh at his old case as they would have 'proper cases'. How deep those words had struck into Flo's heart at the time, the first indication Tom had given that he felt shame about his poor background. Had there been time Flo would have hurried down to the leather goods store in Wood Street and bought him the smartest case she could with the contents of the biscuit tin where she kept the money for the rent, gas and electric bills. But it was too late for that.

The coach hired by the Scout Troop was a full twenty-eight seater and there was only twenty of them going. So they could really spread out: Tom got a window seat with his mate Ronny Briggs from Burton Road sitting next to him for company.

Flo could see that cream and brown coloured charabanc in her mind's eye as clear as the day before yesterday. She remembered how she stood outside St. Luke's with the other mothers and waved Tom off and watched his face pressed to the window disappear up Gibbon Street until it turned out of sight into Richmond Road. How alone she had felt that first evening apart, a frame of mind even half a pack of cigarettes could not dispel.

The charabanc stopped in a big car park in Salisbury which, being market day, was bustling with people. After eating the packed lunches they brought with them they trooped off to visit the Cathedral. On the way they passed through the ancient Market Square. This was the biggest market Tom had ever seen in his life, far bigger than the Monday Market in Kingston Cattle Market which he sometime visited in school holidays. Fortunately they didn't stop to look round or Tom was sure to have spent his whole one pound ten shillings holiday money in one go.

After a tour of the Cathedral, with its iconic spire pointing skyward to the hope of a better world, the scouts were told to buy a penny postcard from the table selling guide books at the main entrance. These were to be filled in and would be posted to their parents that evening to confirm their deliverance from the dangers of the A303 'Highway to the Sun' and their safe arrival at Mule's Field in Teignmouth.

Thirty-four years later, Flo retrieved the card from among the others in her shoe box of memories.

'Dear Mum, We've arrived alright in Devon. On the way down we visited the biggest church you ever saw (see picture on other side). Love, Tom' were all the words he could muster for the postcard the afternoon they arrived. After all, there was so much that was new to see, so much waiting to be explored – and camping in Bell tents under open skies was such fun.

But later that evening Tom still found time to make the first entry of the holiday in the diary. For Saturday August 1st, 1936 he wrote: **"Long drive to Devon, Ronnie Briggs reckons it was over two thousand miles. Really terrific camp site in a big field in the countryside next to the sea. We were allowed on the beach for almost an hour, lots of small ponds in the rocks full of tiny sea creatures. Ronnie and me are coming back to capture some tomorrow. The Bell tents are so big you can stand up in them and we had beef stew with dumplings for dinner. I really like dumplings which I never had before. Two other groups staying here. One is some scouts from up north which should be fun but the other is a load of girl guides worst luck."**

He certainly seemed to be having a nice time despite the presence of the girl guides, thought Flo. But what a pity she had never given him dumplings when she made him stews. They simply weren't something her mother had ever served or taught her to cook. She would have learnt how if only she had known he liked them, Flo thought regretfully more than three decades after the words were written.

Tom awoke next morning to the smell of bacon frying on the camp kitchen fire. He had often had bacon for breakfast at home, but it never smelled so delicious as this, its savoury aroma mixed with the fresh morning air to make it ten times more appetising than usual. After a fried breakfast and being Sunday they set off in crocodile file for the stone-built fishermen's church halfway down the hill towards the town. After morning service they explored Teignmouth and the sea front and then headed back to the beach below the camp site. What a wonderful beach it was: a mixture of clean golden sands and wave-worn outcrops of rock peppered with rock-pools full of sea life in miniature, some familiar and some unknown.

That evening before falling asleep Tom wrote in the plum-covered diary: **'Fantastical day mostly spent on the best beach in Britain. Ronny and me caught tiny crabs, baby fish you could see through and tiny shrimps. We had lots of fun throwing the crabs at the Guides which made them scream but got told off by Mr. Davies the Scout Master and had to stop. Then we had a competition to see who could lever the most limpits off the rocks'**

The other two groups camping at the Mule's Field site that fortnight were a troop of scouts from Birmingham and a company of girl guides from Crystal Palace in south-east London. The next day an excursion to nearby Dawlish had been planned and instead of taking all the three groups' coaches it was decided everyone could squeeze into two. Tom made sure he was in the charabanc as soon as the driver unlocked the door to be certain of getting a window seat, Ronny scrambled into the window seat behind him. Last aboard were the girl guides.

Out of the blue, Tom heard a well-spoken female voice say: 'Excuse me, if this seat is vacant would you mind if I sat here?'

Tom realised the question was directed at him and looked up at the enquiring face of one of the guides. 'Yes, sure,' Tom said and returned to looking out of the window.

The girl broke the silence that followed as the charabanc struggled up the hill in bottom gear towards Dawlish.

'You're with the Kingston scouts, aren't you?' she asked him. 'My name's Katharine, by the way, but my friends call me Kate. You can call me Kate, if you like.'

'My name's Tom,' was all he could manage in reply, still looking out of the window and desperately avoiding eye contact.

She told him she had a cousin called Tom and thought it a very nice name and said she had always wondered why there had never been a King of England called Thomas. There had been Williams and Richards and plenty of Henries but not a single Thomas.

Tom, struggling to keep up his side of the conversation, suddenly remembered a recent history lesson at school.

'Maybe because of Thomas Wolsey and Thomas More and Thomas Cromwell who all had their heads cut off. You know, by Henry the Eighth. Bit of an unlucky name for a King after that.'

'I think you could be right,' said Kate slowly and then added: 'You must be quite clever to know things like that.'

Tom was pleased by this and he turned and smiled and looked at her properly for the first time. She was quite pretty with long brown hair, hazel eyes to match and a flawless complexion devoid of pubescent blemishes that are the curse of most teenagers at that age. But what he liked most was the fact that she went out of her way to show interest in him. When they parked by the seafront at Dawlish she got up first and said to him: 'We're going swimming later so maybe see you in the sea.' Then she gave a big smile and was gone.

Ronny Briggs, who had been sitting behind them and heard it all, shoved his head forward between the antimacassars and said to Tom: 'I think she fancies you, mate,' which both embarrassed and pleased him.

That evening he wrote all about it in the plum-coloured diary: **'Monday 3rd August. Today we went to Dawlish by coach and looked round the shops which were absolutely crowded because it was August Bank Holiday. Then we went to the beach where I went swimming and Ronnie Briggs and me played rounders in the sea with some girl guides and did swimming between their legs which was lots of fun.**

We were given a Cornish pasty for lunch and I ate mine with a girl I met on the coach called Kate. She's quite nice.'

Flo's eyes widened as she read this and she searched through the half-dozen postcards she had retrieved from her shoe box of memories looking for the one for that first Monday. But it said nothing about meeting a girl on the coach or swimming between guides' legs and simply read: **'Dear Mum, Today we went to Dawlish where they have BLACK swans like on this post card. And every other shop is a pie shop selling really great meat pies and pasties. Went swimming and Colin Jarman trod on a jelly fish and Mr Davies spent ages getting the stings out of his foot. Really nice here and food good. Love, Tom'**

Next day all three scout and guide groups took part in a beachcombing competition. They were told to search eastward from Teignmouth along the sands and rocky outcrops and look for unusual shells, flotsam and jetsam – anything that looked interesting. And there would be prizes of bars of chocolate for the best finds.

Tom was examining a piece of driftwood, probably from the root of a tree, that with a little imagination could pass for a galloping horse when he heard a voice behind him.

'Hello Tom, what have you discovered?' asked Kate.

'I found this bit of wood that's sort of shaped like a horse, see. Probably from the Charge of the Light Brigade, I reckon.' And with that he began to rock it backwards and forwards breathing life and movement into it.

'Let me look,' she said taking it from his hands. 'That's really super, how smooth it's been worn by the sea. And look, it even has a sort of a tail. I reckon that's worth a bar of chocolate for certain. You are lucky.'

They walked together eyes down along the beach for quite some time, poking and probing under clumps of seaweed forcing them to reveal their mysteries and upturning stones to see what creatures lurked beneath.

They came across plenty of long narrow razor shells which Tom told Kate mermaids used to shave their beards. She thought for a moment and was about to say that she didn't think mermaids needed to shave when she caught sight of Tom's cheeky smile and knew he was teasing.

But although they also found a massive crab's claw, a seashell that reflected all the colours of the rainbow and an old cigarette lighter that had been in the sea for ages, they never found anything quite as interesting as Tom's charging horse.

Suddenly Tom had an idea. 'You can have it if you like, say *you* found it,' he told Kate.

'That's very sweet of you, Tom. But it wouldn't be fair – and anyway chocolate brings me out in spots. But it was very nice of you to offer.' Then after a pause she said: 'Follow me,' and taking hold of his wrist she led him into the shadow of a large vertical rock rising out of the sand where they were alone and couldn't be seen.

She looked at him for a moment with smiling eyes and still holding his hand said: 'Do you want to kiss me, Tom?'

Before he could answer she reached out and cupped the back of his head in her left hand and pulled his face towards hers until their mouths met. It wasn't a passionate kiss but it wasn't a peck either and whatever it was it gave Tom a feeling he had never known before. Then as suddenly as it had started Kate pulled back and still smiling said: 'Must go, Tom, or the others will think I've been dragged out to sea by an octopus. Good luck with your horse,' and with that she skipped and ran back down the beach the way they had come leaving Tom rooted to the spot.

Later that afternoon Tom indeed won a bar of chocolate for his charging horse. But first prize went to one of the Birmingham scouts who found what might be a Neolithic axe head - which disappointed Tom as it would have looked better in Kate's eyes if he had won top prize. But as he walked forward to collect his bar of Fry's Chocolate Cream he caught a glimpse of her with the guides and she was clapping him for all her worth.

That evening after a meal of sausages, cabbage and mash, they all had a camp fire sing-song. Tom kept looking around for Kate but she was nowhere to be seen. Then just as they were packing up she suddenly appeared beside him. 'See, I told you you'd win a prize,' she said.

Tom smiled and slipped the bar of chocolate from his pocket. 'I want you to have it. And if it does give you spots it doesn't matter 'cause you're pretty enough for it not to make any difference.'

Kate's face lit with laughter. 'How could I refuse such a gallant offer. You're sweet as a bar of chocolate yourself, Tom.' Before he knew it she kissed him quickly on the cheek and with a flick of her long brown hair she turned and disappeared into the darkness clutching Tom's bar of chocolate.

The diary for that day Tuesday the 4th of August read: **'Today we went beachcombing and I found this lump of tree shaped like a galloping horse and I won a bar of chocolate in the competition. Met that girl Kate on the beach, she's a bit posh and her dad has a car. I told her mine died of his wounds after the war.**

'When we reached the end of the beach where the land sticks out we went behind a rock and she kissed me. I think I quite like her.'

Flo was somewhat taken aback by this. How old was he? Of course, he'd had girlfriends when he was much older like Gloria and she now knew about Vera down in Selsey during the War. But Flo never imagined he would have been interested in girls at *that* age, surely he was much too young?

And this girl Kate certainly wasn't backwards in coming forwards. Flo reached for another cigarette and poured the remainder of the teapot into her cup.

Everybody at the camp had eagerly been looking forward to Wednesday for they were all going on a boat trip along the coast. The weather was brilliant once again and straight after breakfast of bread, bacon and beans they all headed off along the Promenade towards the Harbour at the far end of town. The boat had been hired specially and had a covered part downstairs and an open deck on top behind the bridge. Tom and Ronnie Briggs sat just behind the bridge and watched with fascination as the skipper wrestled with the wheel, the hand throttle and the reverse gear to manoeuvre 'The Pride of Devonia' away from the sea wall and out into deeper water.

'Hold on, m'dears, it might be a little bumpy till we clear the 'arbour mouth,' shouted the leather-skinned mariner at the wheel. Soon they were chugging eastward past the entrance to the Mule's Field camp site where the town ran out and before long Dawlish was edging into view. Tom looked across to a giggling gaggle of guides on the other side of the boat and just as he spotted Kate their eyes met.

'Tom, come and sit over here,' she ordered and then added as an afterthought: 'And bring your friend with you!'

They didn't need asking twice and the group of guides parted to let Tom and Ronnie through to the side of the boat where Kate was leaning over the rail staring into the water.

'What's that?' she shouted pointing to some translucent shapes in the sea.

'Them's Jelly Fish,' answered Ronnie: 'The same as stung Colin Jarman yesterday and gave him a poison foot.'

Kate recoiled slightly and brushed against Tom's chest as if she was expecting the Jelly Fish to leap out of the water and attack her.

'What sort of Jelly Fish do you think they are, Tom?' she asked seriously.

'Well you see that reddish one over there, that's a Rowntrees Strawberry Jelly Fish. And that darker one over there, that's a Chivers Blackcurrant Jelly Fish,' answered Tom chuckling at his own joke. Everybody squealed with laughter, including Kate; all except a couple of guides who felt sick at the thought of eating a jelly fish whatever the flavour.

'Let's go over there and look for dolphins, Tom,' said Kate grabbing him by the arm and leading him away from the others to the starboard side of the boat. There they sat looking for the sea mammal's familiar shape and a couple of times imagined they saw one in the distance leaping out between silvery waves. And so they talked together and let their imaginations run wild all the way to Sidmouth.

Tom learned that Kate was a solicitor's daughter and that they lived opposite the Crystal Palace in south-east London. She went to dancing classes every Saturday morning at a private dancing academy, she loved dancing, liked horse riding (though she didn't own a horse) and had been on holiday abroad a couple of times to Deauville in northern France.

Tom was relieved she didn't actually own a horse, every time she told him something about herself she seemed to rise higher and higher above him in social status.

Then just as they were passing the stand of Pine trees to the east of Budleigh Salterton Kate turned the spotlight on Tom.

'So what does your mother do?' she asked directly knowing Tom was fatherless. There was no way he was going to admit his mum worked in the local bagwash laundry so he decided to put a bit of a spin on it.

'Oh, she runs a chain of dry cleaners over our side of London,' Tom lied.

'Where do you like going for holidays?' she asked next.

'Oh, we have a favourite hotel on the front at Bognor Regis, you know, where King George used to stay. We go there whenever we can,' Tom heard himself saying.

Kate showed no further interest in the supposed entrepreneurial activities of Tom's mother and their royal fellow-holidaymaker and suddenly changed the subject.

'Your pal Ronnie seems to be getting on well with my friend Lorna,' she observed.

Just then a fresh breeze caught the boat and Kate complained it was getting chilly and she hadn't brought a sweater. 'Can I come inside your jacket?' she asked.

Tom was only too pleased to oblige. But although Kate pressed close to him for the rest of the outward journey, and he had his arm round her shoulder to keep his jacket in place, nothing more in the way of bodily contact passed between them to Tom's slight chagrin. But he could hardly expect otherwise with all their mates ogling them, he told himself.

The boat moored in Sidmouth at the little quay to the east of the town and they were allowed ashore for two whole hours to stretch their legs and eat their packed lunch on the beach. On his way to buy Kate a choc ice Tom dutifully bought a coloured postcard from a promenade kiosk.

Before they left for the return journey, Tom taught Kate the timeless English pastime of Ducks and Drakes: how to choose the smoothest, roundest stones from the beach and send them skimming across the water. Tom managed to get one to bounce four times whereas Kate only managed twice though she did try hard to make it three. Then Kate decided there was just enough time to cultivate her tan and they lay side by side face-up on the beach.

'Tell me, do you like dancing, Tom?' she asked.

'I don't dance much but I like dance band music,' Tom replied. 'You know, Chick Henderson and the Joe Loss Orchestra, Denny Dennis - and Al Bowlly with Ray Noble.'

Kate sat upright at the mention of Al Bowlly. 'You like Al Bowlly?' she said excitedly. 'He's my favourite singer, I think he's utter bliss. Absolutely the best singer in the history of ever. He gives me goose bumps every time I hear him. What's your favourite song?'

'"Night and Day" and of course "Midnight, the Stars and You"' answered Tom, absolutely delighted that he had found common ground that didn't depend on parental social standing.

Kate lay back on the beach. '"Night and Day" is great!' she replied.

'Do you know, when daddy went to New York on business earlier this year he bought me a new Al Bowlly record that's not on sale over here. It's "Blue Moon" which Al recorded over there and it really is the absolute best.'

'What records do you have, Tom?'

Tom didn't have any nor a gramophone but skilfully avoided belittling himself in Kate's eyes, something he was getting used to having to do, by replying: 'I listen to them all on the continental stations on the wireless, you know, Radio Luxembourg and Radio Normandie.'

Then they fell silent for a while.

After about a minute, Tom felt her unseen hand close on his and they lay there hand-in-hand for another ten minutes. Tom could feel how soft and smooth her fingers were – this hand had never scrubbed a kitchen floor nor blacked a living room grate, nor ever would.

'Isn't this simply Heaven, Tom. I could stay here all day,' Kate said eventually and he agreed.

But all too soon they heard their scout and guide pack numbers being called and they reluctantly made their way back towards the boat.

'I'd better sit with my friends, Tom,' Kate said as she began to climb aboard. 'Otherwise they'll think I'm rude. It's been super talking, perhaps I'll see you at the beach tomorrow. I think it must be full of simply perfect skimming stones.'

Tom said O.K. and tried to hide his disappointment at not having her to himself for the return trip. He watched her cross the rickety gangplank of 'The Pride of Devonia' with all the poise and confidence of a Paris model on a catwalk.

Flo read the entry for that day, Wednesday the 5th. of August: **'Went on a really super boat trip for miles along the coast. Kate and I kept looking for dolphins and reckon we saw at least two jumping out of the sea. I made her laugh about the strawberry-flavoured Jelly Fish. At Sidmouth I bought her a choc ice and we lay on the beach and held hands. I really do like her a lot, she's really super. I think she must like me too. Kate said we should meet tomorrow on the beach near where we're camping and play the stone skimming game which I taught her. Really super day.'**

Flo began to get concerned about Tom's growing passion for this girl Kate. It was as if Flo was reading it in real time, oblivious to the fact that Tom had died in battle eight years later and by now Kate was probably a middle-aged mother. She had noticed that Tom was using a new word too - 'super' – she could guess who he had picked that up from: nobody in Staunton Road, Kingston, that was for sure.

Just as Flo was hoping, there was a postcard for Sidmouth among her little collection but it bore no mention of a girl called Kate: **'Dear Mum, Yesterday I won a bar of chocolate in a beachcombing competition and today we all went on a boat cruise along the coast. The cliffs have wavy lines in them where dinosaurs trod on them millions of years ago and we saw dolphins jumping out of the sea. Played the skimming stone game on the beach at Sidmouth with a new friend. Lots of food in camp but not as super as your cooking. Love, Tom.'**

'Well we know who the "new friend" was,' Flo thought to herself. But he seemed to be having a good time - and he missed her food which pleased her.

The next day there was no chance to play the skimming stone game on the beach with Kate. The Kingston scouts had games in the morning and they were going to the cinema in the afternoon.

Tom did quite well in the long jump and was in the winning team of the relay race. Whilst he was sitting on the grass waiting for the next event, Tom caught sight of Kate competing in the girl guide events: firstly in the high jump and then in the 200 yards sprint.

The guides wore dark navy blue shorts and Tom's attention was soon drawn to Kate's long, slender legs that already showed a slight tan. Those legs seemed to be the most enchanting things he had ever clapped eyes on and he couldn't stop looking at them. What was it about them that fascinated him so, he wondered? But Kate was too absorbed by what she was doing and too far away to notice him.

Come the afternoon and the Kingston scouts walked in file along the Prom to the Riviera Cinema at the back of the green that lay just behind the main beach in Teignmouth. It was a majestic building with a line of white columns and steps that led up to a marble-walled foyer. It was like entering some Roman emperor's palace. The film they had come to see was the latest Hollywood spectacular 'Follow the Fleet'. Up until then Tom had thought it was going to be a war film - but as he looked at the framed publicity photos by the box office he realised it was a new musical comedy starring Ginger Rogers and Fred Astaire.

Tom treated himself to an orange drink and a three-penny bag of sugary pink-coloured popcorn: the latest snack food craze from America. Tom was sure it was going to be a really super film and he wished Kate was there with him to share it - she would specially like the songs and the dancing.

To jaded twenty-first century viewers, Hollywood musicals of the interwar years have lame plots and limp humour. But television had only just begun broadcasting in the mid-1930s and programmes of popular entertainment on BBC radio were few and far between. So almost anything on a cinema screen was considered witty, hilarious and highly amusing.

However, the dance scenes highlighted in those classic Hollywood musicals, usually choreographed by the legendary Hermes Pan, are still considered to be the finest expressions of dance ever recorded - never to be equalled again for pure elegance and grace. Even today, in dance academies around the world, those timeless arrangements are emulated step by step at graduation balls by aspiring young hoofers with the original film projected large on screens behind them.

Once in the auditorium Tom, Ronnie Briggs and their mate Mervyn Jones made straight for the front row and sank back into the sumptuously upholstered cinema seats and began to devour their pink polystyrene-tasting confections.

Soon, the lights dimmed and the Kingston scout brigade, along with an assorted collection of holidaymakers and local residents, were transported away to a glamorous make-believe world some three thousand miles to the west of Teignmouth.

Tom thought the jokes were hysterically funny, as did everyone else, but it was the dance scenes that held his attention most. He imagined himself in the role of Fred Astaire and of course Ginger Rogers was Kate to be whisked around the dance floor, never a foot out of step, with a degree of finesse that was flawless. And whenever he caught sight of a female dancer's legs it was always Kate's lithe sun-tanned limbs he imagined and which he just couldn't get out of his mind.

The evening of that first Thursday in August Tom wrote: 'It's really super here, we had sausage AND bacon for breakfast. This morning we did sports in the field and our team won the Relay and I came joint second in the Long Jump. Only saw Kate doing the High Jump over in the Guides' corner of the field, must have done well as she's got really nice long legs. This afternoon we went to see a super film called "Follow the Fleet" with Fred Astaire, Ginger Rogers and Randolph Scott. The Guides couldn't come. Wish I could dance like that, Kate would love it and the songs were super too, specially "Let's face the music and dance". Mervyn Jones said that in the final dance, if you look carefully you can just see the sleeve of Ginger's beaded dress hit Fred in the face but I couldn't see it. Real meat pies for tea this evening.'

What did Tom mean by 'real meat pies' Flo asked herself feeling slightly miffed? She used to give him mutton pies every week bought from the butchers just past the army barracks in King's Road. Weren't they 'real' enough? Then she remembered they were the cheapest thing you could buy in the shop and felt regret at her parsimony. But that's all she could afford at the time, thought Flo, not like now with Widows Benefit, Housing Benefit, Child Benefit and Supplementary Benefit. She noted the 'super' word was much in evidence again and what was she to make of Tom's comment about Kate's 'really nice long legs'?

There was no postcard for that day or the next. Still, she couldn't expect one every day: he was on holiday after all. Flo closed the plum coloured exercise book, she'd had enough excitement for one day. Better save something for tomorrow.

But Flo was up the next morning just after dawn. She couldn't wait to get at Tom's diary and see what new things she could learn about the short life of her only son. So after a boiled egg and toast, a strong cup of tea and a smoke, she sat at the kitchen table in front of the window and found her place in the exercise book.

On Friday 7th August 1936 a joint 'expedition' to Shaldon had been planned for all the Scouts and Guides camping at Mule's Field. They all had to walk with their own groups so there was no question of Tom walking with Kate but he could see the guides leading the crocodile down the main road into Teignmouth.

Shaldon is a small village of whitewashed houses and fishermen's cottages on the other side of the estuary to Teignmouth. You could reach it by ferry boat or go the longer way round on foot by crossing the long bridge that connects both towns. Naturally, the scouts did the gentlemanly thing and allowed the guides to take the ferry whilst they made the trek over the bridge.

They all joined up again on the estuary front at Shaldon and started off towards the first place of interest: the local Botanical Gardens were holding an open day for the public. By now the column was getting very ragged with the back of one group mingling with the front of the group behind. The Scout and Guide leaders saw it would be an impossible task keeping them apart so simply instructed everybody to follow the route and not wander off – and threatened that anyone caught misbehaving would be sent home on the first fast train to London.

Tom thought Shaldon a pretty village nestling as it did against the side of a cliff and he was surprised by how many shops there were selling meat pies and pasties. After cod and chips and his mum's beef stew Tom thought meat pies were the best kind of food in the world. He half thought of buying one but decided to save his money as he knew they all had a packed lunch waiting. Tom started up the short steep lane leading to the Homeyard Botanical Gardens and as he approached the gate he was pleased to see Kate waiting by the entrance.

'Tom!' she shouted: 'I've been waiting for you, hurry up. I want you to tell me all about that Hollywood musical you saw yesterday.'

'Oh, it was absolutely super, you've no idea!' exclaimed Tom elated by Kate's attention. He told her all about the fabulous art deco stage sets, the funny dialogue and the sensational songs and dancing. And especially the beginning of the "Let's face the music and dance" sequence in which Ginger's beaded sleeve hits Fred in the face by accident. Only the way he told it was as if he had spotted this legendary event when in fact only the sharpest of eyes can spot it.

'And they do the most amazing exit off the stage at the end of the dance – you have to see it to believe it.'

'Sounds marvellous, even better than "Dancing cheek to cheek" in "Top Hat",' said Kate. 'Perhaps when we're back to London you could come over and we'll go and see it together? If you don't mind seeing it twice, that is.'

Tom was delighted to think that she wanted to see him after the camp was over, he was dreading the thought of going home and no more Kate.

'No, of course I don't mind,' he replied and indeed he didn't, in fact Tom would have sat through that or any other film a dozen times if only Kate was keeping him company. They walked through the sub-tropical gardens deep in talk of dance and Ginger Roger's stunning dresses oblivious of the magnificent Banana and Ginger trees, Giant Echiums from the Canary Isles, the Australian Fern trees and the Himalayan Arisaemas. Though Kate did stop once to admire the stunning view across the estuary, across the town of Teignmouth and across Lyme Bay to the Golden Cap beyond.

Just then Ronnie Briggs and Mervyn Jones ran by and as they passed Mervyn turned and shouted to Kate: 'You want to watch him, Miss, he's got wandering hands!'

Ronnie and Mervyn thought this enormously funny and ran off up the pathway laughing.

'I'll get you for that!' Tom shouted after them while Kate just dismissed them with 'What silly boys.'

Before they entered the Smuggler's Tunnel that cuts through the headland to Ness Beach they stopped at a little tea house and bought a bottle of Tizer which they shared. The sun was nearing its zenith and the day quite warm, the climb up from the estuary had been thirsty work.

Tom also needed to buy a card for his mum and went over to the postcard carousel. 'I told her I'd send her one every day and I haven't sent one for two days,' Tom told Kate. 'Which one of these two do you like the best?'

'Send them both and make her day,' Kate answered. 'And get another one for me while you're there, I haven't sent any yet.'

Eventually they entered the long tunnel hewn through solid rock that led to Ness Beach. The temperature dropped suddenly and the walls were dripping with water that seeped down from above. It was also dark with only a few well spaced-out lights of low wattage. The voices of others further ahead echoed strangely against the walls in a distorted sort of way.

Half way through, Kate put her arm round Tom's waist and clung to him: 'Stay close, I don't like it in here, Tom. It's spooky!' she told him.

Tom was happy to oblige. 'Don't worry,' he told her: 'The ghost of Billy Bones hasn't been seen down here for years!'

'Tom!' she shouted digging him in the ribs. 'You're frightening me!'

He held her closer until they emerged into the bright sunshine. Everybody was wearing swimming costumes under their shorts and Tom and Kate entered the warm sea heated by the late-summer sun. They played the swimming under each other's legs game, had a splashing fight and tried to catch small fry with their hands in the shallow water and found it an impossible task. Then they lay perfectly still side by side on the firm red coloured sand.

'Why do you keep looking at my legs?' Kate asked him suddenly.

Tom had to think fast. 'I was comparing them with Ginger Rogers in that film,' he replied. 'And do you know, I think your legs are exactly like her's.'

'I hope you're right,' Kate replied lazily. 'I love dancing more than anything else in the world. I believe we're going to do some dancing next week before we leave.'

'You know what, Kate. With legs like yours, you could become a great dancer just like Ginger Rogers. In five years time you could be making films in Hollywood.'

Tom was learning that if you tell girls what they dream about you can't go far wrong.

'Do you think so? You do say the nicest things,' she answered softly.

Then suddenly: 'But you were horrible in the Tunnel telling me about Billy Bones' ghost.' So saying she scooped up a handful of wet sand and threw it over him which Tom returned.

'No throwing sand!' yelled an Assistant Guide Mistress who until then had been pre-occupied with the attentions of an Assistant Scout Master from Birmingham. 'It can get in your eyes and blind you! Anyway it's time for packed lunches. Everybody get back in your groups.'

That was the last of Kate's company Tom was to enjoy that day. After lunch the Guides played rounders among themselves and they were first to leave the beach when the time came to head back. Though as he passed the ferry stage at Shaldon he looked out into the estuary and saw the ferry boat half way across to Teignmouth. There was a girl standing up waving and he was almost sure it was Kate waving at him so he waved back.

The entry in the exercise book that served as his diary for Friday the 7th of August was full of adolescent joy. '**Terrific day today. We walked across this really long bridge to Shaldon and Kate waited for me specially at the gate to the botanic gardens. She wanted to know everything about the Ginger Rogers film I saw and I told her. I think she really must like me, I think she's very pretty but a bit bossy. We sat and drank Tizer because they didn't have Coca-Cola which she prefers and then we went through a long tunnel built by smugglers to bring barrels of brandy back from the beach. Kate got scared and clinged onto me which I didn't mind a bit. Lovely sandy beach where we went swimming together and caught tiny crabs as small as your thumb nail but we let them live. On the way back with the scouts the tide was out so some of us collected cockles in the estuary under the bridge. Mervyn Jones put them in a rusty old bucket he had found and said he was going to boil and eat them when he got back to camp. Mervyn had taken the micky out of me and Kate earlier on so when no one was looking I peed in his bucket. I'll tell him tomorrow.'**

Flo was shocked by what she read, not just by what she considered Tom's precocious interest in girls but by what he did to Mervyn Jone's cockles. She was discovering a side to him she had never known anything about before. She turned to the more comfortable expurgated version expressed on the next two postcards she had received all those years ago.

One postcard showed the Ness, the distinctive headland at the mouth of the Teign estuary. On the back Tom had written. '**Dear Mum, We went to Shaldon today and walked through a real smugglers tunnel to the beach where we went swimming. On the way back we collected cockles just like the ones they sell in Kingston Market. Love, Tom x.'**

'Not *exactly* like the ones they sell in Kingston Market,' Flo thought to herself. She really couldn't believe he would do such a thing to someone's cockles.

The other postcard showed some fishermen mending their crab pots on the beach at Shaldon. It read: **'Dear Mum, You'd really like it here. One day when I've got a good job and a car I'll bring you here for a holiday. Lots of places do bed and breakfast and the ice cream down here is really scrummy. Love, Tom xx.'**

That was more the message Flo wanted to read. Even when he was enjoying himself, and had made new friends with a girl, he was still thinking of her and wanted her to share in the pleasures. Of course, Flo had seen these places only a short while before on that lovely holiday with Vera and Frank. How much nicer if she'd enjoyed it just with Tom, no disrespect meant to anybody else of course.

A long excursion by coach was planned for the next day which was Saturday. The almost cloudless blue sky promised another warm one. All the scouts and guides were going so that meant taking all three charabancs. Their destination was Charmouth, well to the east, and the plan was to hunt for fossils on the beach which are frequently found there.

Mr. Davies, the Senior Scout Master, made it all sound very exciting.

'Some of these fossils are millions of years old and if you find a really good one you could sell it to a museum for hundreds of pounds.'

'Hundreds of pounds!' thought Tom. 'With hundreds of pounds I could buy a nice house like Kate lives in and in a year or two buy one of those MG sports cars so Kate and I could go driving round Devon and Cornwall and stay at all the posh hotels.'

The Kingston scouts were waiting for the coach door to open when the guides began to pass them heading for their own coach. Tom saw Kate approaching with her friend Lorna.

'Kate, where's your towel. Aren't you coming swimming?' he asked her.

She lent over as she passed and whispered: 'Can't today, time of the month.'

Lorna gave Tom a knowing smile. Tom didn't understand but said 'O.K.' anyway.

Ronnie Briggs was standing next to him. 'What's she mean "time of the month"?' Tom asked. 'Does she mean the tide's out?'

'Are you really dumb, Tom?' chortled Ronnie. 'It means she's having her period.'

'A period of what?' asked Tom.

'Don't you know anything, dimwit?' answered Ronnie sniggering.

'When girls are old enough to have babies they bleed from down there for a few days of every month. You know, where the babies come out.'

'Doesn't the bleeding make a mess?' asked Tom vaguely aware of hearing something along these lines.

'Blimey, Tom. It's obvious you don't have any sisters,' replied Ronnie.

'They use special towels…you know, down there.' And he pointed to 'down there' so there could be no mistake.

'They're called Jam Rags. You know, Red Sails on the Sunset. You really are thick!'

'Oh, I know what you mean, I'd just forgotten,' lied Tom trying to hide his ignorance. And then quickly to change the subject: 'Where's Mervyn, I'm going to see him about what he said yesterday?'

'He couldn't come,' replied Ronnie. 'He woke up sick this morning, he boiled up those cockles we collected yesterday when we got back to camp and I reckon one of them was off. Nothing worse than cockle poisoning, he could be in bed 'til we go home.

'They smelt really gross when he was cooking them, nobody else would touch 'em. But he had to, seeing how he'd lugged them all the way back in that rusty bucket.'

At that moment the coach door opened.

'Just as well I told you about Jam Rags, Tom. Or you might have put your hand up her skirt and got a nasty shock.'

So saying Ronnie ran up the steps chuckling and was first onto the coach.

Tom sat alone for the long drive to Charmouth. Mr. Davies as usual tried to make it interesting by pointing out geological features as they drove along. But what really stopped the Scouts from becoming bored was how the three coach drivers were racing each other to be the first to arrive. But even arterial roads like the A30 were no place to race charabancs in the 1930s and Mr. Davies had to have a word with the driver.

Finally they pulled into a large cinder surfaced car park a couple of minutes after the other two charabancs.

Down on the beach Mr. Davies told them what to look for. He produced one he had prepared earlier: a sea mollusc turned to stone more than a million years B.C.

'It doesn't look like a bit of a dinosaur to me,' remarked Ronnie.

'It's an ammonite, Briggs,' corrected Mr. Davies. 'Like a big winkle.'

'Is it worth hundreds of pounds?' asked Tom thinking of that shiny MG sports car.

'Not this one,' the Scoutmaster explained.

'Ammonites are collectable but quite common. The really valuable ones are the fossils of rare fish, preferably ones that have never been seen before.'

Then he went to the back of the coach to fetch four sets of hammers and protective eye goggles. While he was gone, Ronnie leaned over to Tom and said: 'Mr. Davies has got a big winkle!'

They were both still sniggering when Mr. Davies returned.

'The little metal hammer is to break open the stones to see if anything is inside. But you must wear the goggles or a splinter of stone could go into your eye and blind you.

'I've only got four sets of hammers between all of you so everybody uses one for five minutes and then hands it on to the next. You'll probably have to break open quite a lot of stones before you find one. I'll show you how.'

So saying, he took a fist sized stone and hit it sharply down the middle. The stone opened perfectly to reveal what looked like a tiny starfish. It was enough to whet their appetites and soon the beach at Charmouth reverberated to the frenzied tap-tap-tap of hammers cracking open rocks.

Tom found this so fascinating he almost forgot about Kate for the next hour and a half. It was his sixth five minute turn with the hammer when he made his great discovery. Others had found fossils of small ammonites and seaweed fronds but Tom's was the best of all – it was what looked like a fish with a snout about one-and-three-quarters of an inch long.

Scoutmaster Davies was called to examine the find.

'You look after that, lad,' he suggested. 'It could be worth something.'

Tom's mind was racing ahead: he remembered seeing lots of fossils on a school visit to the Natural History Museum at South Kensington. He would take it there when he got back and would probably get a thousand pounds for it at least. He was already trying to decide whether to buy an MG Sports Car in British Racing Green or Cream. Then he remembered that the previous year they had brought in the driving test which meant he wouldn't be able to take Kate for long drives right away.

Suddenly he heard a voice behind him that sent a tingle of delight through his whole body.

'Tom, they say you've found something interesting.'

He reached out to show his great discovery to Kate.

'What is it?' she asked in wonder, looking at it as if she had just been shown the Holy Grail.

'It's a Sharkosaurus,' replied Tom. 'When they were fully grown they were one hundred feet long and used to bite the heads off cavemen they caught swimming in the sea.'

'Yes and afterwards I suppose they had fruit-flavoured Jelly Fish for dessert,' answered Kate who was wising up to Tom's little wind-ups.

'Mr. Davies said it's probably worth a thousand pounds,' Tom boasted.

Kate was clearly impressed: 'Golly gosh, you are clever. You could buy two houses for that.'

Just then raucous shouts ordered everybody back to their groups for their packed lunches which everyone was delighted to discover consisted of yet another meat pie. Then they were ordered into the sea 'or your swimming trunks won't have time to dry before the coach journey back.'

Tom spent a lot of time splashing about doing an impression of a Sharkosaurus and then he had fun throwing wet seaweed at some of the younger girl guides with Ronnie until the Guide Mistress told him to grow up. Then he spotted Kate sitting alone with her chin on her knees on a low promontory of rock that jutted out to sea. So, slowly and as inconspicuously as possible, he disengaged from the motley of swimmers and joined her.

'Come to keep me company?' she greeted him. 'Sit next to me here.'

'No, I thought I saw a Sharkosaurus, didn't want to take any chances,' replied Tom.

'It's no fun being a girl sometimes, Tom,' Kate said with her chin still on her knees.

'Oh yes, I know what you mean,' he answered in a worldly way.

'But just think, if you didn't have periods you wouldn't be able to have babies and you wouldn't want that.'

Kate was a bit shocked at first by his forthright mention of the menstrual condition but then answered: 'Yes, I suppose so, Tom.'

Just then Lorna and Ronnie Briggs came clambering over the rocks and spoiled everything. But they discovered what great fun could be had with the bladderwrack seaweed that clung to the rocks. If you squeezed the bean-sized bladders until they burst, a squirt of water could be directed at someone up to six feet away, just like a water pistol.

So with this and other simple diversions, the foursome kept themselves amused on the beach until it was time to board the coaches. Who needed surfboards, inflatable dinghies or beach tennis to have fun when you had bladderwrack and flat skimming stones to play with?

Flo stroked her fingers softly across the entry in Tom's diary for Saturday August the 8th 1936 and began to read.

'We went fossil hunting at Charmouth Beach today and I found a prehistoric fish that Mr. Davies said might be worth a thousand pounds. If I can sell it I'm going to buy a real house for mum and me to live in and a cream colour MG.

Afterwards I went swimming but Kate couldn't come in the water because it was her period and she was wearing a Jam Rag. Had lots of fun sitting on the rocks with Kate, Ronnie and Kate's friend Lorna squirting each other with little balloons of water you can find in the seaweed.'

Flo really was discovering that reading other peoples' diaries can have unexpected consequences. She was pleased that Tom wanted to buy her a nice new house with the money from his fossil. But what did he mean by 'a real house for mum'? What wasn't 'real' about the home she had provided for him all his life? True, in those days it didn't have its own front door because they had to share that with the people down stairs. But he had had his own bedroom and there was a bathroom even though the bath had to be filled by boiling up large saucepans of water on the gas cooker in the kitchen when the Ascot heater wasn't working which was quite a lot of the time. Was he ashamed of where they lived?

Ashamed to bring this Kate girl back there! Most probably, that's what he meant. Flo certainly couldn't remember him bringing back a girl called Kate at that time. And what was she to make of Tom's reference to 'periods' and that taboo term 'Jam Rags'? She didn't even know he knew about things like that at his age, she'd certainly never told him.

Flo noted there was no postcard for that day.

The following day in 1936 was Sunday so all the scouts and guides trooped off again to the church half-way down the hill for the ten o'clock service. Then after an early lunch of corn beef, mashed potato and boiled carrots they headed off to the Promenade near the gate to the campsite. There they were all instructed that they were going on a hike to the inland picture-postcard village of Holcombe and it was important for everybody to keep up.

Tom was just approaching the point where the Promenade ends at Parsons Point and the path turns left into Smugglers Lane under a railway bridge beside a babbling brook. He heard a voice from behind him.

'Oi, Tom. I want a word with you,' said Mervyn Jones.

'I reckon me being ill yesterday was all your fault. I think you pissed in my cockle bucket when I had my back turned, you dirty dog!'

'Why would I do that?' asked Tom, clenching his fists ready for a fight.

'Because you didn't like what I said to your girlfriend, you know, Lady Lah-Di-Dah. Is she gonna have your love child, then?' Mervyn asked provocatively.

Tom saw red. He charged at Mervyn bringing him down on the ground. There they rolled in the dust pummelling each other until two older Senior Scouts ran over and pulled them apart. Tom had a small cut just above his left eye where Mervyn's finger-nail had caught him.

'Break it up!' one of them shouted: 'If Mr. Davies knew about this he'd send you both home on the next train.'

'I wouldn't travel on the same train as HIM!" shouted Mervyn who had to be restrained.

'Now listen!' said one of the Senior Scouts. 'I won't tell Mr. Davies about this on one condition. You apologise to each other and shake hands. Whatever started this you must end it now. Or you'll be on the bus for Newton Abbot Station first thing in the morning.'

It seemed to do the trick. Tom and Mervyn reluctantly shook hands, neither of them wanted to spend the next week back in Kingston when they could spend it down here in Devon. But they both kept their other hand hidden behind their back and crossed their fingers to negate the handshake of peace.

Tom was told to walk ahead and catch up with the others whilst they would follow on with Mervyn. After giving him his best death-ray look, Tom continued up the lane to the main road where some other scouts who knew the way were crossing.

About ten minutes later along the path to Holcombe, just as Tom was wondering how far in front Kate must be, he once again heard the familiar voice behind him.

'Tom!' she said: 'What's this I hear about you having a fight over something to do with me?'

News spread fast among the guides and scouts who loved nothing more than passing on gossip of some outrage or scandal just like any adults.

'It wasn't my fault, Kate,' Tom replied quickly. 'Mervyn Jones was saying rude things about you and I let him have it.'

'What did he say?' Kate demanded to know.

'He called you Lady Lah-Di-Dah and said you were going to have a baby.' Tom thought it better not to add that he was supposed to be the father.

'What a beastly boy!' Kate said with a passion, just as a crack of thunder sounded not too far away.

'I think we're going to have a shower,' she added and just then large spots of rain began to fall making a sudden pattering noise on the ground. They both ran for the shelter of a modest oak tree in full leaf and stood leaning against the trunk. Tom looked skyward and pointed out a patch of blue sky fast approaching.

'Enough to make a Dutchman a pair of trousers,' commented Kate.

Just then she noticed the slight gash above Tom's eye.

'Tom, you're bleeding!' she said sympathetically. 'Come here.' So saying she pulled out a small folded handkerchief from the pocket of her shorts, licked it with her spit and began to unhygienically wipe away the excess blood.

Tom suddenly became aware of the closeness of her face to his which gave him a strange but pleasant feeling.

Suddenly she paused and looked at him.

'Do you know, that's the first time any boy has been in a fight over me. I think you deserve a reward.'

Slowly she moved forwards until their lips engaged whilst holding him by the shoulders. He gently held her waist and became aware of her firm body beneath her blouse. Whilst this was going through his head, he began to feel the tip of her tongue probing into his mouth and he rubbed his tongue against her's for a few seconds. All too soon for Tom it was over.

Kate pulled back and said cheerfully: 'That was a French kiss, did you like it?'

Tongue-tied for the first time Tom could only smile his approval.

'Come on,' she said. 'It's stopping raining – we'd better catch up with the others before they scoff all the scones. "Stands the church clock at ten to three, and is there honey still for tea?"'

Tom looked at her nonplussed.

'Rupert Brooke,' Kate told him. 'Don't they teach poetry at your school?'

The sun came out and in the ten minutes it took for them to reach the scenic village of Holcombe, and join up with the other scouts and guides, the rain had evaporated from the rustic wooden benches and tables in the garden of the thatched tea house.

There was a sign offering two scones plus a portion of strawberry jam and clotted cream, and a small pot of tea, for a shilling. The lady who ran the tea house came to take their order and suggested they should have one large pot of tea instead of two small ones if they were together. Tom said 'Yes' and at the same time Kate said 'No' which didn't please Tom.

'Well I can see you're not married, m'dears, but as you're sitting together a big pot will be a lot easier,' said the lady in charge.

Tom had never had a proper cream tea before and thought the combination of scone, cream and strawberry jam tasted scrumptious.

'Mummy and I always have a cream tea in the cafeteria on the top floor of the new Peter Jones store in Sloane Square when we go shopping in town. Do you know it?' asked Kate.

'No,' replied Tom. 'But I went to Harrods once.' He didn't add that he and his mother had walked out after only ten minutes because everything was so expensive.

Kate returned to her favourite subject – dancing. She wanted to know more about the dances in 'Follow the Fleet' and said she was definitely going to see it when she got home. Then she said something that really did please Tom. She repeated her offer that he could come over to Crystal Palace where she lived if he wanted and they could see it together. She hadn't forgotten!

Of course, Tom said he wanted to see it again anyway as it was so good. When they had finished their cream tea she told him she had better rejoin the other guides or 'they'll all start to talk, you know what girls are like.'

Although he had lost her for the rest of the afternoon Tom felt a warm glow. She wanted to see him when the holiday was over, that was absolutely certain. And people were beginning to 'talk' about the two of them. He liked the thought of that.

Tom bought a postcard at the tiny Sub-Post Office and General Stores in Holcombe and then joined Ronnie Briggs for the hike back. Of course Ronnie wanted a blow by blow account of the fight with Mervyn Jones which Tom was happy to supply and embellish.

The entry in Tom's holiday diary for that second Sunday was rather long and left nothing to the imagination. Flo read about the fight and Kate giving him French kisses under a tree and how Kate had suggested they go to the pictures together over at Crystal Palace, where she lived, when they had returned home from the camp.

Of course, Flo thought things were going from bad to worse what with Tom getting into fights and having French kisses with this girl Kate. Even though Flo didn't quite know for sure what French kisses were, she was certain that her Tom was far too young for them and wondered what kind of girl Kate was.

Just then something clicked in Flo's brain and it was the mention of Crystal Palace that did it. She had a near photographic memory for anything to do with Tom and suddenly remembered the time she went through his personal effects, when they were returned to her just after his death, and finding the name 'Kate' and a Crystal Palace telephone number in his address book.

She remembered phoning up the mystery woman and informing her of Tom's death and how shocked and saddened the woman had seemed and how she had called Tom a 'sweet boy'. So, many years after he went to the scout camp Tom must have still been in touch with this Kate and Flo had known nothing about it.

But there was a lovely postcard showing thatch and whitewash cottages with flower gardens in front. On the back of it Tom had written: **'Dear Mum, Yesterday we went fossil hunting on a beach and I found one worth lots of money. We might even be able to afford a home like in the picture. Today went for a long country walk and had a cream tea. Best holiday ever! Love, Tom x'**

'Dear child!' thought Flo. 'Whatever else he gets up to, he never forgets me.'

For a moment, Flo had slipped back into a frame of mind that had her thinking and talking to herself as if her son was still alive.

The next day, Monday 10th of August, there would be no chance for Tom to see the person who, in his view, was rapidly morphing into a cross between movie maiden Dorothy Lamour and the Goddess Aphrodite. It had been arranged for all the Kingston Scouts to go boating in the sheltered confines of the Teign estuary – and they would be away all day.

They walked down to the harbour behind the town where five rowing boats had been hired. There were four Scouts to each boat to do the rowing and either the Scoutmaster or one of his Assistants or a Senior Scout to ensure discipline and that nobody drowned. They rowed round the Salty and the large sandbank in the centre of the harbour a couple of times to get the measure of the boats and then headed up river at a gentle pace.

It was quiet and peaceful once they had cleared Teignmouth with only the splosh-splosh of the oars and the occasional mewing of overhead gulls to be heard. Tom thought how nice it would be to row Kate up here for a picnic, just the two of them, but had to make do with the company of Ronnie Briggs, 'Spotty' Springer and 'Mad' Malcolm Mitchell. At one point they overtook the boat with Mervyn Jones in it that had foundered by going too close to the shore.

As they passed Tom shouted across: 'Good cockle country, Mervyn!' which wasn't appreciated. In fact, Mervyn had to be restrained by a Senior Scout for a gesture that did not involve using all of the fingers of one hand.

Despite the great void in his life that day, Tom was not entirely oblivious to the peaceful tranquility of his surroundings, as Flo discovered all those years later as she read the entry in the plum-covered exercise book: **'Went for a long row up the river, it was so quiet that if you shouted the sound bounced back off the rocks on the other side. We saw big fish underneath the boat the Senior Scout said was a salmon. Landed by the wreck of a wooden boat that 'Mad' Malcolm thought must be an old pirate ship. Explored it and dug around it for chests of treasure but didn't find any. Had a picnic lunch with a bottle of pop each. Going back was easier because of the currant** (sic) **so we hardly had to row.'**

It was so far so good for Flo, all good clean wholesome fun, but then it all went down hill fast: **'When we got back we were given fish and chips from a chip shop for our dinner as a treat. Delicious! 'Mad' Malcolm managed to buy a flagon of cider and a packet of Woodbines and some of us went in the bushes and had a drink and a smoke but Malcolm made us pay.'**

Flo always thought butter wouldn't melt in Tom's mouth and couldn't believe he'd go drinking cider and smoking cigarettes at his age. Still, she supposed it hadn't done him any harm: he was certainly a fine young man by the time he died.

The next day, another beachcombing contest had been planned for all three scout and guide companies. But this time the beach to be combed was the other side of the Exe estuary at Exmouth. The three charabancs set off with the Kingston Scouts' vehicle leaving last.

Once again driver rivalries surfaced as to who could get to Exmouth first. By the time they reached the Exe estuary Tom's charabanc had fallen way behind through getting stuck behind a horse-drawn hay cart on the Dawlish road. But the driver had an idea.

'We'll hitch a free lift on the Starcross ferry that will take us right across to Exmouth,' he announced. 'So long as my old mucker Mick is in charge of her today.'

As luck would have it 'old mucker Mick' was and so they did: the coach just about squeezed aboard the ferryboat and still left space for three waiting cars and a delivery van. This saved them the long detour north along the west shore of the estuary almost to Exeter and then the equally long drive south again to Exmouth. It was a good thirty minutes before the other two charabancs joined them at the end of the eastern esplanade near Orcombe Point. It was here, at the art deco teahouse built into the cliffside, that several decades later Tom's mother and Vera fell into conversation with the couple who told them how

Croydon had been sacrificed to Flying Bombs in World War Two.

Everybody gathered on the sands before the beachcombing began. Suddenly, Tom felt a poke in the ribs from behind and turned to find the adorable Kate standing there.

'Tom – how ever did your coach get here first? We were miles in front of you,' she asked in that ever so slightly upper middle-class voice that Tom found fascinating.

'Our coach has special air in its tyres,' Tom replied tongue in cheek. 'It can drive across water.'

Kate pondered this possibility but not for long.

'Look, the guides have got to stick together for the beachcombing,' she explained. 'But afterwards come and find me and we'll go swimming in the sea.' Tom readily agreed and was glad to hear that the red sails had disappeared into the sunset.

Once she had moved on, Ronnie Briggs who had been close by said to Tom: 'You're in there, mate, I tell you. She must really fancy you.' And then in a poor falsetto imitation of a girlish voice: 'Let's-go-swimming-in-the-sea-Tom-and-I'll-show-you-mine-if-you'll-show-me-yours.'

Tom didn't take offence, on the contrary he was encouraged to find someone confirming his wildest dreams that Kate fancied him.

'How are you and Lorna getting on?' Tom enquired.

'Nah, not really my type after all. So I've given her the Spanish Archer. You know, the El Bow!' Ronnie answered.

The beachcombing was relatively uneventful, Tom found a number of strange oval-shaped objects made of a soft white material that sort of looked prehistoric to him. But when the time came to compare finds it turned out three other people had found them too and they were only the backbones of dead cuttlefish.

'You won't get much for one of them,' Scoutmaster Davies commented.

'The most you could expect is a ha'penny each from someone with a budgerigar - they use them to sharpen their beaks.'

Straight after their packed lunch of a cheese and pickle sandwich Tom went looking for Kate. She was as good as her word and they changed out of their shorts and polo shirts down to their swimwear underneath and charged into the water. The sea was now as warm as it ever gets in Devon having been heated by the unrelenting summer sun for nearly three months. They splashed about and played the swimming through the legs game but soon tired of that.

'I know Tom, let's see if we can swim out to where you can't touch the bottom with your big toe,' Kate suggested. So out they went, further and further, probing the seabed with their toes until they could make contact no more. They turned and faced the shore, the voices of the other bathers were now muffled in the distance.

'Isn't it simply delightful, Tom?' declared Kate. 'To get away from all that noisome chatter for a few moments is pure Heaven.'

So they just floated there treading water, bobbing slightly up and down as the unformed waves rippled past them on their way towards the beach, creating a soft lapping sound as they gently broke against their bodies.

'How did you do in the beachcombing?' asked Kate breaking the quietude.

'I couldn't find anything except a broken sea gull egg that smelled utterly foul.'

Tom's imagination moved into overdrive.

'Well, I did find some strange white crumbly things that Mr. Davies said were the remains of a full grown Sharkosaurus…so they probably didn't die out round here and could still be lurking somewhere on the prowl for unsuspecting swimmers.'

A fixed look of horror appeared on Kate's face and she began to give little yelps of distress that grew louder and louder. Then she began to thrash her arms and legs about in all directions.

'I'm only joking, Kate!' yelled Tom growing concerned by her overreaction to his attempt at humour.

'No, for Heaven's sake! I've got cramp! In my right foot – it's agony and I can't move it!' came Kate's reply just as her head slipped completely below the water for a couple of seconds.

When she surfaced Miss Katharine Harrison felt real panic for the first time in her life and was rapidly losing control. Suddenly, everything he'd been taught for his Scout's Life Saving Badge at Wood Street Swimming Baths in Kingston came rushing back and Tom quickly took hold of her.

'Don't worry, Kate, I've got you! Just do as I say!' shouted Tom sounding as if he did this sort of thing every day. Gently but firmly he turned her on her back, so she was floating head up, with himself behind her and both his arms around her body.

'Just relax and keep your head up, I'll swim you back to the shore!' he added. Although Kate's right leg still thrashed around the rest of her complied and soon Tom's powerful leg strokes were pushing them both towards the beach.

As they moved slowly through the water, Tom became aware of the closeness of Kate's head resting on his right shoulder and even more so of the touch of her near naked body held firm in his tight embrace. It was a most pleasing sensation – but then recently emerged hormones began to pulse through his bloodstream and Tom felt a movement in the region of his swimming trunks that he could not ignore.

Then it was Tom's turn to panic as he realised that if he accidentally brushed against her, Kate was probably enough in the know to realise what was happening and would think him a vile and vulgar beast. Fortunately, the anxiety hormone that accompanied this thought provided the antidote and the danger passed.

As they reached shallow water Kate stood up, lent one arm against Tom to steady herself and began to massage the arch of her foot. They could see figures from further up the beach moving towards them and Kate said with slight irritation: 'I don't want any fuss, Tom! I do wish they hadn't seen.'

It turned out to be Lorna and the Guide Mistress both somewhat concerned but before they could speak Kate told them: 'It's alright, just a touch of cramp – nothing to worry about, Miss Carter!'

'You shouldn't have gone swimming so soon after eating,' the Guide Mistress berated Kate, expressing the received wisdom of the time. Then she added: 'And you know you shouldn't have gone out beyond your depth!'

'It was no problem, Miss,' Tom interceded trying to defend Kate.

'We could almost feel the bottom and I've got a badge in Life Saving.' Miss Carter gave him a dismissive look, he would receive no silver medal from her. Once they were safely on the beach the Guide Mistress left.

'Could you stay with Kate for a minute, Lorna, I'll go and get her a strong sweet tea. It's good for shock,' said Tom in a masterly way, recycling more learning from his course at Wood Street Baths. He was back in a few minutes with a well-sugared paper cup of Lipton's Yellow Label whereupon Lorna diplomatically departed.

Kate cradled the tea in her hands and sat upright on the sand with a towel over her shoulders. She stared up at Tom through wet tousled hair looking so vulnerable and desirable to his eyes.

'Oh, Tom, thank you so much!' she told him. 'You knew exactly what to do…I thought I was going under. I think I might have drowned if it wasn't for you.'

She gestured for him to sit next to her on the sand and gave him a mouthful of the sweet tea. Then after a few seconds she turned and pecked him on the cheek and told him: 'That's the least you deserve, and I don't care if Mervyn Jones does see. You really are my hero.'

The Tuesday August 10th entry in Tom's diary summed up the day's events thus: **'A really great day – we beat the other coaches to Exmuth** (sic) **by cadging a ride on the ferry. Didn't have much luck with the beachcombing but found lots of things budgies use to sharpen their beaks. Later I went swimming just with Kate right out to where our feet couldn't touch the bottom and Kate got the cramp. She almost drowned but I rescued her and swam her ashore. She said I saved her life. She must like me lots now.'**

Tom had no opportunity to buy a postcard for his mum in Exmouth. So instead he sent one he had bought before with the intention of sticking up in his bedroom when he got home. It was hand tinted and showed two Jaguar SS racing cars on the banked wall section of Brooklands Race Circuit. It read: **'Dear Mum, Went swimming at a different beach today. Water really warm and I saved someone from drowning. They keep giving us greens with our dinner. Love, Tom xx'**

That evening the scouts from Tom's bell tent finished the cider and cigarettes under cover of the blackthorn bushes on the edge of the field.

Wednesday the 11th. Of August was not a good day for Tom. For a start the Guides drove off after breakfast to visit an old peoples' home where they spent the day entertaining the residents with song and dance and taking them for woodland walks in Bath chairs. The Scouts went off for a day in Torquay in a trawler that the Scoutmaster had hired. Although advised to take a stroll along the seafront Princess Gardens with its famous promenade lined with Palm trees and visit the local museum, most of them spent the day in a pin-ball arcade and hanging out in a greasy-spoon café that charged ridiculous prices for flat pop and stale cake. Here they studied the female form in somebody's copy of 'Health and Efficiency': a nudist magazine that was read mostly by people who wore clothes.

On the way back Tom bucked up when reminded that that evening a Scout and Guide dance was being held at the campsite. But this event turned to disaster and deep disappointment as far as Tom's courting of Kate was concerned.

It was held on a piece of concrete hard standing where the coaches usually parked. Cream soda and some ersatz cola peculiar to the West Country were provided and the music was supplied by an electric gramophone with a three-valve amplifier powered by a wet battery that the Birmingham scouts had brought with them. As Mr. Davies, the Scoutmaster, was the 'DJ' to begin with the records selected were somewhat sedate consisting mostly of traditional waltzes and foxtrots.

Tom was filling a waxed paper cup with local yokel cola at the refreshments table when Kate spotted him.

'Tom!' she greeted him as usual. 'Someone has some dance band records – wait until this one's finished and you can dance with me if you like.'

'Would you like a cocktail while we're waiting?' Tom asked pouring her a mixture of cream soda and country bumpkin cola into another cup.

Just as they finished their drinks the tempo changed and the unmistakable sound of the Lew Stone Band playing 'Rip Tide' sung by Al Bowlly reverberated across the camp site.

Kate grabbed Tom and led him towards the dance floor where they joined about a dozen other scout and guide couples. Tom tried to lead Kate and avoid bumping into too many other dancers. But he soon began to realise that the few lessons he had received in the course of Music Classes at his school, and the few dances he had actually had at end-of-term parties, had left him ill-equipped to impress Kate. To his further discomfort he was only too aware that Kate was a great dance fan who attended classes regularly every week.

Tom did his best to keep up but there were several minor collisions, caused by him concentrating too much on his feet, and to make matters worse he even trod on Kate's toes at least twice. There was nothing for him to do but tough it out.

The next number 'Let yourself go' increased Tom's anxiety even further – he knew from the first couple of bars that it was going to be an even faster tempo because it featured in 'Follow the Fleet': the film he'd seen a few days previously.

'What's the matter, Tom?' asked Kate halfway through and no longer able to ignore his lack of finesse.

Tom waited until the end of the record before making some literally lame excuse about hurting his ankle during a game of football that afternoon.

'Poor you!' she sympathised leading him off the dance floor towards some wooden crates that served as seats.

'You sit there and recover, I'll fetch some more drinks,' Kate told him and disappeared. Tom's eyes followed her as she walked towards the refreshment table and joined the short queue. Then somehow out of nowhere some tall Rover Scout from Birmingham appeared and with a big smile on his face whispered something in Kate's ear. The movement of people to and fro obscured Tom's view for a few seconds but when he next caught sight of her he could see she was laughing.

Shortly after, she reappeared with Tom's drink.

'There you are, drink this,' she told him, as if it was some miracle medicine that would suddenly make him dance like Fred Astaire. 'Someone over there's asked me to dance and I can't say no. Perhaps we'll dance again when your foot's rested.'

Through the moving figures on the dance floor Tom watched the tall Birmingham scout dancing with Kate and it was obvious he knew his stuff. Not only did he have the confidence of someone who was no stranger to suburban dance halls but he could actually dance and make conversation at the same time. There was worse to come.

The next number the overheating electric gramophone belted out was Cab Calloway's 'Jitterbug Party' – an early cousin of Rock and Roll. This was about the fastest dance known to the civilised world before jive took over in World War Two. To Tom's deep disappointment, both Kate and the Birmingham scout took to the even faster rhythm like ducks to water and the smiles on their faces radiated pure enjoyment. He could see that Kate really excelled at this type of fast dance and knew all the moves.

Tom waited for Kate's return with half hope and half dread. He wanted her company but knew he would be hopelessly lost on the dance floor now the stakes were raised so high. But he needn't have worried, Kate never did return.

In between dances by the flickering light of the camp fire Tom could see her and a few of her guide friends talking with a group of the Birmingham scouts among whom her new dancing partner was always prominent. Several times he saw him put his head close to Kate's ear and say something that always made her laugh.

At least twice more Kate and the now hated Birmingham scout returned to the dance floor to further flaunt their dancing skills in his face. Tom, clutching his cream soda, retreated back to the edge of the undergrowth that fringed the campsite. His last view of her was the most painful of all. Birmingham scout had his arm round Kate and they weren't even dancing.

Tom hardly slept that night in the Bell tent, his mind constantly going over his cataclysmic rejection. How could she drop him for someone else after they had been such close friends? Why did she let him put his arm round her like that? How could she break her promise to return and simply ignore him? He was still asking himself these unanswerable questions when dawn began to show through the opening of the tent flap.

Tom entrusted the secrets of his heart to his plum coloured diary: **'Today we went to Torquay in a stinky old trawler boat and played pinball for a penny a game without the owner seeing us gamble. In the evening we had a dance and Kate danced with me twice but I was no good. So she went off and spent the rest of the time talking and dancing with some scout from Birmingham (where they talk funny) and I never saw her again. She really is a very unkind person and <u>I DON'T LIKE HER ANY MORE</u>!"**

But of course Tom did still like Miss Katharine Harrison from Crystal Palace, south London, as his continuing agonies the following day bore witness. To add to his misery, the Kingston scouts were going off on their own to visit a working farm. So no chance of seeing Kate and no chance for her to come and explain that it was all an awful mistake and she was really sorry and could they kiss and make up?

Kate was on Tom's mind every minute during the farm visit. What wouldn't he have given to get into H. G. Wells' Time Machine and go back just two days so it could all be the way it was. So whereas the other Scouts found some interest in nine piglets trying to suckle from one sow, and smutty amusement from watching the milk maids milking the cows by hand, Tom could only see Kate's brown hair, hear Kate's slightly posh voice and remember Kate's long sun-tanned legs. So much was the disappointment and stress of it all that evening that Tom couldn't stand the banal chatter of his fellow campers any longer. So he left the Bell tent just as dusk was stealing across the land and went and stood half-hidden on the edge of the trees and undergrowth at the top of the field: as far away as he could from everyone else.

He began wishing he was home, away from this place with all its painful reminders. He really missed his mum and wished he was home with her and she had just cooked his favourite Macaroni Cheese with bits of bacon in it the way she always made it for him.

Then something very strange happened to Tom. He saw two people enter the camp site by the gate near the short lane that led to the Promenade. One was a woman he didn't recognise but the other one looked just like his mum. He looked again and although they were about an hundred and fifty yards away he was almost sure it was her. Had his mum heard of his unhappiness and come to take him home? Of course not - how could she? But it certainly looked like her.

The two women were obviously nothing to do with the camp that was for sure. They slowly walked into the field looking around on either side and then after about twenty paces they turned and headed back through the gate. Just before they reached the gate, the one that Tom thought looked like his mum stopped and looked back for a few seconds. And in that moment Tom was as sure as he could ever be about anything that she was looking at him.

Tom's eyes scanned the field momentarily to see if any other of the scouts had spotted them. But when he looked back the two women were gone. He had only taken his eyes off the mystery visitors for a few seconds – it was odd that they had managed to reach the gate and disappear down the lane so quickly. At that point Tom left the shadows of the blackthorn bushes and ran as fast as his legs could carry him towards the gate. Although it meant running the entire length of the field it was slightly downhill so he covered the distance with the speed of a young gazelle. He ran like the wind through the partly open gate and looked up and down the short lane in hope of seeing his mum but to no avail.

Then although no one was supposed to leave the camp site, Tom ran down to the Promenade and looked left and right. Then down onto the beach itself, his eyes searching far into the distance. But the two women were nowhere to be seen. In fact, as most of the summer visitors were back at their hotels and guesthouses relaxing after their evening meals there was hardly anybody about save two dog walkers and a young couple strolling hand in hand.

Tom walked back to the Bell tent deep in thought, he just couldn't fathom it out. Maybe his brain was playing tricks on him. Perhaps it was someone who just looked like his mum. But if it was she looked uncannily like her.

Tom wondered whether it was worth continuing with his holiday diary. Something that had started with so much excitement had ended in a feeling of wretchedness beyond imagining. But as he had started it he thought he'd better continue:

For Thursday 12th August he wrote: **'We went to see a farm where we had to spend all day. Full of pigs lying in their own smelly stuff and cows that went to the toilet standing up. Ronnie Briggs says he's going to become a vegetabelarian. Can't wait to get home from this place. Something really strange happened later on, I was standing by the bushes at the top of the field and I thought I saw my mum and another lady enter the gate like they were looking for something. Just as they left the one who looked like my mum turned round and looked at me. I ran after them but they had gone.'**

Flo dropped the exercise book onto the table and gasped as she read those words some 35 years after they were written. Had it not been just a month or so ago that she and Vera had entered that very field where the camp had been held? And had she not been absolutely certain that she had seen her son standing in the shadow of the trees and undergrowth at the top of the field?

Immediately her mind went back to what the clairvoyant had told her all those years previously: that message from Tom telling her she would see him again both in this world and the next. It wasn't the first time either: she had seen him standing in the street outside her house the day she lost her job at Bentalls, she was sure of it. So why should she be so surprised - after all she had been warned years before it would happen? Flo remembered how she had thought that prophesy had been fulfilled when she answered the knock on her door and found Vera and someone she thought was Tom standing there. But of course it wasn't Tom it was Ray, his grown up son.

So this is what Tom had really meant when he sent her that message at the little Spiritualist Church in Kingston she had visited just the once with Connie. Flo's shock slowly began to turn to elation. Here was proof again beyond shadow of doubt that they would be together once more in the realm of spirit in the life to come. What joy and what relief!

Flo poured herself a fresh cup of tea and lit another cigarette. Vera had often told her she should stop smoking but Flo knew she never would. Flo breathed in the smoke like a New Age traveller enjoying his first burn for a month. Should she suppose that Tom had guided her hand to find this diary, she wondered? After all, here was the proof, if ever she really needed any, that he was with her still: his full and final passing so long delayed.

As she had always believed, her son wasn't really dead and beyond her reach.

This was something to celebrate, thought Flo. So she went to the kitchen cupboard and took down the bottle of Sherry left over from last Christmas. She poured herself a generous measure and knocked it back like a trooper. Her state of ecstacy was complete.

Tom was oblivious of all this future drama back on the aptly dated Friday the 13th of August 1936. It certainly wasn't going to be an ecstatic day for him. The Kingston scouts were given special leave to wonder round Teignmouth - ostensibly to spend what shillings they had left to buy gifts or holiday souvenirs for their parents. Tom was at a loss to know what to buy and anyway he had more important things on his mind. But in a little knick-knack shop he saw a number of tiny china milk jugs with 'Teignmouth' and a jolly sailor adorning their sides. He knew his mum had a few like this on a shelf with 'Littlehampton', 'Arundel' and 'Bognor Regis' imprinted on them. So he had no hesitation in forking out a shilling (five pence) for one.

That last night before they returned home all three of the scout and guide companies came together for a camp fire sing-song. Sufficient dead branches were gleaned from the surrounding woods to create a spectacular blaze and the last of the sausages were grilled beside the fire and handed round as a 'Banger in a Bun'. The word 'barbecue' still had a few decades to go before it crossed the Atlantic and passed into the everyday language of British suburbia.

Tom didn't feel much like singing and he sat round the camp fire just mouthing the words of the well-known scouting songs and sipping the West Country cola that tasted like sweet disinfectant. Due to its lack of popularity this was all that was left that last evening.

Then through the jumping flames of the camp fire he thought he caught a glimpse of Kate. Seconds later he saw her once more - yes it was her alright and, yes, that Birmingham scout was with her again. Tom felt a dull pain where his chest met his stomach. The tall scout was obviously turning on the charm and Kate was either smiling or laughing whenever Tom caught a peek of her. He felt an overwhelming wish for the Birmingham scout to stumble and fall into the fire and be instantly consumed in a roaring furnace of flames. Wouldn't that just serve him right? But even though he sometimes spotted Kate without him in attendance, a minute or so later he was back in the frame.

Tom's misery was now complete and he had quite had enough. He couldn't wait to get home tomorrow: perhaps when he was back in his familiar surroundings he would be able to forget this whole awful business. The last time he looked, Birmingham scout had one arm resting on Kate's shoulder, that was sufficient for Tom who emptied the last of the cola on the ground and went back to his Bell tent. He lay on his bed roll and listened to the chatter outside and watched the light of the camp fire dancing on the canvas walls of the tent.

He couldn't even summon up the enthusiasm to fill in the last entry in his diary. He was mentally exhausted and before the chatter had died completely he was fast asleep; but dreaming strange dreams about Kate being carried out to sea by a large strange fish with a face like the Birmingham scout and he being unable to reach her.

The Bell tents were struck right after breakfast the following morning and the scouts' cases and rucksacks loaded into the boot of the charabanc. Light drizzle was beginning to fall for the first time after two weeks of glorious sun and the scouts congregated around the vehicle's door waiting for it to open. Tom kept his face towards the coach in case Kate caught sight of him in his shame as a clumsy footed dancer and his degradation as a rejected sweetheart.

Just when he least expected it, Tom heard his name being called from behind.

'Tom! Tom! I looked everywhere for you last night before the singsong ended. Where on Earth were you hiding?'

'I was around,' replied Tom in emotional turmoil, his eyes gazing once again on the greatest gift that God had given mankind in general and one teenage boy from Kingston in particular.

'Look, I've written down our phone number,' continued Kate. 'I spoke to mummy yesterday from a call box and she told me that Ginger Rogers film you saw is showing locally soon. I really must see it – we'll go together as we planned...call me when you get back!'

In an instant, Tom was transported from the depths of misery and melancholia to the twin peaks of joy and jubilation. As he replied, there was more than a quaver of tension in his voice as his mouth had turned as dry as the Mojave Desert during a ten year drought.

'Yes, Kate, I'll call,' he warbled.

From the direction of one of the other charabancs he could hear a female voice calling: 'Harrison! Come back here now!'

'Must go Tom, they're calling me,' she said thrusting a scrap of paper into the palm of his hand and closing his fingers around it.

'Don't forget!' And with that she disappeared into the melee of jostling scouts and guides as suddenly as she had appeared.

Tom clambered aboard the charabanc and although he gained a window seat, and although he twisted his head from side to side as the vehicle struggled out of the field and onto the road, he could catch no glimpse of the guides' coach.

But that didn't matter now. Neither did it matter when the rain started pelting down like arrows at Agincourt by the time they reached the Dawlish road. Somehow he must have got it all wrong. She hadn't fancied that Birmingham scout after all – he now saw that he was the one she really wanted to know. Even if he couldn't dance!

Tom felt as if he had suddenly experienced the greatest epiphany since the scales fell from the eyes of St. Paul after his revelation on the road to Demascus. He unrolled the precious scrap of paper from his fist and read it.

"CRYstal Palace 2157."

By the time the coach had reached the A30 arterial road that phone number was etched indelibly into his brain for all time. And if some surgeon had chanced to open his chest he would have also found it engraved upon his heart.

Flo was waiting to meet the coach when it arrived at St. Luke's Church in Kingston. She whisked Tom home and listened to his news while she steamed a steak and kidney pudding she had prepared that morning. But she noticed that Tom didn't want to go into too much detail about what he did on holiday. He was probably just tired, she decided. After dinner, Tom gave her the little Teignmouth jug to add to her collection and she was delighted.

That evening Tom made the last entry in his Scout Camp Diary with the plum coloured cover. On Saturday 14th August 1936 he wrote: **'That girl Kate Harrison does like me after all. Just as the coaches were about to leave camp she came and found me special and gave me her phone number CRYstal Palace 2157 so I could see her when we get back.'**

The next morning Flo gave Tom some good news.

Tom had finished school that summer and was still waiting for the results of his Matriculation, the equivalent of GCSE Ordinary Level in those far off days. His plan was to try to get a job as a trainee car mechanic in one of the big garages that served the growing number of Kingston motorists.

As luck would have it, a friendly neighbour of Flo's worked as the Day Book Ledger Clerk in the Accounts Department of Kingston Hill Motors. She had come round to see Flo specially a few days before to say that a vacancy was coming up for a Junior Trainee Mechanic and thought it might suit Tom.

When Tom heard the news he was really excited. Although the Great Depression was over by 1936, good jobs were still hard to come by. So he phoned the number that the kindly neighbour had given first thing Monday morning and an interview was arranged for the very next day.

The man who ran Kingston Hill Motors, Mr. Nichols, was a dignitary of the local branch of the Labour Party and was one of those early socialists motivated by the unrelenting desire to improve the lot of his fellow man. The neighbour had told him a little of Tom's background. She believed his father had died years ago and he and his mother had struggled but they were good honest, decent folk who weren't afraid of hard work.

Tom's initial nervousness soon receded once he met Mr. Nichols. The first question he was asked was why he wanted to become a mechanic? Why did he think he was right for the job?

Tom answered truthfully that he liked taking things apart and then putting them together again. He had done this twice with his bicycle 'and it still worked!' He was also able to show the results of his Matriculation that by another stroke of luck had arrived by post that very morning and he had passed in all subjects except Geography.

Mr. Nichols took a liking to Tom. Or maybe he just felt he deserved a break because of his deprived background? Either way, he offered him the job, starting the following Monday on a month's probation.

The hours were 8.30a.m. to 5.30p.m. Monday to Friday and he would be paid two pounds five shillings (£2-25 pence) a week to begin with and was required to work every other Saturday morning for which he would receive an extra five shillings (25 pence). He would be entitled to one whole week's paid holiday a year plus Bank Holidays and if he was still there in three months time would be expected to join the Transport and General Workers' Union and pay subs of half a crown (12½ pence) monthly.

Tom ran all the way home afterwards to tell his mum who was just as excited as he was.

'He told me I'd have to be the 'oily rag' to start with - fetching tools, making the tea and washing and polishing cars for sale in the showroom. But I don't mind.' He offered to give Flo all of his wages but she insisted that a pound a week would be enough and he could keep the rest. Although she didn't say it, an extra pound a week coming in was going to make a big difference to her unending struggle to make ends meet.

That afternoon Tom only had one thing on his mind – CRYstal Palace 2157. He went to one of the public phone boxes at the top of his road near the East Surreys' Barracks with a collection of coppers and threepenny bits and dialled Kate's number. A woman answered with an even posher voice than Kate and Tom knew he had to watch his P's and Q's.

'Hello, my name's Tom. I'm a friend of Kate's. Could I speak to her, please?'

The woman said nothing to him in reply but he heard her say: 'Katharine, there's someone called Thomas on the phone asking for you.' Tom thought it rather strange for her to refer to him as Thomas but didn't dwell on it.

'Tom! You've called. How nice!' said Kate. After a few minutes small talk they arranged to go and see a matinee performance of the film 'Follow the Fleet' together. They would meet outside the Granada Crystal Palace at 2.30p.m. next Thursday - Kate explained exactly where it was.

'Are you sure you don't mind seeing it a second time? Are you quite sure you don't mind coming all the way over to Crystal Palace?' Kate enquired. As far as Tom was concerned he wouldn't mind seeing it again fifty times and would travel all the way to Ulam Bator in Outer Mongolia for the privilege if it meant seeing Kate.

Then he told her about his new job, only somehow in the telling 'Trainee Motor Mechanic and car cleaner' changed into

'Automotive Engineer with special duties for car sales'. Kate seemed suitably impressed.

'Golly, you didn't take long! Sounds super!' she exclaimed.

Once the phone call was finished, Tom went straight to Kingston Bus Depot and asked about buses to Crystal Palace. There was a Greenline coach route that went there all the way from Kingston without having to change.

After that, he crossed the road to the Empire Theatre and enquired about dance classes. Yes, he was told, a new class was starting in early September every Saturday afternoon from 3p.m. to 4.30pm.

'Only two bob a week to learn to dance even better than that Birmingham scout,' thought Tom. 'It's a bargain.' He paid his two shillings (ten pence) in advance for the first week to reserve himself a place.

When the big day arrived Tom told his mother he was going to see a new friend he had made at Scout Camp and caught the Greenline coach just after 12.20pm. What with the fares, the price of admission to the cinema and an ice cream sundae afterwards he was going to need that new job the rate he was spending money. It was just as well there were a few shillings left over from his holiday money.

But Tom had never looked forward to anything more in his life and there was a tingle in the pit of his stomach that was half apprehension and half anticipation of a wonderful time to come. He kept checking his wrist watch but the little Greenline coach made good time. Soon Tom could see the shining canopy of the Crystal Palace itself looming into view unaware, as everyone else was, that in little over three months time it would be completely gutted by fire.

Tom got off the coach and headed towards the Granada only stopping on the way to buy a bar of Cadbury's chocolate from a dispensing machine, which he knew from experience would cost half as much again at the cinema kiosk.

For a moment, Tom stood on the opposite side of the road and surveyed the slightly art deco exterior of the Granada with its wide multi-door entrance and huge posters. On these were displayed the images of Astaire dancing in a sailor's suit and Ginger Rogers in a satin trouser suit complete with nautical cap singing into a microphone. A huge banner read '**For two weeks only – FOLLOW THE FLEET – Music & Lyrics by Irving Berlin**'. There was no doubt it was the right place and looking at his watch Tom saw it was ten minutes past two – he was twenty minutes early. He scoured the entrance looking for Kate but it was expecting too much for her to be there so soon. He crossed the road and waited beside the entrance.

Things were fairly quiet to begin with but as it got nearer to 2.30pm people started to enter the cinema in increasing numbers. Tom kept looking left and right up the road - which way would Kate come from, he wondered?

The hands on his watch read 2.30p.m. precisely and Tom checked it against the clock in the cinema foyer which showed exactly the same time. Any minute now she should be here, he told himself.

Over the next ten or fifteen minutes people were entering the cinema in droves: Thursday afternoon was half-day closing for most shops in that neighbourhood so a lot of people were free to go to the movies. But so far there was no sign of Kate.

Once it reached about ten minutes to three fewer people entered and by three it was just the occasional person. Wherever was she, Tom began to wonder? Once they had shown the Pathe News, a few adverts and the trailers for coming attractions the film itself would start. At five minutes past three Tom went inside the cinema, just in case Kate had been waiting for him there all along. But she wasn't. He noticed that 'Follow the Fleet' was listed at the Box Office as starting at 3.15pm - if she didn't hurry they would miss the beginning.

But 3.15pm arrived without Kate's presence, he had been waiting for over an hour but of course he had got there early. Nobody was entering the cinema now: he was alone on the steps of the Granada. Then the idea struck him that Kate may have got the time wrong and thought they were meeting at 3.30 not 2.30pm. Tom looked in the foyer once again just in case she had entered without them seeing each other but it was quite deserted. Just as he was looking inside, the doors to the auditorium opened as someone went to buy something at the confectionery kiosk and for a few moments Tom could hear the soundtrack of Fred Astaire singing the introductory song 'We saw the sea'.

Then 3.30pm came and went and Tom began to face his worse fears. He couldn't believe that he had been stood up by Kate – she was too nice a girl for that. But by twenty to four Tom knew for sure she wasn't coming. After one good look up the road both ways, he began to walk back to the Greenline bus stop. To begin with he started inventing excuses for her. Perhaps she had been taken sick or something important and unavoidable had cropped up. After all, there was no way she could have got a message to him as they didn't have a phone at his house. But before long darker explanations began to come to mind.

Maybe she didn't really want to see him again after all but just couldn't be bothered to tell him? Perhaps she thought so little of him she had been distracted by something else and had clean forgotten? Or the darkest thought of all - that Birmingham Scout had bought a cheap day return ticket to London and they were both doing that thing with their tongues on a sofa in her house even at this minute.

Tom seethed with jealousy and disappointment. But why had she given him her phone number and told him to ring her while they were waiting to board the charabancs? Most likely she was just stringing him along.

On the Greenline coach all the way home Tom felt as wretched and hurt as he had been the evening of the dance at the Camp when Kate had left him for the Birmingham Scout. But once he arrived home he put a brave face on it so as not to upset his mum - even though he could think of nothing else but Kate for days.

But come the Monday and Tom had his new job as a Junior Trainee Mechanic to occupy him and he entered the exciting world of tappits, decokes and timing chains.

The truth of the matter was a lot simpler than he imagined. Tom and Kate had in fact fallen foul of an idiosyncrasy of the English language whereby when some people say 'next Thursday' they mean the Thursday of next week - whereas to other people 'next Thursday' is the Thursday just coming.

This quirk of the spoken word has much to answer for: it has blighted the course of countless budding romances without either side ever knowing.

Though Tom would never have guessed it then, there would be a sequel to his first bittersweet taste of infatuation that came some six years later. And his mother would know nothing about it until the day she died.

It was the cusp of summer and autumn 1942. Tom was in the Army and returning to his unit in Selsey after four days leave in London. He always liked to allow plenty of time for train journeys, you had to in wartime, but when he checked at Victoria Station he found he had over an hour and a half to kill before his train departed.

There was a News Theatre on the Buckingham Palace Road side of the Station so he paid the special armed forces ticket price of sixpence (2 ½ p.) and went inside. At least he could be sure of a comfortable seat. It was all war, war, war – war news from North Africa, war news from the Russian Front, war news about hunting U-boats in the Atlantic and a number of propaganda shorts from the Ministry of Information on the importance of growing vegetables and saving left-over food for pig swill. As if anybody had any food left over these days.

After a while Tom began to get restless and felt the first pangs of hunger. There was no guarantee of a meal in Selsey when he got there, so he decided to stroll over to one of those Armed Forces Canteens that sprang up on large railway station concourses to provide snacks and refreshments for the thousands of servicemen and women who passed through them every day. He had no difficulty locating one manned by two young women from the Women's Voluntary Service.

It wasn't busy so he walked right up to the counter and ordered a tea with four sugars and quipped: 'And I wouldn't say no to a beefsteak sandwich too. Rather on the rare side please, Miss!'

Back came the reply: 'You'll have a spam sandwich like everyone else and like it. With or without mustard?'

While engaging in this light banter, Tom noticed from the corner of his eye that the other young woman who was pouring his tea at the back gave him a couple of furtive glances.

Tom took his door-step sandwich and turned to take his tea when he came eye to eye with…well, he wasn't entirely sure who. There was something familiar about the hazel eyes and permed brown hair that were even now advancing towards him.

'You did say four sugars, didn't you?' the slightly posh young woman asked and at the sound of her voice the penny began its short descent.

'Thank you,' he replied with a smile.

'I know you don't I…some time back?' she enquired: her tired mind, dulled by lack of sleep after three years of war, was grappling with a dozen different faces trying to place his.

'That's it, the Scout and Guide Camp down in Devon before the War. Aren't you Tom?'

Tom stood back and feigned an accusing glance.

'I remember you alright! You stood me up on my very first date.' And he tut-tutted twice in a teasing manner.

'I stood *you* up?' she replied indignantly. 'You were the No Show, if I'm not very much mistaken! I remember waiting an hour in pouring rain for you to turn up - and left cursing your name all the way home.'

Something registered in Tom's subconscious that it hadn't been raining the afternoon he waited for her outside the Granada Crystal Palace all those years ago. Clearly some sort of confusion with the days had thwarted their youthful encounter.

'I turned up alright,' replied Tom with a smirk. 'Left me broken hearted, you did. In fact, I've only just recovered!' And he patted himself twice on the left side of his chest.

He could jest about it now but it had certainly been no joke at the time.

Her laugh seemed to bridge time and distance. It was no longer a dull wartime afternoon in early autumn: Tom could feel the warmth of a far off summer's day with the sun on his back, a gentle breeze drifting in off the sea and waves breaking on a stony shore.

The other tea lady had had enough.

'Look, it's nearly time for your cigarette break, Kate. We're none too busy - why don't you continue your unrequited romance over there,' and she pointed to a nearby row of benches.

As they walked across the concourse to the seats Kate spoke first.

'You used to make me laugh. I remember you telling me that the Jelly Fish came in five different fruit flavours. Do you know that from that day to this whenever I see a fruit jelly I think of those awful slimy creatures.'

'But they are fruit flavoured,' Tom insisted. 'I wasn't kidding. Don't say you've never tried one?'

They sat down on the bench and found themselves sharing Tom's cup of tea. He offered her a cigarette from a pack of twenty.

'Player's Navy Cut?' she commented. 'Some people would kill for these what with all the shortages these days. Wherever did you get them?'

'It's true I had to shoot the tobacconist but he had it coming,' replied Tom. They both laughed. 'No - twenty for a tanner in the NAAFI store. Only good thing about the Army.'

'You know, you've changed,' she said suddenly.

'You reckon?' answered Tom and he looked her full in the face.

'Yes, you're a lot more sure of yourself, I can tell. Not that half-shy boy with the cocker spaniel eyes who I taught to kiss under a tree in a shower. How old were you then, about fifteen?' She looked at him to see if he was embarrassed by her words.

But he wasn't.

'We've all changed, Kate, grown up fast. We've had to. This war has changed all our lives forever.'

'You're right there,' she replied. 'If it wasn't for this bloody war I'd have my own dancing school by now with a service flat of my own and a little car to run about in. And two holidays a year in France.'

'In Deauville,' suggested Tom.

'You remembered!' replied Kate with genuine surprise.

'I'd have thought you'd be married by now,' probed Tom noticing the lack of a ring on her finger.

'Had a few offers but they were all duds. How about you?'

'No. I think those duds all had sisters and I've been dating them one after the other for the past few years,' replied Tom. They both laughed again.

Suddenly she stood up and trod on the butt of her cigarette.

'Must get back now, can't let Veronica hold the fort forever. Look, when you're next on leave why don't you phone me? I'm still with mummy and daddy down at Crystal Palace, give me a ring in the evening.'

She scrabbled in her handbag for a pencil and scrap of paper to write her phone number on.

'CRYstal Palace 2157,' he said beating her to it.

'Good Heavens!' replied Kate with amazement. 'What a memory you have.'

'We might even get to see that Fred Astaire and Ginger Rogers film at last. Or go listen to Al Bowlly sing at the Lyceum?' Tom suggested.

'No, it's Fred Astaire and Eleanor Powell that are all the rage now- in "Broadway Melody of 1940". And Al Bowlly died in the blitz over a year ago.'

'Did he really? I didn't know,' answered Tom in that matter-of-fact manner people did when they heard almost every day of someone dying in an air raid or on convoy duty to Russia or fighting Rommel in North Africa.

Kate pushed the scrap of paper with her telephone number into Tom's hand. Despite his incredible memory she wanted to make absolutely sure he didn't forget it. As she walked away from him back towards the canteen, Tom noticed the lower half of those long slender legs that had given him sleepless nights so many years ago. Then he folded the piece of paper and put it in his wallet, pulled the squashed Spam sandwich wrapped in a serviette from his tunic pocket and began to eat it slowly. So long as there wasn't a raid later he'd be back in Selsey well before midnight and in the arms of heavenly Vera with her long blonde hair (that didn't come out of a peroxide bottle) and her eyes of blue.

About a fortnight later Tom managed to wangle another long weekend pass for a spot of leave. He rang Kate's number well in advance from the coin box in Selsey High Street and the local telephone exchange managed to put him through at the seventh attempt. Phone services were chaotic in wartime – the bombs played havoc with the lines and long-distance calls were worst of all. But they managed to understand each other enough to arrange to meet the following Saturday at Charing Cross Station at four in the afternoon. Under the clock of course.

The moment couldn't come too soon for Tom who felt long forgotten passions beginning to awaken. He spotted her straight away as she exited the ticket barrier: she was wearing a floral pattern frock and a smart knitted jacket, with a matching belt and large patch pockets, that went down to below her hips. Tom could tell they weren't wartime utility issue bought with clothing coupons, she'd clearly made an effort and was wearing her pre-War best. He had on his favourite grey double-breasted suit and a silk tie.

'So you decided not to stand me up this time,' said Tom as they met. She swiped him on the arm with the back of her hand.

'I still haven't forgiven *you* for that!' she chided.

'"Broadway Melody" is playing at the Odeon Leicester Square, what do you say?' he asked.

'Look Tom, I know we said we'd go to the pictures but I'd prefer to go dancing, wouldn't you? Joe Loss and his Orchestra are playing at the Astoria in Charing Cross Road this evening. If we arrive early we're sure to get in.'

'I'd rather dance with you than watch Fred Astaire dance with Eleanor Powell,' replied Tom. It was the right answer - she smiled.

As they walked towards the Station exit Tom warned her. 'You and your dancing, you think you're going to make a monkey out of me on the dance floor, don't you? Well you could be in for a shock. Didn't you see my fancy footwork when I stood in for Fred Astaire in "Flying Down to Rio"?'

'You'd have been twelve years old at the time if you did,' answered Kate.

They decided to go for a bite to eat first. 'There's a Lyons Tea House opposite, they do a stunning Welsh Rarebit,' suggested Tom.

'Cheese on toast? You really know how to spoil a girl, don't you Tom,' Kate teased.

An hour or so later they were among the first dozen couples waiting for the doors to open at the Astoria Dance Salon and they had no trouble getting in. They went straight to the bar to get a drink before the booze ran out.

'Well, it's bottled beer or a fruit punch of dubious provenance?' Tom offered. He was glad she chose the India Pale Ale rather than the other sickly brew.

They found a table and both lit a cigarette. In the background the Joe Loss Orchestra was playing 'Begin the Beguine' without vocal refrain.

'You didn't mind coming here, did you Tom?' she asked. 'When you go out with someone new you don't want to just sit there in the dark in silence staring at the screen. You should talk and have fun! None of us know what's going to happen tomorrow. Do you know, some German Dornier bomber crashed just outside Victoria Station last week about five minutes after I'd crossed the road to collect a quart of milk!'

'Bloody glad you made it, Kate,' answered Tom being serious for the first time. He touched the back of her hand with his fingertips which didn't go unnoticed.

Eventually a singer began to accompany the orchestra.

'Drink up, Sweetness, they're playing our tune,' Tom said suddenly. He grabbed her hand to make sure he wouldn't lose her in the crowd and led her to the octagonal dance floor. It was a slow waltz, Tom slipped his arm firmly around her and became conscious of her body through the thin dress.

Kate was quite tall but she was still a good six inches shorter than Tom. He looked down at her and saw a flicker of self-consciousness on her face. She had felt the moment of close bodily contact too.

'Do you know how lucky we are?' he asked her. 'Do you know who that is singing? That's *the* Chick Henderson and he's singing "Begin the Beguine".'

'Yes I know Tom, it's beautiful,' replied Kate.

'But did you know his record has sold a million copies! Just think of it, a *million*! And now he's singing it in person just for us.'

Kate smiled and all shadow of awkwardness passed. Slowly they circled round the crowded dance floor, the occasional flash from the glitter-ball catching their faces. And in the background the strong, melodious voice of Chick Henderson belted out what is perhaps Cole Porter's most romantic number – the singer unaware that within two years he also would follow his friend Al Bowlly to a wartime grave.

The next song let the more daring dancers really flaunt their prancing skills. It was a faster number: the words of which had special meaning for all present that evening when wailing sirens could bring finality at any time.

Chick stepped forward to the microphone and began to sing:

We'll live a whole lifetime
In one lovely weekend.
We can't wait for Heaven
Or what fate may send.
So meet me at seven,
Now is the hour for love!

Some of the dancers left the floor, less comfortable with the livelier rhythm. Those that remained had more space and were determined to do it justice.

As someone who took dance seriously and practiced twice a week, Kate knew she could handle it. But what about Tom, she wondered? For all his bravado was he capable of anything more than a common or garden slow-slow-quick-quick-slow? He was an unknown quantity, this would be his defining moment.

Round and round the Astoria's eight-sided dance floor they went, whirling and twirling, posing and posturing, more like ballet than ballroom dancers, until there were only six or seven couples left and all the others were watching.

Tom and Kate were among the survivors. Kate was surprised he was keeping up, never missing a step, no matter how far she pushed the envelope. For Tom, all those Saturday evenings spent at Wimbledon Palais, Streatham Locarno and Hammersmith Palais were paying off.

Finally the music came to an end and everybody applauded – Kate was in her element. As they left the dance floor she slapped his arm with the back of her hand and told him: 'Hey, you didn't tell me you could dance, feller!'

'One of us had to,' replied Tom. This time Kate whacked him harder.

'Just remember, Ginger Rogers did everything Fred Astaire did - only backwards and in high heels!' said Kate.

They found a small table and Tom ordered a bottle of sham Champagne. They each lit another cigarette and the smoke drifted up to join the thin haze that hung over the Orchestra and ballroom.

'That was quite something, my lady,' said Tom. 'You weren't joking when you said you could run a dancing school.'

'*Own* a dancing school,' corrected Kate. 'There's a difference. What are you going to do when this damn war is over?'

'I'm going to own a garage servicing cars,' answered Tom.

'You can service my car any time,' she replied coolly. The possible innuendo wasn't lost on him. Was she propositioning him, Tom wondered?

'It would receive my earnest personal attention,' he replied giving it his most seductive Clark Gable impression.

They returned to the dance floor many times, got through at least two more bottles of sham Champagne and flirted outrageously. Their last number was 'Let's Dance at the Make-Believe Ballroom' – another big Joe Loss and Chick Henderson hit.

'Is this ballroom make-believe too?' Tom whispered in her ear as they slowly rotated round the wooden sprung dance floor. 'Are you really here with me?'

'In the flesh, my dear,' answered Kate. 'Are you enjoying it?'

'You've no idea...' he replied and kissed her firmly on the mouth. She responded in kind. Tom put his right hand behind her head to press her closer, just as she had done to him on that first kiss on the beach in Devon the year King Edward abdicated.

Even in the relaxed and carefree context of wartime, long clinches on the ballroom floor were not customary or expected at the Astoria Dance Salon, Charing Cross Road. Other dancers began to give them a bit of space and somebody blew a loud wolf whistle. A few friendly but ribald comments of encouragement were shouted and people began to cheer them on.

But Tom and Kate were lost for a moment in their own private passion and continued their tender attentions until the cheering could be ignored no longer. They left the dance floor smiling sheepishly to a round of applause.

It was getting late and time to leave - after all who really wants to stay for the clichéd last dance of 'Goodnight Sweetheart'? It was simply too non-U.

They stepped out onto the pavement and both welcomed the rush of fresh air but saw nothing incongruous in immediately lighting up another Capstan Full Strength cigarette. There was no brand loyalty in wartime, you smoked whatever you could get.

No searchlights pierced the sky that night and no ack-ack banged away in the distance.

'Looks like the bastards will be late tonight,' said Tom noticing the unbroken cloud that heavy bombers hate.

'Or possibly won't come at all,' Kate hoped.

They continued walking arm-in-arm down Charing Cross Road towards the Station in silence. Tom gave Kate a sideward glance, she seemed deep in thought. Suddenly she stopped and turned on her heels to face him.

'Look Tom, would you think me an awful tart if I suggested we book into the Strand Palace Hotel for the night? People are doing it all the time, the desk clerks don't care. You see, it's this bloody war, I've had enough of it. You meet some nice boy and before you know it he's…he's shipped off to Egypt or something worse.

'Every morning that I catch that bloody train from Crystal Palace I ask myself, will it be the last time? Who knows when the next tip and run raider will strike? Did I tell you my older brother's hunting U-boats in the Atlantic and…and I've had enough of "Keep your chin up and carry on as normal"…' She began to sob.

Tom put his strong arms around her and guided her into the privacy of a nearby doorway.

'Hush now, sweet lady, you've nothing to fear,' he said as he cradled her to his chest. 'Nothing's going to happen, *nothing* I tell you. You're far too good-looking to die.' And after a second's pause he added: 'And so am I.'

He leaned back to look at her and they both laughed at his pretended lack of modesty and Kate's shadows passed.

'Sorry Tom,' she said as they continued to walk arm in arm. 'It's nothing really but after a while it all begins to get a girl down.'

'Did you mean it about the Strand Palace Hotel?' he asked.

She turned to look at him again. 'I've never meant anything more in my life.' So saying she stroked his cheek with her fingers and looked to his eyes for their answer.

'You would make me the richest man in England because for one night I would possess its greatest treasure,' he whispered.

'That's the loveliest thing anybody has ever said to me, Tom.

'What were the words of that song? "We can't wait for Heaven or what fate may send..."'

They walked on faster down the road towards the Strand.

'Do you have anything?' she asked him eventually.

'No, I hate those things,' replied Tom.

'So do I - and I don't give a damn what happens. I'll face that if it comes,' she added.

'I'll make sure it's alright. Just a matter of timing, just like in dancing,' he said.

'You look after your women then,' she replied with a smile.

The elderly desk clerk at the Strand Palace Hotel looked at the guest book and took a sharp intake of breath.

'I don't know, sir, we had a large party of American Officers book in for the night earlier. I've got a nice single room with its own bathroom at the back of the hotel, away from the noise of the traffic, but that's all.'

'We'll take it!' Kate interrupted almost snatching the key and heading towards the lift.

'Room 501. That'll be one pound five shillings in all, including the breakfast,' said the desk clerk. 'Seeing how it's only a single really.'

Tom gave him thirty shillings and told him to keep the change. As he finished filling in the guest book the old man looked at the entry.

'Thank you sir, I hope you and…er..Mrs. Harman have a comfortable night.'

The room wasn't bad for wartime Britain and the bath turned out to be the rare luxury of a shower. There was a stool and a little dressing table with a jug of water and two glasses standing on it.

Kate kicked off her shoes and flopped onto the bed as if exhausted. Tom loosened his tie and stood beside her before sliding a small silver hip flask from his jacket pocket.

'Fancy a brandy, Sweet Thing?' he asked. 'A small night cap maybe?'

She sat bolt upright on the bed. 'Brandy? You're a dark horse! You let me drink Champagne made from pears when you had this all along. I haven't had a brandy since before the War.'

The dark liquid, warmed to just the right temperature by the hip flask's closeness to Tom's body, set their taste buds glowing and slipped down their throats like nectar. They finished the brandy in two gulps as they stood facing each other in the small bedroom.

'That was good,' said Tom.

'Yes, but not half as good as this,' Kate replied slowly turning.

'Unzip me, but be careful. This dress is pure silk.'

Almost an hour later they lay together motionless on the narrow bed. Kate's head nestled against Tom's bare chest and his hand rested gently on her thigh. They basked in the lingering pleasure of the postprandial moment and for the first time since she could remember Kate knew perfect peace.

She broke the silence.

'Sorry for blubbing before, Tom. You know, when we were walking down the street. It's this war, just gets me down sometimes.'

'We're already three years in and no nearer the end than when it started.'

'Everyone has their dark moments, sweet lady,' Tom reassured her.

They both raised themselves up on one elbow until they were facing each other sideways.

'What adorable eyes you have, Tom,' she told him. 'Like doorways to your deepest thoughts drawing me in. A girl could lose herself in the labyrinth of those eyes.'

'Who'd have thought all those years ago in Devon, when you first asked if the seat next to mine on the coach was taken…who'd have thought that half a dozen years later we'd be together here like this, in the middle of a war raging round half the world?'

He continued: 'Tell me, why did you get to know me then, show such interest in a much less worldly soul? You were way out of my league.'

Kate thought back to those carefree pre-War days. 'You were a sweet boy, Tom. You were like the little brother I never had. I wanted to play with you, protect you…even teach you how to kiss.'

Tom felt a flicker of resentment that at the time she saw him as her little brother and not the potential sweetheart he had wished for, even though the triumph of this evening made it all irrelevant.

'So you're saying you've just fucked your brother?' he asked her. Almost immediately he knew he had crossed a line. Kate's countenance changed and there was more than a hint of anger.

'Don't *ever* use that ugly word in my presence again!' she told him firmly.

'I apologise,' answered Tom.

She thought for a few seconds and eventually told him: 'I accept your apology.' They both lay back on the single bed and embraced, each simply enjoying the closeness of the other. There was no time for lovers' tiffs in this war.

After several hours of pacific slumber they rose, showered, dressed and went down to the great dining room of the Strand Palace Hotel. Cracks in the ceiling plaster caused by bombs falling nearby, and marble wall panels in need of a good clean, did nothing to dim the spectacular art deco theme that ran through the Hotel's public rooms.

They broke their fast on a meal consisting of scrambled eggs made from powdered egg, soyabean 'sawdust' sausages, a single tinned tomato and several mushrooms that Tom suggested had been freshly picked that morning in Horse Guards Parade. This was partially mitigated by a large rack of toast, a pat of margarine, a small pot of marmalade made from carrots and a silver pot of steaming hot tea.

Afterwards they strolled down the Strand arm-in-arm towards Trafalgar Square. There had been no raid on London the previous night, that was clear.

'Do you bring all your fellers to the Strand Palace, Kate?' Tom teased.

'Certainly not, I usually take them to the Ritz, it's much more classy,' she replied with such sang-froid that for a few seconds he almost believed her.

Trafalgar Square was preparing for a 'Buy War Bonds' Rally that afternoon. Pushing their way through an army of workmen, they decided not to waste the last warmth of the late summer sun and to take a walk in St. James's Park.

They lingered for a while to listen to some military band playing on a bandstand in the Park. Then they watched the Pelicans on the lake and Tom commented on how thin they looked.

'Who has the spare bread to feed them these days?' Kate pointed out.

Then they sat outside the Refreshment House opposite Duck Island and enjoyed a cup of surprisingly good wartime coffee.

Tom pointed over towards Whitehall where all the major ministries of government were located.

'That's where it's all being decided. See that wall, the other side is Churchill's back garden.'

'That bastard,' Kate said with venom.

'How so, sweet thing? I thought everyone worshipped him,' replied Tom.

'He interned my Uncle Tony for six months without charge or trial. When he was released his business had gone to the dogs.'

'Italian?' asked Tom.

'No, he was one of Mosley's Blackshirts.'

'Wasn't he rather asking for it?' suggested Tom.

Kate's eyes widened.

'Asking for what?' she almost exploded. 'You're told that we're fighting for democracy, free speech and all that, and when you do speak your mind they lock you away. Do you call that fair?'

'Kate, I'm not going to fall out with you over your Uncle Tony,' said Tom barely suppressing laughter.

'No, of course not,' she replied with a grudging smile.

They lit yet another of Tom's cigarettes that seemed to appear from nowhere.

'You're like a magician. Where are you producing all these packs of cigarettes from, Tom?' Kate wondered. 'Your suit must be lined with them.'

They walked on through the Park which was still so perfectly kept that if you half-closed your eyes you could imagine the war was a long time over. Then they sat on the grass on which Tom laid his jacket in deference to Kate's silk dress.

'You should be an Officer, Tom. You're intelligent enough,' Kate suggested.

'Wrong school. Wrong accent. Wrong class. Unfortunately promotion in the German Wehrmacht is purely on merit.'

'Sure that's not just a cop out?' asked Kate puffing on yet another cigarette.

'Go and listen to them talk,' replied Tom. 'That ought to convince you.'

He rolled over on the grass to face her.

'There must have been somebody amongst all those duds you went out with who was more like a Fred Astaire with prospects?' he asked playfully.

'There was one,' admitted Kate. 'But he went to war in a shiny new Spitfire and we decided to knock it on the head for the duration. No point in living for a future that may never come.'

'"Knock it on the head for the duration"?' repeated Tom. 'Doesn't sound like true love to me.'

'You could be right,' she admitted. 'What about you? I dare say you've been round the block a few times since we last shared a cream tea in Devon.'

For a fleeting second their minds flashed back to that serene country scene now so many light years distant from the world at war.

'Before I was called up I had a girl called Gloria,' replied Tom. 'We ran a little wild.' They both smiled.

'Where is she now?' asked Kate.

'The moment passed, another casualty of war of sorts. I think she's seeing another chap now...' he answered.

'Look, I'm not going to lie to you, Kate. Not to you. There's a girl down at Selsey where I'm stationed, pretty thing, name of Vera. We haven't been going out for long but it could have a future. I feel it might.'

'She's a very lucky girl, Tom. And you must thank her for lending you to me,' Kate said smiling to hide her disappointment.

Tom closed the gap between them and kissed her on the lips to which she yielded willingly. His hand was on her knee: part of one of those long, lithe, slender legs he had lusted after down in Devon, if he had known then what lust was. He slid his hand upwards along the side of her leg, enjoying by touch what he had only enjoyed by sight before.

Her hand moved quickly to check his advance.

'Not here, Tom. I'm not a complete tart, you know.'

Tom explained his youthful fascination with her long, attractive legs.

'A dancer has to have good legs,' she explained.

'And a car mechanic must have good hands,' Tom countered. 'Think what a child we could have with my hands and your legs.'

And so they squandered the morning and beyond in idle chatter, mutual flattery and foolish teases.

Then they dozed awhile in each other's arms until the buzz of a late summer bee caused Tom to stir and look at his watch.

'Twenty-five past two already.'

'What time do you have to be back? And where's your uniform?' Kate asked sleepily but waking quickly to the fact that the sand in the hourglass was disappearing fast on their weekend idyll.

'Not until five-minutes to midnight and my uniform's in my case in the Left Luggage Office of your favourite Station. I'll change on the train.'

'Oh you've lost that, they lose everything there,' she suggested.

Then her face brightened. 'Tom, we've enough time - let's go and have afternoon tea at the Ritz in Piccadilly. My treat!'

'So, your other fellers get an all-nighter in a feather bed at the Ritz and all I get is a cup of tea,' Tom pretended to protest. Then he quickly added: 'I'd simply love to.'

It seemed that whatever else wartime Britain was short of cucumbers were not among them. The teatime sandwiches at the Ritz were generously filled with that watery fruit; the tea was hot and strong; and the toasted tea cakes had at least three sultanas apiece.

In accord with the social custom, Kate had slipped the price of tea plus a tip to Tom before they entered the Hotel. Gentlemen always paid the bill.

Afterwards, they walked back across Green Park, still arm in arm, but deep in silent thought. The shadows of the London Plane trees were lengthening. Eventually they were in sight of Victoria Station but neither wanted to take the last few final steps into the great terminus. Instead they headed for the small public garden opposite the Station entrance at the lower end of Grosvenor Gardens where the statue of Marshal Foch upholds the honour of France.

They found a bench, there was time for a last cigarette.

'It's been bliss, Tom, a wonderful weekend…you've no idea how much it's meant to me. Thank you so very much.'

'And thank *you*, darling,' answered Tom, letting slip a term of endearment usually reserved for later in relationships. 'Have you noticed, there hasn't been a single raid, not a single bomb, since we met? Even Goering wouldn't dare disturb *our* weekend.'

Then after a pause: 'Come here, let me kiss you again while I still have the chance before you disappear back into the real world.'

For a short moment he again felt her young body through the thin silk dress as he enjoyed her lush lips one last time.

Then he whispered in her ear: 'In a crowded room my eyes would search only for you.'

'You really are a charmer, Mister Harman,' Kate replied wondering how many other women he had beguiled with those same words.

'Will I see you again, Tom?' she asked as they finally entered the busy Station.

'I'd like that,' he replied. 'But no use trying to ring you, it took ages getting through last time on a trunk call. I'll write. Are you in the telephone directory?'

'Yes, we're in the London book, under Harrison, number forty-two Crystal Palace Park Road – *forty-two,* same as this year. Or simply write to me care of the Forces Canteen, Victoria Station.'

Ten minutes later Kate stood by the tea kiosk and watched Tom and his small case disappear in the direction of the trains. As he reached the ticket barrier he stopped, turned round and gave her a last wave and a smile.

She knew in that moment she would never see him again. It wasn't given for anyone to enjoy too many weekends like that in one lifetime. In hotels all over war-battered Britain during that past couple of days, young people had been trying to fit a whole lifetime of happiness into one short weekend.

As Tom sat on the train gliding through the grey south London suburbs towards Clapham Junction, he knew he must make a decision. He wasn't going to two-time dear Vera with the long blonde hair and the eyes of blue. So there was no alternative. He had exorcised his demons and broken free from the past. He had suffered an enchantment but the witch had flown. Vera would never know and he felt no guilt.

After all, there *was* a war on.

10: Just one more night.

Jeffrey handed in his notice at the National Provincial Bank in East Street, Chichester, and moved into his father's old room at Flo's flat in September 1970. Despite being older than most of the other students, he had succeeded in gaining a place at King's College London to study Computer Science, a relatively new faculty and one that Jeffrey was certain would make him a storm trooper of the new digital revolution sweeping the world of business.

In October, Flo and Jeffrey travelled down to Selsey for the last time the weekend before the rest of the family flew out of Heathrow to begin their antipodean adventure. The cottage down by the shoreline seemed bare and empty stripped of almost all furniture and possessions that had either been sold or packed and sent onto Australia by sea.

On the Sunday lunchtime, they all gathered for a farewell dinner in the large restaurant of Frank's favourite pub, the Fisherman's Joy, which had hosted births, wakes, weddings and other family events for countless generations of Selsey folk. The restaurant was well filled with local seafaring worthies and many came over and wished Frank and the family well in their new life on the other side of the world.

After Cream of Asparagus Soup most of them settled for the 28-day matured beef grazed on the Saltings of Mr. Wakely's local farm 'since the only red meat we'll be eating from now on is lamb if all I've heard about Australia is true' was how Frank put it.

'And loads of rabbit, don't forget the rabbits, the whole country's teaming with 'em!' Ray added in support.

Vera was noticeably on edge, not about the move but about leaving Flo and Jeffrey behind and so many miles between her and them. She kept going over with Flo what the arrangements would be for her to fly out and stay with them when the time came and which of his uncles Jeffrey was to get in touch with should Armageddon arrive in her absence.

The last goodbyes took place back at the cottage and took over half an hour to complete. There were a few tears and many hugs and much good advice given about what to do and what not before eventually the minicab to take Flo and Jeffrey to Chichester Station arrived and they could procrastinate no longer.

Flo was sad on that last journey up to Chi knowing she would never see Tom's old seaside stamping ground again and her extended family, the centre of her universe in recent years, much less frequently. But then she looked at Jeffrey, her new charge and live-in companion, and knew that looking after him would help to fill the void. Her weird energy would not be wasted from now on.

They arrived at Chichester Station with only minutes to spare before the arrival of the London train. Jeffrey dashed off to buy the tickets whilst Flo settled up with the minicab driver.

'That's ten shillings, luv,' the cabby told her. 'Seven bob plus a shilling for each passenger.'

'But there were only two of us,' replied Flo. 'Surely that makes it nine shillings?' The cab driver gave her a funny look.

'Excuse me, but there were two young men in the back. One was wearing blue jeans and the other was in army uniform. They both got out together,' insisted the puzzled driver.

Suddenly the answer dawned on Flo, she was in no doubt about who the third passenger could be. 'I'm so sorry, dear, of course there was. I don't know what I was thinking of,' she apologised giving him a pound note and without waiting for the change hurried into the station. Flo looked both ways up the platform and all around her but there was no sign of anybody in army uniform or any other uniform come to that. Then she went back outside and had a good look round there and after that checked the waiting room but it was all in vain.

Then she heard Jeffrey calling her: 'Come on, Gran, we're going to miss the train!' Just then the engine thundered past the ticket barrier and shuddered to a stop and they both climbed aboard, though Flo continued to scan the platform from the open window of the carriage.

'What's up, Gran? Lost something?' asked Jeffrey perplexed by her strange behaviour.

'No Jeffrey, I thought I saw someone I knew,' she said as the platform guard blew his whistle and the 6.05 evening train to London started to inch forward. Flo sank back in her seat and began to think. 'Why couldn't I have seen him too?' she wondered. It would have meant so much just to gaze on him again, even if only for a few seconds. She would have given anything just to see his lovely face once more. But at least she knew he was always near, he was leaving Selsey for the last time with her and his youngest son. How lucky she was to have a son whose love was so great it even transcended the end of mortal life itself.

Jeffrey soon made his presence felt in Flo's small world, stuck in suspended animation for so many decades, when he replaced Flo's old black-and-white 14-inch Baird TV that could only receive BBC One with Frank and Vera's nearly new Philips 21-inch colour model that offered BBC One and Two and ITV as well. This added a whole new dimension to Flo's life who soon became an avid follower of 'Coronation Street', Tommy Cooper and 'Crossroads'. The goggle box was positioned on one end of the sideboard opposite the sofa and Jeffrey, who was a whiz with anything electronic, soon produced and positioned a much more sophisticated indoor aerial that gave the sharpest, clearest TV picture Flo had ever seen.

Gradually and without discussion or house rules, a division of labour arose that involved Flo doing the laundry and cooking traditional English meals and Jeffrey doing the heavy shopping from Tesco in Kingston and twice a week introducing Flo to the pleasures of Chinese stir fries, Indian Lamb Rogan curries and proper Italian pasta, which basically meant anything other than English Macaroni Cheese.

Sometimes, Flo found the sound of Jeffrey's LPs played late into the night on his Dansette record player somewhat distracting but accepted it as the price of no longer living alone. But he was a thoughtful enough lodger always phoning her if for any reason he wouldn't be coming home that night: something that happened with increasing frequency as time went by.

In the warm summer of 1971 someone at King's College decided to hire a coach for those undergraduates wishing to attend the second Glastonbury Music Festival which, among others, was to feature David Bowie, Fairport Convention and the Pink Fairies. This was the year that UFOs were supposed to have turned up at Glastonbury - though whether they were spotted due to astronomical vigilence or reefer madness has never been satisfactorily explained.

Jeffrey decided it would make a pleasant weekend distraction from the fascinations of ASCII graphemes and Kbytes of data and decided to go. He knew demand was likely to outstrip supply so made sure he was one of the first aboard the coach and took a window seat. It was just as well as the coach soon began filling up fast.

Suddenly, Jeffrey heard a well-spoken female voice ask: 'Excuse me, if this seat is vacant would you mind if I sat here?'

Jeffrey realised the question was directed at him and looked up at the enquiring gaze of a quite pretty young woman. She had hazel eyes, long brown hair and although she was carrying a few spare pounds it would have been churlish of any man to complain.

'Yes, sure,' replied Jeffrey.

As the coach began to move off in a westward direction the young woman broke the silence. 'You're with the new Computer Science faculty, aren't you?' she asked. And then: 'My name's Marissa, by the way, but my friends call me Mez. You can call me Mez, if you like.'

It is enough to say that by the time the coach was hurtling past the sacred sarsens of Stonehenge, and quite possibly long before, Jeffrey and Mez were lovers in thought if not yet in deed. It turned out that Mez was studying Graphic Design and couldn't make her mind up whether to eventually go into the world of fashion or creative advertising. She had a small two-room flat in South Kensington ('Not quite Chelsea but near enough!') that her father paid for and despite being slightly arty found the whole subject of computers fascinating, especially their possible application in design. It was shortly after their meeting that Jeffrey found himself frequently phoning Flo to say he was staying up in town and wouldn't be home that night.

Soon after Frank and Vera arrived in Australia they realised it wasn't going to be a blue-jersey's dream come true. Frank had seriously underestimated how much the cost of buying his own boat and fish processing facilities would be. They would need to save a lot more money to add to the capital they brought with them before he could skipper his own boat again. So Frank had to work as crew on other mens' trawlers and the pay wasn't much more than he had paid his own crew back in Selsey. Vera found a job as a waitress in a beachside restaurant to top up their income and savings; and their move from the migrants' hostel wasn't into the villa with a swimming pool they had hoped for but to a modest one-bedroom rented flat near a busy highway.

Ray and Linda fared rather better. He lost no time in finding a job as a Senior Auto Mechanic at a large garage with a dealership for Australian-built Holden cars, the country's best selling brand. This soon allowed the young couple to move into a two-bedroom bungalow with a large back garden for young Tom to play in.

Frank and Vera's financial struggle to establish themselves began to weigh on Vera's mind for another reason. It was soon apparent that come the British winter they would be in no position to invite Flo over for three months as promised. For one thing they couldn't afford the return air fare - and they didn't even have a spare bedroom. Vera spent about three weeks agonising over the letter explaining all this to Flo and felt very guilty about it. But although Flo had been looking forward to seeing the family, it wasn't quite the disappointment that Vera thought. Unknown to her, Flo was more than slightly relieved. The thought of spending twenty-four hours travelling half-way round the world in an aeroplane, and leaving Jeffrey for three whole months, had been giving Flo sleepless nights. Though if she was completely honest it was 'leaving Tom' rather than 'leaving Jeffrey' that was the real stumbling block. Of course, Flo didn't say any of this in her letter of reply, she just reassured Vera that she completely understood and that the most important thing was for her and Frank to get settled in Australia and that she and Jeffrey were keeping an eye on each other just fine.

A few months later, Jeffrey decided it was time to bring Mez round to Flo's for tea. He told Mez that Flo was a long lost granny and not to expect too much but she had been good to him and he wanted her to meet her. Flo bought a large tin of Red Salmon specially and other dishes included Russian Salad: a mixture of diced potato, carrots and peas dressed with mayonnaise. Jeffrey had insisted on the use of real mayonnaise rather than the synthetic tasting salad cream that Flo usually used. She also baked a fruit cake.

The tea went well and the conversation flowed seamlessly helped as much by Mez's social graces as by Flo and Jeffrey.

Flo wanted to know all she could about this young lady, who she sensed was going to loom large in Jeffrey's life, but she didn't want her enquiries to sound like the Spanish Inquisition on a bad day.

'So do you manage to see your parents often now you're in London?' Flo asked. She already knew about the flat in South Ken and had long since put two and two together about Jeffrey's overnight stays up in town.

'Mummy and daddy were divorced a few years ago,' replied Mez as casually as if it was just another rite of passage.

'Daddy's a test pilot for Hawker Siddeley and lives near Farnborough. I see him for lunch whenever he's in town, which is quite often.'

'Really, dear,' answered Flo. 'I used to work for Hawker's in the War you know. Making them I mean, not flying them.' They all laughed politely at the thought of Flo flying a fighter plane.

'Daddy may well have flown one of the Hawkers you made,' continued Mez. 'He was in the RAF in the War and fought in the Battle of Britain.'

'Then he was a very brave man and we all have a lot to thank him for,' said Flo.

'Thank you, I'll tell him that,' replied Mez.

'And my son was stationed at Farnborough for a time when he was in the Army but he died in the War,' Flo added.

Not sure how to respond to that Mez decided to move the conversation on.

'I see mummy quite a lot too. She owns a number of dancing schools along the south coast. There's one at Brighton and another at Eastbourne but the largest is at Worthing. She lives in Worthing, in one of those blocks of service flats on the front with a view out to sea.

'I like to go down there for weekends whenever I can, specially if the weather's nice.'

Then turning to Jeffrey: 'We had a nice weekend down there earlier in the month, didn't we?'

'It was great,' replied Jeffrey. 'The flat's on the top floor and has a really big private balcony. On a clear day you can even see the Eiffel Tower.'

'No you can't, Jeffrey!' Mez laughed gently slapping him on the arm.

All in all, the tea was a success and later Flo told Jeffrey what a very nice young lady his girlfriend was and he would do well to hold on to her. Naturally, she told Vera all about Jeffrey's new soul mate in her next air mail letter.

The following year Frank and Vera took the plunge and invested in a trawler and also began renting a fish processing unit with a large refrigeration chamber. The boat wasn't new but Frank decided they couldn't wait any longer to buy one – even so Vera had to continue waitressing and they still had to live in the small flat for the time being. So once again Vera had the difficult task of writing to Flo to explain that even though things were looking up they still weren't in a position to invite her over yet – would Flo please forgive them for letting her down once again?

Of course, Flo wasn't in the least disappointed, on the contrary she was only too relieved that she wouldn't have to leave the home Tom and she were happy in for so many years, even though it would only be for three months. The following year all Frank and Vera's hard work was beginning to pay off. They moved to a nice bungalow near the beach, though it didn't have a swimming pool and Frank had to sell the Herbert Truman painting to help provide the deposit. But at least they had the spare room to invite Flo over for the Australian summer at long last. Flo was saved from this prospect by her gall bladder: it had been grumbling for some time and her name came up on the NHS waiting list for an operation at just the right moment.

Flo explained that if she cancelled there was no knowing how long she might have to wait. And in the days before keyhole surgery, convalescing was a long process, especially for someone of her age.

A month or two after the operation, just as spring was banishing the chill of winter, Flo received an offer from Jeffrey and Mez that she wasn't going to refuse. Would she like to come down to Worthing and stay with them at the flat of Mez's mother for ten days over Easter to help her convalesce? Mez's mother was off on a month long cruise to the Canaries and Azores so there was plenty of room and it was her suggestion.

'What a nice lady she must be to think of me,' thought Flo. 'Specially as we've never met.'

Onslow Court is a four storey block of art deco service flats right on the sea front in East Worthing. Each flat has a balcony front and back. 'So when you get tired of looking out to sea, you can move round the back and enjoy the South Downs view instead,' was how Mez put it as she drove Flo and Jeffrey there from East Worthing Station.

'Has your mother been on a cruise before?' Flo enquired making polite conversation.

'Oh, she goes on them every year,' replied Mez. 'This time she's gone with her gentleman friend.'

'Which one?' asked Jeffrey.

Mez gave him a disapproving glance.

'Lorenzo the Painter,' she answered. 'You've met him, Jeffrey, the one with the goatee beard and the oversize green felt hat. He gives me the heebie-jeebies, I do hope mummy hasn't ended up paying for him again.'

'What's wrong with him?' wondered Jeffrey. 'I thought he was...kinda cool.'

'Well for a start he's years older than mummy, nobody's ever seen anything he's supposed to have painted...and for someone who's as English as afternoon tea what's he doing with a name like Lorenzo?'

'I'm sure your mother can take care of herself,' Jeffrey commented. 'She's certainly old enough.'

Jeffrey got his first slap on the arm of the day: 'Mummy's wearing very well, I'll have you know. I see men half her age giving her the eye when we're in restaurants.'

'I think you'll find they're looking at you, gorgeous,' replied Jeffrey in full flattery mode. Mez smiled but said nothing.

During her stay in Worthing the weather was mild and Flo had a restful time: as Mez had the use of her mother's little Mini Cooper car they were able to visit Denman Gardens and Parham House where the flower beds had erupted with spring flowers of every hue. Flo also liked sitting on the balcony just looking out to sea though hard as she looked she never did see the Eiffel Tower. What she did find uncomfortable, though she said nothing, was the way Jeffrey and Mez slept together in her mother's bedroom just as if they were married. She knew conventions had changed, particularly since the Swinging Sixties, but her code of conduct was still based on the Edwardian values of her childhood and it was way too late to change now.

After her stay, Flo sent Mez's mother a large bunch of mixed flowers by Interflora with a thank-you note.

The next autumn Flo decided to take the initiative with Vera about the three month winter/summer stay in Australia and, trying hard not to offend, wrote that she had come to the conclusion that at her age she didn't feel up to the long return journey and all the excitement. Vera replied that they were all disappointed but accepted her decision and that it was their own fault for leaving the invitation until it was too late.

Once they graduated from King's College, Mez and Jeffrey had no difficulty finding well-paid jobs. Mez went to work for J. Walter Thompson, the large ad agency in Berkeley Square, where she landed the job of Assistant Art Director working on Persil washing powder and OXO stock cubes. Jeffrey became a Computer Systems Analyst with the Prudential Insurance Company in High Holborn.

Shortly afterwards, they moved into a terraced house together which they began to buy on a mortgage. The deposit was supplied by Mez's mother and the conveyancing provided at cost by another of her gentlemen friends. The house was located in Norbiton, an up and coming area of Kingston and only a ten minute walk from where Flo lived. Flo was sorry to see her grandson go, she had got used to having someone live with her once again, but knew all along it was only a temporary arrangement. She would also miss the money, as she had only her basic pension and slender savings to live on, and toyed with the thought of finding a lodger. But she eventually went cold on the idea as she couldn't bear the thought of a complete stranger living in Tom's old room.

The following year Jeffrey and Mez decided to marry which pleased Flo no end. It was going to be a big wedding and Mez's mother had taken sole charge of all the arrangements. The labours of childbirth were as nothing compared to her exertions to make sure everything was in place for a perfect day.

Vera and Frank flew over from Australia for a month and stayed with Frank's brother in Croydon. Ray couldn't get that much time off work so unfortunately he and Lin couldn't make it. The very next day Vera and Frank drove over to Kingston in a hired car to be reunited with Flo and Jeffrey and to meet Mez for the first time. Flo was excited to be with Vera and Frank again but she noticed how they both looked much older: victims of the ravages of the unrelenting Australian sun on fair complexions. There was much hugging and 'How many years has it been?' with the general consensus that it had been about five which all agreed was far too long. They all went for a meal at a Chinese restaurant in Kingston where Vera made a great fuss of Flo and told Mez what a treasure Jeffrey's grandma was.

The wedding was held at St. George's Church in East Worthing not too far from Onslow Court. Its honey-coloured sandstone, known as Bargate stone, shone golden in the sunlight as the bride arrived supported by six bridesmaids. Flo was there along with 200 other guests and she thought her grandson looked extremely dashing in his Prince of Wales check suit and waistcoat. It was the first time Flo laid eyes on Mez's mother and noticed she was accompanied by a sun-tanned older gentleman in a white suit whom she presumed must be Lorenzo.

As they stood before the High Altar waiting, the Vicar introduced himself to Jeffrey and his best man, a friend from King's College days.

'Still time to do a runner!' the cleric whispered mischievously. But even as he spoke, the organ began to play the Wedding March and Mez, accompanied by her father and the half-dozen bridesmaids dressed in gold satin, entered the west doorway and swept into the aisle.

It was a beautiful ceremony accompanied by a full choir and it looked as if all the hot houses of Sussex, both West and East, had been plundered to provide the floral decorations.

Afterwards came the photographs. There was a short lull in these proceedings as the photographer went to his car to fetch some film of a different exposure on account of the sun shining so brightly. It was clear the bride was not happy.

'Can you believe it?' she asked her mother as they stood waiting. 'He's dressed completely in white. He's even wearing a white felt hat! What was wrong with his green one? Doesn't he know only the bride wears white?'

'Oh, come now, darling,' replied Mez's mother. 'Lorenzo doesn't mean anything by it, I'm sure. I thought he looks rather...matrimonial.'

'But that's exactly it, Mummy, he's trying to upstage me,' Mez protested. 'It's supposed to be my big day, not Lorenzo's!'

'Just calm down darling, this is all bridal nerves. Don't start having tantrums now and spoil everything,' mother warned sternly.

Fortunately the other 'white bride' heard nothing of this as he had crept away behind a Yew tree to enjoy one of his favourite Panatela cigars hand rolled from Sumatran tobacco leaf.

A large coach had been hired to take the principal guests to the wedding reception and Flo was ushered on board. She took a seat and minutes later was joined by the older tanned gentleman with the goatee beard in a white suit. Just as the coach was starting off he turned to Flo.

'So far, so good! Lovely ceremony, wouldn't you say?'

'Oh yes indeed,' replied Flo. 'Splendid in every way.'

'And the best is yet to come,' continued Lorenzo. 'What better place for the revels than the Beach Hotel. Do you know it?' Flo confessed that she did not.

'Well you've a treat in store. It may only have three stars but it's the best hotel between here and Bournemouth. Family run, of course. It's overlooking the sea and pure art deco inside and out. The bride's mother seems to have a thing about art deco, I've no idea why.

'Oh, and it has the finest cocktail bar on the south coast. You can take my word for that,' Lorenzo added with a wink.

'Sounds very nice,' replied Flo.

Then trying to put on a few airs and graces, and remembering her lovely West Country touring holiday with Vera and Frank, Flo added: 'The Imperial Hotel in Exmouth, the Hannafore Point in Looe and the Carbis Bay near St Ives are my favourites. Do you know them?'

The aging gigolo seemed mildly impressed and smiled approvingly.

'Indeed I do. Takes a bob or two to stay at any of those for any length of time these days.'

'That depends on who's paying,' replied Flo with a mischievous smile. She was going to add that Vera and Frank had paid for her but decided not to go into details.

'Quite so,' answered Lorenzo who, misinterpreting Flo's words and friendly smile, sensed a free summer on the Cornish Riviera coming on.

'I'll be looking for a dance with you later.' So saying he stood up, tipped his white felt hat and headed for the exit as the coach had just arrived at Worthing's Beach Hotel.

'What a nice man,' Flo thought to herself. 'I don't know what Mez has against him.'

As most of the guests had been booked into the Hotel's 115 bedrooms for the night, the management had agreed that the reception could be held in the grand hotel restaurant that was decorated in the Modernist style and whose French windows opened directly onto an elegant tiled terrace overlooking Worthing's pebbled beach. Flo sat with Vera and Frank next to Jeffrey on the high table and felt very important. A flurry of silver service waitresses dispensed the finest 1975 fare the Beach Hotel could muster: Melon and Palma Ham followed by Salmon en Croute with Jersey Royals, asparagus and champignons a l'ail to be followed by a light Belgian chocolate mousse impaled with dark chocolate shards.

Nobody forgot their lines in the after dinner speeches; everybody laughed in the right places; the bride and groom were toasted and re-toasted in Moet & Chandon Nectar Imperial; and a special vote of thanks was given to Mez's mum for arranging everything to a standard that surpassed perfection. Everybody agreed the whole day had gone swimmingly.

Afterwards a space was cleared and those who wished followed Jeffrey and Mez onto the dance floor whilst a four piece rock ensemble played a selection of latest hits and old favourites.

Lorenzo was as good as his word and made a bee-line for Flo through the hubbub of gossiping guests and she graciously accepted his invitation to dance. Vera and Frank suddenly had nightmarish visions of a repeat performance of Flo's wild jungle dance at the Sundowner's Club in Selsey: something totally inappropriate to present company and the occasion. But their fears were groundless as Flo had stuck to one glass of champagne and a white wine and elderflower spritzer. After the dance Lorenzo promised to return later to introduce Flo to the Hotel's secluded cocktail bar and in particular the delights of a 'Hawaiian Hula-Hula Sunset' made with Pacific Rum and real coconut milk.

Just then the time came for Jeffrey and Mez to leave: they had a plane to catch from Gatwick for their two-week honeymoon in Marbella. Before they left, they both came over and thanked Flo for her wedding gift of a Goblin Teasmade: something that had taken up quite a slice of Flo's pension money for the month. She accompanied them to their waiting car and kissed them both. Then she went for a cigarette on the terrace before returning to her place at the table where the remains of her second white wine and elderflower spritzer were waiting.

Mez's mother ordered another bottle of Champagne, why not since her ex-husband was paying the bill? She could relax, nothing could go wrong from here on and if it did nobody could blame her.

Anyway, what possible dramas could unfold now?

Then her gaze chanced to fall on Flo sitting alone.

Clutching the Champagne bottle she crossed over and took a seat next to her.

'Let me freshen your glass,' said Mez's mother and without waiting for an answer filled the crystal goblet to the brim with bubbly. 'We haven't been properly introduced but you're Flo, aren't you,' she continued.

'I am - and I'm most pleased to meet you,' gushed Flo. 'You really are to be congratulated on arranging such a wonderful wedding, it must have meant endless hard work.'

'It did mean burning the midnight oil and the usual last minute cock-ups to sort, if you'll pardon my French. But it's all been worthwhile in the end - only have the one daughter, you see.'

Then after a moment's reflection: 'You're Jeffrey's grandmother aren't you so you must be Vera's mother? I know I should know but there's simply been no time to take anything in.'

Flo laughed. 'No, not Vera's mother - Jeffrey didn't even know I existed until fairly recently.'

'Not too recently I think, you put him up for yonks I remember Mez telling me.' Flo thought some explanation necessary but decided to keep the convoluted family connection as simple as possible. She also decided a little white lie was in order.

'What it is, I had a son called Tom who was killed in the War who was Vera's first husband. They met down in Selsey where he was stationed. They had twin boys: my grandson Ray who now lives in Australia and Jeffrey. Vera married Frank some years afterwards.'

Suddenly, time juddered to a halt for Mez's mother whose brain ceased registering anything beyond 'Tom'...'killed in the War'...'Vera'...and 'Selsey'. It was all such a long time ago but there are some of life's landmark moments that remain crystal clear even until the chiming of the hour. Everything began falling into place - but could it possibly all be coincidence?

Then came the second thunder bolt out of a clear blue sky. Her eyes were drawn to Flo's place name among the table debris, carefully typed out and encapsulated in a clear plastic holder. It had been pushed to one side but she had no difficulty reading it.

'Mrs. Florence Harman.'

'*Harman*'. That was the clincher, it was beyond the leeway of chance. Mez's mother's brain jumped back into real time.

'Did you say that your son was Tom Harman and that he was stationed in Selsey during the War?' she asked.

'Yes,' replied Flo with growing interest: 'Did you know him?'

The mother of the bride was staring blankly into space over Flo's shoulder when she realised she was looking directly at Vera engaged in animated conversation with the Head Wine Waiter.

In that moment she determined that nobody should ever know. It would only serve to sour Vera's memories of Tom, the father of her sons. Why spoil her recollection of rainbow days when the world was young? Why open a hornets' nest that could bring unpredictable family repercussions? But she would have to live with the knowledge that every time she saw her new son-in-law Jeffrey it would remind her that his father was the only man she had ever really cared for.

What luckless fate to fall for a fellow on a one-night stand!

If only she could have had just one more night with him it might have been a different story. Just one more night and she might have rekindled his childhood infatuation with her. She might even have persuaded him to try for an officer's commission in which case he might never have died.

'No!' she lied to Flo, quickly recovering her wits. 'It's just that my parents took me on some lovely holidays to Selsey when I was a child.'

Just then a voice called from across the other side of the room.

'Kate! You're needed over here! We're going to cut the rest of the cake!'

Before they returned to Australia, Vera and Frank took Flo away on a five-day holiday to Jersey. They used the hired car which they took over on the ferry so they were able to visit every corner of that delightful Channel Island.

It was like old times for Flo, reminding her of that memorable tour of the West Country in 1970 and the days when she had a family and second home down in Selsey that she could visit regularly. They stayed in a small hotel right on the beach with a view across the Royal Bay of Grouville to Mont Orgueil Castle. On the first evening they discovered a superb alfresco fish restaurant on the coast road and never bothered to look for anywhere else to eat after that.

All too soon it was over and a few weeks later, after a farewell dinner at Jeffrey and Mez's house in Norbiton, Frank and Vera took their leave and flew back to Perth.

The following year the link with family weakened further when Jeffrey and Mez moved to Bristol. Jeffrey had been offered a highly paid job working for the BBC's Information Technology Department. The following year they had a baby and a year later Jeffrey and Mez started their own company developing computer software for use in graphics, advertising and design. They always invited Flo to spend Christmas and a summer break with them which she always accepted and Jeffrey would pop in to see Flo, and sometimes stayed the night, when he was up in London on business. But other than quarterly visits from her niece Doreen, who had retired with her husband to Hastings, that was the sum total of Flo's social life. It dawned on her that everybody she ever knew had either died or moved away. She was on nodding terms with a few of the neighbours but there was absolutely nobody in Kingston she could call a friend or with whom she could share her joys and sorrows.

These were years of rising prices and although Jeffrey had arranged for Flo to receive Housing Benefit, so she wouldn't have to worry about the rent, she still only had the Basic State Pension and her now depleted savings to live on. Eventually the day came when she had to sell the Mappin and Webb brooch that Connie had given her years before when she was dying: she received over £500 for it from a Kingston jeweller. Flo was surprised it was worth so much and thought how wise and considerate Connie had been to think of her future circumstances like that. It wasn't easy parting with the brooch which, besides its intrinsic beauty, was a link with Connie but it had to go.

About this time, Vera and Frank made one last attempt to get Flo to visit them in Australia. They told her that she only need stay a month if three were too long and that she could travel with Jeffrey and Mez who were also planning to come and visit them. Flo was half tempted but eventually decided she was far too set in her ways and now she was approaching eighty no longer had the stamina for such a long and arduous journey. In the end Jeffrey and Mez visited Australia without her.

The year John Lennon was shot dead in New York, Vera flew to London for a one month visit. She was retired now so her time was her own. Flo was delighted and excited to see her after so long and Vera stayed with her in Kingston for two weeks before moving on to Bristol. Both women thought how much the other had aged, as one does when you haven't seen an older person for some years, but kept it to themselves. Vera was quietly worried that there was nobody on hand to keep a watchful eye on Flo now that she had entered her ninth decade. But other than ask Jeffrey to see his grandmother as much as possible, which wasn't easy given their distance apart and Jeffrey's business commitments, she couldn't see what more she could do.

The years that followed Vera's departure were barren and lonely for Flo. Visits from Jeffrey and her niece Doreen hardly filled a score or more of the days that go to make a year and she reached the point where she didn't know how to fill her solitary hours. There were just so many times a week even Flo could spend re-reading Tom's letters to her from his Army days and looking at the photos in the album that she always kept wrapped up in a tartan woollen scarf on the kitchen table beside the pot plant. Flo had always been content with her own company but sometimes a week would go by without talking to another soul which she felt was no way to live.

How had she ended up like this, she often asked herself? But then she would remember and answer her own rhetorical question: she still had Tom who was with her wherever she went. She didn't need anybody else she reassured herself. The feeling of Tom being physically close to her grew even stronger as each year passed. Eventually she started talking to him and imagining his answers within the confines of her head. After a while she found herself speaking out loud to him and the people downstairs heard her late at night when they knew there was nobody else in her flat.

As time passed, they began to hear another voice coming from upstairs which sounded more like a man's and the conversation became a dialogue. They wondered who the old lady upstairs could be entertaining at such an unearthly hour. But the voices that came from above were always muted and indistinct and eventually they decided it must be the television.

The winter of 1985 had been long and hard and spring came late. The grey sunless days, the one after the other, and the lack of anything purposeful to occupy her resulted in a mild melancholia which was not usual to Flo's nature. Her muscles ached and she moved more slowly, the result of being couped up in her flat by the cold wet weather, she told herself. Flo began to feel her age.

Then spring came again and the sun entered its own, warming the land and bringing snowdrops, crocuses and even early daffodils into bloom almost simultaneously in the small back gardens that she could see from her living room window. Flo felt it was time to get out and that meant the first pilgrimage of the season to Pinehurst Barracks in Farnborough. So one Monday morning Flo packed her shopping bag with a thermos of tea, cheese sandwich and twenty Rothmans King Size cigarettes and headed off towards Kingston Train Station. Flo loved walking and had always gone most places on foot but that day her legs felt leaden: the result, she reasoned, of too long a confinement in her flat.

Even the reawakening countryside and the spring flowers along the railway embankments failed to cheer her spirits that particular day and she almost nodded asleep on the train as it rattled its clackety-clack way along the track. She picked up slightly on the walk south down Farnborough Road but by the time she reached the Barracks she felt distinctly out of breath. So apart from a hurried glance through the main gate she made straight for the bench in the tiny garden sanctuary between the barracks wall and the road. She expected the sandwich and sweet tea would soon revive her but even with a cigarette afterwards she still felt out of sorts.

As she puffed on the Rothmans an older man who lived on the opposite side of the road, and was taking advantage of the mild weather to mow his front lawn for the first time that year, gave her a friendly wave. Half way through he went inside for a cup of tea and told his wife that 'the old lady who lost her son in the War is back.'

Flo mused on how things had changed over the years. The little garden had been repaved and replanted and seen forty summers since she had sat there last with Tom - and the little tea shop up the road they visited together on his afternoon leave was long gone, replaced by a Tandoori take-away restaurant. The English may complain about foreigners but they willingly eat their food.

Even the Main Gate to the Barracks was different now: the wrought iron gates shut closed against terrorist incursions and the kindly Red Cap who often passed the time of day with Flo replaced by impersonal CCTV cameras monitored from some remote surveillance centre. But she could still look through those black wrought iron gates at the tall redbrick blocks within whose shadow she had caught her last precious sight of Tom about this time of year in 1944. This she decided to do next and after carefully stubbing out her cigarette slowly walked the ten yards or so to the gateway and peered through.

All was deserted except for a single soldier walking away from the gate and towards the nearest building. Flo looked at the uninviting blocks of military Victoriana and wondered what went on inside? Was there a nerve centre of well-ordered activity behind those silent walls and windows from which regiments were redeployed across the world and overt operations against foreign foes planned and executed? Or did those closed dusty windows conceal the actual barrack rooms where rows of soldiers slept – among them perhaps the bed space once occupied by Tom?

Her focus was suddenly drawn to the single soldier who was crossing the courtyard. He had suddenly stopped, turned and looked directly towards her. Slowly he stretched out his arms and beckoned with his hands as if to join him. Again and again he gestured but of course there was simply no way that Flo could reach him through the iron gates that separated them. Instead she held the metal rails firmly and called out to him, her voice unrestrained: 'Tom! Oh, Tom!'

His mouth was moving but although he was too far away for her to hear she knew exactly what he was saying: 'It's alright, Mum! I'm here!' repeated over and over again.

Her attention was diverted by intrusive whirring sounds above her head to the left. It was one of the CCTV cameras re-focussing on her, somehow sensing her sound and movement. When she looked back the soldier was gone. Timidity reasserted itself and fearful that the gate would suddenly lurch open and she would be restrained by some elite force of commandos, Flo made a tactical retreat to the roadside bench.

She was sure it was him, she would know him anywhere. His beloved face was as fresh in her mind's eye as the day she last saw him alive. If it wasn't Tom how could the figure disappear the instant she took her eyes off him? The image she beheld was far too real for flight of fancy: it was Tom alright, of that she was in no doubt. Tea from the Thermos and another cigarette started to steady her nerves but no sooner had one cigarette been finished than another was begun.

Then it happened. A series of gentle spasms rippled through her upper body on the leftward side like warning shockwaves before an earthquake. These were followed by two or three more powerful tremors with stabbing sensations. Flo knew for certain something was seriously wrong. Hastily she dispensed with the cigarette and shoved the Thermos into her bag, she knew she must get home and as soon as possible. As she stood up her sense of balance deserted her as a last spasm, painful but not unbearable, wracked her chest and upper arm. She went down like the leading skittle in a frame of bowls – instinctively she thrust out her right arm to break her fall and by so doing saved her head from impact with the pavement.

The man on the other side of the road mowing the last strip of his lawn saw her go down. He pushed the machine aside, shouted 'Doris!' through the open front door and without waiting for a reply dashed between cars rushing in both directions to reach the crumpled body. Immediately he knelt beside her and uttered the usual absurd enquiry: 'Madam, are you alright?'

To his relief he saw she was stirring and with difficulty he returned her to the bench. Just then his wife, who had heard his call and detected urgency, joined his side. 'What's happening, George? What is it?' she asked with growing concern.

Flo was quickly regaining her senses and with them the need to recover her dignity. She began insisting she was alright which clearly was not the case. Whilst his wife recrossed the busy road to bring a glass of water the man began his questioning. 'Did she carry some tablets that she should take?' 'Should he call an ambulance?' 'Was there somebody he could telephone?'

Flo was most insistent that she didn't want an ambulance, she had just felt a little light headed and not to worry. She would catch a bus to the Station and a train home. On hearing that she lived in Kingston the man suggested she was in no fit state to travel there on public transport. Then his wife arrived with the water which seemed to refresh her. The man went into a huddle with his wife.

Afterwards, he insisted Flo should allow them to drive her home, there was no way she could be left to her own devices. A further mention of calling an ambulance soon had Flo agreeing to the kind offer of the Good Samaritan of

Farnborough. The wife stayed with her whilst the man secured his front door and returned in his four-door Ford Escort.

On the journey back to Kingston, Flo successfully deflected further suggestions that they visit the Casualty Department of a hospital 'just to check you over' and began an almost unbroken effusion of thanks. Once they reached her home the kind couple helped Flo up the stairs and sat her on the sofa in her living room. The wife made her a cup of tea whilst the husband continued to enquire who he could ring. But despite the feeling of weakness that overwhelmed her whole body, Flo managed to put on a convincing act that she felt quite recovered. She tried paying for the petrol used on the journey but the man would have none of it. Then, slightly reassured to see that Flo at least had a phone, they reluctantly left accompanied by numerous declarations of appreciation.

Once she was alone, Flo had another cup of tea and a cigarette to buck herself up. 'Whatever came over me?' she asked herself. This was most unlike her usual self. In the end she decided that being almost housebound for so long, combined with the shock of seeing Tom again, had proved too much for her mind and body. She decided to have an early night.

After a fitful ten hours of slumber, waking up in a sweat and then dozing off again, Flo arose and slowly made her way to the living room. She thought it would help if she had something to eat so made herself a couple of slices of toast and marmalade. But no sooner had she eaten them than she brought them up, at that point she knew the problem could no longer be ignored. She decided to call the doctor's surgery and explained she felt too weak and unwell to attend. As soon as she mentioned chest pains the receptionist told her to stay where she was and a doctor would call.

Doctor Green of the King's Road Surgery was puzzled as he pulled up in his Audi saloon outside where Flo lived. His notes showed that Florence Harman had belonged to his practice ever since the National Health Service was formed in 1948 but he had no recollection of ever seeing her. This was not surprising: in all those years Flo had only visited the surgery once about her gallbladder and had seen the other doctor with whom Doctor Green shared his practice. Such was Flo's famous iron constitution.

Horace Green was a Doctor of the old school who had no need for portable ECG machines or blood tests. After taking Flo's blood pressure, checking her pulse and listening to her heart with his stethoscope he knew instinctively there was a problem. He told Flo that he was going to admit her to hospital 'for a short period of observation' and rang ahead to Kingston Hospital to arrange her admission. Flo was a patient of the old school too and would never query a doctor's instructions or ask questions.

For speed and convenience he took her there in his car and soon Flo was tucked up in bed in a small side ward. To begin with there was a flurry of activity as medical staff visited her one after the other, hooking her up to bleeping equipment and prescribing injections of this drug and that. But her almost constant attendant was a large black nurse also named Florence who felt some unexplained empathy with her new patient that was more than just the sharing of a name. It was Florence who spoon-fed Flo at mealtimes, checked her blood pressure and temperature every four hours and helped her wash her hands and face twice a day. In quieter moments on the ward she would sit with Flo for a while and without taxing her would pass the time by regaling her with information about her son and daughter, both at college, stories about her childhood in Ghana and the rising price of fish.

It was Florence who phoned the Hospital's Lady Almoner and suggested she visit Flo. During the meeting that followed, the Lady Almoner discovered her next-of-kin was a grandson who lived in Bristol and insisted he should be told. Flo began to get distressed because she hadn't brought her address book with her but the Lady Almoner said not to worry and soon found Jeffrey's number from directory enquiries. Out of Flo's hearing, she lost no time in telling him that his grandmother had suffered a heart attack and was very weak. Jeffrey immediately phoned long-distance rousing his mother Vera at her home in Western Australia in the middle of the night.

Flo lost all track of time, the medications befuddled and muddled her mind, but she felt safe and peaceful just lying there and knew she was in good hands. She appreciated the kind attentions of Nurse Florence and felt somewhat guilty that a few decades before she had been fearful and disturbed by the sudden appearance of black faces in Kingston: people whom her upbringing had taught her to think of as little more than savages.

Vera lost no time in catching a flight from Perth to London and Jeffrey met her at Heathrow Airport with his car. Before they set off for Kingston Hospital from the car park, Jeffrey produced a mobile phone and rang the hospital for the latest news. The phone was the size of a house brick and it was carried around in a base station the size of a coal scuttle. Vera had never seen anything like it before but wasn't surprised that Jeffrey of all people would be among the first to have such a novel device.

And it was there in the car park of Heathrow Airport's Terminal Three that Jeffrey and Vera learnt that Flo Harman had passed away peacefully in the early hours of that morning in the second week of April 1985. Vera shed a quiet tear, a door on the past was closing shut for her. Jeffrey regretted that he would see the old lady who had always treated him so kindly no more. He had been fond of Flo and was sad that she had died - but she was 85 and for him that's what 85 year old people do.

They drove to the Hospital where they were shown into the Lady Almoner's small office and given tea. Then Florence the nurse took them to see the old lady for the last time. On the way, Florence said what a lovely person Flo was and that they had had many conversations and Flo had told her that just before the heart attack she had seen her son again after such a long time. Vera and Jeffrey exchanged glances. Then Florence said that when she came on duty the evening before Flo died the old lady had said something she didn't understand. Vera asked her what it was.

'I'd just arrived on the ward and was doing my round before the lights were dimmed for sleeping and I said to Flo: "How are you, dear?"

'It was her answer that puzzled me, just two words.

'"Missing Tom"'.

At the funeral at Kingston Crematorium three days later the turnout was small. There was Vera and Jeffrey and Flo's niece Doreen. There was the couple who lived downstairs from Flo and there was Florence the nurse from Ghana and the Hospital Lady Almoner. And there was Mez who knew nothing of the close affinity of her own mother with Flo's son Tom.

After inviting everybody back for a drink and a pork pie at The Albert Tavern on Kingston Hill, just a few yards away from where Tom had worked as a Motor Mechanic, Vera thanked them all for attending. Jeffrey and Mez drove straight back to their home in Bristol, they had a child and a business to attend to and neither could be neglected for long.

Vera walked back along Park Road to the flat in Staunton Road and unknowingly passed the Italian delicatessen that had almost provided Flo with an escape from the pathos of her lonely life. A few minutes later she passed the spot where the flying bomb had fallen and Flo had found it within her to become heroine for an hour.

Once inside the flat she quickly checked each room: the thirty pounds she would pay to the man with the van to clear the flat would be well spent, there was little of value here. Then she went to the living room and noticed the potted plant on the table in front of the window had died and shed its leaves. Vera made straight for the v-shaped corner cupboard and took down the old biscuit tin and the shoebox. The letters written to Flo when Tom was in the Army she would show to Jeffrey and then take back to Australia for Ray so they would know their blood father a little better. In the biscuit tin she was relieved to find Flo's Rent Book and quarterly statements with reference numbers from the gas, electricity and telephone companies.

She also found Tom's Scout Camp diary for 1936 with the plum coloured cover and decided to give it to Jeffrey to see what he could make of it.

In addition there was a Post Office Savings Bank book with just two hundred pounds and thirty-seven pence in it. Vera had no way of knowing that this was almost exactly the amount that Flo's aunt had left her in her will and with which she had opened the Post Office Savings account back in the 1920s. Before she closed the cupboard door, Vera was aware that while removing the biscuit tin it had knocked against something solid but unseen behind it. She moved a kitchen chair to beneath the cupboard and raised herself up so she could reach it. Vera took down the object from the back of the cupboard and read the label.

It was an old jar of Crosse and Blackwell's Pickled Walnuts.

Flo became conscious that everything around her was pitch black. She felt she was moving at high speed through infinite darkness but was not in the least afraid. Gradually she became aware of a blinding white light growing closer and closer until it glowed all around her. Then everything suddenly stopped.

Flo was standing on the side of a small valley covered with lush grass that was the most vibrant green she had ever seen, trees with beautifully shaped leaves and giant shrubs covered in the most exquisite flowers imaginable. A small group of people was standing about 20 yards away on the left smiling towards her.

Flo recognised Stan and then her sister Ada who was standing next to him. Behind them she could see her mother and father, their faces free from the wan look and weary expression she knew of old. And then she spotted Connie standing slightly apart to the right. Dear Connie, her very dearest friend who had kept her going through the period of her greatest tribulations.

Flo started to move towards her but Connie raised her left arm and with outstretched palm gestured towards a lone figure further down the valley side.

Even though its face was turned away, Flo knew who it was in an instant and hurried in that direction, overwhelmed by a feeling of euphoria and great expectation. As she approached the figure turned and stretched out its arms to envelope her in an embrace of unbounded love. Then he spoke.

'Hello, Mum.'

Or was it all just Flo's last dream?

11. Glossary

Antimacassar: a piece of cloth or lace fitted to the top of an armchair (or a seat on a coach or train) to prevent men's hair cream (i.e. Brylcreem) marking the chair.

Bagwash or dampwash laundry: a laundry that took in dirty washing in a large cotton bag, washed it and returned it in the bag damp for the customer to dry.

Bath chair: a large invalid chair that was pushed by an attendant.

Blighty: a slang term for Great Britain.

Bob: a slang term for a shilling (5-pence)

Briny: a slang term for the sea.

Capon: a chicken that had been castrated so that it grew large.

Charabanc: a touring coach.

Chi: the local abbreviation for Chichester.

Coal scuttle: a special fireside bucket containing coal to replenish the fire.

Demob suit: a cheap suit given to servicemen when they were demobilised and returning to civilian life.

Ducks and drakes: a game played by the sea that involved skimming flat stones along the water surface to see how many times they could be made to jump.

Flag days: special days approved by the police when charities could collect money in the street in return for a small flag on a pin.

Flagon: a large bottle of alcoholic drink containing beer or cider etc.

Great War: the First World War (1914-1918).
Guinea: One pound and one shilling (£1.05)
Labour Exchange: the Job Centre.
Lady Almoner: a social worker who helped hospital patients with their non-medical problems.
News Theatre: a small cinema that showed non-stop newsreels (like CNN and Sky News on TV today).
Pantechnicon: a large furniture removal lorry.
Pop: Any soft sparkling non-alcoholic drink such as Tizer, lemonade or cream soda.
Public Bar: Pubs had two bars: a Saloon bar that was carpeted and had upholstered chairs and a more sparsely furnished Public bar where drinks were slightly cheaper.
Quart: two pints.
Rag and Bone Man: a man who toured the streets with a horse and cart taking away unwanted domestic items which he recycled.
Receiving hospital: a hospital that accepted into its wards sick and injured people without prior arrangement i.e. accidents and emergencies.
Reefer: a marijuana cigarette.
Service flat: a purpose built block of flats with a resident caretaker; central hot water and heating system; and often a restaurant and a resident's lounge.
Shorthand typist: An office secretary who could take dictation in Griegs or Pitmans shorthand before typing.
Squaddie: a low ranking soldier.
Tallyman: someone who collects instalments on loans or credit door to door.
Tanner: a six pence piece (2 ½ pence).

Ten Bob: ten shillings (50 pence).
The Old King: King George V.
The Old Queen: Queen Victoria.
The Smoke: London.